The Reverend

The Reverend

❖

Roger J. Zimmermann

To order additional copies of this book, contact:
Xlibris Corporation
1-888-795-4274
www.Xlibris.com
Orders@Xlibris.com
85765

Contents

INTRODUCTION

The *New York Times* writer, Joseph P. Fried wrote: "*He ran a house of God*," he said, "*but it turned out to be a house of horrors.*"

Sometimes, not often, there comes along someone who embodies malevolence. He gives off an aura of piety and virtue. Often, too, this person's behavior is the opposite of those who gave him birth. Such a man we shall call Casius Anthony LeMans.

This is a work of fiction but based in fact. The preacher does exist; he did kill numbers of young Black girls and women. He is a handsome, charismatic global thinker who finally outsmarted himself. He began serving four consecutive life terms in Sullivan Correctional Institution then transferred to Shawangunk Correctional in New York State where he has gone to pay for his atrocious crimes. So far, he has had one unsuccessful parole hearing.

"Not one of us knows what effect his life produces, and what he gives to others; that is hidden from us and must remain so, though we are often allowed to see some little fraction of it, so that we may not lose courage. The way in which power works is a mystery."

—Albert Schweitzer

CHAPTER 1

END OF TOUR

Bedford-Stuyvesant, also known as Bed-Stuy, for decades has been the cultural center for Brooklyn's 140,000 ethnic mixes of African-American populations. The main thoroughfare in this enclave is Nostrand Avenue, but the commercial thoroughfare is Fulton Street. This section of Brooklyn consists of three old neighborhoods: Bedford—Stuyvesant Heights, Ocean Hill and Weeksville.

Law enforcement protection to the community comes through Brooklyn North Borough Command, in general, the 77th Precinct patrol and detectives of the New York City Police Department in particular

The detective squad commander, Lieutenant Lance Carpenter, signed that last document on his desk, placed it in the outgoing box and stood, preparing to leave for the night. He turned off his desk lamp then shut the overhead lights before closing the door to his office, his suit jacket slung over his left shoulder. The squad is now in the hands of his second in command, Sergeant Mark Berryman.

Detective Sergeant Maria Soriano was waiting for him. She was leaning back on another desk in the squad room, with her hands on the desktop, her long legs stretched out in front of her, her raven hair falling free to her waist.

"Are you ready for dinner, Maria," he asked? Everyone in the squad knew they were living together but thought nothing of it.

"I'm starving, Lieu. I hope you have deep pockets."

"Listen," he called to everyone in the squad office, "If anyone is looking for us, our tour is ended. In case it's important, we'll be at the Starving Artiste restaurant on Halsey Street."

The Starving Artiste Restaurant on Halsey is a favorite dining location for many residents in the area and members of the squad as well. Tonight this couple, Lance and Maria occupy a corner candlelit table.

They were finishing dinner with a glass of the red wine and a cup of demitasse coffee. It is seven-thirty with the night air hot, still and muggy. Both are in good spirits having finally brought an intensive homicide case to closure. The case had been in the active file for more than twenty years. They worked on it for the last three years, with a host of other cases, and it had ended with the arrest and conviction of their chief suspect, the Reverend Casius LeMans.

The dining room of the restaurant with low lighting, the tables tightly compacted; the rear of the restaurant had a rack holding various wines. On their table were two empty bottles of Chianti, one of which had a half burned candle stuck in its neck. The flame of the candle flickered sending dancing shadows against the wall, the other bottle had a splash of wine remaining at the bottom.

"Lance," Maria said in a low voice, "this was a great idea having dinner at the *Artiste*. This is the first we've relaxed in months."

Lance reached across the table to take her hand. "Maria, you've done an outstanding job and besides, I wanted to be with you and this was a good excuse."

"Why don't we go home and celebrate some more?"

"Besides being a good detective, you're also clairvoyant."

Dinner had been something of a celebration of the detective squad's success in bringing that case to closure. Among their accomplishments, they had affected the arrest and, as a result, secured four convictions against the Bishop, as LeMans preferred to be called. They had affected closure of his church, imprisoning the pastor, reassignment of the church and its collected properties to fitting State and local agencies, elimination of religious women working there. Placement of forty children adversely affected during their formative years, were given to Child Protective Services.

Lance and Maria had been enjoying a subdued euphoria but looked forward to renewing the celebration at home. Against department policy they had become involved in a liaison and were sharing an apartment on Brooklyn Heights. Both were adult and single but supervisor and subordinate, working in the same assignment, and living together, was prohibited by department hierarchy, policy and its rules.

Both had been in a quiet celebratory mood as they exited the restaurant. They started walking on the shaded side of Halsey Street; the east side is in waning sunlight. Car traffic was light and the street was empty of evening strollers.

Lance suddenly tensed as he stopped to look up Halsey Street. Maria noticed at once Lance's sudden rigidity, stopping just outside the front entrance of the restaurant. She turned to see what he was looking at when she too tensed.

Nonchalantly strolling down the Halsey Street were Darryl and Nevatro LeMans, two of the older sons of the killer they had helped in putting behind bars to serve four consecutive life sentences.

Oddly, both young men wore what, in the jargon of the neighborhood are called 'dusters', beige lightweight long unbuttoned raincoats. It was a scene out of a B western movie. The officers watched their approach uncertain of their intent; slowly, their training kicking in, they started to drift apart. The brothers were not hesitant, but evinced a certainty about their behavior. Darryl, the older of the two, was the first to move. He pushed aside the right side of his coat, reached behind his back then pushing forward a .9mm automatic held parallel to the ground.

At that movement and sight of the automatic, Maria pushed Lance further away from her side as she too reached for her automatic held in a waist holster. Darryl, however, holding the weapon as he did, fired the first shot striking Maria in the left breast. Maria had, in a swift movement, fallen into the proscribed combat position, fired her weapon striking Darryl in the throat. As he turned to fire at Lance, she fired a second shot that struck him in the center of the forehead, killing him but simultaneously with his firing a off the shot that struck Lance in the shoulder. She collapsed to the pavement mortally wounded calling softly, "Lance."

Lance, pushed hard by Maria, fell to the pavement. There had been three, possible four shots, he was uncertain who had done the firing. He saw Darryl go down with a third eye, when he was almost simultaneously struck on the side of his head by a grazing bullet and again in the shoulder. He had seen Nevatro take out a weapon, also holding it sideways, and fire at him, giving him, he thought, that grazing blow to the side of his head. He is hit a second time, this time in his right shoulder and felt that it must have been Darryl that shot him. He returned fire hitting Nevatro in the mouth but his second shot had gone unseen where it had gone or if it had struck his assailant. He saw Nevatro step back and fire twice more. Both shots struck Lance in his abdomen. Lance got off another round that struck his assailant in the left eye. Nevatro fell to the ground fatally wounded.

Lance collapsed to the pavement, got to his feet wavering, assured himself there was no longer any threat of danger from these two assailants, and then turned to look after Maria. He saw that she too was on the sidewalk, her right arm extended, her raven hair lying in blood from her chest wound. He tried to move toward her but fell back unconscious, smashing the back of his head hard on the pavement, making him lose unconsciousness.

He momentarily regained consciousness, his thoughts still focused on his partner's well-being. He felt cold, clammy and bathed is sweat.

"Maria . . ." He whispered her name, tried to right himself. He moved to assist her before he passed into a hazy state, not unconscious, but out of it. He looked to the onlookers begging them to send for help.

"Call 911!" He managed to say before he too fell back. "Ask for police and an ambulance," he asked of them. "My partner has been shot."

He collapsed to the pavement.

CHAPTER 2

THAT WAS NOW—THIS IS THEN

It was an ominous, rainy, dreary day. The clouds had opened releasing huge rain drops that continued to cover everything with drenching water. Puddles formed here and there, tiny rivulets crisscrossed Police Plaza. It had been raining like this for three days showing no signs of relief.

A police lieutenant, in mufti, assigned to the Seventieth Squad Detectives, stood in the arch that was part of the Municipal Building. He was daunted by his failure to figure a way to negotiate between this building, across the open plaza and into police headquarters.

"Lance," someone called out. "Lance Carpenter!" He turned to see an old friend from the Tenth Precinct, Sergeant William Defoe.

"Hey Will, how're you doin'?"

"I'm dryer than you are." They moved toward each other to shake hands. "What are you doing here? I thought you were in the seven-oh precinct."

"I still am. I got a summons yesterday to report to the Chief of Detectives Office at 0800 this morning. It's almost that now and here I am. I think I am being reassigned somewhere."

"Luckily," Sergeant Defoe said, "I brought my golf umbrella. You can share part of it if you want."

"Let's do it."

They walked at a brisk pace across the plaza before Police Headquarters. He barely noticed Bernard Rosenthal's huge 'Five in One' red metal disks that rose 30-feet in the air beside him and on into the "Puzzle Palace." He made straight for the building's entry, eager to learn why he had been directed to report here. He identified himself to the officer at the door, unimpressed by the security to this important bastion of police operations.

"Lieutenant Lance Carpenter to see the Chief of Detectives." He announced.

He went into the Chief's office, surprised to see his friend and mentor, Chief Francis X. Mannion, the Chief of Detectives seated with Chief Matthew J. Pender, Deputy Chief, Special Investigations Unit. They were at a small table by a double window.

14

"Come on in Carpenter," Chief Pender called. "Have some coffee and a pastry."

Carpenter helped himself then took a seat. "This is ominous, two Chiefs ganging up on one peon. Do you fellas have something in mind for my future?" He asked brazenly.

"Specifically, I have something in mind," Chief Pender said. "The Chief of Detectives and I had a meeting last night about a problem in the 7-7 squad. Interested?"

Carpenter leaned toward, his arms bent on the table, his hands opening and closing. "More, give me more information please."

"It seems like the interim commander," the COP began, "Sergeant Blasé Matiere is something of a thug, an asshole and a lousy commander. His records are so screwed up that no one wants to do an inspection of his management of the squad."

"So you want me to go in, clean up his act and his records so the borough can come in and find fault. Man, oh man, you find me one good assignment after another." After a short pause he continued. "That's a plush assignment you're offering," he said sarcastically. "What comes next after this, cleaning toilets in headquarters?"

"Hold on, Lieutenant," Chief Lutz said, "that's just background and keep in mind who you are talking to. What we want you to do is to bring a specific case to closure that has been going on for far too long. I'm talking about a serial killer who is also a protestant minister in a storefront church. At least we think he's protestant. He's been killing young Black young women for over twenty years and we don't seem to be able to stop him. Everything else we mentioned is extraneous to that."

"That's crazy, sir. Just have someone arrest him, what's so hard about that?"

"He has been arrested many times," Chief Mannion said. "Each time a case comes up for trial, something happens to the complainant or the victim or both."

"Something, like what?" despite his many questions, Lance found he was interested.

"Something like they show up dead, usually with a broken neck and their fingers missing," the COP said.

"Does the precinct or squad or whatever have all the records on these events? I'll want to look them over to see what, if anything can possibly be done."

"I'll have Central Records put together a package for you; UF 61s, DD5, DD13s, DD14s and anything else you can think of to supplement what they have. Is there anything else?"

"Get me the jacket on Sergeant Matiere and the other squad members. I want to know what I am up against."

"Oh, there is something else, you will keep as low a profile as you can. The minister is Black and the community is Black, most of the Detectives in the squad are Black. We want no racial issues provoked."

"And the hits keep coming."

"Yes, I understand. When do the orders come down?"

"I'll have them published as soon as I get in the office," Chief Pender announced,

"Am I allowed one more question?" He asked.

"Yes," Chief Mannion replied. "What is it?"

"I've heard no mention of the Homicide Squad. Isn't something like this within their purview?"

Chief Pender leaned forward. "They are doing a lateral investigation but are unaware that this is going on. Apprise them of this when you take command and seek their cooperation. Is there anything else?"

"No, sir."

He left the office. As he stood waiting for an elevator, Chief Mannion came to stand next to him. Come up to my office, Carpenter."

Once inside the chief's office, they sat to continue their talk. Chief Mannion was a close family friend and someone Carpenter respected.

"Lance, take this assignment. I'll watch your back and give you whatever support you believe necessary. The people there need a good supervisor."

"Uncle Frank, I'll do what I can."

"How are your mom and dad? I haven't seen them for some time."

"They are doing fine. I'll tell them you asked. Why don't you and Aunt Marjorie come to dinner soon"

"I'll get with your mom and dad and arrange something."

CHAPTER 3

ASSIGNMENT: 77ᵀᴴ SQUAD DETECTIVES

Two days later Carpenter reported to the Desk Officer at the 77th Precinct, flashed his shield and was directed to the Precinct Commander's Office. He knocked on the door and walked in. He was holding his personal belongings under his left arm.

"Good morning, Captain, I'm Lieutenant Carpenter the new whip of the squad," he said holding out his hand.

Looking up he said, "Welcome, Lieutenant." The offered hand was ignored. "Your office is on the second floor." Carpenter held his hand out waiting for something to happen. When it did not, he turned to leave.

"Nice to meet you captain," he called over his shoulder. What did I do to piss him off? The precinct boss is a hard ass. Wonderful, simply wonderful, he murmured too himself.

On the second floor he noted the Homicide Squad was on the right and Detectives were on the left, Anti Crime was in the southern part of the floor. He entered the squad and met with the civilian receptionist slash clerk.

"Good morning, young lady. I'm Lieutenant Carpenter, the new whip."

"Good mornin' Lieu," she replied as she turned the command log in his direction. "I'm Gloria Phillips your secretary and receptionist. We saw the transfer in the orders last night." Gloria was a Black woman in her early thirties and slightly overweight, comely dressed with a quick smile. She wore her hair in "corn rows" that set off her face. She smiled with her eyes and mouth.

He signed into the Squad Command Log as taking command of the squad and lined off the page below his signature. "Where can I hang out?" Carpenter asked lightly.

"You're in the northwest corner, there," she pointed to where it was. "Sergeant Matiere is in there now. She turned in her chair and called out: "Hey Sergeant Matiere! The new whip is here!"

A formless voice answered, "Be right there!"

"Gloria, Gloria," Carpenter said soothingly, "Does the phone on your desk not work?"

A quizzical look came over her face. "Sure it works. Why do you ask?"

"Well, instead of shouting across the office, it would have been more professional if you had called Sergeant Matiere on the phone to advise him."

"Oh, I get it, call, don't yell."

"Exactly."

He looked around and saw the squad room was open with eight steel gray desks with green Formica tops; all had Smith Corona typewriters on stands that were scattered throughout the room. There were nine gray and green file cabinets against a wall that turned out to be the commander's office. The room was illuminated by overhead fluorescent lights and four windows dominated the west wall. On the south wall were two corkboards with flyers of different sorts pinned on it and by the entrance was a round cardboard waste bin. On an inside wall was a rack for recharging radios and for hanging car keys. He also noted there were no detectives present.

In what would be Carpenter's office, two walls had windows casting bright natural light on the room through opened blinds. The overhead fluorescents had not been turned on. The room was large enough to allow two desks and near the entryway was a bathroom. Found between the two desks was a locked upright olive green locker.

As he entered, a man he assumed to be Sergeant Matiere, was sitting at the far end behind a desk in the left corner. He did not look up but kept reading and signing reports.

"Sergeant," Carpenter called softly from the doorway.

Matiere looked up annoyed. "Yeah, what?"

This was not a good beginning, Carpenter thought. "I am the new whip, Sarge, Lieutenant Carpenter and you are seated at what must be my desk, are you not" he asked curtly?

"But I had . . ." Aw shit, Matiere thought, one of those guys. "All right I'll move my ass to the other desk." He let Carpenter know that he was not happy.

"Sarge, let's start off on the right footing. Did you hear Gloria shout that I was on board?"

"Yeah, I did," he said hesitantly.

"Do me the courtesy of responding to messages you receive, no matter how you receive them, in the proper manner."

"Yeah, I can do that," his annoyance was still obvious.

Carpenter deposited the box with his belongings on his desk.

"Tell me all about the command," Carpenter said as he sat. "How many detectives are assigned to the squad?"

Feeling the tense moment had passed, Matiere said, "There are eighteen. Seven detectives work day duty; seven work night tours, and four on the late tour. I supervise the day tour and Sergeant Maria, the feminist Soriano is the night tour supervisor. She's a female Italian but good at her job. There is no supervisor on the late tour. And we have one civilian clerk and secretary, Gloria Phillips. She wears both hats as secretary and receptionist.

Soriano, Carpenter mused, where have I heard that name before?

"Listen, why don't we go somewhere and grab a cup of coffee? We can talk and relax at the same time," Carpenter suggested trying to put the man at ease.

Matiere asked, "Here, in the precinct?"

"Sure, why not," Carpenter wondered what he was getting at?

"Well, I usually go over into Queens or Brooklyn North to eat."

"That's too far. Let's grab something nearby." Carpenter wondered if Matiere was uncomfortable eating in a local establishment.

The men walked toward Atlantic Avenue. A simple sign over the storefront saying "Eats" identified the store. The smells were mouthwatering and delicious as they entered the crowded diner. Many of the patrons looked up as they walked in. Carpenter pointed at a table to the counterman who nodded. He sat with his back to the front door while Matiere sat himself where he could see the entrance, Wyatt Earp fashion. The counterman came to the table wiping his hands on his apron.

"You guys are cops, right?" He asked but already surmised their occupation. He handed them

Well-worn menus.

Carpenter turned to look at him, "Do you have decaffeinated coffee?" He asked.

"Yeah, we do," he replied taking a pencil from its perch behind his right ear.

"I'll have a cup of decaffeinated, two eggs over easy and a toasted English. What are you having Blasé ?"

"Just coffee," he replied sullenly, "in a clean cup." The counterman took back the menus and left.

While they had coffee, eggs and English, Matiere gave Carpenter relevant information about the squad, their strengths and weaknesses, as he saw them and his view of a situation involving a Minister, his church, and the entire M.O. The minister he identified as Reverend Casius LeMans. Carpenter got the impression, as they spoke, the sergeant liked to paint himself as a good guy with the men of the squad. Listening to him give his briefing on the squad and its members, he made it seem as though everything that went on did so because *he* supervised it and approved of it. He wondered what Sergeant Soriano would be like.

Later that day when he was getting himself settled in, there was a soft knock. Carpenter looked up and saw a woman standing there; he got to his feet. She stood, he guessed, at five feet seven inches, with dark black hair and blue eyes.

"Lieutenant," she said, "I'm Sergeant Maria Soriano the four to twelve supervisor. Welcome on board."

"Thank you, Maria. Come in I'd like to speak with you if you are not busy."

She entered the office and took a seat. "Shall I give you some of my background on-the-job," she asked.

"Yes, please. Give me a cameo sketch."

"Well, I have eleven years on-the-job, the first two in plainclothes in the 14th Precinct. I transferred to the 5th Precinct on patrol. When promoted, I went to the 70th for two years and later assigned here. Lieutenant Giuseppe Petrosino, the only police officer killed in the line of duty outside the country, is my great-uncle and the reason I became a police officer."

"Joe Petrosino, you said? That's some background. Well I look forward to working with you." Now he understood why she had seemed so familiar to him, she had been a patrol sergeant in the 70th Precinct while he was there.

Several days later, Carpenter sat behind his desk, a pile of file folders and jackets in front of him, stopping only to rub his eyes and stretch. He had been reviewing a build-up of UF61 Complaint Forms, After Action Summary Reports, and DD5s dating back more than twenty-five years. He first had to match up the DD5 with the correct complaint. He also matched Activity Log, Aided Reports worksheet, Missing/ Unidentified Persons Reports trying to make some sense of this hodgepodge. At best, it was tedious work but provided much insight into the LeMans operation. He did notice was that all dealt with the *Rehoboth Bethel Church* of God or its pastor, Casius LeMans.

Seated in front of him were his squad supervisors, Sergeants Soriano and Matiere discussing different facets about several of the complaints.

"Maria," he asked, "how well versed are you on the LeMans complex and its inhabitants?"

Maria Soriano is a raven-haired handsome Italian-American woman who underplays her graciousness by having her hair pulled back, loose shirts or blouses and little or no makeup; she was wearing slacks and flat rubber soled shoes. Despite that, her good looks came through, and as he now recalled she is a supervisor with street experience.

Her counterpart, Blasé Matiere, an Italian-American fireplug, looks to be forever in need of a shave, balding, seemingly without a neck, with a look of subdued power and an inherent inferiority complex.

"Well, Lieu, Blasé and I review and sign the DD5s, especially those dealing with young women disappearing, or those that are found dead with a broken neck, or we have an incident where the group has suspected involvement, "she replied matter-of-factly.

"You mentioned 'the group.' Do you have a specific group in mind?"

"Yes I do, the church group headed by the Reverend Casius LeMans. By the way, the Coroner estimates that all the young women had their necks broken in the same manner and by a left-handed person. There is one other peculiarity; all the women we've found have had their fingers removed."

"That's just bullshit, Maria. It has no significance," Blasé said.

"That's good input, Maria. As I read the reports," Carpenter said pointing to the stacks of reports, "a couple of interesting facts stood out. One you have already mentioned, Maria, about the broken necks. That is significant. The other oddity is the one you just mentioned, that all be missing their fingers. I find that most unusual. This latter fact suggests the perp had taken time to remove the fingers and most killers do not take the time to do that."

"Now that you mention it, Lieu," Matiere was quick to pick up on his oversight, "it did seem strange."

"Maybe someone is collecting coups," Maria ventured. "You know, like collector's items."

"We're talking about ghouls here," Carpenter remarked. "Each of the fingers had been cut off with some unidentified instrument. Assign someone to find out what the instrument was. That will narrow the field somewhat. Let's keep all these tidbits to ourselves."

"Why should we do that; I mean keep that info secret Blasé wanted to know?

"Its ghoulish and some the media would jump all over," Lance explained. "Besides, with the notoriety these murders will attract, we can identify the real killer from the wackos."

Turning to another subject he said, "If you two don't mind, in the future anytime we have an incident involving LeMans or his church, keep me in the loop. This bullshit has gone on long enough," Carpenter announced. "Also, I paid a visit to the Homicide Squad across the hall," he stressed, "to see what paper they have generated on the church," he said looking unwaveringly at Matiere. "They were kind enough to duplicate what they had to date. Those stacks of papers on the chair are copies of their files. I want to match them up with what we have and add anything new so we can look at it."

"Maria, would you ask Gloria to requisition a couple of white boards so we can start diagramming the church, its hierarch and its occupants?"

"Sure Lieu, I've wanted to get at their files for some time. Now that you have them we can begin." She had glanced at her partner giving the impression she had mentioned it to Matiere and was discouraged in her attempt.

Sergeant Matiere took an immediate offense feeling his supervisor was voicing adverse criticism of their actions about LeMans and the others. "Lieu," he said defensively, "we do all we can, every time. The bastard is too slick. He has too much clout."

"I'm not being critical, Blasé. It has been almost twenty years since he made the scene. If these records are accurate, and I have no doubt they are, it's time to shut him down!"

"As you settle in," Matiere said, "you'll find that is easier said than done."

"All right, Blasé, Maria, I'm sure we'll talk again about this. I want to review what has been done so far, consolidate these records and then perhaps we can discuss strategy."

"I'll give you a hand with these records if you want," Maria offered.

"That would help a lot. On another matter, when we are alone, my name is Lance. Otherwise keep it at Lieu before the troops."

Both sergeants got up to leave, Matiere made kissing sounds as he got ready to leave for the day and Maria settling in to begin her tour.

She gave him the finger mouthing softly, "Fuck you asshole."

Once they had gone, Carpenter began taking Complaint Reports from the folders to read. He found that the records had been gathered from various sources: precincts of occurrence, Missing Persons, the Harbor Squad, Housing Bureau, Transit Bureau, and other commands. He began to separate them in their crime category, then their location, time and date of occurrence to learn if there were some distinct pattern, and finally separating the records by the age and sex of the complainant. He compared these with Arrest Reports. He immediately noticed the person complained of was either LeMans or one of his offspring or connected with the church.

He was certain that some of these records were not the work of LeMans or any of his offspring. Some did not match the profile; some looked like copycat cases. It would be necessary to separate those that were someone else's criminal activity and those that dealt with only the LeMans clan. He further determined that although arrests had been made, there had been no recorded convictions. He selected one.

Complaint Number: 77-334
Complaint: Aggravated Sexual Battery, Unlawful Detention
Date and Time of Occurrence: 4:15 p.m., October 22, 1960
Place of Occurrence: 144 St. Mark's Street, Brooklyn
Date of Birth: July 22, 1945
Description: Female, Black, 120 pounds, 5'6"
Complainant: Dorothea Blessard
Residence: 4414 Albemarle Road, Yonkers, NY
Suspect: Reverend Casius LeMans
Details: *On date, time and place of occurrence Complainant Blessard states that she was taken to the Rehoboth Bethel Church of God where she was promised shelter, food and clothing. She alleges she was sexually assaulted for two weeks by one Reverend Casius LeMans, pastor of Rehoboth Bethel Church of God.*

CHAPTER 4

BEGINNINGS

Casius LeMans' biography began in Louisiana specifically in the lower bayous of Plaquemines and Lafourche Parishes. Plaquemines Parish is located in southeast Louisiana in the Mississippi River and its Delta, with a long coastline along the Gulf of Mexico. The state and the parish have a rich heritage that incorporates an intriguing blend of American Indian, Spanish and African cultures.

In the 1700s French trappers set up a trading post on the Red River, above Plaquemines that flows down from Arkansas into Louisiana and finally into the Gulf of Mexico. The finicky river changed course but the outpost there in north central Louisiana known as Natchitoches stayed put, predating New Orleans by four years making it the oldest permanent French settlement in the Louisiana Purchase.

The senior of the LeMans clan, a guy by the name of Lucas was born into slavery in Plaquemines and the property of a generous, well-liked French cotton farmer named André Petain who had his slaves reared in the French Jesuit Catholic religion. After the Civil War ended, Petain endowed each freedman with a small stipend, whereupon Lucas moved north to Natchitoches. He would move again to Addis on the Mississippi where it was rumored there would be enough work on the proposed railroad for that region. Sure enough, in 1871 Congress granted a charter for a transcontinental railroad. The charter specified that the railroad would be a Military and Post Road. It would later be called the Texas and Pacific Railroad.

Lucas was kept employed by the railroad while at the same time sought an education at the Leffert Street—Delphine School. With an education, albeit scant, came an understanding that the Negroes along the river did most of the heavy labor and were, for the most part, bereft of religious leadership. He apprenticed as a minister and, it seemed, found his calling for the time being. Once he had been recognized as a minister of the Word, he struck off on his own.

Chapter 5

Life in the Bayous

After work on the railroad petered out, Lucas, had to work at menial jobs along the Mississippi River to eke out a living. He lived, for the most part, in corrugated metal buildings or abandoned slave quarters that were blistering in the summer and frigid in winter. His only son, Marcus Judah, came from the union with another former slave, Jamalia that he had not bothered to marry. He had been reared French Jesuit Catholic, and they raised their son in that faith placing his education in the hands of the French Jesuits who had a mission nearby. Marcus, as he grew older, had another path to follow. He became what he considered a Southern Black and Indian minister. His mother had been an ignorant poor woman who died early in life of swamp fever presumably from the miasma in the bayous and his father had later been arrested and jailed for murders committed throughout lower bayou country.

Marcus, was then raised by foster parents, Ned and Amelia Cathcart, he became a biblical scholar and at the age of eighteen stuck out on his own. At first he worked his way over to New Roads on a bend in the Mississippi River loading and unloading river barges. The work was hard and long, paying very little. New Roads is a poor river area, with most of the housing rotting and falling apart and there were few paved roads.

On his twenty-first birthday he moved to the fabled city of Baton Rouge. It was here that he learned he had a talent for preaching the word of the Lord. He apprenticed with a licensed minister for seven years until he felt he was ready to go off on his own. He started his ministry along the river: Port Allen, on the west bank of the Mississippi; Addis, a railroad town used primarily by the Texas and Pacific Railroad the former employer of his father; Plaquemine a rich delta area made up of a landmass and wetlands; and Donaldsonville whose claim to fame is that it was a site in the Civil War held by the Yankees.

In Iberville Parish, while spreading the word to his scattered flock, the Reverend LeMans met Honore Marchman, the daughter—it turned out—of a well-to-do Southern Baptist minister, the Reverend Casius Marchman. Theirs was truly a whirlwind romance over which there was great controversy. Lucas was a Black man, after all, and she was of quasi-noble French and English stock. The men, father and suitor, found commonality in that both were preaching the word of the Lord. They arrived at an understanding and the couple would be married. True to his word, Pastor Marchman walked his daughter down the aisle about a year later. Marcus and Honore were married in the pastor's church in Gardere located just south of Baton Rouge.

Honore rode the circuit with her husband in a small one-horse carriage, a wedding present from her parents. The couple was quite happy moving from one parish to another, living mainly off the largess of each congregation. Honore learned to modify her wardrobe in order that she did not hurt her husband's parishioners. She had become quite an asset to him playing the piano beautifully when there was one to be found and leading the choir in their hymn singing whether there was a piano or not. Honore conducted a popular class in Bible study where she garnered a large following. Before long, however, the parishioners began noticing that the preacher's wife was great with child. She continued in her duties though until she became too large to continue. There came a time, then, when she needed confinement being too swollen to move about easily and she was tired all the time. On their return to her parent's home, they were offered and accepted a home with the Marchmans in their antebellum home.

On July 7, 1930, Honore went into strenuous and difficult labor supervised by her mother and a local midwife from which labors she did not emerge. She did, however, give birth to an eight and a half pound fair-skinned healthy boy who was given the name Casius Anthony, in honor of her father.

"*Sacrée boucane!*" Marcus exclaimed on hearing the news of the birth of his son. "What of Honore?" he asked anxiously. "How is she doing," he asked quite concerned?

"The midwife did all she could," his mother-in-law answered solemnly. "The Lord called her to be with him. We're sorry Marcus," Pastor Marchman said dolefully. Marcus and his in-laws clasped one another and broke down, their beloved Honore was gone, but praise be for the son and grandson!

Later, when the family gathered at the family cemetery to place Honore in the family crypt, the Pastor conducted the service. Afterward, the Marchmans noticed that a subtle change had come over their son-in-law; he seemed to have lost his vitality. Young Casius was later taken to the local hospital to have his birth recorded and a physical checkup. He was pronounced hale and once released from the hospital, it was decided amicably that Casius would remain with his grandparents to rear while his father continued his ministry on the road.

The Marchmans brought in a wet nurse, a member of the Pastor's congregation, who also served as his nurse and nanny. She was a *mamam*, or priestess of a *Vodou* cult, clad in white clothing and a white covering for her head. She cast a spell over the infant praying to the *Bon Dieu* to protect him from the evil *Loa* spirits. She cast another spell to bring him health, wealth and a bond between him and his mother. The Reverend had to let her go when he learned that she was doing *Vodun* or Voodoo dancing in the house. Another member of the church took over her duties.

Marcus would stop by every time he was on this leg of his circuit, to see the growth of his son. Each visit brought pride and pleasure to his eyes and a gleam to his grandparents' eyes. As the boy grew, he became a favorite in the church among the parishioners. All wanted to hug him and smother him with affection. Young Casius was light skinned, like his mother, with pale blue eyes and light brown curly hair. He was quite the handsome child.

CHAPTER 6

APPRENTICESHIP

There was nothing remarkable about Casius' childhood until he began his schooling in the Baton Rouge Christian School—there he excelled. He seemed to have an instantaneous grasp of the most complex concepts, consistently taking top honors in English, history, mathematics and most of his other school subjects. He was, however, particularly interested in his Bible studies, perhaps this was due to his working with his father. The children in his classes, especially the young girls, found him likable, handsome, and a powerful charismatic force.

Casius was also familiar with the Cajun tongue spoken in the bayous and among the poor in town. He would frequently go to town in order that he might converse in that tongue with the people there. He became quite proficient.

Always curious, Casius was sitting on his bed while his father undressed. "Poppa," be asked, "Where did the name of Baton Rouge come from? Is it somebody's name?"

"No, Casius, a long time ago the flags of seven nations flew over Baton Rouge—those of France, England, Spain, West Florida, and Louisiana. The French had great influence and it was the French that called the settlement Baton Rouge or in French, 'red stick' of 'red staff' after the cypress trees when they are stripped of their bark an' used to mark the boundaries of hunting grounds between two Indian tribes. I guess the name just stuck."

"What a weird way to name a town. So then, Grandpa and Grandma live in Red Stick?"

"Yep, I guess so."

He grew to be a handsome youth, well-liked by the others in his class and by his teachers. He appeared to make friends easily, especially with the young ladies.

The boy looked forward, though to each summer and his father's return at the completion of his circuit. The two would spend a great deal of time together bantering about with Bible verses:

"David sang to the Lord the words of his song when the Lord delivered him from the hands of all his enemies and from the hands of Saul."

Marcus would look up from his Bible to his son, waiting for his response.

"2 Samuel, verse 22," came Casius' quick reply. "*The Lord is my rock, my fortress and my deliverer . . .*" he finished. Marcus had randomly selected that passage from the Old Testament and was astounded by the boy's knowledge of the Scriptures. He would then play a game where he would begin a passage and Casius would have to finish it giving chapter and verse. Or, he would begin to narrate a biblical story and Casius would tell him where the story was found and who was involved, as well as the theme of the text.

> *"And thou shalt number seven Sabbaths of year unto thee,*
> *seven times seven years;*
> *and the space of the seven Sabbaths of years*
> *shall be unto thee forty and nine years."*

Casius was quick to respond: "Leviticus, Chapter 25 verse 8 the year of jubilee:

> *"Then shalt thou cause the trumpet of the jubilee*
> *to sound on the tenth day of the seventh month,*
> *in the day of atonement shall ye make the trumpet sound*
> *throughout all the land."*

As far back as he could remember, after those earlier years with his grandparents, Casius had traveled the circuit with his father, basically that of a Southern Baptist minister who brought the Bible and its teachings to the poor Blacks of rural Louisiana. Wherever they went the people seemed genuinely pleased to see the Reverend and his handsome mulatto son with the piercing blue eyes. There was always a roof over their heads—although sometimes it was a hayloft—and there was always lagniappe—a little food to eat. At each stop on the circuit his father, Pastor Marcus, as he was now called, would conduct Bible study during the day and at night he would preach the word of God trying to give the word meaning to them and their meager existence. After the service was started, the Reverend would call on his son to recite the evening's Bible verse and explain its meaning, giving his interpretation of the passage to the congregation. It would appear to be extemporaneous but father and son had carefully rehearsed both the passage and his response.

The people in each hamlet thought Casius was a godly young man and carefully taught by his father. Each time the collection plate, although in most places the people had very little, it would be passed around, bills and coins would be piled high. No one knew about the passing of the preacher's wife and no one spoke of her although rumors were rampant. However, young Casius made frequent mention of her to the appropriate audiences. If there were mainly matronly women at the meeting, young Casius would describe her, her refined French-English good handsome looks, and her lady-like poise and charm. He would also tell them of her passing, not in childbirth, but later on with some mysterious malady and with her dying breath ask him to recite the 23 Psalm, her favorite:

> "The Lord is my shepherd,
> I shall not want;
> He makes me lie down in green pastures.
> He leads me beside still waters;
> He restores my soul.
> He leads me in paths of righteousness
> for His name's sake."

His rendition, coupled with tears he was able to muster up each time as he collapsed into a nearby chair, drew additional tears from the congregation every time and many times larger donations at the end of services. They were well aware that these poor folks had little to give and each coin and bill was all the more precious.

He did have a secret that he shared with no one. During one of his free times, he went off to a deserted lonely spot along the river where he took delight in taking a stray dog with him. He was going to cut up the creature and torture it to watch it die. He enjoyed tormenting the animal until it would no longer respond to his torture, watching the animal intently to see how it behaved. He made a ritual of the session and took great pains in burying the creature. After that, he did not take animals often, but every once in a while he felt an irresistible impulse to do it. Of course, if he had gotten the animals' blood on his clothing, he merely had to go for a swim to clean off. Afterward he would often ask himself why he did what he did, but had no satisfactory answer. He took solace in the fact that he did not do those things often.

Marcus had finished his service in Terrebonne Parish when his son approached him. "Poppa," he said, "where are we headin' for next?"

"Well, bless me boy," Marcus said. "We got a fair piece to go. From here we're headin' for Vermillion, then on to Natchitoches, we'll do well in Grant Township there, but that's only a third of our journey. Why you ask boy?"

"Jus' curious Poppa. Why do you go to so many places," the boy inquired.

"Well, see here. In any of the places we've been, you see any other preacher anywhere?"

"No, Poppa, none at all."

"And you won't either. We're the only ones bringin' the word of the Lord to these folks. So there's a lotta souls we got to reach. Each trip we will bring God's word to ten different parishes all along the river and bayous."

"Don't you never get tired, Poppa," the boy asked?

"Not when your Momma was with me an' not with you by my side."

Casius was having one of these morbid bouts as they traveled from Grant to Lanceandria in Rapides Parish.

"Poppa," the youth asked, "You said Momma was buried in a crypt."

"Yes, I did son."

"Since you told me, I see lots an' lots of crypts. Why do they put people in crypts an' not in the ground,?" he asked as they drove past a cemetery.

"See there," Marcus said pointing? "They are called 'Cities of the Dead."

"How come, Poppa?" he boy asked.

"Well, let's see. A long time ago they used to bury people under the ground but there were problems with coffins bursting through the ground an' floating away in times of hurricanes, heavy rains an' floods. In those areas with high water tables underground burials were not practical. That's when they began using crypts for burials."

"But," the boy pressed, "I see maybe a dozen names in the stone. Where do they put all of them," Casius asked?

"Many of them are large enough to handle two coffins but after a year, the crypts are reopened, with the permission of the family, an' the old coffins and bodies are broken up. Then these busted up remains are stored in the hollow area under the bottom of the crypt. That's because there's little left after a year because of the extreme heat; the crypts become little ovens, nearly cremating the remains. Then the crypts are laid out in rows resemblin' city streets an' that's where the name came from, 'Cities of the Dead."

"That sounds awful, Poppa," the boy exclaimed.

"Yeah, but it's practical, son."

CHAPTER 7

MOREHOUSE COLLEGE

In western New Orleans, Marcus met with his father-in+law to discuss Casius' education and future. The Reverend Casius Marchman informed Marcus that he was on the board and Advisory Committee of Morehouse College in Atlanta, one of the oldest Black colleges in the United States. He offered to contact these people to make arrangements to have him enter as a freshman if he was sure he wanted his son in a Black college.

"Ah think he could be a force for the Black people one day." Pausing he continued, "Yes, he should attend Morehouse if he can. Where is it located, Casius?"

"It's up in Georgia. Ah'm sure we can work out some sort of scholarship for the boy." Reverend Marchman asked. "I know Honore would be pleased. Would he be willin' to study the word of the Lord?"

"Casius is a natural preacher n' will do us proud," Marcus's replied.

"Well then," Reverend Marchman countered, "Ah'll take care of the housin' an' tuition, you take care of his food an' such. Can you handle that, Marcus?"

Excitedly Marcus replied, "That Ah can handle!" And so it was that Marcus and elder Casius discussed young Casius' schooling, his future and the changes that would be necessary.

Several months later, father and son were walking and chatting together.

"Come September," Marcus said to his son, "you'll be on your way to Atlanta up in Georgia. Your granddaddy pulled some strings an' got you enrolled in an Augusta Institute which is called Morehouse College an' its tuition free. But, listen here; you must maintain at least a "C" grade. Do you think you can maintain that grade? It means study an' lots of it."

"Sure, Daddy!" came the boy's confident reply. "How long will I be there?" Casius asked but he was already looking forward to the move. "What kind of school is it? When will we see each other? Can you afford it?"

"Slow down," his father begged. "You're askin' a jumble of questions all at the same time.

Ask me one question at a time. Morehouse is the oldest Negro church in the United States and is now a Baptist college. As to your second question, you'll be there for four years but at the end of that time you'll have a bachelor's degree in whatever field you choose. As far as affording your upkeep, remember that Prince Albert tobacco can I had? Well, I got it stuffed with bills an' then I stuffed another an' another. We can afford it! I'll just have to dig them up from you're your grandpa's back yard an' hand it over to him. Granddaddy is payin' for your room an' board an' books. You will also have an allowance."

"When will I get to see you and grandpa and grandma?" Casius asked.

"We'll get together," Marcus answered, "on holidays, Easter, Christmas an' such."

"Poppa, I don't know," Casius said his voice quivering, suddenly filled with misgivings. Doubts began to enter his thinking.

His father put his arm around Casius' shoulders, reading his thoughts. He said, "You do the best you can, that will be enough."

Convinced all would be well, father and son purchased a basic wardrobe in Baton Rouge with all the extras, shoes, socks, and underwear and an inexpensive suitcase. They kept to their routine making the circuit rounds only now Marcus had something to crow to his congregation about.

"My son here," he would inform them proudly, "is goin' over to Morehouse College up in Atlanta to learn to be a proper preacher." He placed his arm around his sons' shoulder and hugged him close. "An' you people," he said to his flock, "are responsible!"

"Praise the Lord," came the collective response! Father and son noticed that the collections were much improved with the news.

When September came Marcus, Casius, and the Marchmans were at the Greyhound bus terminal in Baton Rouge. The large gathering of people, the smell of the bus's exhaust fumes was frightening and almost sickening. At last the luggage was loaded underneath and all waited for the signal to board. Marcus was seeing his son off to a better future; the Marchmans were seeing their grandson off to get the college education their daughter had missed, and Casius was full of plans and ideas for his future.

CHAPTER 8

DEATH OF MARCUS

In the fall of 1945 the fifteen year old Casius LeMans entered Morehouse College as a freshman. He noticed that his skin coloration was not the same as most of the other students. He felt different, but it was not just the skin coloration. He got himself settled in the freshman dormitory and later, he discussed his class options with the freshman advisor. He decided to take up the study of Sociology with minors in Comparative Religions and Biblical Studies. College was something he had hoped for and here he was—it defied belief! His ability to make friends served him well and he developed a captivating personality with a quick wit. He was a global thinker and the four years he spent at Morehouse helped him develop and refine his thinking.

The freshman year was spent in establishing a routine; attending classes and scheduling time for study in order that he might do well. In his sophomore year, he maintained the same sort of schedule, adding oratory to his class studies. There was one other addition; he met Angelica Newman, a pretty Black girl who worked in the local Food Lion supermarket where he purchased his foodstuffs. At first he just said hello and goodbye and once in a while called her 'Brown Sugar.' Then, he would arrange to meet her after her shift at the store and they would walk along tree-shaded Parsons Street, then onto shaded Raymond Street, along Milton Street and back to Parsons. It was a route seldom used in the evenings and one where they could be alone. Often they would lie among the trees in a park area off Raymond Street. Not too many walks went by before he was fondling her abundant breasts and getting her aroused. He would break off the petting just as soon as her breathing quickened. He was learning to manipulate this girl's emotions.

"Casius," she whispered one evening, "don't you like me?"

"Sure I do, Brown Sugar," he replied, making his voice waver as he kept petting and caressing her.

"Well then," she pleaded, "why don't you take me? You know I want you to."

"I can't, Angelica," he moaned, "I don't have any protection. I'm trying to think of you."

And so it went, the petting getting more and more passionate. Finally, he thought she was ready. He took her on their usual walk and laid her on a blanket he had previously placed there. She reached into her blouse pocket and withdrew a foil prophylactic. He was dumb struck.

"Angel," he said with husky voice, "what are you going to do?"

"Hush, sweet boy." He reached into his trousers and pulled him out. She could see that he was aroused. She tore open the pouch and began unrolling it on him. Soon, they were frantically removing each other's clothing. It turned out to be a most satisfying encounter for both of them. Afterward they lay naked wrapped in the blanket looking up at the plentiful stars.

"Brown Sugar," he whispered while caressing her lightly with his finger tips around her nipples, feeling them swell under his touch.

"Yes, Casius," she answered snuggling closer.

"You can't tell anyone about us," he went on gently stroking her face and shoulders. "If the college finds out we're lovers, I'd be finished here. This is a religious college and something like this, well. I'll be thrown out of school without so much as a bye your leave and I'll be back in Louisiana."

"Oh, ah wouldn't say a word," Angelica answered earnestly, "not until you say so."

"Have you told anyone about seeing me?" he asked.

"No, baby, you told me not to," she gave him another reassuring reply. She couldn't bear to think of losing this precious boy.

"Well then, Brown Sugar," he said feigning ardor, "let's go again."

These clandestine trysts continued. She was aglow having this handsome college man shower her with attention, affection, and love. She was concerned, however, that they were now taking no precautions against her becoming pregnant. They never talked about it. She was deeply concerned but with his loving assurances, she put her concerns aside.

In his senior year, Casius was doing quite well with his studies, he was certain to graduate with high honors. He had secured a part-time job working for a local minister printing tracts. He had been able to set aside enough money to buy an inexpensive auto from one of the minister's flock.

One fall day, he received a telegram from Grandpa Marchman: "Casius," it read, "your father has had a sudden heart attack in Assumption Parish. He passed away quietly. Funeral—on Saturday—Tickets waiting you at depot—We are sorry, son."

He told Angelica of his father's passing and his need to return home, promising to see her on his return. The following Saturday, in the Reverend Marchmans church, with his father's casket in the aisle draped in a religious flag, he spoke eloquently at his father's passing.

"William Shakespeare said, "Some men are born great, some achieve greatness, and some have greatness thrust upon them'. My father was one of the latter. Many of you heard him preach the Lord's word and let me tell you, he always spoke from his heart. Always!" His shoulders shook, he bowed his head, and he could go no further.

At the gravesite he was not talkative as they placed his father in the crypt with his mother. Upon their return home, his grandfather asked him to join him in the study. It was a room Casius enjoyed with its dark paneling, mullioned windows and the lingering smell of his grandfather's pipe, which the pastor was lighting.

"Son," his grandfather began, "we need to speak of your future. After you graduate, what are your plans?"

"I'm working hard to achieve high honors in hopes that a scholarship might come through to go on to graduate school. Nowadays you need credentials to achieve anything."

"You are to be congratulated for your fine work in college. Your father told you that he would put money in my hands for your schooling and he did. A great deal of money! And we will continue to help you out as best we can. You will have enough to see you through graduate school.

The young man breathed a quiet sigh of relief; this was exactly what he had been planning. In any event; his father's death had made him cautious about mentioning it, fearing it would have appeared too presumptuous. Upon reflection of these thoughts and his relationship with his father, Casius was surprised that he felt no more remorse than he was feeling. They had been close after all.

"How will it be worked out, grandpa?" the young man timidly inquired. "Will I get a lump sum for the tuition and housing expenses?"

"Well, son," Grandpa Casius explained, "if you have no objections, I will continue making payments on your tuition. That will remove a burden from you. On top of that I will send you weekly checks to cover your housing and other living expenses. If that is not enough, you let me know and it will be raised. However, these are not limitless funds so spend wisely."

Relief swept over him. If he could secure a job tutoring or some other thing, he would be in good shape. "I don't need much, grandpa and I would like to go on to graduate school."

With his father's ranch settled, the papers signed, and a new larger wardrobe purchased, Casius returned to Morehouse College and to Angelica. It was as if one door was closing in his life and another was opening.

On their first drive together after his return, she said that she had some news for him. He immediately felt as though someone had struck him a low blow sensing well in advance of her telling him her news. They arrived at their spot and began disrobing.

"Casius," she began hesitantly, "Ah have somethin' to tell you."

He turned toward her anticipating the worst. "What is it, Brown Sugar?" he asked.

"Well, ah was supposed to have my monthly friend cuppla weeks ago, but it hasn't showed up. Ah think Ah'm gonna have a baby." He did not immediately respond, staring intently at her. She went on fearing rejection, "Are you pleased, Casius honey?" she asked anxiously.

This was not exactly what he had been planning. In any event; his father's death rather liberated him. He didn't need this complication in his life, not now. "Why don't we lie down," he said smiling, "and make sure you are." His mind ran on frantically!

Gleefully, and quite relieved, she quickly undressed and lay down on the blanket. "Oh, Casius," she cried relieved, "Ah'll make you happy, Ah promise. Look here," she hurried on, "My nipples are tender to the touch."

He began taking off his clothes his mind racing with the news and its ramifications and at the same time he was aroused. He knew what he had to do. He was aware that he again felt quite analytical, with no remorse. They entwined and he quickly, powerfully broke her neck giving no thought to the child she was carrying. He held her until he could feel her body begin to cool. Well after dark he bundled her and her clothing in the blanket they had lain on. She was flung over his shoulder and carried to the car he had purchased. He drove north on State Road turning off to Jones Bridge Landing. He buried her body in a shallow grave by the bridge, covering it over with twigs, leaves, rocks and some dirt. With a small tree limb he erased all trace and telltale signs of their having been there. He folded up the blanket, threw it in the trunk of the car and quietly drove back to the campus. The following day he laundered the blanket then had it laundered professionally and finally stowed it away in moth balls, forgetting the little inconvenience as he did so.

His senior year was spent in preparation for graduate school. He applied successfully for college grants and with the assistance of several of his professors, was successful in his quest. He joined the debating team and consistently was the school's leading speaker and debater. He was back on the career path he had outlined for himself.

He met another young lady, Kandi Kidman, more practiced than Angelica. It was a welcomed union since both of them entered the relationship for sexual gratification and nothing more.

CHAPTER 9

GRADUATE STUDIES

Casius graduated with high honors in Sociology in 1949. Without much of a layover, he once again boarded a Greyhound bus to make his way north to Crozer Theological Seminary in Upland, Pennsylvania.

Walking down the gray stone wide pathway to the imposing grey structure, he thought the attendance here to be surreal, only dreamed of in the past. A few short years ago he was stomping through the bayous now; here he was finished with undergraduate school and entering graduate school at Crozer.

He had applied earlier with letters of recommendations from many of the Morehouse College faculty. He was accepted and also awarded a full academic scholarship. Here, too, he did well. He met another young lady, a fellow student, also attending classes at Crozer. She too was studying for the ministry. Unlike Angelica, the young lady, Noel Bramford, was most aggressive in her pursuit of him and in her love making. She taught him to think of and take care of a woman's needs and desires. He was an apt student. Her voracious sexual appetite had to be held in check if he were to survive and keep his goals.

One of Casius' favorite teachers was the Reverend James B. Richards the chair of Old Testament History and Exegesis. This man did a great deal to mold the religious insights in the eager student. They became fast friends; probably the only friend Casius would ever know.

In 1955 he graduated with honors in the Master of Divinity program. Casius and Noel had an energetic farewell party and said goodbye. Both had gotten from the relationship what each had wanted. In days and years to come, whenever he thought of her, a smile etched his face in fond memory.

He wrote his grandparents asking their advice on going further for his doctorate in theology, this time in far away Boston, Massachusetts. They were immediately enthusiastic and offered their support. He applied for admission and entered Boston University where in three years; he earned a doctoral degree in Systematic Theology in 1957.

The Reverend Casius LeMans, as he was now recognized, had notable public speaking ability which would later become well-known, improved and developed from his circuit stomping days in Louisiana through his collegiate years and into manhood. He had taken a second in a speech contest while at Morehouse and had won high honors in public speaking and rhetoric while at Crozer. During his senior year at Crozer, his professors were praising Casius for the powerful impression he made delivering his public speeches and oratory discussions. He excelled in Biblical and Historical Studies as well as in Philosophy, Theology, and Ethics but could only achieve average grades in religion, culture and personality. He walked proudly away with a doctorate in Theological Studies.

In each of the institutions of higher education he attended, his professors thought highly of him and each felt he would make a fine minister. They were impressed with his social skills and love of the Bible and its teachings.

His Cajun drawl was completely gone. He had trained himself to speak as the others in his classes. To accomplish this, he had attended speech, rhetoric, oratory classes. He felt ready to launch himself in his chosen field.

CHAPTER 10

CASIUS RIDES THE CIRCUIT

Casius had given no further thought to Angelica although he had ardently followed her disappearance in the local newspapers and on television. Her body, as far as he knew, was never found. After a time she was completely forgotten by the media and as was their hunt for her slayer. He returned to Louisiana and his grandparents. When they saw the tall, lean, handsome, adult young man before them, there was no question of his color; he was family. They were thrilled to see him and listened intently as he regaled them with stories of his travels in Atlanta, Upland and Boston as well as his studies. Pastor Marchman, with great pride, introduced his fully grown grandson to his congregation.

"Today's services will be conducted by my grandson, *Doctor* Casius LeMans!" Their greeting was warm and enthusiastic, his sermon, "Christ's Teachings in Their Lives," enthralled them. After services they clamored to greet him and introduce their unwed daughters to him. He was gracious, charming and each person went away thinking they had known him all of their lives and they had been great friends.

Like his father, he began circuit riding wherever a preacher was needed in an effort to learn if this was his calling. His next romantic encounter took place in Marksville on the Atchafalaya River. She was a light skinned Black woman who was clearly smitten by the handsome Dr. LeMans. Whenever she had dreamed of a young man entering her life, she thought of someone exactly like him. After service she brazenly waited around helping him collect hymnals and tracts.

"Lord, have mercy," he said smiling as he walked up to her. "What is your name?"

She started at the sound of his deep resonant voice and his ice blue eyes. "Rosemary, Doctor LeMans, Rosemary Boston," she replied having difficulty breathing, her small breasts heaving.

"Please call me Casius, Rosemary," he said as he looked deeply into her brown eyes. "If ah'm not bein' too presumptuous," he said feigning a local accent, "may I walk you home this evenin'?"

Rosemary could only manage a nod of her head.

It was oppressively hot in town that night and instead of walking her home; he took her down by the swamp near the river, where the air was much cooler with a soft caressing breeze and the slight smell of magnolia wafted around them. If she had noticed where they were walking she raised no protest. When he had her far from prying eyes, he began gently disrobing her, softly kissing her neck and her shoulders. She shivered under his touch. Casius knew instinctively what needed to be done to claim his prize. He gently brushed her eyes, neck, and shoulders with his fingertips as he unbuttoned her blouse; she wore nothing beneath it. Her breasts burst from their confinement. He bent to kiss each one. His kisses became more ardent, demanding, and she responded appropriately.

"Is this your first time, Brown Sugar?" he asked removing his shirt.

"Yes," she answered holding him tightly to her.

"It's mine too," he lied. "Ah'll be as gentle as Ah can. Is that alright?"

"Casius," she breathed, "you can do anything you want."

He did what he wanted. Afterward, as he lowered her body into the water he could hear the bellow of 'gators nearby. He stood by watching to see if anyone had seen them. Satisfied that there were no onlookers, he picked up her clothing, bundled them in a wad, and dumped them separately in highway trash bins along the roadway. He returned to the meeting ground and finished packing away the hymnals.

Oddly there were no mention of her disappearance and no hue and cry raised for the capture of her assailant.

In Hamburg, he conducted services to perhaps his largest gathering; in Simmesport there was another conquest, Crystal Mason, a youngish Black girl with small breasts, slim waist and broad hips above slender legs. It was getting so easy, so predictable. She too went into the bayou swamp for 'gators and crabs to feast on. Finally, at Fordoche he decided that he needed a rest. He returned to Baton Rouge and home to discuss his plans with his grandparents.

The three of them sat on the veranda, the sun going down in the west and frosted iced tea glasses in their hands. They sat for a while, listening to the evening sounds waiting for Casius to say something.

"I can't do it," Casius said breaking the silence,

"Can't do what, son," Grandfather Marchman asked?

"What my father did all his life," Casius replied.

"But Casius, honey," his grandmother offered, "at least we get together to visit every couple of months."

"I know, grandma," Casius retorted. "But doing circuit preaching is a waste of my education and my degrees," he said in exasperation. He needed their support and didn't want to alienate their feelings.

After a pause, his grandfather said, "He's right, mother, we didn't send him off to Atlanta, Pennsylvania and Boston to have him spend his time in *beaucoup des marais* and the bayous." Turning his attention to his grandson he said, "Where you figuring ongoing, Casius?"

"Well sir," Casius replied with growing excitement, "I thought I would try Chicago, then maybe New York."

"But Casius," grandma pitched in, "who's gonna make your *tourte de pēcan* for you?"

"You are devil, grandma," he replied leaning over to give a loud kiss on her cheek. "You're going to feed me every time I come back home."

The matter was settled and he had their support.

CHAPTER 11

ELOHIM BAPTIST CHURCH

Greyhound Bus Lines transported him from Baton Rouge in Louisiana to Chicago in Illinois. Sightseeing a new and different part or of the country fascinated him but the length of time it took wearied him. As he exited the coach on the outskirts of the city, he sought assistance from *Traveler's Aid* to find the nearest Southern Baptist meeting center only to learn that about two percent of the population was Baptists. He had given this some thought, deciding on this brief stint in Chicago. Perhaps he would join with the *Salvation Army* for a while or some other religious group. He had been preaching to bayou people for a long time, perhaps preaching to people with a little more sophistication would be a good place to start. He knew where he was going; he was a little unsure of the way to get there.

Elohim Baptist Church was an old, worn, ivied covered place of worship. He walked in the darkened nave to savor the feel of this house of God with its blend of incense and candle wax still lingering in the air. All lights were out except for a mini wall lamp illuminating paintings and statuary.

"May I help you young man," came a voice from the darkness?

"No ma'am," Casius responded. "Ah'm lookin' around appreciatin' the wonders that God can do," he said in his deepest Louisiana drawl.

She moved from the darkness into the dim light. She wasn't exactly beautiful—more like a captivating presence. She seemed to glide in his direction. She had long jet black hair, an oval face that had no makeup, a long flowing casual gown that swept along the floor completely covering her slender frame. Casius could feel his breath quicken and his mouth became dry. She was of an indeterminate age; not young but not old either.

"Are you a member of the congregation?" she asked. "I don't recognize you."

"No ma'am, Ah'm from Louisiana near Baton Rouge. Ah'm the Reverend Gregory Wallace," he lied, "here in your city to begin gatherin' my flock."

"A man of God," she exclaimed, "beginning God's precious work. Welcome, young man. You are most welcome. Where are you staying?" she inquired obviously taken by this handsome young man with the beautiful pale blue eyes and winning smile. "I am Luella George, secretary to the Reverend Jeffrey Bollard, pastor here at Elohim."

"Ah just arrived in town an' haven't found a place yet," Casius countered.

"And I will just bet you haven't eaten yet either."

"You are a most engagin' woman, Miss Luella. As a matter of fact I haven't eaten. How did you guess," he said moving on her.

"Well, you just come with me. The pastor just finished dinner but I'm sure there is plenty left over. I'll fix you a plate," she coaxed taking him by the hand and leading him to the parish house. "You don't mind leftovers, do you?" she asked.

"Ah'll eat whatever you have and praise the Lord for your kindness."

While he ate, she drank a glass of red wine with him. As a matter of fact, added to the two glasses she had had at dinner, she was beginning to feel their impact.

"Gregory, may I call you Gregory?" She asked, not wait for a response. "I think I have had a little too much to drink. When you are through, would you mind walking me to my apartment? It's not far from here."

"Miss Luella, Ah would be honored."

He rinsed his dish in the sink as she cleaned up the kitchen. Once done they went out the back way onto the street. As they reached her apartment building she took his hand leading him into the building and into the elevator. Alone in this space she grasped his shoulders and kissed him fiercely. He found it impossible not to respond. Nearing her door they began removing each other's clothing. Her speech might have been slightly slurred but it did nothing to dampen her ardor. A line of clothing, his and hers, led the way to the bedroom. Later, as she slept, he lay there panting, covered with a dim glow of sweat.

"Wow!" he thought. "Wow!" He got up to go to the bathroom and later walked around her apartment. It was richly furnished with find furniture, original paintings and artwork, everything about the place said 'money.' He looked around opening drawers and searching through purses. He found some bills packaged and coins encased in wrappers, in the amount of thirty-seven hundred dollars with a deposit slip to some local bank.

'This must be the Sabbath's collection money,' he mused. "Well, it's mine now." He got dressed and quietly left.

He then tried Naperville, Aurora, and Joliet with the same negative results. His money was adequate for now but the formidable mystique of Chicago held no charm for him. He would try New York.

In July, the seventh month of 1958, fate took a commanding step forward in the life of the Reverend Casius LeMans. The sun had been up for some time and it was just beginning to warm up. The sky was clear and fresh as he walked slowly, deliberately, with his hands swinging effortlessly at his side. It was his twenty-eighth birthday and he had a feeling of great things happening.

He was a tall man, an erect man; he head held high, his vivid ice blue eyes missed nothing. He had a look of confidence and self-assurance. He was in New York where he wanted to be. The fruitless months he had spent in Chicago, convinced him he needed a larger arena. While there he had made two additional conquests who were excellent sex partners but who made the mistake of placing demands on him. Both had died of broken necks and paid dearly for their impertinence. With this behind him, he was seeking a place where he could begin his ministry. "The Lord will provide," he assured himself, "the Lord will provide."

Casius was dressed in an inexpensive black suite with a starched white clerical collar at his neck as befitted his calling. He wore black socks with a pair of highly polished black shoes. His attire had cost everything he had except for seven dollars in his pocket.

"Mystical," he said to himself. "That's what it is, mystical." Seven had always held some high religious meaning for him. He was born in the seventh month, on the seventh day; it had always been his lucky number. Something life-altering was about to happen, he just knew it.

Casually strolling down St. Mark's Avenue in Brooklyn, Casius' right index finger was bent in half and resting on his pursed lips as if pondering some serious matter. He was in a section that was known as Bedford-Stuyvesant, probably had some Dutch origins, he thought. It was an all-Black lower middle class neighborhood, he reckoned; both sides of the street had five and six story apartment buildings; on one side there was a mini-market, a dry cleaner, there were garbage cans standing sentinel by the apartment steps, and garbage lay in the gutters and some on the street. Some children were playing stickball in the street; a fire hydrant had been turned on a garbage can turning the gushing water to a spray. People sat on their stoops watching the children at play; young boys playing stoopball, another group played stickball in the center of the street.

Bedford-Stuyvesant was not a rich area, to be sure, but its residents seemed well enough off. He nodded and smiled to passersby who cheerfully nodded and smiled back recognizing his clerical garb. Suddenly he saw it, a four-story building with a store front chapel and modest appointments. He walked past, not wanting to call attention to himself but just a brief surveillance of the place. He carefully noted the location and address. He recalled a saying by Confucius, "A journey of a thousand miles begins with a single step." He would take that step toward his destiny.

Casius begins his paroxysm by becoming a familiar figure in the neighborhood and around the chapel. For the next several days he observed the comings and goings of the church people, the dirty plate glass window with Rehoboth Bethel Church of God painted in black faded Gothic lettering, "Bishop Jonathan Brown, Pastor." He watched the church during the daylight hours and in the evening. There were, he noted at least fourteen quasi-religious nuns—he thought nuns rather than sisters because they were not cloistered—women wearing course black twill habits and bibs, a black cord tied at the waists that held a black string purse. On their heads were small white starched hat covering close cropped hair; each wore sandals on their feet and all carried tambourines at their sides, no doubt their collection plates. He followed them at a distance as they solicited donations from people on the street, wondering if that were the only source of their income. Casius had always been a global thinker and this talent went into overdrive.

He noted that when the nuns had collected what he estimated to be about five dollars apiece, they were through for the day returning to the chapel. Quickly calculating what he estimated about seventy dollars for the day and that would, he guessed, average four hundred twenty dollars for a six day week and they only worked about half a day. That could easily be doubled. At their present rate they sustained themselves, but only just; at double that amount there could be growth. A plan was beginning to formulate in his mind, a plan that he built upon each night in his Y.M.C.A. room—a room given him in exchange for his holding nightly prayer meetings. When the plan was completed, he wrote to his grandparents quoting 1 Kings: 15:

"Your son whom I will put on the throne in your place will build a Temple for my Name." He told his grandparents he would build a temple in their name in Brooklyn, New York.

He had studied the church; his next task was to study the neighborhood. The people, he noted, spoke many dialects and he questioned people in stores and on the street about these differences. His best source of information was a Black police officer he encountered walking his beat.

"In this neighborhood," the officer informed him, "there are several ethnic mixes of Black and none of them are rich, but they make do. For instance, there are Jamaicans, Hondurans, Puerto Ricans, Columbians, and Guatemalans, some from the Virgin Isles. They spend their evenings sitting on their stoops watching the kids playing in the street or jumping rope. Or some of them play dominos on card tables for money but I'm not supposed to know that. The apartments are too hot so they hang out their windows or on the stoop. And weekends are the worst. The work week is over, the beer begins to flow and without doubt, fights follow, stabbings or shooting are the end result. Nowadays," he went on, "narcotics, heroin mostly are the abuse substance of choice."

"Why are all the houses attached?" Casius asked.

"I was told that they were built as row houses" he informed him, "all have pretty much the same floor plans, and all were built at the same time. It was cost effective and they went up quickly. For a time, we had a major problem with the kids eating the lead based paint that had peeled off the walls. Lots of kids died from that, but not so much anymore."

"Thank you, officer," he said as they parted.

CHAPTER 12

REHOBOTH BETHEL CHURCH OF GOD

In July, the seventh month of 1958, fate took a commanding step forward in the life of the Reverend Casius LeMans. The sun had been up for some time and it was just beginning to warm up. The sky was clear and fresh as he walked slowly, deliberately, with his hands swinging effortlessly at his side. It was his twenty-eighth birthday and he had a feeling of great things about to happen.

He was a tall man, an erect man; his head held high, his vivid ice blue eyes missed nothing. He had a look of confidence and self-assurance. Here he was in New York where he wanted to be. The fruitless months he had spent in Chicago convinced him he needed a larger arena. While he had made two additional conquests who were excellent sex partners but who made the mistake of placing demands on him. Both had dies of broken necks and paid dearly for their impertinence. With this behind him, he was seeking a place where he could begin his ministry.

"The Lord will provide," he assured himself, "the Lord will provide."

Casius was dressed in an inexpensive black suit with a starch white clerical collar at his neck as befitted his calling. He wore black socks with a pair of highly polished black shoes. His attire had cost everything he had except for seven dollars in his pocket.

"Mystical," he said to himself. "That's what it is, mystical." Seven had always held some high religious meaning for him. He had been born in the seventh month, on the seventh day; it had always been his lucky number. Something life altering was about to happen, he just knew it.

Casually strolling down St. Mark's Avenue in Brooklyn, Casius' right index finger was bent in half and resting on his pursed lips as if pondering some serious matter. He was in a section that was known as Bedford-Stuyvesant, probably had some Dutch origin, he thought. It was an all Black lower middle class neighborhood, he reckoned; both sides of the street had five and six story apartment buildings. On one side was a mini-market, a dry cleaner. There were garbage cans standing sentinel by the apartment steps, and garbage lay in the gutters and some on the street.

Bedford-Stuyvesant was not a rich area, to be sure, but its residents seemed well enough off. He nodded and smiled to passersby who cheerfully nodded and smiled back recognizing his clerical garb. Suddenly he saw it, a four story building with a store front chapel and modest appointments. He walked past not wanting to call attention to himself but just a brief surveillance of the place. He carefully noted the location and address. He recalled a saying by Confucius, "A journey of a thousand miles begins with a single step." He would take that step; toward his destiny.

Casius began his research by becoming an even more familiar figure in the neighborhood and around the chapel. For several days he observed the comings and goings of the church people, the dirty plate glass window with *Rehoboth Bethel Church of God* painted in faded black Gothic lettering. "Bishop Jonathan Brown, Pastor." He watched the church during the daylight hours and in the evenings. There were, he noted, at least fourteen quasi-religious nuns—he thought nuns rather than sisters because they were not cloistered—women wearing course gray twill habits, white bibs, a black cord tied at their waists that held a black string purse. On their heads was a small white starched hat covering close cropped hair; each wore sandals on their feet and all carried tambourines at their sides, no doubt their collection plates. He followed some of them at a distance as they solicited donations from people on the street. He wondered if that was their only source of income. Casius had always been a global thinker and this talent went into overdrive.

He noted that when the nuns had collected what he estimated to be about five dollars apiece, they were through for the day returning to chapel. Quickly calculating what he estimated about seventy dollars for the day and that would, he guessed, average four hundred twenty dollars for a six day week and they only worked about half a day. That could easily be doubled. At their present rate they sustained themselves, but only just; at double that amount there could be growth. A plan was beginning to formulate in his mind, a plan that he built upon each night in his Y.M.C.A. room—a room given in exchange for his holding nightly prayer meetings. When his plan was completed, he wrote to his grandparents quoting 1 Kings 15:

"Your son whom I will put on the thrown in your place will build a Temple for my Name." He told his grandparents he would build a temple in their name in Brooklyn, New York.

He had studied the store front church, his next task was to study the neighborhood. The people, he noted spoke many dialects and he questioned people in stores and on the street about these differences. His best source of information was a Black police officer he encountered walking his beat.

"In this neighborhood," the officer informed him, "there are several ethnic mixes of Blacks and none of them are rich, but they make do. For instance, there are Jamaicans, Hondurans, Puerto Ricans, Columbians, and Guatemalans, some from the Virgin Islands. They spend their evenings sitting on the stoops watching the kids playing in the street or jumping rope. Or some of them play dominos on card tables for money, but I'm not supposed to know that. The apartments are too hot so they hang out their windows or on the stoop. And weekends are the worst. The work week is over, the beer begins to flow and without doubt, fights follow, stabbings or shootings are the end result. Nowadays," he went on, "narcotics, heroin mostly are the abuse sub stance of choice."

"Why are all the houses attached to one another," Casius asked?

"I was told that they were built as row houses," he informed him, "all have pretty much the same floor plans, and all were built at the same time. It was cost effective and they went up quickly. For a time, we had a major problem with the small kids eating the lead based paint chips that had peeled off the walls. Lots of kids died from that, but not so much anymore."

"Thank you, officer," he said as they parted.

CHAPTER 13

CASIUS MAKES HIS MOVE

Casius began his research by becoming an even more familiar figure in the neighborhood and around the chapel. After a short period of time, waiting for what he felt was the right moment, he asked for an audience with Bishop Jonathan Brown.

Late one afternoon he strode up to the chapel, knocked loudly, polishing his patent leather shoes on the back of his trousers and brushing some imaginary flecks from his suit jacket. Soon, the door was opened, a nun answering his knock. She held the door ajar while at the same time noticing his clerical collar.

"Can I help you, reverend," she asked?

"Doctor Casius LeMans, sister," he responded elevating his station. "I have an appointment with his eminence," as he spoke he smiled a smile that lighted up his face, winning her over immediately.

"The Bishop is in his study," she replied, returning his smile. "If you will follow me, please," she asked. As they walked down the hallway he was aware of the smell of years of burnt candles, cooking and burnt incense pervading the air. Not an unpleasant smell at all. There were few icons, pictures or statuary and in the chapel he noticed stacks of folding chairs—about fifty he guessed, not a large congregation by any means. The nun knocked on the study door, opening it as she did so.

Casius took in the room, the same dark paneling, the smell in the study was the same as in the hallway plus the aroma of old pipe tobacco and was dark except for a desk lamp, a couch and no side chair.

"Doctor LeMans to see you, Bishop," she announced.

A white-haired, an elderly man wearing a white long sleeved shirt opened at the neck sat behind the old, worn and polished oak desk. The man stood up slowly saying, "Come in, Doctor LeMans, and please come in." The men shook hands while the nun moved to a corner lamp to turn it on for them before leaving.

"Casius LeMans, your eminence," Casius said placing them on a person-to-person basis. "Who is in awe in your presence."

"Sit down, Casius," he said indicating a chair that had been brought in. Bishop Brown again said, "Sit down, Casius. Please be seated." Both men seated themselves. The Bishop continued, "How may I help you?"

Casius noticed the man's weary demeanor, his apparent stoop, snow white hair, and a slight tremor in his blue veined hands. He quickly gets to the point of his visit. He outlined for Brown, in part, his sacerdotal ambitions for the future. He needs at this point in time, he said, the help and assistance of a sponsor, mentor and friend. He continued for some period of time telling the elderly cleric how his humble start in this church can be developed, improved upon and become a religious center in Bedford-Stuyvesant. As he continued weaving his spell, he suggested that Brown take a well-deserved sabbatical leave for a year. At the end of that time, when he returns, if there is not a vast improvement in the church and its operation, he, Casius will move on. If, on the other hand, there are the promised changes and improvements, the Bishop will hire him as an assistant cleric.

LeMans turned his attention to the staff at the church, asking about their hopes and dreams, their feelings, all that he can elicit from the older man. What he hears he absorbs.

Bishop Brown tells him that there are indeed fourteen women who are devoting their lives to God in their humble way. They belong to no recognized religious sect but wear clerical garb nonetheless. Brown, caught up in LeMans verbal trance agrees to take a year's sabbatical leave. In his absence LeMans will run the church operation with the agreed stipulations. Whatever the outcome, Brown will have had a well-deserved paid vacation. A rough contract is drawn up, so glib, spell-binding and convincing is the younger man's hypnosis, and it is signed by both men. As they leave the Bishop's office, one of the nuns is walking by.

"Sister Agnes," Brown asks, "would you please have the others join us in chapel? I have an announcement to make." Sister Agnes hurries off.

The men stand to one side of the old chapel as the nuns gather, setting up the folding chairs. Once they are all present and seated, both men move to the lectern. LeMans is introduced to the gathering.

"Sisters," Brown begins a bright smile on his face, "I have the honor to introduce Doctor Casius LeMans." He turned to LeMans and introduced each of the nuns who stood up as their name was called. Once done, he turned back to LeMans to continue.

"We," indicating LeMans and himself, "have been speaking at some length. As a consequence, I have decided that Dr. LeMans will be taking over my duties for at least a year while I enjoy an overdue sabbatical leave. I have been waiting for an opportunity like this. Now I must go for a while and get some rest."

There is an immediate hubbub among the nuns who had not been expecting the announcement. There had been no indication of any change; no hint of the bishop's leaving. The bishop had confided in no one about his intentions. And, who was this interloper, this new preacher? What kind of person was he?

"Bishop," Sister Ruth asked, "what's to become of us?" There was a nodding of heads and the nuns murmured amongst themselves. Bishop Brown raised his hand quieting them.

Turning to LeMans, Bishop Brown once again identifies the questioner as Sister Ruth Johnson. "Sister, you will go on as before," Brown assured them. "Dr. LeMans has expressed some new ideas that I find exciting. The Lord will be guiding his hands I assure you."

"We know that you need the rest," Sister Claudine stated. "We all know that. But will you be returning?"

To Casius he says, "That is Sister Claudine James. "Yes, Claudine," he answered her reassuringly." I will be back in a year. If the church has prospered in that time, I will hire Dr. LeMans as an assistant cleric. If it has not, we will continue as we have done and Dr. LeMans will seek another appointment elsewhere. Now let us pray for his success as your new pastor and for our church."

The nuns immediately become quiet. They clasp their hands; Bishop Brown and LeMans bow their heads.

"Heavenly Father," Brown intones, "we are about to undertake a change in our church and in our lives. We ask your help and guidance for our new pastor and our church. May both prosper. Amen."

That night at dinner—

"Doctor LeMans," Sister Claudine asked hesitantly, "what changes are you expecting to make?"

"Please call be Pastor or Reverend," Casius responded, establishing a hierarchy, "straight away there will be none," he smiled warmly. "I want to get a sense of our short and long term goals. After that, you will be told of any impending change."

Sister Lynnette Mann called out, "Are you expecting to work us harder that we have been?"

"Once again, Sister," he said smiling pleasantly, "I cannot tell you. We will talk together to see where the church is going; where we can anticipate going. I look forward to working with each of you." His hands swept the entire room. "Let me say this, the Rehoboth Bethel Church of God will, I hope, become a force in the community for God's work."

The women looked around the room, heads nodded and all smiled approvingly. Casius left the table with the Bishop sated in many ways.

CHAPTER 14

BISHOP JONATHAN BROWN, PASTOR

Bishop Jonathan Brown, at age sixty-seven, has been a preacher for thirty-five years. He is a pious man, born in Tennessee, ordained in Texas at the Dallas Theological Seminary and had served in Dallas, Enid, Oklahoma, Jersey City, New Jersey and now in Brooklyn, New York. He was aging he knew, without the vigor he once had and with little to show for his labors. The Rehoboth Bethel Church of God was barely surviving and he had no thought on how to better its prospects. He was, however, progressive enough to recognize the place of youth in his ministry and in his work. If everything turned out as it appeared it might, with this new preacher, he would be the prelate of a larger church and well content to groom someone else to take the reins.

He and Casius had spoken at length of the church and its struggle to survive, about the nuns who went out each day pleading for alms, where he would to go on his sabbatical leave and it was learned that he had often spoken of and yearned to see the Holy Land. His bank account was of sufficient strength to afford such a trip for the year's duration.

Arrangements were made, his tickets delivered. He said his goodbyes, took up his luggage and left in a waiting taxicab. In its wake, the nuns waved until it was out of sight. Casius stood in the doorway smiling. The nuns returned saddened faces but Casius still had a smile on his face.

"In such a short amount of time," he mused, "here he was with his own church. God is good!"

CHAPTER 15

PHASE TWO—ESTABLISH DOMINANCE

Phase one, making an entree, was over and done. Phase two, establishing his dominance, was about to begin. He studied the building's plans and structure, the available records of the church itself. The first floor housed the chapel, kitchen, bath and laundry; the second floor held the church's offices, dining room and bath. The third and fourth floors housed the sleeping quarters of the nuns and a private bedroom and bath for the pastor.

In the following weeks, he held evening services in the small chapel where he was introduced to the congregation, such as it was; seventeen pious souls. The church continued for the next few days with business as usual. The nuns and congregation were taken in by his charm and charisma, his warmth, and apparent piety. He was a forceful advocate of the word. One believer after another came to the chapel to hear and see this new man of God, those that came stayed.

Casius leaned forward his elbows on the pulpit. The chapel hushed, waiting for him to speak. He remained in that position with his eyes shut and his hands clasped in from of him. Then, speaking softly he began . . .

"I want to tell you a story about Job.

> *"Well, Satan wanted God to test Job and his faithfulness. And God agreed. So Job's servant told him his oxen and servants were killed. Another servant told him that lightning had killed his sheep and servants. Still another servant said the Chaldeans had taken his camels and killed his servants. And finally another servant said that a great wind had blown down his house and all his children were slain. Well old Job fell on his face but he did not turn away from God. Even when his friends turned away from him and he was covered with sores he remained faithful to God."*

"My friends, this church are like old Job. It has seen hard time, it has foundered many times, people have turned away but the church endures. Amen?" The few people there were in the church shouted 'Amen!' Casius concluded: "With your help the church will endure. God be praised!"

Pastor LeMans, in his newly assumed title, was out and about in the Bedford-Stuyvesant community. He took an active role in community life, and in local politics. He held meetings where he discussed the church's growth, the number of services were increased to accommodate his burgeoning flock, and there were Bible studies held during the day. The Reverend was becoming known, well known, respected and revered.

At the end of the month, he was preaching in the local high school band room, having stirred religious fervor as never before. He was what the community had been searching for. His devoted congregation grew rapidly. There were now four hundred souls in the congregation.

Behind the scenes the story was somewhat different. After that first week, Casius assembled the nuns in the chapel to inform them of a change he was incorporating immediately. They met in the chapel to discuss these proposed changes.

He stood at the dais his hands clasped in front of him, his eyes closed in meditation. He lifted his head and spoke.

"Up to now, each of you had been collecting about five dollars a day," he informed them. "There are fourteen of you so that totals seventy dollars a day and four hundred twenty dollars each week."

They were looking up at him then at one another a collective smile like the Cheshire cat appearing on their faces.

"On top of that," Casius continued raising his voice slightly, "you only work half a day!" he paused letting these facts sink in. "Henceforth," his voice even louder but not threatening, "you will each collect seven dollars a day. That will net us ninety-eight dollars a day and five hundred eighty-eight dollars a week, increasing our revenue by one hundred eight dollars weekly."

The nuns were stirring uneasily, unwilling to change the status quo.

"Sisters," LeMans went on, "you have been merely surviving on the pittance you have been collecting. With these additional monies we can improve the chapel, clean up our surroundings, and perhaps, put some money aside for a rainy day."

He let them ponder his words, knowing that they would ultimately agree to his proposal. On their first day out on the street with their new incentive, they were able to bring in the stipend asked for and they had not had to work much longer. This increase had not been all that bad.

LeMans was also a virile man. First one then another was invited to share his room for the night. None resisted or complained. Those chosen were flattered and made to feel honored, special and they felt that they truly were. It was also universally felt that it was the obligation of the servant to satisfy the sexual needs of the pastor. He was, after all, a pious man, a religious man, and a man of the Bible. Refusal of his advances would have been unthinkable. Besides, he was a better than average sexual partner. They had blushed coyly at his inference about 'getting into the habit.'

The nuns discovered that the two dollar increase was not all that difficult. Another week went by when they were once again called to the chapel. Casius was to introduce another innovation.

Once again he posed at the rostrum, his hands clasped before him. He raised his head.

"You all are working hard for the church. Now, I want to try something we have never done before." He could see that their interest was aroused. "After I have delivered my evening sermon and before the hymns are sung, I want two of you to pass tambourines among the gathering to collect donations." He instructed them to "plant some seed money—a dollar bill and some change in your tambourines."

Sister Juanita Evans voiced a protest, "We've never done that before!"

"No," he said agreeably, "you never have. All I'm asking is that we give it a try."

That evening in chapel he delivered his mother's favorite psalm passage with the same introduction that he had used at her death.

"The Lord is my shepherd;
I shall not want.
He makes me to lie down in
green pastures . . ."

Several people in the audience cried out, "Praise be!" and "Tell us, Pastor." The words of the psalm rang out in the chapel mesmerizing his listeners. He finished the psalm making its words fit into and enrich their daily lives. He had orchestrated their responses to almost a fever pitch. Unnoticed were the tambourines passing from hand to hand. When he was finished he knew that the experiment had been successful, the tambourines were almost overflowing.

Some days later, Casius, who was all smiles these days, called for another household meeting in the chapel, he had something else to ask of them.

At this meeting there was no preamble.

"We have been doing reasonably well," he began his understated remarks. "The front plate glass window has been scraped, washed, cleaned and the church's name made larger. We have newer hymnals to accommodate more parishioners. And, I notice, even with the additional income you are generating you are still working only about five hours a day. Therefore, you are now going to bring in ten dollars a day and you know that that is not a great deal of money. In so doing, that will give us a total of one hundred forty dollars a day and eight hundred forty dollars weekly or translated in broader terms, we will have about forty-three thousand six hundred eighty dollars annually. Just think of what *we* can do with that amount of money! And that does not include what we are taking in the collections."

"No, no pastor!" Sister Anne Soriano called out. "That is too much! It can't be done!"

He glared at the offending nun and then thought of an old hokey adage and thought it fit here appropriately. He leaned forward on the rostrum and said softly, "Edgar Guest, in his collected verses, included a saying that fits this situation:

> "Somebody said that it couldn't be done,
> But, he with a chuckle replied
> That "maybe it couldn't," but he would be one
> Who wouldn't say so till he'd tried.
> So he buckled right in with the trace of a grin
> On his face. If he worried he hid it.
> He started to sing as he tackled the thing
> that couldn't be done, and he did it."

He was trying to be patient. "Sister Anne," he forced himself to remain calm, "that's all I'm asking, that you try. We need to expand our facilities," he seethed. "Our congregation is rapidly growing and before and after every meeting you have to set up and put away our metal seats. I know it will mean that you will have to work harder or maybe longer, but it needs to be done!" Then we can install permanent seating."

"We'll be out all day," Sister Ruth complained.

"Ruth," he countered, "you need new sandals or maybe shoes for the winter months. You all need new habits and I want you to have them. I'm not spending any money on myself. We can't do any of those things with our present checking balance. This increase is needed! I sincerely wish there was another way but there isn't."

After further debate, Casius gave them logical arguments against their objections. Finally, they agreed to try to increase the income. Their first day on the street, they found to their collective surprise, that it could be done. They spent more time on the street but it really wasn't that strenuous. In addition, the people seemed to be more generous when they learned that they were collecting for the now well-known *Rehoboth Bethel Church*. In a demonstration of their achievement, construction began on expanding the chapel, pews were set in place that would almost double their capacity, and the pastor's study was brought to the second floor. The women had new clothing and shoes and all had a sense of accomplishment.

CHAPTER 16

CHARISMA

With all the construction going on, the church was a beehive of activity. In the height of the hubbub, a local businessman came to the church asking to see the Pastor. Sister Anne ushered him into the Pastor's new study to the sound of hammers and radial saws at work.

"Good afternoon, Pastor," the tall, distinguished man in a grey Brooks Brothers suit said. "I am Isaac Montgomery. I own Montgomery Motors on Eastern Parkway."

"Yes, Mr. Montgomery, please come in. Sister will bring us some tea." He said nodding to Sister Anne who was standing nearby.

"Let me get right to the point," Montgomery said once seated, "I know how busy you are."

"Please do."

"I own the two building adjacent to this one."

"I didn't know that."

"Anyhow, we have been noticing how hard you and your sisters have been working in recent weeks and how quickly your church has been growing, making your need for space more acute."

"Amen to that brother Montgomery." Casius felt he knew where Montgomery was going but tried to rein in his excitement.

"Pastor LeMans," Montgomery went on, "We would like to make a gift to the church of those two buildings."

"Sacrēe boucane!" exclaimed LeMans reverting to a Cajun exclamation. Then, noting the confused look on Montgomery's face, he hastened to explain. "It is an old Louisiana exclamation of surprise, Mr. Montgomery. It means roughly 'holy smoke!' In spite of himself, Casius grinned as Sister Anne poured their tea.

Montgomery grinned as well. "Pastor," he said, "it's a win-win situation. In addition to our getting an income tax deduction for the contribution, the company will also realize a tax credit. All we have to do is sit down with my lawyers, some of the state representatives and complete the title transfers. The buildings are fifteen years old and have been maintained quite well. There are some tenants but most of the buildings have been kept vacant in recent months."

Using the royal title, Casius said, "We are most grateful to you, Brother Montgomery. What you are proposing is overwhelming and extraordinarily generous."

"I will be back in touch with you to complete the transaction. May I suggest that you secure the services of an attorney to watch out for the church's interests? We might also have to meet with some politicians to get the tax credits but I am informed that it should be no trouble."

The men chatted over tea for some time then warmly shook hands. Montgomery gave Casius an embossed business card as Casius saw his visitor to the door bidding him farewell. With the door closed, he did a jig causing several of the nuns to stare in amazement. It was time for phase two of his plan, building his family.

CHAPTER 17

PROPERTY ACCUMULATION

Quite naturally the media got word of the church's windfall, especially since it was advantageous to Montgomery to let the word out. It gave them press and television attention for several days. Those members of the congregation who were apparently better off than the others, a fact learned from careful observation and astute questioning, were asked to a Sunday tea with the Pastor and a select group of nuns. The dining room had been cleared and tables set up.

Inroads and progress were measured and examined by the group as measured by the additional services being offered and the increase in local participation in all the church's functions. There was something going on day and night. He presented to the group a critical self-assessment and he asked for their assistance in moving forward. They wanted to know what the church's most critical needs were and he prefaced their needs by informing them of the acquisition of the two adjacent buildings. They were astonished. He went on . . .

"What we need now is money to refurbish these buildings, have classrooms built in order that we might start up a day care center and perhaps a preschool to accommodate the church's growing need to better serve the community. That will require hiring appropriate staff, hiring teachers, checking their credentials or getting them credentialed, and someone to supervise these schools. We have the opportunity to really do some community good."

One member of the assembled group, one Clarence Barton spoke up. "Dr. LeMans, I work in an agency that needs venture capital on a continuum for a number of projects. I have the background and the knowledge of where to write and who to write to in securing grants from local, state and federal agencies. It does not and will not represent a conflict to my firm. If you wish, I can get started on drafting several grant proposals and making a few contacts to see how much we can get done for the church."

"Mr. Barton," Casius humbly replied, his right index finger bent and placed against his lips contemplating the offer. "You are most generous. I did not know there were such funds available for an undertaking such as we have in mind."

"There is, sir, especially for a minority religious undertaking such as you propose," Barton informed him.

Another of the assembled group spoke up.

"Mr. Barton, Pastor, I am Jeffrey Grantland, an attorney dealing in acquisitions here in the city and community. I would be honored gentlemen, to give whatever legal support you might need at no immediate cost to the church. If matters move along favorably, and I'm sure they will, then I would like to be considered as legal counsel."

"Gentlemen, I am truly astonished. The Lord is good, the Lord is great," he said as he tented his fingers.

"Clarence and I can meet separately," Grantland continued, "in my office and get the ball rolling for your project." Others in the ad hoc group voiced their willingness to assist in whatever way they may. The meeting was adjourned and he was alone, Casius seated himself contemplating with his index finger pressed against his lips, what had just taken place. Suddenly he looked up. Of course, he thought, it was the seven day of the month. He should have known.

Chapter 18

FRUITS OF THEIR LABORS

With everything moving along so well, Casius added a new item to his wardrobe, a large gold cross with an amethyst centerpiece on the outside of his clerical vest. Too, he felt that it was time to ratchet up his plan a notch. The nuns were pleased with their contribution to the overall success of the church and the enormity of the gifts that the church had received. He knew that they were please to be part of the *Rehoboth Bethel Church of God*. He called them into assembly where he divided them up into seven families, once again reverting to that mystical number. He was doing this, he said, with a view toward future growth.

He began by saying, "Our family has grown in recent months and it shows signs of further development (Sister Anne and Claudine were pregnant). For that reason, we need to establish a sense of legitimacy for the church and for ourselves."

LeMans began the meeting with a quote from the Bible: "In [Psalms 119:164] 'Seven times a day I praise you . . .' in [Luke 11:26] 'Then he goes and takes with him seven other (sic) spirits . . . and they enter and dwell there,' and in [Acts 6:3] 'Seek out from among you seven (wo)men of good reputation.' With these core families," he explained, "I shall start families. Seven of you will be the mother of children we shall produce and seven of you will assist in their upbringing."

"What nerve you have," Sister Naomi Randolph said nonplused. "To assume we would go along with such a thing; seven families, indeed!"

"Alright Sister," he interrupted soothingly, "that is something for you to think about and for the future. On another matter, your daily alms collections are being increased by another five dollars. We have a lot of work to do and we need the extra money. By the way, these monies would amount to better than sixty-five thousand five hundred twenty dollars a year. This will probably be the last increase asked of you."

He walked out of the assembly, leaving them to discuss both issues among themselves. At first the group was against both proposals, they were aghast at his seven core family's concept. As the discussions wore on it was learned that two of the nuns, Sister Anne, Claudine and Sister Ruth were already pregnant. Since this was the case, they decided that the seven family concepts could be tolerated. In fact, it might make him more understanding of their situation.

"Well he is very good when you are invited to spend the night with him," Sister Anne laughed. "In fact," Anne continued, "he called me 'his brown sugar!' Several others joined in the laughter.

Sister Ruth added meekly, "He calls me that too."

"Yeah," Sister Rhoda Cummins said, "all that's well and good but what about this added income we are now responsible for? How are we goin' to manage that? People just won't give us that kind of money."

Sister Anne interrupted, "Wait a minute. We said the same thing about the other increases and we managed to get the money and people out there are willing to help. Since he came here, aren't we better off than we were?"

Sister Claudine suggested that they give it a try to see if it would work. "If it doesn't," she said, "we can ask him to reconsider." Several of the others joined in. It would take some hustle on their part, they decided, but maybe it could be done. Some asked about the monies that had already been brought in. How was it being spent? No one volunteered to ask him about it. At last, it was agreed, they would try their best. They saw the obvious changes that had taken place, but had the money gone to pay all of that?

CHAPTER 19

ASSIGNMENT FAILURE

Everything was moving forward for about a week. On Tuesday evening of the second week of the latest edict, the nuns learned another, more grievous lesson. Sister Oprah Thomas turned in her collections; she was, however, one dollar and twenty-five cents short. The nuns were required to put their collections into a wicker basket where it had been counted by the pastor and noted in a ledger. Visibly the Reverend—as he was now being called—was quite annoyed and upset. He had known beforehand that this was bound to happen. It had only surprised him that it had not happened before this. He needed this to happen in order to move forward. It was the opportunity he had been waiting for. Casius called the others into the dining room. Up to now, they had been unaware of Oprah's shortfall.

The Reverend's face and manner displayed absolutely no emotion. "Sister Oprah," he announced tonelessly, "did not meet her obligation today. She has let us all down and that is quite unacceptable!" He raised his right hand pointing in her direction. "Oprah, remove your clothes," he demanded!

Visible shaken, Oprah looked to the others for someone to stand up for her. A sea of downcast eyes could not meet hers. All were sympathetic but all were too frightened to say or do anything.

"Reverend," Oprah said pleadingly, "you don't mean for me to take all of my clothes off in front of everyone."

"I do mean it! I mean do it now!" he roared at her, his face turning livid.

"Reverend," Sister Ruth was the first to speak up, "how much is she short. We can make up the difference between us."

"No!" he said emphatically, "I will not allow that!"

Haltingly, timidly Oprah began to disrobe. A growing pile of her clothing was laid at her feet. Now she became angry. She stood erect, threw her shoulders back, looking Casius in the eyes, defying him. Her shoulders shook as she quietly removed her habit and undergarments.

He recognized the rebellion there; it had to be stopped immediately. There were pocket doors from the dining room to a small meeting room. He went to the doors, threw open one side and disappeared inside. He returned with a length of fiberglass fishing rod the eyelets removed, which he used to cut through the air as he walked to the offending nun. The women stepped back reflexively. They saw what was coming but could not believe he would do it. Casius went over to Oprah, some of her defiance withering. She was bound hand and foot with duct tape. He forced her mouth open to shove a handball into her mouth, which he also lashed in place with duct tape. Casius began to lash her about her body, each blow bringing agonizing screams now muffled by the gag and she could not run from the blows. The others watched in unbelieving horror moving further away from the Reverend and Oprah. Casius continued beating her until mercifully she fainted, lying still on the floor. There were angry red welts all over her body. He turned abruptly to the others.

"When you are told to bring in a specified amount," he said raising his voice, his eyes ablaze, "you *will* bring in that amount!" He cut the tape and removed the handball; turned to return to the meeting room leaving Oprah to the others to care for her.

"Can you believe it?" Sister Anne whispered when he had gone.

"Yeah," Sister Aquida Cruz said quietly, "he's a mean sommna bitch!"

Sister Ruth, daubing Oprah's wounds as she also helped her to get dressed added, "You got that right!"

"Wait'll the Bishop gets back," Sister Anne offered.

"One thing though," Sister Charlotte Williams observed, "Until he does get back, we had better hustle our bustle unless we want some of the same."

The women went with their companion back to her room where they washed her and applied aloe vera on her welts. Each kept their private thoughts about what had just taken place. However, there had been no outcry against it, merely tacit acceptance. Another macabre message had been transmitted and received by all and when they thought about it, not one of them spoke out or moved in her defense.

Casius came back into the room to see how they were progressing and to squelch any discontent there might be. Sister Ruth advanced toward him unafraid.

"Reverend, why don't you beat us all right now?"

"Why should I do that?" he asked but had an inkling of what was to come.

". . . 'cause each of us will be short at some time or another, so beat us now and get it over with. It's gonna happen anyhow."

"What you say is no doubt true. May I suggest an alternative?" he said offering appeasement.

"Like what, for instance?" Ruth asked.

"When you find that you are unable to achieve the day's goal, one of you find a runaway, preferably a light-skinned Black girl with no family ties and bring her back to the church."

Sister Agnes argued, "How are we to get them to come back with us?"

Patiently he murmured, "Invite them to have a meal with us, or a place to stay for the night, or both."

"What will happen to them when they get here?" she asked.

"We will feed them, clothe them and see if they want to be part of the church," Casius answered exasperated at being quizzed.

"That," Agnes said, "doesn't sound like such a bad idea."

"It isn't, think of it as a recruitment drive," he said.

CHAPTER 20

THE DEMISE OF BISHOP BROWN

Several days later, and exactly one year to the day, Bishop Brown returned to his church on Brooklyn Avenue. He was warmly received by his nuns. They held off telling him about the monster he had left in charge, opting instead to allow him to get comfortable. For his part, the Bishop was overwhelmed by what confronted him. This young zealot had performed nothing short of a miracle.

Coming out to meet the cleric, Casius held out a hand in welcome a smile on his face.

"Bishop," he called out, "welcome home! You have been missed, sir."

"Thank you, Casius. It's good to be home," the elderly man replied.

He took the bishop on a brief tour of the buildings making note of each change. The last stop on the tour, he took him to the adjoining buildings newly furnished as schoolrooms. When the tour ended, he led the older man upstairs, he saying, "You look well-rested and fit."

"But eager to get back in harness," he said trying to assure his colleague.

For his part the Bishop was overwhelmed by what had confronted him. This young zealot had performed nothing short of a miracle. He noticed the larger chapel, the relocated prelate's office, the enlarged dining area, the large oval picture of praying hands that dominated the hallway. Now there was statuary, the lighted bulletin board outside the front entrance, the additional pew seating instead of metal chairs, icons, pictures, and the fresh painted look of the place. Everything said newness. What had been a meager abode for God's house was now a revitalized religious chapel. One of the most attractive features was a large mahogany dining table covered with a lace cloth and a shining silver platter that added a sense of elegance. He felt renewed religious fervor.

He was shown to a spare bedroom to unpack and freshen up. Casius asked the bishop to join them at lunch. Brown accepted and as he seated himself beside his assistant at the head of the table, he brought the gathering up-to-date on his travels but he also had many questions about the church and its development; and sought answers. Brown seemed pleased with all the answers he was receiving, the acquisition of the two adjacent buildings; the plans for as education center; the increase in revenue, and the expansion taking place. Much was under construction to be sure, but it was taking place.

Casius continued speaking of certified teachers in their classrooms, of federal, state and local funding they were receiving to aid in the running of the schools. He spoke of the multiple plans he had for the future of the church.

As the women left the church after the midday meal, the men retired to the study to continue their chat, they had the house and chapel to themselves. Idle chatting turned to a more pointed discussion about the future and who would hold what position in the church. Casius escorted the elder cleric throughout the church explaining the changes that had been wrought. He lured the bishop to the basement to discuss the architectural plans for that area. Some of the construction work had already begun. They took seats in the bleachers.

"What is the purpose of these bleachers?" Brown asked.

"They are for large assemblies. We can seat more people this way."

"And what of the steel table in the floor's center?" he probed.

"That Bishop is the altar for the services we conduct here. To another matter, now that you have seen what has been done in your absence, where do you see me in your scheme of things?"

"Casius, it has taken be more than thirty years to have this church operational. What you have done in my absence is truly remarkable. You foresight obviously surpassed mine. I would like you to stay on as the assistant pastor of the church. You can keep doing as you have been doing only I will be by your side throughout. How does that sound?"

"More than I had thought." No, I will not be your assistant, Casius mused, and there will be a change in leadership in this church. You, old man, have outlived your usefulness.

Bishop Brown looked around at the well-lighted basement. It was deeper than he had remembered. Now, it looked as though it had been built as a miniature amphitheater with tiered seating around three sides and in the center of the floor; a stainless steel altar-like table was bolted in the concrete beneath which was large grated sewer plating.

"That's an altar in the center there?" he asked his assistant as he turned away from him to point to the table.

Bishop Jonathan Brown never felt the blow that ended his life. His lifeless body fell to the floor. This was the first of many blood lettings that would take place in this part of the house. Casius unhurriedly hefted the body to the table and began disrobing his mentor. Swiftly, with no sense of emotion he dismembered the body and packaged it in heavy-duty plastic for disposal later. Bishop Brown's head was washed and saved; it would serve another purpose later. Next he turned his attention to the table and surrounding area that needed to be washed and cleaned. A high-powered hose did the clean-up efficiently. This done, he returned to the study.

Later, when the women returned, they noticed that the pocket doors to the dining area were closed and locked. It would have been unthinkable for any of them to open what the Reverend had obviously closed and secured. Not long afterward they were all summoned to the chapel. They thought they were to receive another increase in the solicitations. The door was flung open allowing Casius to burst into the room. The women quickly, quietly seated themselves. He began the meeting by walking to the pulpit, took hold of it with one hand and with the other clasped the cross around his neck. The women noticed that the bishop was not present. Perhaps he would be there later, they thought. Casius began the meeting with quotes from the Bible dealing with his mystical number. He explained, "The number seven is used in the Bible eight times: in Psalms 119:164; in Luke 11:26 and 17:4; in Acts 6:3; in Revelations 1:4; in Daniel 9:24; in Matthew 18:22; and in Luke 10:17." Using these passages as his theme, Casius told the gathered women that seven had always been a mystical number with him and told them of the events that centered on that number.

"Therefore," he continued, "seven of you have been selected with whom I shall procreate. These seven women will represent an inner core family grouping and they will be accorded special privileges. The remaining seven will continue as usual and only be called upon as needed."

The expected murmuring and discontent began. The Reverend glared at them from his pulpit. Turning quickly away from the group he strode to the dining room. Casius always believed in taking swift and immediate action whenever disapproval or a threat became manifest. He did so now. He motioned them to follow him to the closed pocket doors. Pausing for effect, his index finger bent across his lips contemplating something momentous, he threw the doors opens.

Collectively the women took a backward step. Many put their hands to their mouths while others covered the faces completely. All let out an audible horrified gasp. Many of them began crying uncontrollably; two fainted. There was the mahogany table covered with the lace table cloth and lighted by a spotlight focused on the center of the table. And there on the silver tray bathed in the white light was the head of the former pastor of the Rehoboth Bethel Church of God, Bishop Jonathan Brown, his eyes wide open and his mouth closed. Casius turned to see if all of them were looking at his presentation and if it was having the desired impact. They were and it was.

"I will dispose of this," Casius said as he lifted the tray, "you others, get dinner started." He said no more; nothing needed to be said. If they did not get what he asked for, the consequences would be dire indeed.

Two more of the women collapsed to the floor, the rest stood about in shocked horror and disbelief. This could not be happening. It had to be a cruel nightmare. The crying was heart-felt and became a mournful wail.

Sister Lynnette Mann fell to her knees, her hands clasped together. "Oh, Sweet Jesus, Oh, Sweet Blessed Jesus."

CHAPTER 21

NEW ASSIGNMENT INTERVIEW

On the tenth floor of Police Headquarters, at One Police Plaza, three men sat at a small wooden table, inside a small conference room. The room was windowless but well lighted. At the head of the table sat Deputy Chief Inspector Matthew Pender, Commanding Officer of the Special Investigations Division, on the right side was Deputy Inspector Donald Cowan, administrator of that division, and facing the Deputy Chief was Sergeant Lance Carpenter, commanding the Brooklyn South Anti Crime Unit.

"You have been asked to meet with us, sergeant," Chief Pended opened, "to discuss an undercover assignment dealing with a Puerto Rican subversive group, known colloquially as the FALN. I am looking for a man I can trust," he said pompously. "Are you the man I am looking for?" he asked almost rhetorically.

"Chief," Carpenter replied brushing a strand of hair from his eyes, "my reputation in the department should answer that. As for the FALN, it's the abbreviation of Spanish Fuerzas Armadas de Liberación Nacional, or 'Armed Forces of National Liberation." It is a separatist organization in Puerto Rico that has used violence in its campaign for Puerto Rican independence from the United States.

Deputy Inspector Cowan opened a folder before him. "In Anti Crime, where you are now, your team has an outstanding arrest and conviction record. In the Second Division as the plain-clothes supervisor, you also had an outstanding record. In fact, sergeant, your records sounds like that of a most dedicated and capable police officer."

Carpenter, for some inexplicable reason thought of the last time he had seen his friend. They were patrol officers in the Tenth Precinct on Manhattan's lower west side, an area known as Chelsea. Carpenter had been asked by the precinct commander, Captain Sanford Garfield, to retrieve some cocktail frankfurters and buns from a distributor and put the boxes in the Captain's car trunk. There were three boxes each three feet long, a foot wide and deep. Juggling the three boxes he walked out of the station house, he tripped going down the three steps and off balance fell in the street scattering hot dogs and buns in the roadway. He got to his knees, scooping up hot dogs, buns and dog shit at the same time. Each arm full was thrown into a box. Patrolman Cowan sat is a patrol car laughing at the comic scene before him.

"Get out here and help me," Carpenter called to the officer.

"And get myself with shit all over me, no thank you," he rebuffed.

Twentieth Street is one way westbound and vehicles began moving down the street to the police officer on his hands and knees. The cars forced him to stand and stop traffic then resumed his task. He gathered up what he could, opened the car's trunk and threw the boxes into it and slammed the lid.

The next morning, as he was turning out to begin his tour, Captain Garfield called to him to remain behind.

"Were those the boxes you put in the trunk the ones that Rocco Panetta gave you for me?" he asked.

"Yes sir, three boxes marked 'Sabrett."

"You should have seen what I got. There was dog shit, dirty papers and cups and other garbage. Wait until I see him!" he snarled

The Chief bent to the briefcase on the floor beside him, muttering, "We'll see whether he's a dedicated police officer," responding to Cowan's observation. He removed what appeared to be a 4.5 inch by 3.5 inch booking photograph of known felons stamped with departmental markings on the back. He selected one.

"Do you know this man?" he asked as he slid the picture across the table face down, it read: Police Department City of New York. It listed the crimes of assault and robbery, it listed the pedigree of the person arrested, listed the date of the arrest as March 20, 1942 and disposition: 'Not guilty,' over forty-five years ago.

He turned it over and looked at it. "Yes, sir," he answered. "That is my wife's uncle Antonio LaRosa," he said handing back the photo. He is known to the Department as 'Toni Brighton.' He turned to look at the deputy inspector who had asked him to come to this meeting. Inspector Cowan shrugged his shoulders almost imperceptibly as if he didn't know what this was all about.

The Chief continued, "Are you aware that this man is in usury in Brooklyn? He's a loan shark, for God's sake. He's with Jimmy Epps aka Bath Beach's outfit. And are you in this man's company a great deal," the Chief continued edging closer to the table? He looked as though he were angry about something.

Carpenter knew immediately that he was not to be considered for any assignment. He decided he would play a little head game with this nasty supervisor.

"Well, sir, I do know of the man's background in loan sharking but he has never conducted business in my presence. And I would suppose the answer to your other question is that it would depend on one's interpretation of 'often'. I see him once or twice a month, depending on the occasion."

Chief Pender glanced at Cowan, a trace of a smile on his face. "What would make that determination?" He sat back knitting his fingers together behind his head.

"Well, sir, we would see one another at family weddings, a wake, holidays, or someone's birthday; those kinds of gatherings. Oh yes, we meet once a year at a family outing. If there is other than family members at any of these gatherings, I am always introduced as Carpenter the cop."

"That's it?" he said annoyed. "Those are the only occasions?" the Chief said loudly, glaring at his subordinate. "There are no other occasions that you might meet with this man?"

With complete innocence, he responded, "Why else, Chief? Those are all that come to mind. I thought I was ordered to be here to discuss an undercover assignment."

Ignoring Carpenter's remark, Chief Pender went on, "You said there would sometimes be other than family there at the gatherings. What were they there for?" Chief Pender inquired.

Pausing as if considering the question, he put his left forefinger alongside his cheek, the other fingers cradling his jaw, he said, "Each time I noticed their presence, it was to pay their respect to the person being honored. You know at weddings, at birthdays and similar occasions. On rare occasions he would show up to take his sister, my mother-in-law out to dinner and we would go, along with my father-in-law."

The inspector slid another photograph across the table. "Does this look familiar?" he snarled.

Carpenter saw that it was a long distance surveillance photograph and that it had been taken of the elevated front porch of Uncle Toni and Aunt Rosa's house on Shore Road in Brooklyn. There was a red, green and white awning overhead and on the central table was a large birthday cake. "Oh, yes, this looks like the gathering we had for Aunt Rosa's sixty-seventh birthday. We had been invited to celebrate with them."

"Oh, very cozy," the Chief remarked. Sensing that this man would not cave in immediately, Chief Pender changed his tactic. "Have you ever received any gifts from this man?"

Carpenter paused as if thinking, his index finger along his right cheek, and his fingers under his chin yet carefully guarding his answer. "Yes, sir I have received numerous gifts from Uncle Toni and Aunt Rosa," he said without guile.

Chief Pender smacked his hand on the table as if he had scored a point. "You know that members of the force are not allowed to receive gratuities, especially from known felons? What sort of gifts have you received?"

Trying to appear overpowered, "These were not gratuities," he stammered. "He has taken my in-laws and my family to dinner on the occasion of someone's birthday, as I've said. He has also given birthday gifts to my children and again at Christmas."

Pender interrupted, "Monetary gifts?"

"Oh, no sir, he has given underwear, sweaters, socks, that sort of stuff, to my wife and children."

"No sergeant, monetary gifts to you personally!" came his annoyed rebuff stressing the fact that Carpenter was a subordinate and he a Deputy Chief.

Carpenter had to stifle a laugh, "Oh no, sir, that would be illegal and a violation of Departmental Rules and Regulations."

"Get the hell out of here!" he ordered. "Return to command."

"Am I to take it Chief that I am not to be considered for this undercover assignment?" Carpenter asked, his face the mask of innocence.

"No, sergeant you are not being considered for any assignment."

Carpenter rose and glanced again at his friend. Cowan was mute. He left the meeting wondering why he had been asked to go on this fishing expedition in the first place.

CHAPTER 22

ASSIGNMENT: PISTOL LICENSE BUREAU

Back in his office, the telephone rang. "Sergeant Carpenter, Anti Crime, may I help you?"

["Carpenter?"] It was the familiar voice belonging to Deputy Inspector Donald Cowan. ["What are you doing for lunch?"] the caller asked.

Carpenter knew that his friend wanted to talk. "I have no plans," he did not identify the caller.

["If you want to meet me at the Corner House Restaurant in the Six-Eight, I can be there by twelve-thirty."]

The phone went dead, the appointment made. At the appointed time the two men met. They were seated in a corner booth and after they had ordered lunch, they enjoyed their drinks of Chianti wine. The Corner House was a neighborhood Italian restaurant and bar owned and occupied by the same owner, Giuseppe Grappa, for seventeen years; he was known to both men.

Cowan spoke first. "Carpenter, I didn't know that old sonofabitch was going to sandbag you. I was as surprised as you were."

"Don't sweat it, Don," Carpenter smiled at his friend. "I know you wouldn't chop my legs off without a heads up."

"I liked the way you handled him, though," came Cowan's reply. "That's the good news."

"What's the bad news, Don?"

"The Chief thinks you're a smartass and is having you transferred to the Deputy Commissioner Legal Matters, License Division forthwith, the PLB specifically."

Carpenter was incredulous. "The Pistol License Bureau," he queried? "He's taking me off the street and sticking me in PLB? What did I do wrong besides pissing him off?"

"You did nothing wrong, Carpenter. The Chief thinks you bested him and he doesn't like being bested in anything. But he is sweetening the pot for you. You're on the Lieutenant's list and he's bumping you up so that you will be the whip in the PLB," Cowen said trying for appeasement.

"The best part," he went on, "you'll be assigned at Centre Street, you lucky guy."

"Yeah, lucky, that's me." Carpenter was obviously disappointed at this turn of events. "Great, I'm to be the whip in a dead ass desk job." Carpenter said despondently. "We used to be friends, weren't we, Don?"

Ignoring the rhetorical question, Cowan responded, "Do you penance and we'll work something out for you. By the way, what kind of guy is Uncle Toni?"

A smile crossed his friends face. "Uncle Toni is an old-world Italian and not too bright. To give you an idea, one day he calls me, he says: ['Lance,'] in that gravelly voice of his, ["I tink my phones are up,"] he said mimicking the man.

"You mean wiretapped?" Cowan asked disbelieving the stupidity of such a statement.

"Yes, exactly so I ask Uncle Toni, 'where are you calling from?"

He answers, ["from da house, where else?'] I hung up on him."

"Nah," Cowan said. "Nobody is *that* stupid!"

"Oh, no? One night he calls the house, he says:

['You know who dis is?]

'Yeah, I said.'

[I got some swag," he says, "you want some?']

I said, 'What?'

He says, ['You know C U T T Y S A R K,' spelling it out.]

I ask him, "Uncle Toni, don't you think whoever is listening knows how to spell?"

["Awright," he said, "furgedabodit."]

For the remainder of the luncheon they spoke of past memories. "Do you remember Lock 'em up Reilly?" Cowan asked.

"Oh yeah," Carpenter said. "The Mounted Cop who chased the sunbathers off St. Vincent de Paul church steps with his horse."

"That's the one! He came into the house to write out his summonses and when he went to the bathroom, we filled his fountain pen with water, pinned his badge on his jacket upside down and filled his hat with dead cockroaches. His eyesight was going bad and when he came out and started writing the ink faded. He mumbled, "These goddamn glasses," and got up, put his jacket on and his hat and went downstairs. We called the desk officer, Lieutenant Otto Von Odtstadt, and told him what he did. When Reilly was leaving the station house Odtstadt said, "Reilly, you look like shit. Your badge is upside down, and your hat in on crooked. Straighten yourself out before you leave here." Reilly adjusted his badge and when he removed his hat, the cockroaches spilled down his head. After that, he never came to our office to write out his summonses. I wonder why." The men enjoyed a laugh together before leaving.

Two days later the department Personnel Orders were published, Sergeant Lance Carpenter was promoted to Lieutenant and assigned to the License Division, Legal

Matters. He was to report at 0800 hours the following day, the promotion ceremony to take place the following week.

When he reported to his new assignment he was told that the PLB was the central repository for all pistol carry permits in the city. Everyone who carried a firearm had to be licensed and that license was issued by the division after a thorough background investigation. For special carry licenses, these were issued according to the provisions of article 400 of the New York State Penal law. His assignment was to oversee the entire operation. The only good feature of the assignment was that it was a 0800 to 1600 hour tour and weekdays only.

CHAPTER 23

ATTEMPTED BRIBERY

Three months went by with little excitement except to see if an investigation of a license's and or applicant had been completely conducted: two photographs, birth certificate, proof of citizenship or alien registration, military discharge where applicable, proof of residence, fingerprints taken and read, the recommendation by the investigator, letter of necessity, and the fee paid; a very mechanical process. It surprised him that many of the police investigators were almost illiterate or abundantly careless, and did not know how to write clear sentences and their spelling was atrocious! Once the applications were reviewed, he stamped 'Approved' or 'Disapproved' and sent them forward for issuance or filing. He was in the midst of this when a man dressed in a captain's uniform stood before his desk. "Lieutenant Carpenter?" the tall man asked. He was wearing dark sunglasses indoors and was still wearing his uniform hat.

Carpenter looked up. "I'm Carpenter, what can I do for you, captain?"

"A man called Rocco DioGuardia has filed an application for a carry pistol license. He is the president of the Milk Wagon Driver's Union in Manhattan," the captain intoned.

Carpenter remembered the name and the application he had disapproved. DioGuardia, as he recalled, had appeared before the McClellan Crime Commission and had taken the Fifth Amendment on fifty-five occasions. He was suspected to be a member of the August Vitale Crime Family in Brooklyn. "Yes, sir, I recall his application." Before he could speak another word the captain reached into his pocket to pull out a pack of bills and began peeling twenty dollar bills from a folded thick wad and letting them fall to the desk top. "Tell me when to stop," he said.

The Internal Affairs Bureau was constantly pulling integrity testing which took on different methods. Carpenter thought this might be one of those tests.

He got to his feet saying, "Whoa, captain. You must think I'm crazy or you are," Carpenter told the brazen man. "Where do you get off offering me bribe like this?" Carpenter's annoyance was apparent.

Confused, the captain stepped back asking, "Is it not enough? Should we go somewhere private? I can give you a thousand but no more."'

Gathering up the bills with a blotter and pushing them toward the captain, Carpenter said, "No, Captain, I do not want a nickel from you or him or whoever. You are involved in an act of malfeasance, Attempted Bribery, captain. Quit while you're ahead," he advised. "That license will never be issued! He's an Organized Crime soldier. And, Captain, the department will never sanction him to carry a weapon!"

Feeling he was on safer ground, the captain ordered, "Alright then, I'm giving you a direct order, Lieutenant! You are to issue that pistol permit and do it forthwith!" He snatched the money from the Lieutenant's hand.

"That's an illegal order, captain." Carpenter was really angry now and threw caution to the wind. He leaned forward saying, "You put that order in writing and sign it and I will be glad to issue the permit on your say so."

"Lieutenant," the Captain snarled, "I'm sending an inspection team down here to go over your records. For every error they find, I will stick a complaint up your ass a team of Chief Surgeons can't remove. You will be through in this job!" His face was flushed as he turned and stormed out.

Carpenter sat down to telephone his friend in SID and asked him to lunch. They met at an outdoor restaurant, The Bistro on Canal Street. Carpenter recited the episode of the license bribe:

"The bills came floating down like leaves from a tree," he said. "I turned him down, of course and then he threatened to send an inspection team to go over my records and if I was found off base, I would need a team of surgeons to remove his boot from my butt."

Cowan shook his head in disbelief. "I doubt you will see him anyone. Put the facts on a 49 letterhead and send it to my attention. I'll take it from there."

The next day, Carpenter was once again engrossed in reading applications and investigations when the telephone rang. "Lieutenant Carpenter, Pistol License Bureau may I help you?"

There was an audible 'ahem' as if clearing a throat before a voice came on the line. ["Lieutenant, this is Inspector Henry Howe, Headquarters Division."]

"Yes, sir, can I help you?" Carpenter rubbed the back of his neck. There was something eerie going on, he could sense it.

["You have a pistol license permit in the name of Rocco DioGuardia and you are to issue it forthwith."] Carpenter reached for the portable tape recorder and turned it on placing the microphone near the mouth piece and a suction cup adapter on the ear piece.

Carpenter paused, "That's Rocco DioGuardia, Inspector Howe?"

["Yes, dammit, issue it forthwith!"]

"We have no permit issued in that name. But if we do, I'll be glad to issue it Inspector. Just send me a signed release from your office relieving me of my responsibility and I will certainly issue the permit when it is issued."

["Is CYA all you care about? I don't have time for this bullshit, Lieutenant. I'm ordering you to issue it on my say so,"] the voice ordered.

"Sorry, inspector, I can't do that, but send me a release on department letterhead and I will." The line went dead. Carpenter sent a follow-up report to Cowan as he checked the roster of supervisory officers in the department. Not surprisingly there was no Inspector Henry Howe on the roster. To himself he said, "Curiouser and Curiouser."

CHAPTER 24

FAMILY PICNIC

That weekend, there was the usual family picnic at Uncle Jon and Aunt Rosalie's house in Oakwood on Staten Island. It was located on three acres that were mostly wooded with the two story wood framed house set back off the road and a graveled driveway leading up from the street. The children were running around playing different games, the women gathered preparing the tables with food and the men sat around drinking beer and smoking.

Family friends Dolly and Blasé Formica were seated with Carpenter and his in-laws. The Formica's owned a mausoleum business and were quite well to do. Dolly, a short heavy set woman with teased grey hair piled high on her head, dressed completely in black was telling them how she wanted to be buried.

"Will the coffin be open, Dolly," Carpenter said urging her on?

"Nah, I want a closed coffin with the best pitcher of me on top of it. And I want someone seated at the foot of the coffin with a guitar playing "Hello Dolly." What made the statement even more hilarious was that no one was laughing.

Uncle Toni approached Carpenter. In a gravelly voice he commanded, "Hey Lance, let's take a walk." The two men walked away from the group. They seated themselves on a wooden bench on the edge of the woods. Uncle Tonio removed a cigar pouch, offered him one and lit both cigars.

"Carpenter," Uncle Toni said softly, "you're a stand up guy and I like that."

"What are you talking about, Uncle Toni," Carpenter asked confused.

"That assignment you interviewed for with SID," he said with emphasis. "You know cuppla weeks ago."

"I don't know what you're talking about. I didn't interview with anyone."

"Yeah, you did. See, that what I like. Chief Pender and Deputy Cowan interviewed you for an undercover assignment dealing with the FALN."

Stunned Carpenter asked, "You're telling me that I had an interview and I don't know about it?" he could not believe what he was hearing. The man knew who, what, where, when and why. He decided to turn the information over to the Intelligence Division and let them handle the fallout from this revelation.

"Yeah, I know about that. Listen, Lance, you want da job? If you want it I can get it for you. Just say the word," he said making it sound as though he had great influence in departmental affairs.

Incredulously Carpenter asked, "Uncle Toni, you can get me an undercover assignment?"

"Or any other job in the department you want," he said with complete confidence.

"Uncle Toni, with all due respect, if you can get me a job, then I don't want it. If I took you up on your offer, I would be in your pocket and that will never happen. You go your way and I will go mine. Just make sure you don't place me in a position where I have to take action because you will be a collar." Carpenter got up, turned and walked away from the man.

"Don't be a jerk, Lance," he called after him!

Several months later, Grandma LaRosa passed away and her funeral was being held in Marcuse's Funeral Home in Bay Ridge. It was a two-story business with grandma being laid out on the second floor. Flower arrangements were everywhere. Carpenter showed up with his wife, Susanne and in-laws to pay their respects. After greeting Uncle Toni and Aunt Rosa, he walked around while the others consoled with one another. In a smoking room he saw a Who's Who of Organized Crime with some goon standing guard at the door. He walked past him as a hand was placed on his arm. "Ya can't go in dere right now," Muscleman announced. "It's a private meeting of the relatives."

Carpenter removed the man's hand saying, "I'm one of the relatives." Uncle Toni came rushing over. "Lance, go downstairs and have a smoke. This is private."

"Uncle Toni, I told you once not to have your business and mine interfere with one another. According to the Penal Law of the State of New York, any known felons meeting together are prima facie evidence of a conspiracy. In that room," indicating the smoking room, "there are about fifteen felonies being committed and that means your business and mine are in conflict. I'm going in to say goodbye to your wife. When I come out, if there are still any of you still there, I will drop a dime and call 911. Then I will arrest the nearest one of you. Please don't let it be you."

"But Lance, you're puttin' me on the spot. Let up won't cha?"

"You and your friends have put me on the spot and gave no thought to it. You have maybe ten minutes." He walked away.

He was standing in the hallway speaking with an aunt when he saw a tall man with slick black hair, wearing an expensive suit, a cashmere coat draped over his shoulders, with pointed black shoes, a white-on-white shirt with French cuffs, and sporting a Star Safire pinky ring in conversation with several other men. Carpenter walked over to the parlor where grandma was laid out. He approached Uncle Jimmy saying, "Hey, Jim, why don't you take a break and I'll relieve you here?"

"Thanks Lance. I gotta go bad," he said as he walked away.

The tall man he had seen earlier, he now knew as Charles Cheech Mancuso, a Brooklyn organized crime figure dealing in usury. He approached Carpenter putting out his hand.

"I'm sorry for your loss," he said as he handed Carpenter a thick envelope.

"Would you like to sign the register," Carpenter asked innocently while trying to stuff the envelope in his inside jacket pocket.

The man smacked his forehead and hunched his shoulders. "Waddaya nuts," he said as he turned away. Uncle Tonio, who must have been watching, came over quickly.

"Lance, give me that envelope. That's for the funeral expenses. I'll stand here and you can go and take a break."

"But Unc, I just got here."

"Lance, the guys are leavin' and I got nothin' else to do."

Later, after he and the family had said their goodbyes, Carpenter noted that there were no other known felons in the funeral parlor. He wanted to tell his wife and his in-laws but decided not to. As he left, he wondered if the funeral parlor was under surveillance.

CHAPTER 25

ASSIGNMENT: INTERNAL AFFAIRS

About fourteen months later, Carpenter was transferred to the Internal Affairs Bureau. At first he was reluctant to throw himself into the work, uneasy at taking action against police officers. He came to learn, however, that it was the active officers who received the most complaints and the majority were cleared by the officer's actions. Approximately three percent of the complaints were substantiated, but three percent of thirty-two thousand was still nine hundred and sixty cases. On further review he learned that the majority of these were for minor infractions—being discourteous, unnecessary abusive language and other minor violations. He came to the realization that of those three—percenters, the first charge should have been 'stupidity.'

One Friday morning he was summoned to the Inspector's Office. Inspector Ralph Finley was known as a hardass and a tough supervisor. He had come up through the ranks and if not respected, he was feared.

"Siddown, Carpenter," the supervisor directed. "We got a situation in the Six-Eight Precinct. A young Hassidic youth was taken in a sweep and while in police custody, he was hung, burned with cigarettes and his legs broke. I don't know what those guys think they're doin' out there. Go to the station house and write up the desk officer, the station house supervisor and the turnkey. We do not run Gulags in the department. Those three guys are waitin' for you."

On entering the 68th Precinct Station House, a reasonably new three-story building at 333 65th Street, in Brooklyn, he reported to the desk officer.

"I'm Lieutenant Carpenter, IAB."

"Hey, Carpenter, Paulie Spinelli we were in the academy together, remember?"

The last time he had seen Paulie was when they were assigned in the Tenth Precinct to check open doors on Fifth Avenue because of a rash of burglaries there. Dusk had just turned to darkness when they found an open door at Twenty-Second Street and Fifth Avenue. There was no sign of an AIR—Artist in Residence—so they began their floor by floor search. In the hallway it was pitch black requiring them to use their flashlights. As the ascended the stairs, Paulie fell behind as Carpenter went on ahead. On the top floor, it always happens on the top floor; Carpenter shone his light on a door knob and found it had been forced open. He flashed his light down the stairwell and cautiously opened the door. He pointed his flashlight into the open doorway and it centered on a white shirted male figure seated in a chair with a sword sticking out of his chest!

He went to the stair railing to call down to Paulie but no sound came out. He thought, 'I'm a four year veteran and I shouldn't be scared. But no sound had come from his throat!' He decided to wait for Paulie. Finally he was there and said, "Waddaya got?"

Carpenter pointed the light into the room saying, "In there."

When Paulie saw what he had seen he said, "Holy shit!"

Carpenter' voice had returned. "Paulie, you take the wall on the right and I'll take the wall on the left and see if we can find the panel box for the lights. Be careful."

"Gotcha," he said and moved into the room with Carpenter following.

Carpenter felt his way along the wall until he came to the metal panel box. He opened it and threw every switch in the box. Immediately the loft was lighted brilliantly. He looked to Paulie who was flat against the wall. He then looked around the room. There were bodies everywhere! A body was on a couch, four or five on the floor, another handing from the rafters, others seated in chairs and at the back of the room was a pile of bodies!

Another 'Death House,' Carpenter thought, "just like the one the police found uptown years ago. He stooped to examine the first body he came to. He sat on the floor and began laughing in relief.

"What the hell are you laughing at, asshole?"

"Examine one of the bodies, Paulie."

"Why?"

"Because they are manikins, that's why! They are all dummies!" It was then they discovered a sign on the wall identifying the loft as the NBC prop studio. The remainder of the tour was spent in a local bar and grill and the next day Carpenter was transferred.

"Sure I do, Paulie. I remember you. How have you been?"

"Same oh, same oh. You here on that beef?"

"Yes, I am. Are the officers here?"

"Yeah, they're back in the Muster Room. If you need anything, let me know."

"Paulie," Carpenter asked, "is the captain's office being used? If not I would like to offer these guys some privacy."

"No, no one is using it Carpenter, the boss is at a COMPSTAT meeting in Manhattan. He'll be gone all day. I'll have the guys sent in one at a time.

"I wonder if that program on Comparative Statistics will work out as they hope. Anyhow, see you later, Paulie and thanks." He went to the office and prepared for the interviews. He had left the door open.

A tall, grey haired man stood in the doorway. "Lieutenant Robert McDonough" he said annoyed at having to answer questions of someone who would be second-guessing them and their actions. Without being asked, he took a seat.

Carpenter stood up and leaned across the desk offering his hand. The gesture was ignored.

"I am Lieutenant Carpenter, assigned to the Internal Affairs Bureau. This is an official investigation into the death of one Seymour Blount while in police custody. For the record, would you repeat your name and assignment yesterday?"

Peeved at having to repeat himself, he said, "Lieutenant Robert McDonough and I was assigned desk duty on the 4:00 p.m. to 12 midnight tour here in the 68th Precinct."

"What took place, Bob, in your words," he tried to put the men at ease so that they would not revert to legalese or departmental jargon.

"Is this conversation being recorded," he asked?

"No, it is not and it is not 'off the record' either. It is, however, an official departmental investigation and I will be taking notes."

"Okay. About six o'clock we held a roundup, you know a sweep, of narcotic addicts that were hanging around in parks, on street corners and in alleys. They were brought into the station house and when it was determined that some of them were in need of medication, they were transported to a medical facility for treatment by the Patrol Wagon Operator and a cop ridin' shotgun.

"I logged them into the blotter; they were brought to detention and signed them out when they were taken for treatment. I signed them back in when they returned and back into detention again. They were held temporarily in the cells while waiting for transportation. My log entries reflect that and are all correct," he said handing Carpenter the Blotter for the day in question.

"Most desk officers don't bother to go to such trouble but I like to have everything accounted for."

"I'll look this over in a bit. I need to ask you, did you and did anyone else strangle the prisoner in your custody, burn the prisoner with cigarettes or break his legs?"

"Hell no!" he yelled. "I'd have written them up in a heartbeat, if not arrest them!"

"Did you examine the PD244-145 and initial your inspection?"

"You mean the Prisoner Roster book? No, I didn't examine it, we were too busy."

"Is there anything else you want to add?"

"No, that's it."

"Okay, would you ask the sergeant to step in?"

Lieutenant McDonald went to the Muster Room announcing, "You're next Sweet."

The sergeant entered the room as Carpenter indicated the chair. He introduced himself and the reason he was at the station house. This is an official investigation into the death of one Seymour Blount while in police custody. For the record, would you repeat your name and assignment yesterday?"

"I'm Sergeant Samson Sweet, Station House supervisor here in the 68th Precinct. I was helpin' both Bob, the desk officer and Matt, the attendant in charge of the cells. It was a zoo here at that time. We had prisoners comin' in, prisoners logged in the cells and prisoners out to get medical attention and then logging them back afterward. I didn't have time for a dump. They all had to be frisked before putting them in the cells and we collected their ties, belts and shoe laces."

"Just a few more questions, sergeant, did you make the appropriate entries in the Prisoner Roster register?"

"No, I started to but we just got too busy."

"Did you or did any member of the department strangle the prisoner in your custody, burn the prisoner with cigarettes or break his legs?"

"What? Never! That kid killed himself!"

"Did you notify the desk officer of what was taking place in the cells?"

"I don't think so, we were just too busy and when the shit hit the fan . . . all hell broke loose!"

"Alright, sergeant, you may leave. Please send in the police officer."

The patrolman entered and sat beside the desk. "Please state your name and assignment yesterday."

"Do I need my delegate here," he asked?

"You may have your delegate, if you want one. Do you want to have one present during this interview?"

Nah, the lieutenant and sergeant said you was alright."

"Okay. This is an official investigation into the death of one Seymour Blount while in police custody. For the record, would you repeat your name and assignment yesterday? If this turns accusatory, I will advise you to obtain a delegate and an attorney. It is not off the record but an official inquiry into the death of a prisoner in your care. Do you want to tell me what happened?"

A very despondent officer sat at the desk. "We're gonna get harpooned anyways, Lieu, so why bother?" he asked.

"No one will get anything they don't deserve, officer. Just tell me in your words what took place."

"Like I'm sure the Lieutenant and sergeant said we had a round up, about eight or ten junkies at a clip."

"Matt, I need to get your name and assignment. Give me that first, okay?"

"Yes, sir, I'm Patrolman Matthew Bonds assigned to Attendant duty at the 68th Precinct. First they, the prisoners, had to be logged in at the desk then they was turned over to me frisk and put in the cells. Well, sir, there was so many of them, after I searched them, takes their ties, if they were wearing any, their shoe laces and their belts. I put four in a cell at one time after I entered their pedigree and arrest number in the cell log. I had one kid, Seymour Blount who had been arrested earlier for playing with himself in a school yard. He was waitin' to go to Central Booking. He was by himself in a cell. I had removed his belt, his shoe laces, he had no tie and I had him empty his pockets. That stuff I put in a multiuse envelope."

"What happened next, Matt?"

"Well, the bus came, that's the patrol wagon, when it came to take the junkies to the hospital, I logged each one of them out. Then the next batch came in and I repeated the process. By the time the third batch came in I saw a foot sticking out of Blount's cell. I went there and saw him squatting with his pant leg tied around his throat and his legs folded under him. It looked as though he tied his pants to the upper cell bars and hung there until he choked himself to death. I ran to the desk officer and asked him to call an ambulance. He got the 124 man, [in police jargon the command clerk assigned to the station house under Rule 124], to make the call while he came back to the cells with me."

"How long, would you say, the entire process took?"

"You mean from the time the junkies came in and left and so on?" Carpenter nodded. "About two hours, I guess."

"And in all that time, you made no inspections of the cells as required by the Rules and Regulations and no entries in the Prisoner Roster?" he said testing the officer's reactions.

"I just didn't have the time, Lieu! I wish to God now that I had taken the time but I had no time then. I was busier than a one legged man in an ass kicking contest. And, Lieutenant I did not fudge the record either. There were no inspections and I did not falsify the record saying that I had.

"We examined the prisoner and he was not breathing and there was no discernable pulse and his face was discolored. We did notice that he was covered with puckered wounds that looked like cigarette burns but they were old wounds of some unknown origin. When the ambulance arrived, they pronounced him DOA and released his body for removal. His parents were notified and quite understandably they were upset. The bus hadn't removed his body yet. They accused us of breaking his legs, lynching him, and burning him with cigarettes."

"And did you," Carpenter asked?

"No, I didn't and none of the others did either."

"That seems pretty straight forward. Anything else any of you want to add?" Carpenter inquired.

Sergeant Sweet entered the office to say, "Seymour Blount's family will be in shortly to sign some papers and to pick up his belongings."

"I'll wait around for them, sergeant," Carpenter informed him. "In the meantime, you men can go back to whatever you were doing."

"What action is going to be recommended, Lieu," Sergeant Sweet asked?

"Before I return to the office, I will let you all know."

Almost an hour later, Carpenter was informed of the Blount's arrival by the 124 man. He said, "Will you ask the Blounts to step in the office and give me a statement?"

"Yes, sir," he said as he left the room.

A short time later the parents walked into the room. "Lieutenant Carpenter?" they inquired.

"Yes, I'm Lieutenant Carpenter. Won't you please have a seat?" They took chairs on either side of the desk. Mrs. Blount was plainly dressed in black and Mr. Blount was wearing a dark suit with a yamaulka.

"I want to express my condolences at the loss of your son, a sad and unfortunate situation. May I have your names for my records?"

Mrs. Blount took the role of spokesperson. "I am Sophie Blount and this is my husband, Seymour and the death of our son is more than unfortunate. It is an example of police torture and uncalled for brutality!"

"Yes, we'll get to that. May I have your address?"

"We live," Mrs. Blount t said, "in Park Slope." She had not given her address for some reason and Carpenter did not push the issue. He would get it later from department records.

"Have you any idea why your son was arrested?" Carpenter asked.

Mr. Blount spoke for the first time, "No one has told us."

"He was arrested for indecent exposure and masturbating in front of children in a school yard," Carpenter told them. "There are a number of witnesses who saw him do that and one of them called the police."

"Oh, my God!" Mrs. Blount exclaimed. "Exposing and masturbating himself like some pervert! What a disgrace! What shame!"

"Has young Seymour received any medical attention recently for any medical malady? I was wondering if there had been any . . ."

Mr. Blount said, "He recently had a rash of boils all over his body. We thought it was some dietary thing. The doctor at Coney Island Hospital lanced the boils and took some blood tests. We haven't heard back from him."

"How long ago was that?" Carpenter asked.

Mrs. Blount responded to his question in a quiet voice. "That was about a week ago. Listen, Lieutenant, we were upset when we filed the complaint, now, we have to think this situation over, what with this new information and all."

"I understand. I will send you a copy of my report when this investigation is over. In my opinion, with your religious background, the boy was mortified at being found out and took his own life because of the humiliation. Let me again offer you my condolences for your loss. We should not out-live our children."

"Lieutenant," the father spoke for the first time, "we wish to withdraw our complaint," he said as he looked toward his wife.

"Are you sure of this," he said looking at both parents.

"Yes, we are," Mrs. Blount answered.

Carpenter later spoke with the Medical Examiner's Office, Doctor Joseph Weingarten who said that the wounds did in fact look like healing lanced boils, the legs had been folded under the youth and rigor mortis was beginning; the legs were not broken, and the youth had died as a result of strangulation that he apparently accomplished on his own.

On returning to IAB, Carpenter reported to the Inspector's office as directed.

"How many of them did you write up?" was his first question.

"I'm not writing up anyone, Inspector." Carpenter replied waiting for the explosion. It came.

"What? I told you to get three of them. Why did you disobey my direct orders?" His face was flushed and he had gotten to his feet.

Carpenter paused, attempting to defuse the situation. "I did not write up anyone because, in my judgment, no one did anything wrong."

"Lieutenant, are you crazy? No one did anything wrong? We have a lynching, burning with cigarettes and breaking legs. If that's not something wrong then I wonder what your definition of wrong is."

Carpenter deliberately took a seat, removed his notebook and slowly opened it while the Inspector fumed. "To begin with, the desk officer, Lieutenant Robert McDonough, had entered thirty seven arrests in the Blotter of persons charged with various narcotic violations. According to department guidelines, he had them shipped to a medical facility for treatment, signing each one out to that facility, and then reentered them when they returned." Inspector Findley flopped into a chair.

"Sergeant Samson Sweet, Station House Supervisor acting independent of the desk officer, assisted in frisking each and every prisoner, vouchered their property, helped in placing them in holding cells until transportation could be provided to the medical facility, escorted them out when it arrived and escorted them back on their return." Inspector Findley leaned forward his head cradled in his hands.

"Regarding Patrolman Matthew Bonds, the so-called turnkey at the station house, he searched Seymour Blount before placing him in a cell. He had removed his belt, shoe laces, and there was no tie. He made the appropriate entries in the Prisoner Roster. He then was inundated with a total of thirty-seven prisoners being booked in; they had to be searched then signed out to the medical facility and brought back in. The prisoners being brought in were done piecemeal requiring all of them to be busy for more than two hours. The desk officer did not make any records inspection, the station house supervisor likewise and the turnkey ditto. There just was not enough time. They sacrificed their meal in order to accommodate everyone." Inspector Findley sat back, his hands clasped behind his head. "Lastly, I spoke to the parents of the deceased and at first they were quite upset at what they thought was misconduct on the part of the officers.

When I explained the facts of their son's arrest, they withdrew their complaint."

"Seymour Blount," Carpenter went on, "is a male Hassidic, age seventeen years, had been arrested for exposing himself and I'm told, masturbating in front of school children. He expressed great shame at what he had done. Left alone in the cell, he felt—I'm sure—shame, humiliation and embarrassment at his action which subsequently took possession of his mental faculties. Overcome with guilt, he removed his trousers, tied one end to the cell bars and the other end around his neck. He had to be quite intent on hanging himself in such a manner causing his death. The alleged burns were in fact healing lanced boils attested to by his parents and by a medical doctor. His legs were in fact not broken but had been folded under him to put pressure on the pant leg. It is all a sad state of affairs but that's what will be in my report and a copy will be sent to the boy's parents, who by the way, had been informed beforehand."

"Much of this is supposition, Lieutenant. You offer hardly any proof," the Inspector said resignedly.

"Much of it is verifiable, however and I see no reason anyone should be punished for an understandable yet unfortunate series of events, Inspector."

"Okay, we'll let it go at that. But the next time you are told to do something, god dammit, you do what you're told!"

CHAPTER 26

DETECTIVE SERIAL KILLER

Assigned to IAB, Carpenter was especially proud of an arrest he had made of a police officer who hired himself out as a hit man. The officer, a detective in the Auto Squad, had been caught on a wiretap laying out the parameters for his taking the job. He was to be paid five hundred dollars up front and another five hundred on completion. His modus operandi in his execution for hire was to have the victim tied up; kneel before a full length mirror so that they could watch themselves die as he cut their throat.

Carpenter called the suspect detective at his squad office. "This is Doctor Monahan of the Medical Records Bureau. I'd like to speak with Detective Abraham Norris. Is he there?"

["This is Norris, Doc. What can I do for you?]

"Your force records show that you have not had a physical examination for eight years. We need to update your file and your 10 card. You are directed to report to the Police Academy at 0800 hours tomorrow morning for that physical. That's on Twentieth Street in Manhattan."

["I guess I can do that. I am to report at 08000 at the Police Academy. What room number?]

"It's on the ground floor, the Medical Office. See you there."

The following morning at 0730 Carpenter and three detectives were in place in the Medical Office. One of the detectives was a the clerical desk, two others sat on seats as though waiting to be called, and Carpenter, dressed in a white coat with a stethoscope around his neck, was seated at another desk writing on a yellow pad. At the assigned hour, Detective Norris walked into the room. He spotted Carpenter in his coat and stethoscope and approached him.

"Doctor Monahan? I'm Detective Norris reporting as directed."

"Yes, good Norris. Sorry to get you up so early. Please go to the next room and remove all your clothing and place them in the receptacle provided. Put your shield and weapons in the lock box on the wall, and keep the key. I am a registered nurse and I'll be right in and we will make this as quick as possible. Do you have any questions?"

"I guess not." He moved to the door and entered the room. Norris was a male, Black, about six foot in height, and weighed in the neighborhood of one hundred ninety pounds. A short time later, Carpenter looked into the room through a plate glass in the door. Norris was completely nude. It had been found by Carpenter through previous experiences, that in order to make an arrest of someone with the violent tendencies such as Norris displayed, it was best to have that person in a position where they felt helpless and vulnerable. Carpenter turned to the others saying, "Let's go. Don't take any chances."

As the four men entered the room, Norris looked at them surmising what was happening. He looked at his clothing in the receptacle, at the property locker on the wall, decided against any overt action, opting instead to remain motionless, resigned to his fate. As Carpenter moved in to handcuff him, he asked, "How bad is it?"

Carpenter placed cuffs on his wrists before replying. "It doesn't get any worse. Detective Norris you are under arrest . . ."

CHAPTER 27

INCIDENT AT THE WORLD TRADE CENTER

There followed an incident that spelled the end of Carpenter's stay at Internal Affairs. He and the others under his supervision had produced a training film on and entitled, Corruption Hazards Within the New York City Police Department. The video dealt with the gamut of hazards that included bribes, shakedowns, pads, free meals and others errant behavior. The video instantly became quite popular at the Police Academy where it was shown to recruits. Other jurisdiction in the metropolitan area heard of the video and asked for it to be shown at a closed circuit conference with the Inspector to discuss it and its implications.

Arrangements were made and the conference was to be held on the 68th floor of the World Trade Center in a television studio that provided linkage to law enforcement in the metropolitan area. The agenda called for the video viewing, then a question and answer session dealing with police corruption, its hazards and impact. Carpenter and his squad had been visiting the precincts in the five boroughs for several months and were familiar with the frequently asked questions.

Carpenter and Inspector Finley were seated behind a small conference table with lavaliere microphones hung about their necks. The Inspector brought with him a stack of papers about a foot in height while Carpenter laid a thin folder on the table.

The station manager, Mrs. Gwen Forbes, signaled them to introduce themselves and invite questions which the two men did.

The first questioner, Chief Clement from Patterson, New Jersey introduced himself and asked, "What is the estimated percentage of the department that you believe to be corrupt?"

Inspector Finley began going through his stack of papers and when the delay became uncomfortable, Carpenter leaned over to the Inspector, covered his microphone saying, "About three percent."

Inspector Finley repeated the statistic, "keep in mind though, we are not only focusing on the corruption issue but on allegations of police brutality. Sergeant Carpenter has more specific data."

Carpenter faced the cameras and presented the department's misconduct picture.

"The three percent the Inspector mentioned amounts to ninety-six allegations out of a base of 32,000 officers. Not all of those deal with corruption but also brutality, abuse of authority et cetera.

"Of that number about 42 have charges and specifications prepared and last year, the department was compelled to turn over six cases to the District Attorney. What gets lost here is that the vast majority of the people in the department are outstanding public servants."

Chief Williamson of Toms River, New Jersey was the next questioner. "What are some of the steps we in law enforcement can take to prevent corruption?"

Again the Inspector went through his stack of papers. When the pause became tedious again, Carpenter leaned over, covered the Inspector's microphone saying, "Education and awareness. We educate the officers on the potential hazards and the proactive measures being taken to thwart its growth."

Finley repeated what he had been told. And so it continued for about fifteen minutes. When a Chief from Jersey City, New Jersey asked a question and when Carpenter leaned over to give the Inspector the answer, Pender jumped to his feet. He turned to Carpenter shouting, "Shut the hell up! Keep your damn mouth shut!" He turned to the cameras addressing the Chiefs, "I want to thank yez all for bein' here an' I'll see yez all again." With that he stormed off leaving everyone dumbstruck. The cameras were shut down, the monitors turned off and Mrs. Forbes came onto the set.

"I'm so sorry for what happened," she said solicitously.

"It wasn't your fault, Mrs. Forbes," Carpenter said. "We should apologize to you."

"Oh, that's alright. It happens. The Inspector said for me to tell you to see him when you return to your offices."

Carpenter took the subway to Poplar Street and went directly to the Inspector's office. His secretary stopped him in the outer office.

"What happened? She asked. "The Inspector came back fuming and sent for the deputy and the captains to come to his office. What's going on?"

"I'll tell you later, Sophia."

He opened the door to the Inspector's office and was confronted by a conference table where the Inspector sat at the head, one empty seat was close to the boss and five captains sat in the other chairs. Carpenter went to the empty chair and sat. Everyone was silent, waiting.

"Just who the hell do you think you are?" Finley hissed. Before Carpenter could answer, he continued. "Subordinates do not give Inspectors answers."

"They do, Inspector when the Inspector doesn't know the answer. It is incumbent on him to protect the inspector from embarrassment."

"Shut your mouth! You're through here Carpenter. You did embarrass your superior and that will not be tolerated!"

"I have no superiors, Inspector only supervisors."

"I told you to shut up! I'm going to have you transferred to the worst shithouse in the city. Get out of my sight!"

"You can't have me transferred to the worst shithouse in the city, Inspector. I am already assigned to it." Carpenter got up and left the office. He went to his office, closed the door and telephoned Inspector Cowan to tell him what had happened.

["Carpenter, stay out of his way for a few days and let me try to work out something."]

Carpenter took some vacation time spending it on Staten Island pondering his future and wondering why he hadn't kept his mouth shut. He took advantage of the free time to begin work on a gazebo he had been planning to build. He had the plans, the foundation had been laid and he had the requisite lumber and shingles to complete the undertaking. The work would take his mind off his predicament.

When he returned to the IAB office the following Monday, there was a call from Deputy Inspector Cowan. He returned his call on his private line.

"Hello, Inspector." He had not identified himself not knowing what his call had been about.

["How about lunch, Carpenter?]

"When and where?" he asked mimicking his friend's tone.

["Same time, same place as before."]

Seated in the New Corners Restaurant, both men made themselves comfortable, sipping their cold beers. Carpenter waited for his friend to start the conversation.

"Have you had enough of IAB, Carpenter?" he asked sincerely.

"So far it's kept me off the streets and out of bars and allows me to piss my bosses off. You got something else in mind?"

"As a matter of fact I have. Chief Mannion, who is I understand is a very good friend of yours, and my boss had a meeting about a situation in the 7-0 Precinct and it's detective squad slot. It will mean squad commander's money. Interested?"

"I'm always interested in extra money. Let me get this straight. I get the Inspector of IAB on my case threatening me with disciplinary action and you're having me transferred to God knows where and you are offering me a plum with extra money? How bad is it out there in the hinterlands?"

"The place is going to hell in a hand basket. There's not much you can do with the precinct situation but you can put the squad on the straight and narrow."

"You're full of clichés; be specific."

"The guys out there in Brownsville like to ride rough shod over their prisoners. We've had some brutality suits and they seem to be getting worse. If something changes in the squad then maybe it will trickle down to the precinct."

"You sweet-talking Irish hump. If I see what can be done, do it and if nothing changes, I don't want to get burned for trying to help."

"I'll watch your back like I always do."

"As you always do."

CHAPTER 28

ASSIGNMENT: 70TH SQUAD DETECTIVES

That weekend, a Friday evening, it was bitterly cold and drizzly. Carpenter parked his car in front of 154 Lawrence Avenue, the Seventieth Precinct Station House. He stopped at the desk, informed the desk officer that he was the new whip and asked directions to the squad office. He walked through the Muster Room and found it a bedlam. The ceiling was hammered tin; the floor seemed to be made of terrazzo with an iron hand railing on the stairs and over that hanging from what looked like a cast iron cluster of grapes, they had jerry-rigged a rack, on which was a Black man who appeared unconscious.

An officer was seen coming down the stairs. He whacked the man with his night stick. Two others were walking up the stairs and they too whacked the unconscious man. Carpenter could not believe his eyes. This place was worse than Cowan had suggested! Carpenter stopped the officer who had recently descended the stairs taking note of his name plate on his uniform jacket.

"Go to the Desk Officer Blake," he ordered, "tell him to order an ambulance for that man!"

With a wave of his hand, the officer retorted, "Up yours, Jack."

Carpenter stopped the officer, took out his shield and repeated his directions. "While you're at it, have the patrol sergeant report back here to see me."

A short time later a big bulky sergeant came into the room. His hat was on the back of his head, his gut seemed to be waiting to burst through his jacket that reminded Carpenter of the Smiling Jack comic strip, and he had a red bulbous nose indicative of a heavy drinker.

"Just who in the hell do you think you are, bucko?" he demanded of Carpenter.

"I'm Lieutenant Carpenter the new squad commander. I want that man," he said indicating the hanging man, "taken down immediately. I've directed an ambulance be called. When it arrives see that he is taken care of."

"Not that hump, Lieutenant. He and his buddy killed an officer this afternoon and this one is being tuned up before going to court."

"The tune up is ended. I will be writing up the man who fetched you and I will be charging him with brutality of a prisoner in police custody. I have his name from the name plate on his jacket and I'll get whatever additional information I need from the clerical office. Now, get that man down!"

"Geez, we got us a bleedin' heart. Here, you two," he called to two officers walking by, "get that man down from there and lay him on the floor." He turned back to Carpenter, "Are you happy now, Lieutenant?"

"Just do your job, sergeant. I'll check on him later" He walked up the stairs to the squad office. If the sight that greeted him when he entered the station house had bothered him, the next sight bothered him even more. A second Black man, bare-chested was handcuffed to the radiator; arms spread to each side, his chest against the cast iron vanes. The man was moaning and immobile in an unnatural position.

Carpenter removed his handcuff key and unlocked the cuffs. He helped the man to a seat. He turned to the two detectives seated at desks presumably typing reports.

"You," he called out indicating the larger man, "call for an ambulance and get this man taken care of. You," indicating the second detective, "get this man's clothing and get him dressed." The pair of them sat unmoving.

"Hey, smartass," a larger man thundered as he emerged from an office, "Just who in the hell do you think you are ordering my men around like that? Get the hell outta here!"

"Are you Sergeant McDonald?" Carpenter asked.

"Yeah, I'm McDonald. Whatsittoya?"

"Let's talk in the office, sergeant." McDonald did an about face and Carpenter followed. He turned back to the detectives. "You men, do as you were told!"

"I'm Lieutenant Carpenter," Lance began, "the new whip of this office. What I've seen here tonight, both downstairs and here, pisses me off. Brutality is never condoned! Let's get that understood from the start. What kind of an example are you setting for your subordinates?"

"Yeah, but those mutts ambushed and killed a cop this afternoon. They deserve whatever they get."

"In case the message hasn't come across to you and the others yet, getting your kicks by beating these men only opens the door for their release. I know, I know they were resisting arrest but how can you justify the burns on that man's chest," indicating the man in the squad room, "and the broken bones of the man beaten downstairs. Cops are never in the punishment business!"

"Listen Lieu," McDonald said apologetically, "so we got carried away a little. It won't happen again. Now, if you want to unload your personal gear, I'll see to the cleanup of this mess."

"First see that the man outside gets medical attention and check on the other one downstairs.

"I'll get right on the clean up."

Carpenter looked around the office; it was not much larger that a closet. The two desks faced each other and there was one beat up file cabinet. He took a seat facing the door making himself comfortable.

McDonald returned to report that everything had been taken care of.

"I'm sorry for the welcome you got on your first day with us. These guys in the squad are really a great bunch, but you will have to learn that for yourself. Is there anything I can do to make you more at ease?

"When we are alone, let's use first names. Otherwise we need to be more formal."

"Sounds like a plan."

"Give me the rundown on the command and, our strengths and weaknesses."

McDonald decided it would be best to be up front with this guy and so he gave him what he had asked for. Carpenter learned that the workload was quite heavy, the men had heavy court time but their reports and paperwork were up to date.

The following day he was being given a tour of the precinct by Detective Lenny Adams, one of the squad's detectives.

"Len," Carpenter asked, "can you give me a condensed rundown on the precinct?"

"Let's see Brownsville," the detective began, "was part of the organized crime families' area and they included Meyer Lansky and Lucky Luciano who started here; Margaret Sanger's first birth-control clinic; and Danny Kaye, and Mike Tyson also lived here."

The detective drove him around pointing out the more famous or infamous sites in the precinct. As they drove on, Adams made a sudden stop.

"Follow me, Lieu and have your gun handy." They both got out of the car when Adams threw a young Black man against a chain link fence. The youth looked emaciated, he wore a full length raincoat and a baseball cap turned backward. Adams took the coat off the boy by pulling it down immobilizing his arms. Carpenter saw a sawn off shotgun, on a short rope loop through its stock hanging from the boy's right shoulder.

Adams removed the shotgun, threw it to Carpenter then patted the boy down. From his pockets he removed two glassine bags, a wallet, a wad of money and a switchblade knife; all of which was handed to the Lieutenant.

"Lookin' to get your bones, Slick?"

"I ain't telling' you nothin' asshole!"

"Well, you missed out on your bones today, Homeboy." He put the youth in handcuffs, turned him around pushing him toward their car. "Get in the car, Homer." He held the man's head down as he was put into the rear of the car.

When they were in the car heading to the station house, Carpenter asked, "I heard you call the kid by three names; how come?"

"Homer, is his real name; Homer Anthony Jethro. The others are street names. You get to know them after a while."

Two days later Carpenter was driving with two Black detectives, Carpenter and Walters, who were acquainting him with the nuances of the command and; the power brokers, the runners, the musclemen and a bevy of others.

The car's radio blared out. ["In the seven oh, signal ten thirty, man with a gun at Floyd Bennett Houses. What seven oh unit is responding?"]

"Seven Oh squad supervisor responding, Central," Carpenter informed the dispatcher.

["Ten four,"] the dispatcher responded.

Carpenter was the first out of the car running into the building. He ran past a young boy sitting on the stairs. He started up the stairs but stopped short. He heard one of the detectives talking to the boy.

"Stand up you little shit." Carpenter turned back to see the youth get to his feet. "Why is your hand inside your shirt?" He pushed the boy's arm out to his side saying, "take your hand out of the shirt and it had better be empty." The boy did as he was told. Carpenter put his hand into the shirt and came out with a .9mm Beretta automatic. He gave the youth a quick pat down before placing him in plastic cuffs.

"Words to the wise, Lieu," Walters warned, "never run past anyone, young or old, with their hand in their shirt or pants pockets without first checking them out. You could have been hurt and second, always let the detectives go first."

"A useful lesson," Lance replied," thank you."

The detectives began kicking the wall panels with their feet as Carpenter stood by dumbfounded.

"I got one her," Carpenter exclaimed.

The two men pulled the panel away from the wall revealing a cache of various weapons. There were pistols, automatics, shotguns and other assorted weapons with the requisite ammunition.

"See, what happened is, this kid saw some older guys puttin' their guns in here and he decided to try one of them out. It was just an educated guess but, as it turned out, we made a good one. I'll call it in and get some help carting this stuff off. The kid is a collar for the discharge."

Later that day, Carpenter and McDonald were heading to meal walking downstairs to leave. A female sergeant was turning out a special detail of officers in the Muster Room. She stood at a rostrum facing the troops. She was in uniform, had black hair pulled back and braided, she looked rather tall and slender.

"How do you like that, Lieu?" McDonald said quietly indicating the sergeant.

"Very pretty, what's her name?"

"Maria Soriano, she's been here for about a year and her people have her in high regard. She can put her shoes under my bed anytime."

"Will wonders never cease? A woman who knows her job," he said sarcastically. "What a concept!"

After lunch Carpenter was in the office catching up on the never-ending paperwork when the phone rang.

"Lieutenant Carpenter."

["Patrolman Jackman, Lieu, I'm over at the Housing Project on Monroe. I have a situation here that requires BIG help."]

"What is the situation, Jackman?"

["I got a homicide I was guardin' and some Lieutenant from the Housing Authority relieved me and told me to return to my command. He doesn't have the authority to do that, does he?"]

"What are his people doing?"

["It's just him, Lieu. He's takin' tenants into the crime scene two at a time. It's like a circus side show."]

"Is there anything unusual about the scene," Carpenter inquired?

["Yeah, see, the victim's wife cut off his head with a serrated knife, grabbed him by the hair an' walked down the hallway bashin' his head against the walls on both sides. There are blotches on either side of the hall. As soon as the Lieutenant seen it he took command and turned it into a freakin' circus."]

"Oh, my God," Carpenter exclaimed nonplused. "And now he's taking people through the scene two at a time?"

["Yeah, two at a time and get this, he put the severed head on the kitchen table facin' the guy's body, stuck the knife she used into the table at an angle so that the blood would drip off. And oh yeah, he took the victim from the floor and sat him at the table too!"]

"Jackman, I'll be right there," Carpenter exclaimed and hung up.

Carpenter and McDonald drove to the housing project with flashing lights and an occasional siren blast to warn motorists and pedestrians. At the Housing Project there were additional patrol cars on scene, an ambulance and a Housing Authority patrol car. As he entered the building he called to one of the officers:

"Notify Central we have enough backup on the scene."'

"Okay, Lieu," an officer replied.

"What floor is Jackman on," he asked another?

"Fifth floor," someone called back the response, "along with everyone else!"

As they exited the elevator on the fifth floor, there were twelve people standing two abreast against the wall waiting their turn to see the gore. At the end of the hall, outside an open door, Patrolman Jackman sat on the window sill, a forlorn look on his face. He got to his feet.

"Lieu, Patrolman Jackman," he said by way of introduction as he saluted. "They are in there," indicating the open door and the people waiting to get in. Two people emerged from the room holding handkerchiefs to their faces. They were followed by a short pudgy Housing Authority Lieutenant in uniform. He ignored Carpenter and to the others cried out, "Next!"

Carpenter stepped forward, his right hand raised toward the waiting viewers. "Hold it, Cowboy," Carpenter demanded! To the others standing in the hall he said, "You all go about your business. This show is over!"

The Lieutenant grabbed Carpenter by the arm forcing him to turn. "Who the hell do you think you are," the Lieutenant demanded? "I'm in command here!"

McDonald grabbed the Lieutenant, pulled his hands behind his back, placing him in handcuffs. He said, "No, sir, you are not. This is the jurisdiction of the New York City Police Department. I am Sergeant McDonald and he is Lieutenant Carpenter and you, you hump, you are under arrest!"

"What in hell am I being arrested for?" the Lieutenant demanded indignantly.

"The willful destruction of a crime scene, interfering with governmental process, attempted assault on a police official and the deliberate altering of physical evidence and I will think of some others, you cretin!"

McDonald removed the prisoner from the scene while Carpenter reviewed the scene to determine, if possible, the damage that had been done. With no added attractions the scene would have originally been a horror. Now, however, with the dramatization the scene was surreal. People had run their fingers through the blood on the walls, the alleged killer was seated in the living room handcuffed and on view for all the onlookers, the headless man was seated at the table his body facing his head which was on the table along with the knife embedded in the table dripping blood. Carpenter instructed the woman to come with him. On leaving, he directed Jackman to safeguard the scene until the arrival of the Crime Scene Unit and the Patrol Supervisor.

"You did good work here today, Jackman," he informed the officer.

"Thank you, Lieu."

As he entered the station house, Lieutenant Jacob Kohlman, the Station House Supervisor, informed him that Housing Authority brass was in the squad room waiting for him. Carpenter used the telephone at the desk to call the Borough command requesting their presence and assistance. He then called the Action Desk informing them of the situation and requesting they notify the ADA. He informed them that a Housing Authority lieutenant was at the command under arrest.

After several hours of heated debate between the Housing Authority, the New York City Police Department and the Brooklyn District Attorney's Office, the Lieutenant was released despite Carpenter's forceful protests and the arrest voided, Carpenter and the Department were held harmless and Patrolman Jackman became the arresting officer of the irate housewife. Just another day, he consoled himself.

The lieutenant kept his job with the Housing Department and there was no word of any punishment being meted out, if there had been any.

The next day, Lance received notification to report to Police Headquarters that would bring about changes in his career.

During Carpenter's watch, the incidents of unnecessary force had been reduced significantly by the squad members. There was also a decline at the precinct level for which he could no responsibility.

He was just getting settled in when he received a telephone message to report to the Office of the Chief of Patrol. A lieutenant assigned there informed him that he was to report the following morning at 0800 hours. Carpenter told McDonald of his summons and asked him to 'mind the store' in his absence.

CHAPTER 29

ASSIGNMENT: 77TH SQUAD DETECTIVES

Two days later Carpenter reported to the Desk Officer at the 77th Precinct, flashed his shield and was directed to the Precinct Commander's Office. He knocked on the door and walked in. He was holding his personal belongings under his left arm.

"Good morning, Captain, I'm Lieutenant Carpenter the new whip of the squad," he said holding out his hand.

Looking up he said, "Welcome, Lieutenant." The proffered hand was ignored. "Your office is on the second floor." Carpenter held his hand out waiting for something to happen. When it did not, he turned to leave.

"Nice to meet you captain," he called over his shoulder. He didn't even introduce himself; very curt. What did I do to piss him off? He would have little to do with him, he decided.

On the second floor he noted that the Homicide Squad Office was on the right and Detectives were on the left, Anti Crime was in the southern part of the floor. He entered and met with the civilian receptionist and clerk.

"Good morning, young lady. I'm Lieutenant Carpenter, the new whip."

"Good mornin' Lieu," she replied as she turned the command log in his direction. "I'm Gloria Phillips your secretary and receptionist. We saw the transfer in the orders last night." Gloria was a Black woman in her early thirties and slightly overweight, comely dressed and a quick smile. She wore her hair in 'corn rows" that set off her pretty face. She smiled with her eyes and mouth.

He signed in as taking command of the squad and lined off his name. "Where can I hang out?" Carpenter asked lightly.

"You're in the northwest corner, there," she indicated where it was. "Sergeant Bonaventura is in there now. She turned in her chair and called out: "Hey Sergeant Bonaventura! The new whip is here!"

A formless voice answered, "Be right there!"

"Gloria, Gloria," Carpenter said soothingly, "Does the phone on your desk work?"

A quizzical look came over her face. "Sure it works. Why do you ask?"

"Well, instead of shouting across the office, it would have been more professional if you had called Sergeant Bonaventura on the phone to make your announcement."

"Oh, I get it, call don't yell."

"Exactly."

He looked around and saw that the squad room was quite spacious with eight steel grey desks with green Formica tops; all had Smith Corona typewriters on stands that were scattered throughout the room. There were nine gray and green file cabinets against a wall that turned out to be the commander's office. The room was lighted by overhead fluorescent lights and windows dominated the west wall. On the south wall were two cork boards with flyers of different sorts pinned on it and by the entrance was a round cardboard waste bin. On an inside wall was a rack for recharging radios and for hanging vehicle keys.

In Carpenter's office, two walls were windowed casting bright natural light on the room through opened blinds. The overhead fluorescents had not been turned on. The room was large enough to accommodate two desks and near the entryway was a bathroom.

As he entered, a man he assumed to be Sergeant Bonaventura, was seated at the far end behind a desk in the left in the corner. He did not look up but kept reading and signing reports.

"Sergeant!" Carpenter called.

Bonaventura looked up annoyed. "Yeah?"

This was not a good beginning. "I am the new whip, Sarge, Lieutenant Carpenter and I think you are seated at my desk," he said curtly.

"But I had . . ." Aw shit, Bonaventura thought, one of those guys. "Alright I'll move my things to the other desk." He let Carpenter know that he was not happy.

"Sarge, let's start off on the right footing. Did you hear Gloria shout that I was on board?"

"Yeah, I did," he said hesitantly.

"Do me the courtesy of responding to messages you receive, no matter how you receive them, in an appropriate manner."

"Yeah, I can do that," his annoyance was still evident.

Carpenter deposited the box with his belongings on his desk.

"Tell me all about the command," Carpenter said as he sat. "How many detectives are assigned to the squad?"

Feeling the tense moment had passed, Bonaventura said, "There are a total of eighteen. Seven detectives are assigned to day duty; seven are assigned to night duty, and four on the late tour. I supervise the day tour and Sergeant Maria Soriano is the night tour supervisor. She's a female Italian but good at her job. There is no supervisor on the late tour. And we have one civilian clerk and secretary, Gloria Phillips. She wears both hats as secretary and receptionist."

Soriano, Carpenter mused, where have I heard that name before?

"Listen, why don't we go somewhere and grab a cup of coffee? We can talk and relax at the same time," Carpenter suggested trying to put the man at ease.

Incredulous, Bonaventura asked, "Here, in the precinct?"

"Sure, why not," Carpenter wondered what he was getting at?

"Well, I usually go over into Queens or Brooklyn North to eat."

"That's too far. Let's grab something nearby." Carpenter could tell that Bonaventura would be uncomfortable eating in a Black establishment.

The men walked toward Atlantic Avenue. A simple sign saying "Eats" smelled delicious as they entered the crowded diner. Many of the patrons looked up as they walked in. Carpenter pointed at a table to the counterman who nodded. He sat with his back to the front door while Bonaventura sat himself where he could see the entrance, Wyatt Earp fashion. The counterman came to the table wiping his hands on his apron.

"You guys are cops, right?" he asked but already surmised their occupation. He handed them well-worn paper menus.

Carpenter turned to look at him, "Do you have decaffeinated coffee?" he asked.

"Yeah, we do," he replied taking a pencil that was perched behind his right ear.

"I'll have a cup of decaffeinated and a toasted English. What are you having Blasé ?"

"Just coffee," he replied sullenly. The counterman took back the menus and left.

While they had coffee and English, Bonaventura relayed to Carpenter pertinent information about the squad, their strengths and weaknesses, as he saw them and his view of an ongoing situation involving a Minister, his church, and the entire operation. The minister was identified as the Reverend Casius LeMans. Carpenter got the impression, as they spoke, that the sergeant liked to paint himself as a good guy with the men of the squad. Listening to the sergeant brief him about the squad and its members, he made it seemed as though everything that went on did so because he supervised it and approved of it. He wondered what Sergeant Soriano would be like.

CHAPTER 30

BACKGROUND INFORMATION

Later that day when he was getting himself settled in, a soft knock was heard. Carpenter looked up and saw a woman standing there. She stood, he guessed, at five feet seven inches, with dark black hair and blue eyes.

"Lieutenant," she said, "I'm Sergeant Maria Soriano the four to twelve supervisor. Welcome on board."

"Thank you, Maria. Come in I'd like to speak with you if you are not busy."

She entered the office and took a seat. "Shall I give you some of my background on the job," she asked.

"Yes, please. Give me a cameo sketch."

"Well, I have eleven years on the job, the first two in plainclothes in the 14th Precinct. Then I was transferred to the 5th Precinct on patrol. When I was promoted, I was sent to the 70th for two years and then assigned here. Lieutenant Giuseppe Petrosino, the only police officer killed in the line of duty outside the country, is my great uncle and the reason I became a police officer."

"Petrosino, eh? That's some background. Well I look forward to working with you." Now he understood why she had seemed so familiar to him, she had been a patrol sergeant in the 70th Precinct while he was there.

Several days later, Carpenter sat behind his desk, a pile of file folders and file jackets in front of him, stopping only to rub his eyes and stretch. He had been reviewing an accumulation of UF61 Complaint Forms, After Action Summary Reports, and DD5s dating back more than twenty-five years. He first had to match up the DD5 with the correct complaint. He also matched Activity Log, Aided Reports worksheet, Missing/Unidentified Persons Reports trying to make some sense of this hodgepodge. At best, it was tedious work but provided a great deal of insight into the LeMans operation. One thing he did notice was that all dealt with the Rehoboth Bethel Church of God or its pastor, Casius LeMans.

Seated in front of him were his squad supervisors, Sergeants Soriano and Bonaventura discussing different aspects about several of the complaints.

"Maria," he asked, "how well versed are you on the LeMans complex and its inhabitants?"

Maria Soriano is a raven-haired handsome Italian-American woman who underplays her femininity by having her hair pulled back, loose shirts or blouses and little or no makeup, she was wearing slacks and flat rubber soled shoes. In spite of that, her good looks came through, and as he now recalled she is a supervisor with street experience.

"Well, Lieu, Blasé and I read and sign the DD5s, especially those dealing with young girls going missing, or is found, usually dead with a broken neck, or we have an incident where the group is involved," she replies matter-of-factly. "By the way, the Coroner estimates that all had their necks broken in the same manner and by a left-handed person. There is one other peculiarity; all of the girls we've found have had their fingers removed."

"That's just bullshit, Maria. It has no significance."

"That's good input, Maria. As I read the reports," Carpenter said indicating the stacks of reports, "a couple of interesting facts stood out. One you have already mentioned, Maria, about the broken necks. That is quite significant. The other oddity is the one you just mentioned, that all seem to be missing their fingers. I find that most unusual. This latter fact indicates that the perp had taken time to remove the fingers and most killers do not take the time to do that."

"Now that you mention it, Carpenter," Bonaventura was quick to pick up on his oversight, "it did seem somewhat strange."

"Maybe someone is collecting coups," Maria ventured. "You know, like collector's items."

"We're talking about ghouls here," Carpenter observed. "Each of the fingers had been cut off with some instrument. Assign someone to determine what the instrument was. Let's keep all these tidbits to ourselves."

Turning to another subject he said, "If you two don't mind, in the future anytime we have an incident involving LeMans or his church, I would like to be placed in the loop. This bullshit has gone on long enough," Carpenter announced. "Also, I paid a visit to the Homicide Squad across the hall," he emphasized, "to see what paper they have generated on the church," he said looking directly at Bonaventura. "They were kind enough to duplicate what they had to date. Those stacks of papers on the chair are copies of their files. I want to match them up with what we have and add anything new so we can look at it."

"Maria, would you ask Gloria to requisition a couple of white boards so we can start diagramming the church, its hierarch and its occupants?"

"Sure Carpenter, I've wanted to get at their files for some time but now that you have them we can get started." She had glanced at her partner giving the impression she had mentioned it to Bonaventura and was shot down in her attempt.

Sergeant Bonaventura took an immediate offense feeling his supervisor was voicing adverse criticism of their actions regarding LeMans and the others. "Lieu," he said defensively, "we do all we can, every time. The bastard is too slick. He has too much clout."

"I'm not being critical, Blasé. It has been almost twenty-five years since he made the scene. If these records are accurate, and I have no doubt they are, it's time to shut him down!"

"As you settle in," Bonaventura said, "you'll find that that is easier said than done."

"Alright, Blasé, Maria, I'm sure we'll talk again about this. I want to review what has been done so far, consolidate these records and then perhaps we can discuss strategy."

"I'll give you a hand with these records if you want," Maria offered.

"That would help a lot."

Both sergeants got up to leave, Bonaventura made kissing sounds as he got ready to leave for the day and Maria settling in to begin her tour.

She gave him the finger mouthing softly, "Up yours asshole."

Once they had gone, Carpenter began taking Complaint Reports from the folders to read. He found that they had been gathered from a variety of sources: precincts of occurrence, Missing Persons, the Harbor Squad, Housing Bureau, Transit Bureau, and other commands. He began to separate them in their crime category, then their location, time and date of occurrence to learn if there were some discernable pattern, and finally separating the records by the age and sex of the complainant. He compared these with Arrest Reports. He immediately noticed that the person complained of was either the Reverend Casius LeMans or one of his offspring. He was certain that some of these records were not the work of LeMans or any of his offspring. Some did not match the profile; some looked like copy-cat cases. It would be necessary to separate those that were someone else's criminal activity and those that dealt with only the LeMans clan. He further determined that although arrests had been made, there had been no recorded convictions. He selected one.

Complaint Number: 77-334
Complaint: Aggravated Sexual Battery, Unlawful Detention
Date and Time of Occurrence: 4:15 p.m., October 22, 1960
Place of Occurrence: 144 St. Mark's Street, Brooklyn
Date of Birth: July 22, 1945
Description: Female, Black, 120 pounds, 5'6"
Complainant: Dorothea Blessard
Residence: 4414 Albemarle Road, Yonkers, NY
Suspect: Reverend Casius LeMans
Details: *On date, time and place of occurrence Complainant Blessard states that she was taken to the Rehoboth Church of God where she was promised shelter, food and clothing. She alleges she was sexually assaulted for two weeks by one Reverend Casius LeMans, pastor of Rehoboth Bethel Church of God.*

CHAPTER 31

DETECTIVES' OBJECTION

The next afternoon, there was a knock on the office door that startled Carpenter, so wrapped up in his research was he and as he looks up, Detective Marchand entered.

"Lieu," Marchand said, "have you got a minute?"

"Sure, Denny. It is Denny isn't it? Have a seat." He puts the files aside, clasped his hands in front on the desk, tenting the index fingers.

"Yeah, well, I'm sorta the Guardian Association delegate for the detectives in the squad."

"That's nice to know, Denny. You're speaking of the Black officer's fraternal organization. I assume?"

"Yeah, well, we want to welcome you to the squad and to tell you that we object to taking action against our brothers and sisters, like we've been doin'."

"You lost me. What do you mean when you say you 'object to taking action against your brothers and sisters?" Great, Carpenter thought, the seat is hardly warm and I have dissention in the ranks.

"You know, Lieu, we're all Black and we're arresting Blacks."

"You are not all Black but I get your drift."

Carpenter needed some time on this one. He paused digesting the news. "Denny, can you call a squad meeting for tomorrow morning at 0800 and get all the Black detectives here? We need to get this matter straightened out."

"Yeah, I think so; sure I can," he said confidently.

"Well do that and let's see what needs to be done. When you leave would you ask Sergeant Bonaventura and Soriano to step in here?"

"OK, thanks, Lieu." The detective got up and went out the door.

Blasé and Maria walked in a questioning looks on their faces. Carpenter motioned them to be seated.

"Denny Marchand just presented us with a problem. Are either of you aware that the Black detectives are unhappy about having to arrest their brothers and sisters?"

"Lieu," Maria began . . .

"Carpenter," Bonaventura interrupted bruskly, "Marchand is a rabble rouser as well as a royal American pain in the ass. I wouldn't pay no attention to his ramblings."

"Maria, is there something you wanted to say?" Carpenter asked.

"Marchand is trying to impress you. He's looking to establish his turf with you."

"Well, is this the first time this problem has surfaced? If it isn't, why hasn't something been done long before this?" Carpenter wonders what else has been kept from him as he looked at his supervisors.

"Lieutenant," Maria speaks first, "this is something new. I have heard nothing. Perhaps they are testing you to see how far they can go with you," she offers.

"I've called a squad meeting for tomorrow morning to see how universal the problem is. You two," indicating both supervisors, "know them better than I do. Do you have any suggestions on a course of action I might take?"

"Don't take any bullshit!" Blasé thundered. "I've told them all about you and what a bad ass you are."

Another thunderbolt has landed! "You told them *all* about me? You don't even know me. And what do you mean 'bad ass? What have you told them, Blasé?"

"Well," Blasé began squirming uncomfortably, realizing that he may have overstepped his bounds, "that you have done plainclothes duty in the city, you were a supervisor in the 7-0 in Brownsville, did some time in PLB, 'n worked in Internal Affairs for three years."

"That's the sum total of what you know about me? You . . ." Carpenter, clearly annoyed, changed his mind on what he was going to say, he held back with Maria there. He would have to watch this man and speak privately with him.

"Is there anything we can do, Carpenter?" Maria asked trying to change the subject.

"No, I don't think so. We'll talk again after the meeting. You two do not need to be there unless you want to. Thanks." Watching their backs as they left the office, Carpenter wondered: what do I do now? What should I do?

CHAPTER 32

SQUAD MEETING

As Carpenter drove through the brick entryway and into the parking lot, he noticed for the first time that the lot was walled in. What is this, he thought, Fort Apache in Bed-Stuy? Then he recalled that the last time he had parked on the street and had not been near the parking lot. Once inside the station house, however, he waved to the desk officer, checked the latest department issuances and messages, picked up squad mail and went directly to the squad office. He stopped at the civilian clerk's desk to ask for some Inter-Departmental forms.

"Good morning, Gloria," he said, "are the detectives in the Interview Room?"

"Good morning, Lieutenant. Yes, they are all there waitin' on you. Can I know what's goin' on?"

"I'll talk to you later and tell you all about it but right now I need about thirty Requests for Transfer forms. When you get them, would you bring them in to me? I'll be in the room."

"I'll have them in about three minutes, Lieutenant."

He called 'thank you' over his shoulder as he made for the room. Entering the room he saw the members of his command gathered together lounging around. He wasted no time.

"Good morning, I have not met all of you yet. I'm Lieutenant Carpenter the new squad commander here in the Seven Seven. I know many of you are on your day off so I will be brief. Marchand here," indicating the detective, as Gloria Philips delivers the forms, "informs me that you all object to having to take action against your brothers and sisters." Carpenter walked from one detective to another, handing each a Request for Transfer form.

"If that is the case," he continued, "then I don't want you here. I will not ask you to do something you find repugnant. I am well aware that each of you is assigned to a high crime hazard command and when you go home at the end of the day, many of you return to another high hazard area, with, a few exceptions. So it may seem at times that there is no let up. Does anyone have anything to say?"

"Lieutenant," Detective Binghamton said as he looks at the form, "we don't know what this is all about."

"Okay," he said pausing. He realized that he had been standing; he now took a seat. "Detective Marchand informed me yesterday that as your delegate, he wanted me to know that you each object to having to take action against your brothers and sisters. I think he was referring to arrests of Blacks for criminal acts. This meeting is to see if we can do something about that."

"He ain't our delegate," Detective Jackson pointed out apparently quite annoyed.

"In any event, those of you that feel as Marchand does make a valid point, complete this form and sign it and I will have you transferred. It may not be right away, but I will see that it happens.

If I may I would like to ask you a couple of questions. What is the ethnic mix of this command? Who is it that is being assaulted, raped, robbed and beaten? The answer to both questions is Black. So, that being the case, it seems obvious that your allegiance, if you resent having to take action, is with the 'bad guys' and not with the 'good guys.' If that's true, I certainly don't want you here. Sign those forms and turn them in to Gloria as you leave." Carpenter waited for some time but no one had anything to say. He turned and went to his office. As the door closed he heard a number of loud voices directed at Marchand.

He stopped at Gloria's desk to tell her that some of the detectives would be giving her some signed request for transfer forms. He told her everything that had transpired and what had precipitated it.

"When you have them all, would you bring them into the office?" He started to the office when Sergeant Bonaventura intercepted him.

"How did it turn out, Lieu," he asked.

"We'll see, Blasé. We'll see. Would you ask Maria, when she comes in, to see me and I will want to talk with you at the same time."

Later that day both Maria and Blasé walked into the office and took seats. "I met with the troops this morning and we spoke of transfers. I don't think the mood is as widespread as Marchand would have us believe."

"I told you that was bullshit!" Bonaventura said emphatically.

"On another matter," he paused as he picked up a folder, "the 61s we have compiled reflect that the fingers from all the girls are missing. To the best of my knowledge, no one has made much of that fact and the media hasn't been screaming their heads off about a serial killer."

Maria moved forward in her seat. "Up to now it was just a statistic added to the report. We didn't think that that fact had any significance."

"It is a discernable pattern, Maria," Carpenter advised them. "It will allow us to distinguish which crimes are our concerns. When our people get to the scene and the fingers are missing, have them cover the body as quickly as possible. Now, let's brainstorm on what course of action we should take with this new information. Oh yes, Maria, get one of the detectives to look into the method used to cut the fingers from the hands. Perhaps speaking to one of the pathologists they can give us more information in that area. Also, find out if the same instrument was used in all or most of the cases. If so, than that will become another part of the pattern."

CHAPTER 33

"GIMME ALL YOUR MONEY!"

Shortly after lunch, one of the detectives came into his office. "Lieu," Detective Jerry Michaels said, "What do you make of this?" holding up a slip of paper.

"What is it, Jerry?" he asked.

"We've been having a series of gas station stick ups and each time the perp hands the attendant a note like this saying: 'This is a hole up. Gimme all your money,' and then signs it 'Bobby Jones."

"Let's see that note." Jerry handed it over and Carpenter read it. "Where did you get this note?"

"I got it from a Chevron station operator, Jerry Bittner. He's over on Marion and Ralph."

"Is Bittner still here?" Carpenter asked.

"No, he left some time ago. He just wanted to report the robbery. He says he didn't have much cash on hand but felt it should be reported."

"Do we have anything on 'Bobby Jones' in the Name Check file that you know of?"

"Yeah, we have him in the precinct Name File and his picture too. He's some mope over on Decatur Street, a small time hump."

"How many of these stick up notes do you have and have those who were robbed been shown Jones' picture?"

"Five or six holdups, I think but they haven't been shown his picture that I know of."

"Go with your partner, put together a photo array and show it to all the complainants. If they pick him out, scoop up this Bobby Jones and see if you can get the other notes if they still have them. Then, let's see what he has to say.

The detective leaves and Carpenter returned to reading and signing the various reports. Gloria Philips entered with one request form. "Only Detective Marchman has signed a Transfer Request. What shall I do with it?"

"Give it to me and I'll speak with Marchman about it. Thank you, Gloria."

About an hour later, Michaels and Harv Truter return with Bobby Jones in tow. He is placed in the interview room in handcuffs. The officers move to the Lieutenant's office. "Lieu," Truter says, "we got the "golfing pro" and we're batting a thousand on the IDs. You want to talk to him?"

"Have you given this guy a toss?" Both men nod and say "Yeah" in unison.

"Gather up all the notes we have on these robberies, save this as a writing exemplar for the D.A. If there is a match, charge him with all the armed robberies," Carpenter said. "If you found nothing on him, have the ADA seek a search warrant for his apartment. If Mr. Jones used a firearm in the commission of these robberies, we need to find that gun. That will change the severity of the crime. You might also ask him where it is."

"Michaels takes the note saying, "Hot damn this is gonna work!"

CHAPTER 34

EXEMPLAR EVIDENCE

"Are either of you," Carpenter asks, "familiar with 'exemplar evidence,'" he asks.

Detective Truter answers, "Yeah, we've had that in training but I've never gotten any of that evidence before."

"Me neither," Detective Michaels said.

"Well, you guys handle the questioning; you decide among yourselves who will lead. Place all the notes face down on the table. The lead detective will hand Jones a piece of paper and a pencil. Ask him to write: 'This is a hold up. Give me all your money,' nothing else. If he agrees, let him write the note. Then we'll see what happens. If the note matches the others then that note becomes the exemplar. Are there any questions?"

"We've got it, Lieu," Detective Truter said. All three walk to the Interview Room. Jones is seated at the head of the table, Detective Michaels and Truter sit on either side and Carpenter takes a seat in the rear of the room. Michaels hands Jones a slip of paper and a ball point pen.

"Mr. Jones," he said, "we would like you to write what we tell you."

"Why do I hafta do that," he asked?

"You do not have to do anything. We're asking you to do this which will go a long way to clear up the case."

"Oh," Jones mumbles as he bends to write. "What you want me to write?"

"Just this, 'this is a hold up; give me all your money."

Jones scratches on the paper and when finished, he hands the paper to Michaels who read it. He handed it to his partner who also read it then passed it on to Carpenter. The note read: This is a hole up gimme all your money. Bobby Jones.

"Mr. Jones," Detective Truter announces, "you're under arrest for armed robbery," as he began to read the Miranda Warnings. Detective Michaels leans forward to ask:

"Mr. Jones, did you use a gun in these robberies?"

"Nah, I dint."

CHAPTER 35

DETECTIVIE MARCHAND

As the prisoner is taken to Central Booking, Carpenter continued his investigation into the comings and goings at the Rehoboth Bethel Church, while at the same time, continuing his work as the squad supervisor. In his reading of the DD5s, in certain cases cataloguing the investigative activity, he conducted random call backs to listed complainants, to see if anything was missed. When reading the DD5s of Detective Marchand, he noticed that every time Marchand placed a statement in quotation marks, it is a clear indication that he never interviewed the witness mentioned. It was an obvious quirk of Marchand's that even he himself was probably not aware of. Carpenter mentioned the phenomenon to Bonaventura and Soriano.

"Have you noticed Marchand's use of quotation marks?" he asks them jointly.

"Yeah," Bonaventura says before Soriano can. "He does that a lot."

"Well," Soriano said, "I do not let him slide on that. Every time I get one of his 5s, I notice that he usually hasn't interviewed anyone. In those cases, I have him conduct a re-interview."

"Wha,?" Bonaventura begins. "Why are you bustin' his horns for?" he asks Soriano. "It's no big deal."

"Blasé," Carpenter interrupts, "these DD5s, as I'm sure you know, are official records. If you let him get away with falsifying a record and with a lie, it only continues. Call him on it each time he does it. Okay? And if it continues to happen, write him up on charges. On the way out, please have him step in here."

Marchand entered the office asking, "You wanted to see me, Boss"

"Yes, Denny. I've been reading through your DD5s and something has come up."

"Yeah, like what?" He is both annoyed and curious to learn what the Lieutenant has learned.

"Every time you put a statement in quotations, it usually means that you never talked to the complainant as you said you did."

"No, that's not true! How are you findin' that?"

"It is true, Denny and I want it to stop. If I see it again, you will be assigned to every rotten detail that comes up and if it continues after that, I will have you arrested for falsifying official records. You seem like a good investigator and I don't want you to louse it up with something like this. Just don't do it again, alright?"

"No, that's the last time you'll see that."

"Just one other thing, you are the only one to put in for a transfer because of your racial resentments. Are you still interested in another command?

"Nah, you can tear it up." Carpenter nods agreement as Marchand walks out as the telephone rings.

CHAPTER 36

AN UNUSUAL AIDED CASE

"**77**th Squad, Lieutenant Carpenter"

["Lieu,"] Gloria said, ["there's an officer asking to speak to one of the detectives. Who do you want me to give it too?"]

"Who is catching?" he asks.

["Detective O'Brien, but he's out with his partner."] Gloria informs him.

"Let me speak with the caller and then I'll pass it on to O'Brien." The call is transferred to his line. "77th Squad, Carpenter."

["This is Patrolman Grady, Lieu," the officer said. "I got . . ."] he continues and pauses.

"Is there a problem, officer?"

["I dunno, Lieu,"] the officer says.

"Tell me about it, Grady," Carpenter says trying to get the patrolman to talk.

["Well, sir, see. I was sent here on an aided case and when I get here the aided case is a dead baby. And it don't smell right."]

"You mean the baby soiled its diapers?"

["No, Lieu, nothin' like that. There's something fishy about the whole thing. See, the mother and her boyfriend say the baby fell out of a dresser drawer and was killed in the fall."]

"Have you seen the dresser?"

["Yes, sir, I have."]

"How tall is the dresser?"

["It's six drawers and the top drawer is used as the baby's crib."]

"Did you ask how old the baby was?"

["Yes, sir I did. He's about twenty months old."]

"That's a little old for a dresser drawer but if there is no money for better, then that is what they use. It's most unfortunate, officer. Sometimes, in poor neighborhoods the people have to make do with what they have."

["Could someone come and take a look just to make sure I haven't overlooked anything? I'm reasonably new on the job an' I don't want to screw up."]

"Alright, officer, I'll be there in a few minutes. What's the address?"

["It's the only high rise on the northeast corner of Herkimer and Troy, apartment 804."]

"Has a call been made for an ambulance?"

["I dunno, I'll ask."]

CHAPTER 37

INFANTICIDE

Detective Maureen O'Brien asked if she might go with him, Carpenter agreed. She walked to the driver's side of the unmarked car. He briefed her on the way to Herkimer Street. As they arrive she noticed that an ambulance was on the scene and points it out to Carpenter. Walking into the building, they are met by a concentrated smell of stale urine, feces and decayed garbage that caused them to catch their breath. In Apartment 804 the baby was found lying in soiled bed clothes. In the room was a patrol officer, a small Black female in her early twenty's wearing a housecoat and tall, thin Black male dressed in boxer shorts, and two annoyed ambulance attendants.

One of attendants came forward. "Are you the Lieutenant?" he snarled.

"Yes, is there a problem?"

"The cop here," indicating the uniformed man, "wouldn't let us do anything but pronounce the kid dead. He said he wanted to wait for you. What's the big deal? We ain't got all day!"

"Simmer down. Let me speak with the officer." Carpenter said as he moved toward the uniformed patrolman. "Are you Grady?" the officer nodded his head. "What doesn't feel right about this infant?"

"Look at this, Lieu," the officer said as he turned the infant over lifting its night shirt, "I just noticed them." On the infant's back running from its left shoulder to its right buttock were a series of pencil-line bluish-red welts. There were eight such welts sketched on the infant's back.

To the woman he said, "What are those welts from?"

The woman shrugged her shoulders and threw her up arms. Just then the tall Black man stepped forward. He looked to be about six feet two and about 220 pounds. He is quite muscular; slim waisted was wearing his hair in tight corn rows. He is wearing boxer shorts.

The man said, "I'm Shantelle's boyfriend and I live here. See, the baby shit its diaper and I beat him with a length of fishin' rod for doin' a bad thing."

Carpenter thought to himself, using a fishing rod on an infant is a cruel means of corporal punishment but not enough to cause the death of the child. He bent over the infant to examine the baby's body more carefully. There did not seem to be other visible injuries but a slight bulge in the right scapula area. Standing he said, "Did anything else happen?"

"Well, yeah, see. I got really pissed off and punched the kid until my hand hurt."

Carpenter stepped back raising his left hand to have the man stop. "Do not say another word! You are under arrest. You have the right to remain silent . . ."

The man was confused and upset. "I know my rights," he shouted, "I've been there before. What you mean I'm under arrest? I'm allowed to punish my own kid for Christ's sake!"

Carpenter turned the man around, took his left hand and placed handcuffs on his wrist. He took the other and secured that arm as well. He turned the man back. "You sir, are much bigger than this infant and I believe you may have caused internal injuries. For now you are arrested for aggravated battery and when we get the medical report, you may be charged with Manslaughter." Carpenter turned to the officer and attendants. "Grady, accompany the baby to the Medical Examiner's Office, these drivers" indicating the ambulance men, "will take you there. Ask the duty doctor to do hurry up post and you call me with the results. Do you understand what is needed here?"

"Yes sir, Lieu!"

Maureen took the prisoner by his arm and led him out of the room. "I'll get the paperwork started. Do you want Grady and the arresting officer," she asked?

"Yes, the experience will do him good."

Back at the squad, Carpenter stopped at the clerk's desk.

"Gloria," he said, "would you please call for the sitting ADA and ask him or her to stop by on a baby's death and beating?"

"Yes, sir, is the baby dead?"

"Yes," was all he could manage to say.

CHAPTER 38

DIFFERENCE OF OPINION

Assistant District Attorney Robert Tannenbuam was shown into the office where he took a chair in front of Carpenter's desk.

"What have you got, Lieu?" he asked. "I'm covering all of Brooklyn South."

Carpenter pushed forward a UF61 and DD5 on the arrest and the death of the infant. "The baby is at the ME's office," he informed Tannenbuam, "and we're waiting to hear from them."

Tannenbuam read the reports then looked up. "What are you waiting for? Has there been an arrest made?"

"I thought you should read the report. Yes, there was an arrest made for the unlawful death of an infant."

"Well, Lieu, I do not authorize you to make the arrest."

The Lieutenant stood up, placed both fists on his desk and leaned toward the man. "You do not what?! You do not authorize me to make an arrest? I do not need your authorization!" His voice had risen, he brushed a wisp of hair from his forehead, and his face became reddened. "That man is arrested for breathing the same air I'm breathing. He punched an infant until his hand hurt. Have you fallen on your head, you moron?"

"Lieutenant, there is no need," he stammered. The telephone rang interrupting the confrontation.

Carpenter picked it up. "Carpenter," he said. He sat down to take up a pencil and a piece of paper. He began writing several items on the paper. "Anything else?" he asked and began writing again. "What is the bottom line, an accidental death from the fall or a homicide?" He again wrote on the paper. "Thanks, Grady. Listen; when you get back here, the collar is yours and the prisoner is in the cell waiting your return. That was heads up work today." He hung up the telephone.

He sat looking at the paper for a time then leaned forward reading: "Broken clavicle, broken vertebra, broken back, ruptured spleen and punctured lung. Cause of death from a series of blows about the body, an infant homicide." Having finished reading the paper, Carpenter bunched the paper into a wad and threw it into the ADA's face.

Tannenbuam slowly bent to pick up the paper and read it. "Well, alright. You can go ahead and make the arrest."

The office door opened and Detective O'Brien entered. "Lieu," she began, "the media, Channel Four and Seven have gotten wind of the baby's death. They want to come up and get a statement."

Tannenbuam rose from his chair. "I'll go and meet them downstairs. I'll make the official statement on the death and its cause."

"Detective," Carpenter said to the Maureen, "Go with Mr. Tannenbuam. If he makes any statement to the press or media or anyone else, place him under arrest for Interfering with Governmental Process." He snatched the paper back from the ADA who stood nonplused.

"You can't to that Carpenter!" he screamed.

"Yes, I can." He moved to stand in front of the man. "This is an on-going investigation and the department is unprepared to make any official statement at this time. When and if we do, it will come out of Press Relations. That's all."

"You're an asshole, Carpenter!"

"Sticks and stones . . . , Tannenbuam. Sticks and stones . . . ."

CHAPTER 39

CARPENTER IS GUNNED DOWN

A year passed quickly in the 77th Precinct and in the squad. Carpenter has survived one attempt on his life. He and Sergeant Soriano had gone to lunch in a small restaurant on Jamaica Avenue. As they emerged from the restaurant a glossy grey compact car came careening around the corner. The driver's window rolled down and someone in a ski mask pointed at gun at him and fired almost point blank. He had seen the movement and dove left taking Maria with him. Only one of the three bullets fired hit him high in his right shoulder. Maria was unhurt. Both had drawn their weapons but the car had screeched away. They both noticed that there was no license plate on the vehicle. Maria went to their unmarked car and called a 10-13 officer shot, asking for an ambulance.

"Carpenter," she said reassuringly, "you caught one high in your right shoulder. An ambulance is on its way. Stay on the sidewalk until they get here."

"You're being a pushy broad, Maria," he said through clenched teeth.

"Yeah, that's me, pushy, pushy."

Carpenter spent the next two days in Coney Island Hospital recuperating and another month in rehab before he was returned to duty. On her visit, Carpenter and Maria discussed the shooting.

"Who do you think it was taking the pot shots at us?" he asked.

"My money's on one of the LeMans clan. They're the only ones I've pissed off lately."

CHAPTER 40

CITY-WIDE BLACKOUT

In his absence, the bodies of two young black females were found; both were killed in the same fashion as the others. Their fingers were missing as well. One of them was found nude in an empty building on Park Place and Brooklyn Avenue and the other was found with panties only wrapped in an old rug on Brown Street and Albany Avenue. These cases were added to the other open homicides.

Then one hot August evening there was a citywide power outage. An order came down from Borough Headquarters that all members of the squad will turn out in uniform and be out on the streets assisting the patrol services. They are briefed on the tactics to be used on the streets at dusk for rounding up looters. From the last blackout like this there was a population explosion nine months later. It was the cause of a massive love in. Not so, this time. Word is sent out that Armories and sporting goods stores have been broken into and weapons taken, all of which means that the police must now deal with looters and armed bands. "Wonderful." Carpenter murmured, "Simply wonderful."

Carpenter and the detectives are assigned to sweep the one area of the precinct's streets between Rochester and Saratoga Avenue. He has the detectives, armed with batons, form a vee or wedge with patrol wagons trailing behind them. At the head of a street, he announces over a bull horn that there will be a sweep in five minutes and anyone found on the street after that will be subject to an arrest. The detectives move forward. Whenever an arrest is made for looting, the prisoner is searched, the officer is photographed with his prisoner, and the prisoner's name, time, date and location are entered into a log along with the property seized or vouchered. The prisoner is handcuffed with plastic cuffs and placed in the wagon. As the wagon fills, it returns to the station house where the prisoners are booked to await matching up with the officer later. The station house supervisor separates them by sex and age. The children are placed in the sitting room and given whatever food is available.

At the head of Buffalo Avenue, Carpenter warned people on the street through a megaphone. "This is the New York City Police Department," he announced, "You have five minutes to clear the street. Anyone found on the street or found looting will be arrested." Fortunately there is a three-quarter moon that provides enough light for the officers in their work despite the stifling heat and humidity. At the end of the prescribed time, the wedge slowly moves forward. It was almost comical watching people scurrying this way and that to avoid being arrested. Quickly one van is filled and returned for another load.

"Joab," he calls out to one of the detectives, "see that little Black guy with the baby carriage?"

"Yeah, Lieu," Detective Jackson replies, "That's 'Bebop' he's the local purse snatcher."

"He's got televisions and other audio equipment in the baby carriage. Take him in unless he has receipts for those things."

"Gotcha, Boss." Detective Jackson hurries after the looter.

In front of Mason's Haberdashery the officers see Mr. Mason sitting on an inexpensive lawn chair with a Remington 870 Wingmaster shot gun across his lap. His store is a narrow structure with a limited inventory.

"Mr. Mason," Carpenter walks over to talk with him, "you can't sit here with that gun. Someone will get hurt."

"Ain't no one bustin' in my place," Mason replies. "I work hard and no punk is takin' it from me tonight or any other night!"

"We can't allow you to threaten anyone with that shot gun," Carpenter informed him. "Please put it away. You can sit out here but without the gun."

"Okay, Mistur pooleece man." Mason gets up from the chair and enters his store, the gun with him. The officers move on. Once they are well down the street, Mason returned to his chair, his shotgun across his lap.

Carpenter noticed that there are perhaps a dozen or so kids sitting atop mopeds puttering around the neighborhood. He turned to Maria to ask: "What's with the mopeds?" he asks, "And why are they out tonight?"

"There's a dealership on Eastern Parkway," she answered knowledgably, "and these have probably been taken from their lot. They'll ride them around until they run out of gas."

"Wonderful, simply wonderful," Carpenter says once more. "Would you remind me to call Sanitation to pick up the abandoned mopeds? We can trace the owners through the registration or VIN numbers."

At about three o'clock in the morning the looting has waned and few people are on the street. Carpenter took the squad back to the station house to get them started with photo matching and report writing. A long day is promised. At about 0830 the next morning a tall, slender black haired woman with hair pulled back tightly and tied in a bun, is brought into the squad room by Gloria Philips. She is wearing expensive skirt, blouse, and shoes carrying a clipboard clutched against her breast.

"Lieutenant," she says, "This is Adrienne Heitzman of the A.C.L.U. to see you."

Carpenter and the others have been on duty for more than sixteen hours and weariness has begun to show gaunt on his face. "Thank you, Gloria. Ms Heitzman, may I help you?"

"*Missus.* Heitzman, Lieutenant," she said coldly. Carpenter observed 'no bullshit from this one in her attitude or in her demeanor. She appeared to not have heard him or deliberately ignored him.

"It is *Missus.* Heitzman, Lieutenant," she corrected him.

"Whatever, I'm waiting, *Missus* Heitzman," he's not going to stand for much bullshit either.

Referring to the clipboard clutched in her arms, she says: "We have many complaints of gross prisoner mistreatment," she states quite appalled.

"Already?" Carpenter asked incredulously.

"Yes," she is now indignant. "The first complaint, for instance, is about over-crowding . . ."

"Sit down, Mrs. Heitzman, sit, sit." She remained standing. "Yes, we have experienced some overcrowding. We have facilities here for a total of sixteen prisoners in this station house and last night and early this morning we have arrested nearly six hundred in this precinct. We have had them separated by sex, age, and children were recently sent to a separate shelter. So, divide five hundred or so by sixteen and you have overcrowding. What's next?"

Mrs. Heitzman, seeing that she cannot intimidate this man, frostily continues. "We have multiple complaints that none of your prisoners were given any food. That's over a twelve hour period!"

"*Mrs.* Heitzman," Carpenter had taken almost all he can. "I'm going to say this slowly so that you can grasp its meaning. We had a blackout which means there was no electricity in the Borough of Brooklyn and most of Manhattan! All the restaurants, bars, dinners and bodegas closed shop until the lights come back on. There was no food to give the prisoners or the police officers either and police officers get quite testy if they are not fed regularly! So you are quite correct, there was no food. What's next?"

Clutching her clipboard pressed to her breast, an annoyed Mrs. Heitzman says: "You seem to have a haughty, cavalier attitude, Lieutenant. No wonder the police department has the terrible reputation it does with Bolshevik bullies like you. I will have to report your attitude to my superiors."

"That sounds like a very good idea, *Mrs.* Heitzman. Put your complaints in writing and send them or hand carry them to the Brooklyn South Borough Command where they will be properly adjudicated. Good morning. I have some prisoners to beat." The woman walks off in a huff. Before she gets out of the door, Carpenter called out: "Don't let the gate hit you in the ass!"

A smiling Detective Jackson, who had been waiting until this tête-à-tête was over, approached Lieutenant Carpenter. "Hey, boss. Remember that guy Bebop we took in last night?"

"Oh, yeah, Bebop, what about him?"

"You were right. He had a television, cameras, hifi equipment and some other shit."

"That's not unusual. What else?"

"Only a baby maybe eight months old who was under all that stuff!"

"Is the child alright? Has the child been harmed?" he asks alarmed.

"No, she's quite alright. Social Services have taken the child to find its' parents. Bebop says that he never knew the baby was there. Should I charge him with kidnapping as well?"

"No, hold off on that. But talk it over with the ADA's office and get their opinion. Also ask what should be done about the parents and their abandonment of the child. Where were they?" He turned away when Jackson shrugged his shoulders, saying, "What a night!"

CHAPTER 41

THE WITNESS

Carpenter was on the telephone giving a summary of the squad's activity during the blackout and subsequent arrest processing to the Borough command. As he speaks, Gloria walked into the office placing a message on his desk. He picked it up to read: "Sergeant. Bonaventura wants to talk to you on line two."

"That brings you up to date, Inspector. Our written reports will follow. Thank you, sir. Have a good day." He depressed the button and punches line two. "Blasé, this is Carpenter. What have you got?"

[*"Another fifteen year old light-skinned Black girl,"* he said tersely. *"it's part of that pattern we've been working on,"*] the sergeant reports.

"Have any of the media been inside the frozen zone?"

["No, we cordoned off the area then covered her up."]

"Was her neck broken, Blasé ?"

["Yup an' her hands are the same as all the others. It looks like she was brutally violated and it looks like it was done post mortem."]

"Where was she found, Blasé?"

["Over on Revere and Prospect Place. Some old lady walkin' her dog found her in a tiny pocket lot. It's been estimated she's been dead for about three days at least."]

"Was she carrying any ID?"

["There is no ID but she has a bright red rose tattooed between her shoulder blades. No other papers or distinguishing marks."]

"We need photographs and Blasé, have them take footprints impressions, if there are any. Maybe we'll get lucky again. I'll be there to help in the investigation."

When he arrived Carpenter saw that the pocket park was an area used by the locals for walking their dogs. It was now crowded with portable lights, photographers, police and medical personnel. Everyone else was kept at a distance. The media, annoyed at being kept from the scene, were yelling questions at him. The medical people were getting ready to put the frail young girl into a body bag.

"Hold it, fellas," Carpenter called out to them. "I would like to have this body carefully wrapped. There may be fingerprints on her neck that we may be able to recover. I also want to know if she has been violated and how recently." Turning to his sergeant, "Blasé, have a female officer go with the ambulance and remind her to have a rape kit examination done."

"Lieutenant Carpenter," a uniformed officer approached. "We might have a witness to the dumping of the body," the officer reports.

"Is that person here?" the Carpenter asked.

Turning to reveal an elderly woman standing behind him, the officer introduced her. "Lieu, this is Mrs. Sophie Blanchard who lives across the street." Mrs. Blanchard wore a babushka over her grey hair, a knitted shawl around her shoulders, a long thin dress and sensible shoes.

"Hello, Mrs. Blanchard. I'm Lieutenant Carpenter and this is Sergeant Bonaventura. We are given to understand that you witnessed the body being placed in the park. Is that correct?"

With a very frail voice the woman responded. "Yes, Lieutenant, I saw them just the other day putting the body there," she pointed to the park.

"You say 'them' Mrs. Blanchard. There was more than one?" Carpenter inquired.

"At least three of them," she said. "When they came out of their space craft, they took off their helmets and took hold of her body. I knew they were in the area because of their airwaves interference. The waves came right through my window pane. That's how I know about them."

"You have been most helpful, Mrs. Blanchard. I'll have an officer take down you statement."

"I hope I can help, officer."

After she was led away, Carpenter turned to his sergeant. "Blasé, what kinds of vehicles are at the church?"

"Let's see, two sedans and an SUV. Why"

"Is the SUV black?"

"Yeah."

"Might a black SUV look like a spacecraft?"

"It's a stretch but it might, who knows?"

CHAPTER 42

HER DAUGHTER IS MISSING

The blackout is history now and the precinct has slowly returned to some sort of normalcy. On his watch there have been three new homicides of young Black girls and all were brutalized. Their investigations into the homicides have met with little progress. Carpenter experienced first-hand the frustration that this case engendered.

Carpenter was on the telephone speaking with a friend, Margaret Carmody.

["Carpenter, I'm so sorry to hear what has been going on," she says sympathetically.]

"What are you talking about, Maggie? What are you sorry about?"

[*"About your divorce, I heard you and Susan were getting a divorce,*] she announces.

"A divorce," he asks incredulously? "We haven't been arguing. Why would we get a divorce?"

[*"I'm sorry, Carpenter. I must ha've you mixed up with someone else,*] she hurriedly says.

Gloria knocks on the office door and entered. "Lieutenant, a Sister Ruth Johnson of the *Rehoboth Bethel Church of God* would like to talk to you."

He holds up his hand. "Listen, Maggie, I've got to go. You scared me on that one."

[*"Sorry, Carpenter, so long,*] she says and both hang up.

"Do you know what it's all about, Gloria?" Carpenter inquired.

"No, sir, but she seems upset."

"Show her in."

Sister Johnson, a short woman in her late thirties, early forties, still wearing her black habit, is shown in and took a seat before Carpenter's desk.

"Lieutenant," she blurts out on seating herself, "my daughter is missing and 'Doc' is responsible!" The woman makes a production of smoothing out her habit.

"Sister Johnson, what is your daughter's name?" Carpenter asks cautiously.

"Yolanda, Yolanda Johnson an' she be fourteen years old."

"Give me her description including the clothing she was wearing when you saw her last."

"She is fourteen years old, a Black chile, under five feet tall, 'bout a hundret pounds an' she's wearin' a yellow sun dress with white sneakers."

As Carpenter makes note of this information, he looked up and asked: "What do you mean 'Doc's responsible? Who is Doc?"

"Why, Doctor LeMans a course. He's a doctor of religion or somethin' like that. We call him 'Doc' or Reverend or whatever," she explained."

"Well then, how long has Yolanda been missing?"

"Since yesterday," Sister Ruth calls out excitedly!

"Sister, she could have stayed over at a friend's house," he explained.

"No, she's dead! I know she is." Johnson was nearing hysteria.

"I'll have a Missing Person's Report prepared, and I will also alert the officers on patrol and my detectives to be on the lookout for your daughter. Did you bring a photograph of her?" The woman reached into the folds of her habit and brought out a snapshot of her daughter and handed it to Carpenter.

"But, what do you mean 'she is dead?" Carpenter asked.

"We have rules in the church and anyone that breaks those rules is punished. She broke one of the rules and Doc had killed her, I know it."

"You don't know that. She could be anywhere," Carpenter replied.

"No, no. Doc killed her for shacking up with a Puerto Rican boy, Pablo Salazar an' I think she's been smokin' some weed."

"Maybe Yolanda's with Pablo," Carpenter tried to reason.

"Why aren't you listening? She's dead and Doc killed her!"

"We will begin an investigation into this missing daughter of yours. Does she have any outstanding features, and do you have a recent picture of her," he repeated?" Carpenter continued taking the pertinent information from Sister Johnson. When the form has been completed Carpenter says: "If Yolanda shows up, please let us know. In the meantime, if we learn anything about her or her disappearance, we will contact you."

"Thank you, Lieutenant. Remember though, she is dead."

CHAPTER 43

"YOU GOT FEETS?"

For several weeks there was no information learned in the disappearance of Yolanda Johnson. There was just no trace of her. Early one Sunday morning though, Carpenter was in his office reading through the LeMans file again and jotting notes to himself on a sheet of brown wrapping paper tacked to the wall in his office, for follow-up action. The paper was six feet long and three feet wide, the schematics on it resembled an organizational chart. As he was reading and making notes he overheard one of the detectives in the outer office on the telephone.

"You got feets," the disembodied voice was saying. "You got two feets," it said. "What kind of feets are they? They be Black feets. Listen, Buddy, is this some kind of put on?"

Carpenter's interest had been piqued. He turned from the chart and walked into the squad room. Detective Kulik was on the phone. Kulik cradled the telephone between his shoulder and chin raising both his arms in the air. "Yes, sir, I'll ask the Lieutenant and see what he says." He put the phone on the desk to face Carpenter.

"Boss," he began, "this janitor over on Saratoga says that the found two black 'feets' in a black plastic bag in his garbage and wants to know what he should do with them?"

"Benji, why don't we take a ride over there and see what he's got? It's probably nothing but you never know."

"Gotcha, Boss," he picks up the phone. "Mr. Carmoda, we'll be right over to take a look."

A short ride put them at the curb where Mr. Carmoda was waiting for them. He was a short dumpy man wearing soiled coveralls and workman's boots. When Detective Kulik got out of the auto he asked: "Are you Mr. Carmoda?"

"Yes, officer and here is the bag." He handed the officer a black plastic trash bag that Kulik took and opened.

"Phew!" he moaned as he turned away. "Oh, Jesus." he said grimacing and holding the bag at arm's length.

Carpenter could smell the bag and its contents and knew instinctively that it was rotted flesh. He asked: "What do you have, Benji?" seeking verification.

"There are two black feet in here, Lieu. It looks as though they were cut off just above the ankle with a saw or something like it and they belong to a Black kid by the looks of them. I couldn't tell too much," he said as he closed the bag and sealed it off.

"Alright, Benji, let's get them bagged and tagged then put them in the trunk." They thanked Mr. Carmoda and reenter the car. Enroute to the station house, Carpenter said, "Let's get them to the ME's office to give us a run down on what they are. Ask him to let us know ASAP."

Later that afternoon, Detective Kulik returned to the Interview Room, which had been converted into a war room of sorts, to report on the ME's findings. They all met sitting in a rough circle because Carpenter wanted everyone's input on this recent finding.

"Well, sir," Kulik began, "the ME says that to the best of his knowledge the feet were cut off with a saw, probably electrical, and that they belong to a person between the ages of 14 to 16 years, probably a Black female. More than that he said would take more time."

"Benji, were footprints taken?"

"I took them myself. I got them here," he replied.

"Why don't we get them read by BCI then we can transmit copies to all the hospitals in the metropolitan area and see if we can get a hit on them? Ask all of them to respond positively or negatively so that we have some sort of record of what we're doing."

"I'll get on it."

On Friday of the following week, Detective Kulik reported to Carpenter and Bonaventura.

"All the hospitals have been heard from and we have no hit. The girl is still a phantom."

"Get the others in the interview room," Carpenter directed the detective. "Let's brainstorm the situation and see what we have to do next."

Six detectives crammed into the room. Carpenter brought them all up to date on what had taken place and what steps the office had taken. He showed them the wrapping paper schematic. "Any suggestions," he asked of no one in particular.

Joab Jackson offered a recommendation: "Why don't we send copies of Yolanda's footprints to the Department of the Army and all military facilities in the area. They might be able to help us. They keep their records on microfiche."

"It's a thought, Lieu," Tony Romano said, "although there is no indication of any military background for LeMans."

Detective Kulik said. "I'll take care of that."

When nothing further was brought up, they returned to their work.

The next day the ordinary hubbub of the office was shattered with a loud "Yeah!"

Kulik rushed into the office bubbling with what he found out. "The U.S. Marine Hospital on Staten Island gave us a hit! The footprints have been identified as belonging to one Yolanda Johnson and date back almost fifteen years."

"Benji, you and your partner take a ride to Staten Island and the Marine Hospital and get copies of any documents they have on the birth. If there's a fee, pay it; if they want a subpoena, we'll get one. Also, stop at the 1-2-0 Precinct and see if they have aided cards on the delivery." Carpenter and the others, with Borough approval for the overtime, have been on duty for more than sixteen hours and weariness has begun to show. He pointed to the door saying, "On your way, Maria and tell the others to get some rest." Wordlessly she left the office.

Several hours later, Carpenter had all of the relative information on the severed feet. He had a copy of the footprints from the Marine Hospital and the Department had and a copy of the footprints of an infant child, with accompanying paperwork. He called Detective Kulik to his office. "Benji, before you report out, you and your partner take a ride over to the LeMans place and ask Sister Johnson to join us. If she won't, we'll try something else."

Chapter 44

THE DIKE SPRINGS A LEAK

Later that day, Kulik returned with Sister Johnson. She was brought to the office and asked to have a seat. The detective moved to leave when Carpenter asked him to stay.

"Did you have any problems?" he asked the detective.

"No," Kulik responds, "the Reverend is off somewhere and the Sister here came voluntarily.

"Lieutenant?" Kulik added.

"What do you need?"

"I'm going home; I'm fallin' through my ass."

"Okay Benji, thanks."

Turning his attention to the nun, he said, "Sister," he began consolingly, "I'm afraid we have some bad news for you."

She sat bolt upright. "She's dead, right?"

"Well, we don't know. You see," he handed her a copy footprints of the feet. "These are the footprints of a fourteen year old. We subsequently learned," he handed her the copy of the footprints of the Marine Hospital, "that they belong to a Black female known as Yolanda Johnson, possibly your daughter."

"She's dead, I knew she was dead," she wailed.

"Sister Johnson," he went on, "just having these footprints are no proof of death. In all likelihood she is, but these," indicating the copies on the desk, "are not proof of that."

"She's dead and Doc done it." She sat down heavily and was quiet for some time her hands folded in her lap then straightening out her habit then back to her lap. Finally, she said, "Alright," coming to a decision, "I got something to tell you."

"What do you mean? What else have you got to tell us?"

"'bout Doc and what has been and is goin' on. That bastard needs to pay!" Carpenter could see the anger that gripped her.

"Let me get a stenographer to take your statement," he said. He picked up the telephone to call Gloria into the office.

138

"Gloria," he asked, "do you take shorthand?" There was a short pause. "You do? Come in here, please and bring your steno pad and the portable tape recorder with you. Make sure you have batteries and clean tapes. Thanks."

Gloria entered and sat down next to the Lieutenant.

"Gloria," he began, "Sister here is going to make a statement and I would like you to take it down for me, type it up and we'll have Sister sign it. The recorder will help you if you don't get it all in shorthand. Can you handle it?"

"Yes, sir, I can," Gloria answered confidently.

"Good, let's get started. 'This is Lieutenant Lance Carpenter," he began, "Squad Commander, 77th Squad Detectives and I am present at the squad office, 127 Utica Avenue, Brooklyn. With me are Ruth Johnson of the *Rehoboth Bethel Church of God* and Gloria Philips, civilian clerk at this office. Today is Thursday, October 18, 1971, the time is 4:20 p.m. Absent mindedly he brushed aside fair from his face.

CHAPTER 45

ANATOMY OF A NIGHTMARE

"About fifteen years ago," Sister Johnson began fingering her waist cord, "I was pregnant and it was almost time for me to deliver. We had an outing planned on Staten Island, three of the children and me. We got there by ferry, had lunch on South Beach in the Amusement Park, and we were supposed to come back here. Well, when we got there, on the island, I knew it was time. I sat on a bench and began constrictions. Someone called the police and they called for an amb'lance. The amb'lance was from the United States Marine Hospital. I no sooner got to the hospital when I started to deliver. Sure enough, here comes Yolanda. I didn't know they had taken her footprints though."

"We thought it was something like that," Carpenter said.

"When I came back here, several days later," she went on, "Doc was pissed off that I had the baby over there. Darryl, that's Anne's oldest son, had come to take the kids back but he never saw me. Doc beat me something fierce an' besides, I hadn't brought any girls in for some time nor any money either."

"Why would he do something like that?" Detective Kulik asked. When she didn't answer the question, Carpenter asked: "What do you mean; you hadn't brought in any girls for some time?"

"Well, see, he has this rule if you can't bring in the amount of money he told you to get, we were supposed to bring in a young, unattached Black girl, around fourteen or fifteen instead."

"Why? What reason did he have for that?" Detective Kulik asked incredulously.

"Let me tell it my way," taking up her waist cord. "When they was brought in, he would take them to his room after we fed 'em and have sex with them every day until they either had their minstrel [sic] period or they had become pregnant by him. He would then assigned them to a family and have a sit down with the girl."

"Sister," Carpenter asked, "we need some clarification here. He kept them there against their will? Like kidnap them? What sort of 'sit down?'" He silently chastised himself for asking multiple questions.

"Yeah, that's what I'm tellin' you. Some stayed willingly but others didn't."

"Go on."

"He'd tell 'em they was welcome t'stay and become part of the church family an' some of them did. If they wanted to leave he said they could but if they said anything about what happened to them, he would kill them. If the girl had a baby, he legally adopted the chile and the mother was given the same choices but the baby had to stay."

The nexus of all the complaints of sexual abuse, kidnappings, assaults and rape now began to make sense.

"Were there, to your knowledge," Carpenter inquired, "any of the girls that left the church and who complained to the police, later killed?"

"Sure, the police would show up, question Doc 'bout some girl's complaint but he never got any jail time. The witness, we were later told, had disappeared. Yeah, right," she said skeptically. "He killed them or one of his boys did."

"One of his boys?" Carpenter asked unknowingly.

"Yes," Ruth continued. "Anne Soriano had seven sons by Doc and each of them was sent to some sort of specialty school to help him. Darryl helped him screw the girls we brought in; Jeremiah was sent to butcher's school; Marcus is a pimp in Manhattan; Shasta is a burglar; Yunki is a packaging specialist; and Jesse, Gideon and Moses have other jobs. Doc told us a long time ago that seven was a mystical number for him and he took Anne's having seven sons as a mystical sign. She also had a girl but she didn't count."

Carpenter and the detective looked at one another nonplused. "Well that accounts for many of the children but there are a lot more," he observed. "There are about twenty five to thirty children that we know of."

"Some of them I had, some Anne had, Juanita had one, and the others came from the girls we brought to them."

"Sister," Carpenter asked her, "would you be willing to go on record with what you have told us here today?"

"What does that mean?" Ruth asked uncertain now.

"I want to call in the Assistant District Attorney for Kings County to have your information recorded so we can take action."

"Well, I guess so, sure. Where would this take place?"

"Probably in the ADA's office here in Brooklyn," he opined.

"No. Can't it be done here?" she now began fingering her waist cord anxiously and becoming quite agitated.

"Well, sure. If that's what you want. Is there anything else you want to tell us?"

"That's it for now."

"Thank you for coming in and we are sorry for your loss. What do you want us to do with the feet?"

"I don't know. They are not Yolanda, only part of her. What do you suggest?"

"We can, I think, have them cremated, but I'll have to check."

"Okay." She stood up to leave the room. She paused turning, "You know the girl who got killed on Revere Place?" She did not wait for an answer. "Her name is Clary," she said as she started to leave.

"Ruth! Is that her first name or last?" Carpenter asked.

"Clarisa Anne Murray. She was brought back to the church cuppla months ago. She was let go an' tole to keep her mouth shut. Guess she didn't." The nun walked out of the room.

The trio sat in silence for several minutes. Kulik was the first to break the silence that had fallen over them. "That's quite a story. Do you believe her?"

"She seems to have a great deal of specific and pertinent information. After her session with the ADA we'll get with them to plan out next step. In the meantime let's check the complaints and reports to see if we have one made by Ms Murray against the Reverend."

CHAPTER 46

LACK OF CORROBORATION

Sister Johnson repeated essentially the same story to an ADA and his staff as she did the detectives. She added new information to what she had already given them. She said that the Reverend was judicial tribunal in the church; if he found anyone guilty of violating his laws, they were condemned and appeals from the process were non-existent. She also said that the disposal method for the disposal of the bodies had always bothered the Reverend since it took at least four hours to dispose of a corpse and that was a risk each time, no matter the incendiary used.

"There is one nagging question," Carpenter observed, "that we cannot find an answer to. We have found better than ten young female bodies in our immediate area. If he is killing them and burning them, why are we finding these bodies? Do you see where I'm coming from?"

"I don't keep count Lieutenant," the nun said. "I only know about the bodies he gets rid of upstate."

Once she had gone, ADA Stephen Bostik asked, "Does she offer any corroboration to her allegations?"

"We asked her for someone to back up her story but she refused to give us anyone. She said they were all too terrified. I noticed that you did not ask for any. Was there a reason for that?" Carpenter inquired.

"I thought, I assumed you had gotten corroboration."

"We have had nothing to move against the Reverend with. Don't forget, he's a clergyman and we can't just go and arrest him on someone's say so. They might be having a personal dispute. You need that corroboration."

"Yes," Carpenter said dejectedly. "I know; I know."

CHAPTER 47

DETECTIVES ARE GUNNED DOWN

When everyone had left, Carpenter asked his two supervisors to fill in any gaps they may have discerned in the nun's narration.

Bonaventura mentioned that the nun had held them all in her spell. He suggested they all absorb what had taken place so far and rehash their findings at their next brainstorming session.

Carpenter agreed.

"Maria, would you touch base with the New York State Police?" He consulted his rolodex. "They are located at 5591 State Road 19 or 22 North Main Street in Belmont. Here is there phone number 845-344-5300. Ask them if they would copy us with any paperwork they may have generated regarding raids to the LeMans ranch. We need anything and everything they have."

"Okay, Lance, I'm on it."

"Blasé, work your magic and put together a team of four detectives to work exclusively on this investigation. You will head it up. Whoever you choose will be taken off the chart to work with us."

From the overhead speakers the police radio blared out. ["In the 7-7 Precinct. A man known as 'Red' is selling narcotics in Maurice's Bar and Grill on Ralph Avenue. Any 7-7 units responding?"]

["77th Squad is nearby Central. We'll respond."] Two of the squad's detectives were nearby.

Red West is a scrawny Black male who was a known street dealer. He got his name from his bright red dyed hair and red shirt he always wore along with his red socks. He was also well-known to Detectives Michael Cummins and Phil Mason, the detectives responding. They drove to the bar and on entering, saw Red sitting at the bar in conversation with another man. The detectives approached, as the man got up walked away sitting at a distant stool.

"Red, my man," Detective Mason said. "What's shakin'?"

"Same oh, same oh," came the dealer's reply as he turned to greet them.

"On your feet, Red," Mason directed. "We've got some talking to do." Detective Cummins was standing back taking in the encounter.

Red stood up, turned his back to the officers, allowing Mason to handcuff one of his wrists to his. All three turned to leave the bar. Unobtrusively another man slid off his bar stool to come up behind the three men exiting. The man drew a semi automatic, pointed to the back of Mason's head and fired a shot. Mason collapsed to the floor. As Cummins turned drawing his weapon, the man pointed the gun to his face firing another shot. Both detectives fell to the barroom floor dragging Red with them. The man stood over the detectives, removed Cummins weapon and walked out of the door as Red screamed to be released. The bartender at first shocked, moved and picked up the bar telephone to call 911.

The police radio blared: ["In the 77 report of shots fired in Maurice's Bar and Grill, officers down. What units responding?"]

Carpenter and Sergeant Bonaventura were in the supervisor's car, going to meal when the call came in.

"Central, 77 Squad Commander will respond. Has an ambulance been requested?'

Central Dispatch answered: ["10-4 commander. It's on the way."]

On arriving at the bar, they saw the detectives and Red on the bar's floor in the entryway, the officers lying in their own blood. Red was screaming his head off. Bonaventura swiped Red in the mouth then bent to undo the handcuff from Mason's wrist. He attached it to his own, yanking the prisoner to his feet.

Carpenter saw the two were grievously injured, he also saw that there was nothing that could be done for them; one had the back of his head blown away and the other had caught at least one round under his left eye. Other units arrived. Carpenter stood up to confront the arriving officers.

"Secure the scene," he directed the second unit on the scene. "Get the names and addresses of any witnesses. Detectives will be here to assist at the scene later," he said to another.

"Okay, Lieu," one of the uniformed officers said. "Are the detectives alright?"

"It looks serious but we'll know better after the ambulance arrives." He turned to the next unit on the scene. "You officers direct traffic and clear space for the ambulance." They moved to carry out his directive. Turning to Blasé he called, "Notify Central that we have enough units on the scene.

A minute or so later, the ambulance arrived and two attendants went to the assistance of the fallen officers. One of the medics stood. "This one," indicating Mason, "is dead. I'm sorry, Lieutenant. The other is still with us. We'll get them outta here." Both officers were removed.

As his injured detectives were removed on gurneys; he spoke a silent prayer. He turned to Sergeant Bonaventura. "Blasé," you take the prisoner to the station house and start the processing. I'm going to stay here for a bit to see this is handled correctly."

"Okay, Carpenter. I'll see you at the house."

Some time afterward, Carpenter returned to the station house, he was still upset. His clothing was soaking wet from sweat. He had to notify the officers' family of their injuries and make notifications to the Borough and those in the big building. He had already secured the name and a description of the shooter and transmitted it to Central for broadcast. Solicitous officers said their condolences as he walked through the station house.

He was walking past the interview room outside the detective squad office and happened to glance in. The room had one-way glass where the occupants could be seen and heard through an attached speaker hung on the wall, but they could not see out. The speaker had not been turned on. Sergeant Bonaventura had Red handcuffed, his arms through the chair rungs, and the sergeant's service revolver jammed in his mouth. Red's eyes were wide in terror.

"Oh shit," Carpenter thought, "that's all we need."

Later he could not recall moving to the door but he went in and shouted to Sergeant Bonaventura, "Blasé! Don't shoot! Take your gun away! Do it now!" Slowly the gun was removed and slashed across Red's mouth. Carpenter grabbed him by his shoulders. He violently turned him away from the prisoner and removed the weapon from Bonaventura' hand.

"Go to my office, Blasé! I'll see you there in a minute." He watched as Bonaventura left reluctantly.

"Red," he said to the prisoner, "I don't want you to say a word. We do not want anything from you. Do you understand?"

Red nodded his head muttering, "That summa bitch is a crazy mother."

"Shut up! That slash with the revolver split your lip. Do you want any medical attention?"

"Nah, I've had worse."

As he walked to the office he found he was shaking. Bonaventura should have had more sense than that. I hope he hasn't screwed up the case with that shit, he thought.

When officers are injured on duty, other officers have a strong desire to punish those who are responsible for the injury. Far too many cases have been lost in court because the urge was not held in check.

Entering his office he said, "Blasé, sign out and go home. You are suspended. If I deal with you now it will mean your job. I may have you arrested yet. Your behavior in there today made no sense at all. The greenest rookie knows better than that."

"Listen, Carpenter . . ."

"Shut up and go home. If you have ruined this case, I will see you are charged. Get out of here!"

Bonaventura walked out as Carpenter flopped into his chair to begin making notifications after which he had to write up the Unusual Occurrence Report and Charges and Specifications against Blasé.

CHAPTER 48

RENEWING ACQUAINTANCES

Maria walked into the office to see whether Carpenter needed any assistance. Truth be told, she wanted to be with him, help him if she could.

"Yes, thanks Maria. Would you please follow up and see if any of the officer's family members are in need of the Trauma Counseling Program? If so, please make the necessary arrangements?"

"Okay, Lance, I'm on it."

"Maria," he called after her before she left the office.

"Yes Carpenter, was there something else?"

"This sounds like an old pick up line but, haven't we met somewhere before?"

"As a matter of fact we did. You had the squad in the 7-0 and I was one of the patrol sergeants. You caused a ruckus on your first tour there. Our paths crossed several times."

"Yes, now I remember," he said animatedly. "You looked great in uniform! Thanks for reminding me."

CHAPTER 49

KILLER'S LOCATION ESTABLISHED

The shooting had taken place on the day tour prompting a search for the shooter which had been on-going all the hot, sweltering day. The four-to-twelve tour officers came on duty and joined the search while the day tour officers stayed around looking to help. They had gathered in the parking lot awaiting orders to go somewhere, or do something. Yet, there was nothing to do and nowhere to go so some of them bought six-packs of beer and cooled off. As the day wore on the six packs grew in number, talk became louder and slurred but the zeal remained.

At eleven o'clock that evening a call came in to the detective squad. Sergeant Soriano answered the phone.

"77ᵗʰ Squad, Sergeant Soriano, how may I help you?" she asked the caller.

["This is Mrs. Jamison,"] the caller said [and my son is the one who shot the officers today."]

"How do you know your son shot the officers, Mrs. Jamison?" she asked loud enough for all to hear.

["He called me and tole me,"] she answered. ["He said he wanted to give himself up but was afraid of being kilt."]

"Mrs. Jamison, hold on please while I connect you to the squad commander, Lieutenant Carpenter." Maria made the transfer. "Mrs. Jamison is on the line," she informed Carpenter. "Her son did the shooting this morning."

He took the call. "Lieutenant Carpenter, may I help you?"

["Yes, sir Lieutenant. My son Jaime, I'm his mother, he was the one who shot those officers an' he wants to give himself up but he's afraid he's gonna get shot by your policemans."]

"How do you want to handle it, Mrs. Jamison? If he gives himself up quietly and does not resist, I guarantee he will not be hurt."

["He wants you to get him here in my apartment,"] she offered, ["with me present."]

"Where do you live, Mrs. Jamison?" he inquired.

["I live in the Kingsboro projects, apartment 717,] she replied.

"When is he coming home?" she was asked.

["In about half an hour,"] she said. ["'bout eleven-thirty."]

"We'll be there before that and arrange to have him taken into custody." He broke off the conversation with Mrs. Jamison and informed the officers of what had taken place.

As promised Carpenter, Sergeant Soriano, Denny Marchand and Jim Kelly were at the Jamison residence; Marchand and Kelly were armed with shotguns while Carpenter and Soriano carried side arms. There was the delicious smell of recent cooking, the aroma reminding him that he had not eaten since lunch. His stomach growled.

Carpenter spoke with Mrs. Jamison once again reiterating: "If he surrenders quietly, he will not be hurt. Did you tell him that?" She nodded her head. "But if he resists, we will use force to take him into custody. Have you told him that?"

"Yes, I did an' he says he will not resist." Tears were streaming down her weathered face. She sat at a kitchen chair, her hands folded in her lap.

Several minutes later, there came a plodding foot tread on the stairs. Marchand and Kelly posted themselves on either side of the door, Marchand with shotgun at the ready, and Kelly with his weapon on the opposite side of the door jamb. The door opened slowly. Jaime walked in cautiously. Kelly dropped the shot gun into Jaime's ear saying very quietly: "Do you want to die?" There was no sound for several minutes, no noise whatever.

"No," Jaime said raising his hands. Kelly kept the shot gun in his ear while Marchand relieved him of his weapon and the slain officer's gun as well. Maria placed him in handcuffs reciting the Miranda warnings.

Mrs. Jamison thanked them for not hurting her son. "He did like he said he would," she said. "Don't be hurtin' him, please."

"He'll be alright," Mrs. Jamison, Maria said. "I will call you later and let you know what's next." The officers filed out with Jaime in custody.

There was no conversation as they drove to the station house, each keeping his or her own council. Driving into the parking lot, they were confronted by a gang of drunken off duty officers that surrounded the car. Maria removed the prisoner, moving toward the station house door. Several of the officers blocked her way.

"Let's lynch the son of a bitch!" shouted an unidentified officer.

"Lynchin's too good for him," another called out. "Let's make him suffer first!"

"Kill the bastard!" said another.

"Move away," Carpenter directed the men. Marchand and Kelly also stepped out of the car, audibly jacking rounds into the shotguns. "Move away," Carpenter repeated. "Let us pass. I do not want to take action against policemen but I will. Move away!"

As he said that, Maria moved forward once more, the officers reluctantly parted. The prisoner was removed to the squad room and the processing begun. The sitting ADA was called. While they waited, Carpenter said: "I want you all to prepare DD5s on what took place as you remember it. I don't want this shooter to walk on this. You can leave out the confrontation in the parking lot."

A short time later, Carpenter was at his desk reviewing the paperwork generated thus far. He got a telephone call from the precinct commander.

["Lieutenant, this is Captain Coughlin, get your ass down here forthwith!" he commanded.]

Turning to Maria who was in the office, he said: "I wonder what that's all about?"

"What whats all about?" she asked.

"I just got a forthwith from the precinct commander."

"Want me to come with you?" she asked.

"No, you oversee everything here. I'll be back."

Walking down stairs, he went to the precinct commander's office.

"Come in, Carpenter!" he ordered getting to his feet.

Carpenter entered, closing the door behind him.

"Listen to this, lieutenant and listen good. I want you to appear at the next ten consecutive roll calls and tell the troops why you didn't kill that son of a bitch you brought in here tonight. He killed at least one of your cops! You got that?"

He could not believe what he was hearing. "You want me to do what?" he asked not believing what he had heard.

"Goddamit!" the Captain yelled. "If you will not take care of your men, I damn well will! You are to appear at the next ten consecutive roll calls and tell the people why the prisoner was brought in on his feet! And, lieutenant, your people will prepare PD429-065 on each of your people."

Carpenter was angry, as angry as he had ever been. He stood with his back against the door, silently seething in his anger. Finally, he said: "Hear this Captain. I have an action verb and a personal pronoun for you. If you want, I will repeat it in front of the desk officer. Call him in here." He waited for some action on the Captain's part. When none was forthcoming, he continued. "We made a good untainted arrest tonight and this shooter will stand trial under the laws of the State of New York. It is a tragedy that police officers were gunned down but I will not alibi to anyone why I did not personally, or any officer under my command did not execute the prisoner. He offered no resistance and gave up quietly. We are the good guys, not executioners, Captain. Now, let's put this in writing and let's go to the trial room, you monumental horse's ass! We'll see who gets burned on this." Carpenter turned and walked out then turned back to include, "I know my responsibility to prepare reports on injuries to members of the department."

CHAPTER 50

AN UNUSUAL CIRCUMSTANCE

Carpenter had Maria secured the personal belongings of the officers to have them turned over to their families. He had Gloria prepare the Line of Duty Death report while he made the notifications to the Action Desk, the Borough Command and the detective's resident precincts. He called the Chaplain's Office requesting that he make the notifications to the families.

"Gloria, please contact the Operations Unit to see if they need extra copies of the Unusual or Line of Duty Injury reports. They have to notify about twenty different offices and if we can be of any help, let's assist them."

"I'm on it Lieu."

The bullet, a .32 caliber projectile, had entered above Cummins' eye and had, evidently, bounced back and forth inside his skull reducing the greater part of his brain to pulp, was turned over to detectives as evidence.

The hospital was keeping him alive on a resuscitator. The family had directed the hospital not to resuscitate and take no unordinary measures to save him since the prognosis was just a matter of time. The detective was removed from the machinery. About five days after Jamison's arrest, Carpenter received a telephone call from the District Attorney's office.

"Lieutenant Carpenter, 77th Squad" he said answering the telephone.

["Lieutenant, this is ADA Silverman, Kings County Criminal Court,] the voice on the other end said identifying himself.

"What can I do for you, Mr. Silverman?"

["I just got off the phone with the attorney for Jaime Jamison. He is informing us that the hospital has been asked to pull the plug on your detective with the family's consent.]

"That is probably best. There is no way he can survive his wound."

["That's not the point. His attorney said that if the hospital does that and the officer dies, he wants the charges reduced down from felony murder."]

"What is your position on this possibility?"

["He might have a point. I haven't researched it."]

"Coupled with the other detective's shooting death, how can you possibly have doubts? These were felony murders. Both men have died in the line of duty as a result of a felony in progress. Keep me posted on what you will do, but understand this, the perp had better not walk on this or you and I will have harsh words."

Before any action could be taken by the hospital to shut down the life support apparatus, Detective Mike Cummins died as a result of a gunshot wound he received in the line of duty. That attorney's search for leniency for his client became moot.

CHAPTER 51

INSPECTOR'S FUNERAL

The funerals were held at St. Rose of Lima Catholic Church. Their brother officers were joined by others from the metropolitan area. Also attending were was Chief of Detectives, Brooklyn South Borough commander, the Department Chaplain and other ranking dignitaries. Both families had Roman Catholic funeral services conducted by the Chaplain. Such funerals are awesome events. The flag draped caskets were removed from the hearses as everyone stood at attention and rendered the hand salute. They were escorted into the church by six uniformed detectives, their shields blocked with black bands; the families following them.

When the services ended, the cortège left the church. When the coffins appeared at the doorway, hundreds of white gloved officers again rendered the hand salute until the caskets were placed into the vehicles. As the doors closed, the hands were slowly lowered

At the gravesite on Long Island of Detective Cummins and Detective Mason in Queens, taps were played with an echoing bugler in the distance, accompanied by the Emerald Society pipers playing a Scottish dirge. There were few dry eyes. The chaplain made some appropriate remarks; the services ended.

CHAPTER 52

COMPELLED VIEWING

Several months later, Ruth Johnson returned to the squad offices to find out what was happening in the investigation into her daughter's death. She asked to speak with the squad commander and she was announced.

As she entered Carpenter's office he rose from his chair to greet her.

"Sister Johnson, hello," he said as he rose to greet her.

"What's happening with my daughter's case?"

Returning to his seat, he said, "No positive identification has been made from the little evidence we have. We have interviewed her boyfriend, Pacho, and he could shed no new light on the matter. I'm sorry; I wish we could do more."

Without being asked, she took a seat, made herself comfortable before speaking again. She began to nervously finger her waist cord, which apparently was a nervous habit of hers.

"You might want to bring in recording equipment," she said, "or someone to take down what I am going to tell you. I want Doc hurt like he's hurt me."

Carpenter picked up the telephone to speak with Gloria never taking his eyes from Sister Johnson. He thought here was a woman dreadfully hurt and possibly seeking revenge. He acted quickly.

"Gloria," he said. "Please come to my office and bring your pad and the recorder with you. I have another statement I want recorded."

Gloria entered the office setting up the equipment then took the only other chair. "Hello, Ruth. How's Anthony and Raymond?" she said to the seated woman.

"They're in school and they're doing well. Thanks for asking, Gloria."

Nodding to Gloria, the Lieutenant began the interview with the predicate statement. Then, "Alright Sister, begin wherever you like," he said.

"In the church," she began, "we have seven families that Doc has created. I am the head of one of those families. If any of the kids or any of us breaks a rule that Doc has created, that person and his or her family are summoned to the basement for punishment where there be bleachers and a metal table. Then, when everyone is there, Doc straps the guilty person to the stainless steel table. He tells that person's

154

family what it was that this person did. He then reads his finding on the matter and the person is always found guilty."

"When you say his or her family," Carpenter interrupted, "do you mean everyone in that family, young and old?"

"Yes," she continued, "everyone and we take seats in the stands to watch. We are forced to watch while he kills that person before our eyes and then begins to cut that person up. He or one of his boys packages the pieces and they are taken to the ranch upstate."

"Hold it, hold it," Carpenter said incredulously, running his hand through his hair brushing away a strand from his face. "The pastor kills them and you have to watch? Why hasn't anyone told the police or someone about this?"

"Who will do that? No one! We all were too terrified to speak to anyone about it. Anyhow, he cuts them up and wraps the parts in plastic so he or one of the boys can take it upstate. After he showed us the bishop's severed head on that platter, you think anyone wants to join him? Ha! Not likely!"

"Oh my God," Gloria gasped.

"I don't like interrupting like this," Carpenter said, "but you are giving us information no one knew about or we only had partial information. He has property upstate?"

"Yeah, not him specifically but it belongs to the church. Years ago someone in the community made a gift to the church of a ranch in White Sulphur Springs, I think. He calls it the ranch. It was supposed to be used for retreats and such. Anyways, the parts are taken up there where he burns them in an old enamel bathtub on the property. He's always complaining that he can't get the parts to burn up completely in less than four hours no matter what the accelerant, he calls it, he uses. When the tub cools off, he dumps the ashes and whatever into a smaller pail or bucket that he loads that in a boat to take out on the lake where he dumps the ashes. Now that the boys are old enough, the older ones help him either cutting up the bodies or they help upstate."

Carpenter sat riveted to his seat, his mouth open. Finally he said, "This is a fantastic story you're telling us. You've told us part of it before. It's hardly believable. Are you sure of your facts? I mean, this is unbelievable!"

"All of us," Sister Ruth says matter-of-factly, "have had to go to the basement and watch what happens there at least once and some, much more. And all of us have been upstate to watch what goes on there. What's not to believe?"

"Well, for one thing," Carpenter pauses assorting the many questions he has, "when he cuts up the bodies, there must be lots of blood. How does he get rid of that?"

"Oh, yes. Well over on the side wall there's a big hose that he uses to wash down the table and floor. In the center of the room there is a large drain that takes it all away. When he's finished, he wipes everything down and puts the rags in one of the packages."

"Okay then, when he burns the bodies and it takes four hours, hasn't anyone smelled the burning flesh. I mean, that is a smell you can't easily forget as you must know."

"The State Police have been there acting on all kinds of complaints but no arrests have ever been made. And no, the ranch is off by itself in the woods up there. I don't know how close the nearest neighbor is. And he never uses a huge fire to begin with."

Ruth continued to give additional details of events within the church basically reinforcing what she had already told them. When she finished, she asked: "Can you use any of that? I want to hurt him for what he did to my Yolanda."

"What determines whether he will cut up the body and burn it, or just break the girl's neck and dump her somewhere?"

"Usually the girls that have left and later filed charges against him are dumped with their necks broken as a warning to others," she replied.

"To the best of your knowledge, does the Bishop or any of his sons, do anything with the hands or feet of the victims?"

"No, not that I ever seen or heard."

"Okay then, as we have told you before, we need corroboration of what you have said. We believe you but the law requires that we get similar information from an independent source. Isn't there anyone willing to come forward?" She said that there was no one. He made no promises but promised to keep in touch with her. He thanked her for coming in.

When she had gone, he turned to his clerk.

"Gloria, did you get all that?"

"Yes sir," she said, "I can't believe that the Reverend could do such a thing! He is an evil man!"

"Gloria, do not tell anyone of this interview. Type up your notes and get with me. We'll have a notary come in and we will both sign the papers. After that, it's up to the District Attorney and his staff. Keep your notes under lock and key."

Once he was alone, Carpenter sat with his thoughts. In order to conduct a search here in town or upstate, there would have to be corroboration; if he were able to get that, could search warrants be gotten; how would anyone go about searching the lake bottom; who's going to believe this horror story?

Lance made notes to himself to include the basement in any search warrant, plus the metal table, floor and drain.

CHAPTER 53

REVISEWD PLAN OF ACTION

T he interview was completed, copies made of the transcripts, signed by all, and notarized. Carpenter made an appointment to see the Deputy Commissioner of Legal Matters. He was given an appointment for 0900 the following morning. He presented himself to Police Headquarters at One Police Plaza, known in the department as the Big Building, in the heart of downtown Manhattan, with some of the more pertinent records on the LeMans church operation, the collection of complaint forms and the typed statements.

"Good morning, Lieutenant," Deputy Commissioner Clarence Ruark said. Ruark was a tall man in his middle 50s with black hair growing white at his temples. He was nattily dressed in uniform, standing tall.

"Good morning, sir."

"Have a seat Lieutenant. Help yourself to some coffee. I use it every morning to give my heart a kick start."

"Thank you, sir." He helped himself to the coffee and sat at a small conference table with the deputy commissioner seated opposite.

"What do you have, Carpenter? It is Carpenter, isn't it?"

"Yes, sir," he answered as he sorted out his files. "The other day a woman came into the office with a fantastic horrific tale. I had a stenographer take notes and then had those notes signed and notarized. These papers," he said as he passed over the statements, "are the interviews in their entirety. I also have some of the more pertinent records, complaint forms, DD5s, et cetera, indicating the other papers he had brought with him."

"Let me scan this interview and then we'll talk." He read through the papers thoroughly. "Carpenter," he said when finished, and pushing his glasses on top of his head, "your cover sheet identifies this alleged fiend the Reverend Casius LeMans. Is he a true man of the cloth?"

"There records," Carpenter said indicating the other folders, "document his education at Morehouse College, where he achieved his Bachelor's degree, at Crozer Theological he was given his Master's degree and Boston College School of Theology he apparently earned his doctorate. So it appears that he is a 'man of the cloth. Allow me to give you a synopsis

"There is no available record or documentation of his ministering anywhere but in New York City, Brooklyn specifically. What we can document is his beginning in the *Rehoboth Bethel Church of God* which was then pastored by Bishop Jonathan Brown who has since disappeared. I'll come back to him later.

"The church has fourteen religious who solicit money throughout the city. They wear Black habits but as far as we have been able to determine, they belong to no recognized religious cloister. They reportedly range from Bed-Stuy to Jersey City in New Jersey.

"In his tenure he has fostered great growth to the point that the church congregation has grown, the number of buildings trebled, he has a day-care center, a preschool, and a middle school. All his teachers are licensed or certified and he receives assistance from the City, the State and the Federal government.

"That's the plus side of the ledger. The antithesis of that he has a violent criminal record, his nuns bring him runaway light-skinned Black girls that had been kidnapped, raped and many of them have been killed with their necks broken by a left-handed person. He is left handed. In addition, he has cut off the fingers of the girls we've found but we haven't learned what he has done with them.

"The statements you have before you allege that numbers of girls have not only been killed but mutilated and their bodies burned on his fifty acre ranch in upstate New York."

"As I understand it, you want to go after a church leader in a Black community with the backing and support of the department? That's a major problem you are asking us to take on."

"This woman says that this church leader has kidnapped young light-skinned Black girls he has raped, committed unlawful detention, he is guilty of murder, unlawfully disposing of dead human bodies, aggravated assault and who knows what else."

"What is this allegation about kidnapping light-skinned Black girls? I saw nothing in your records about that little tidbit."

"During an earlier interview with Sister Ruth Johnson she stated that the nuns go out every day to solicit funds; she alleged that there had come a time when the women could not bring in the amount of money in solicitations that he wanted. One of the nuns was beaten senseless. She thinks he knew that that would happen. In any event, Anne Soriano, one of the other nuns went to him telling him that he needed to beat every one of them because his demands were too high to fulfill every day. She thinks he knew this was bound to happen because he had a solution for them right away.

'When you are not able,' he allegedly said, 'to bring in fifteen dollars you can make up the difference by bringing home a light-skinned Black girl who is a runaway or who has traveled into the city or who is available and who is a young teenager."

"You bring them home with you," he said, "and I will make arrangements to have them become part the family, if they want. They will be assigned to one of the families.'

Instead, the Lieutenant went on, he kept them against their will and there we have kidnapping charges of unlawful detention; he had non-consensual sex repeatedly with them—they were too young to consent, and in any event, we had rape allegations and sexual battery. The guy's not a pious holy man, he is a fiend!"

"Carpenter," the Deputy Commissioner interrupted, "you're saying he has nuns working for him?"

"Well, yes sir. As far as I know they are not members of any recognized religious organization or sect, or any affiliation, except for *Rehoboth Bethel Church*. If they had been part of an organized group I would have gone to the Mother House or whatever it is called to get some help."

"Carpenter," Deputy Ruark said, "I'll show this to the boss but I know he will want corroboration of these allegations. This, unfortunately" holding up the paperwork, "is not enough. Let's nail the bastard and get him good."

"Commissioner," he said trying to show his urgency, "this case is more than twenty-five years old and there has never been a window of opportunity as there is now."

"Thank you, Carpenter. Let's do it but let's do it right. I'll be in touch."

CHAPTER 54

BERSERK

Carpenter returned to the station house, stopped at the desk to pick up squad mail, when the desk officer, Lieutenant Mickey Markham walked over. "Hey, Carpenter, while you were out, Sergeant Bonaventura picked up a Gimme." Bonaventura had been found guilty of the abuse charges leveled against him, he had been suspended but because the complainant would not press charges, he appealed to the Civil Service Commission and was reinstated and returned to his command.

"I haven't heard anything about it. What did he catch?" Carpenter asked.

"Some mope bludgeoned his wife and hung around waiting to be arrested. Bonaventura was first on the scene and he made the collar. They're upstairs now."

"Thanks, Mickey for the heads up." Carpenter said as he walked toward the stairs. As he moved past the Interview Room, he saw Blasé in conversation with a male, Black, middle aged man who looked disheveled. He walked into the room, standing at the back observing the sergeant's technique.

"Wadda ya want, sergeant? I ain't-tellin' you nothin'," the small man said defiantly. He wore shoes with no socks, dirty camouflage pants, and a dirty undershirt.

"Listen here, scumbag," Bonaventura snarled, "you're gonna tell me everything. Ya hear? Everything! You're so fucked up," he said quietly, "you're gonna start squealing like a stuck pig."

"I ain't fucked up, man. I'm cool," the little man insisted.

Blasé sat back staring at the man intently. He said quietly, "No, shitface, you're so fucked up you can't sit straight."

Forcing himself to sit erect, he replied, "I'm cool and you're a fool." He grinned at his pathetic rhyme a smile crossing his face.

"No, my man, I'm gonna tell the neighborhood, you're so messed up you can't balance this thin telephone directory on your head." From the floor under his chair, Bonaventura picked up a small telephone book and handed it to the man who looked at it then placed it on top of his head. He centered the book, balanced it and smiled broadly. "See, you mother . . ."

Seemingly from nowhere, Bonaventura's right hand held a baton. As he stood up, he brought the baton down atop the man's head with a dulled *thwack* as the man stopped speaking in mid-sentence and pitched sideways falling face first to the floor. He lay there quivering terribly, oozing from every opening in his body; a small puddle spreading at his waist.

"Blasé!" Carpenter shouted as he rushed forward seeing the baton coming down on the man's unprotected head. "Have you gone crazy? You stupid thug! Give me that baton!" Carpenter yelled as he moved on the sergeant.

Bonaventura turned and said: "Where . . . where did you come from?" asked the incredulous sergeant. "Chill out, Lance, this hump will be okay. I just gave him a little attitude adjustment. He'll come around in a cuppla minutes." It was obvious that the sergeant saw nothing wrong with what he had done.

Gloria burst into the room, a concerned look on her face. "Lieutenant," she called, "is everything alright?"

"No, Gloria it isn't. Please call for an ambulance to report to the squad office."

"Yes, sir," she said as she hurried away.

Carpenter knelt beside the stricken man checking his vital signs. "Blasé," he said forcing his voice to be calm, "the concussion you inflicted on this man has got to be unbelievable, besides being uncalled for and a criminal act. What is the man's name?"

At first Bonaventura didn't answer, trying to figure out what the problem was. Finally, he said, "Sylvester Santos, he killed his wife."

The man on the floor began to stir. His eyes opened as he gingerly touched his head. "Wha happened?" he asked still in a fog.

"You fell down," Bonaventura lied.

"What do you want from me, sergeant?" he said looking in his direction.

"Did you kill your wife, Sylvester?" he snarled at the man.

"I already tole you I did."

Two ambulance attendants walked into the room and were shown to the stricken, still dazed man. They did an examination of him, asked him several questions and one of the attendants walked over to Carpenter and Bonaventura. "He has a severe concussion," the attendant said, "but we find no injuries on him or serious trauma. We'll know better when we get him to the hospital. Is this guy a collar?" he asked.

"Yes he is," Carpenter responded. "I'll have one of the detectives accompany him to the hospital." He turned to Gloria. "Will you have whoever is in the squad room step in here?"

Gloria ran from the room. Marchand walked in. "Did you want to see me, Lieu?" he asked.

"Yeah, Denny, I would like you to accompany the prisoner to the hospital. Have him checked out. If they keep him overnight, let me know and I'll make the necessary arrangements to have him guarded. In any event, report back here to me."

"Sure, Lieu." The attendants placed Santos on a gurney and took him from the room.

"Listen, Lance . . ." Bonaventura tried to explain.

"Go," was the response he got, "go to the office. You and I need to talk."

Carpenter closed the door while the sergeant sat at his desk. "You will not see Santos through the arrest processing tomorrow. I will turn the collar over to Marchand. Give me your shield and all your weapons. You will turn in your papers," he said glaring at his subordinate.

"Like hell I will!" Bonaventura screamed.

"You will retire sergeant or I will prefer charges against you for gross malfeasance and brutality of a prisoner in police custody. I will also have you arrested and throw in that incident when our detectives were shot. Either way, you are finished. It's your choice."

"Carpenter," Blasé said whining, "You're upset. I was wrong but give me another chance."

"No, Blasé you've brought two men close to death. There will be no other chance. I will be at the hospital tomorrow and if Mr. Santos wants to file a complaint, your ass is grass."

Reluctantly, sullenly Blasé handed over his badge, a service revolver and a Beretta automatic.

"You don't want to reconsider?" he asked hopefully. "No, Blasé, you're stressed out. You need to be away from this. Give me the key to your locker. I'll have your property catalogued and sent to you."

When the sergeant had gone, Marchand returned from the hospital.

"Mister Santos is okay," he said. "He's got a concussion but they want to keep him under observation overnight," he said to his supervisor.

The following morning, as promised, Carpenter was at the hospital interviewing the prisoner.

"The doctors say you will be fine. You are, however, under arrest for the murder of your wife. I don't want you to make any statements until you have spoken to an attorney. On another matter, last night you were unlawfully struck by the sergeant who brought you here. You have the right to prefer charges against him. You do not have to decide right now."

"No, Lieutenant, I don't wanna make a complaint. I got to be punished for what I did, I had it comin'."

"It's not the policeman's job to punish you. He was wrong."

"Let it be, Lieutenant. Let it be."

When Carpenter returned to the squad office, Gloria spoke out. "Lieutenant, Sergeant Bonaventura turned in his papers, he is on terminal leave. I guess he is retiring." To everyone in the squad office the retirement came as a surprise. Sergeant Bonaventura retired after twenty-one years of service.

CHAPTER 55

INFANT RAPE AND ITS AFTERMATH

Carpenter had been hoping for some action to be taken or some break in the LeMans situation but he was a realist. There was a great deal that had been uncovered but not a word of corroboration. He returned to the precinct to find that it was business as usual taking place. He needed to replace the three men the squad was down.

Sergeant Bonaventura, who had had charges preferred against him for abuse of authority, malfeasance and misfeasance, after Carpenter had reported the incident to Borough command and Internal Affairs, was on terminal leave waiting for IAB to decide his fate. Sergeant Peter Townsend, Detective Samuel Martin and Detective Justin Jones had been assigned as replacements the following Monday.

All the replacements were Black officers and all were fast becoming acclimated to the command and its nuances. Townsend greeted him as he entered the office.

"Lieu," he began, "we have a mother and her boy friend in the interview room under guard. Patrol had been called to the Albany Housing project on an alleged assault. The mother complained of her boy friend screwing her twenty month old baby daughter. The baby was taken to St. Mary's Hospital as a rape victim and the rape kit verified the child's assault. Also, the infant has gonorrhea."

"How did we get the case if patrol was first on the scene?" he wanted to know.

"The responding officer is going on vacation tomorrow and asked if we would take it. Was that wrong?" Townsend asked.

"No, not if we were asked. I just don't want to be accused of stealing arrests."

"What was that you said?" Carpenter exclaimed, "Did I hear you correctly? Gonorrhea? This is not the first time then or was the child born with it?"

"It doesn't appear that the child had it at birth. The mother says that she did not know about it though. She thinks her boyfriend has it."

"Has the ADA been called?"

"Yeah," Townsend replied, "a friend of yours Robert Tannenbuam. He's on his way." Carpenter looked at the newcomer to see if he was aware of his relationship with the ADA. He apparently did not. "Let me talk to him when he gets here. We have a history. The mother saw the boy friend with the child?"

"That's what she says," Townsend replied.

"After the ADA gets here, let's have both of them checked for venereal diseases."

About thirty minutes later, the ADA walked into the squad room. "Hey, fellas and girls," said jovially. "What major mystery have you got you want me to solve?"

Detective Aquila spoke first. "The Lieutenant would like to speak with you first, Mister Tannenbuam. He is in his office."

Tannenbuam walked into the office with no preamble. "You wanted to speak with me, Carpenter?" he asked.

"Yes, Bob. We have a twenty month old baby who, the mother alleges, has been raped by her boy friend. The hospital verifies that the infant was assaulted and the baby has been diagnosed with gonorrhea, we do not know about the mother. The baby is in St. Mary's Hospital and I would like to have both of them checked out for venereal diseases, along with the boyfriend."

"So, what's the problem?" the ADA asked. "You want to make an arrest? It can't be done."

"Are you out of your mind? The infant was raped by the mother's boyfriend! We want to know the best way to go about this; that's why you were called," Carpenter said his annoyance apparent.

"You can't arrest him, Lieutenant. Who is your complainant, a twenty month old baby? Get real. It would never stand up in court."

Carpenter sat down, tented his fingers trying to calm his growing anger. "Mr. Tannenbuam," he said quietly, "the mother of the infant is the complainant, not the infant, you roaring asshole!"

"Oh, that's different. You didn't say that. Charge him with Statutory Rape and I'll follow up on it. By the way, whatever happened to that other baby case, the one where the baby was beaten to death? One of the other prosecutors took over the case because I had an emergency leave."

Carpenter still had his hands tented in an effort to keep from strangling this pompous fool. "He was convicted but the case was appealed."

"Oh, yeah, on what grounds was it appealed?"

"On my alleged, 'Failure to give the Miranda Warnings before questioning," Carpenter replied.

"Didn't I tell you that? I warned you, Carpenter."

"Yes, you did, Bob. However, the Supreme Court overturned the appeal in that case and upheld the conviction. It was their considered opinion that up to the time I was questioning him about events surrounding the child's death, the matter was in the investigatory phase. When he blurted out what he had done, it then became accusatory and Miranda applied. I had done the right thing after all."

"Go figure," the prosecutor replied completely missing the point.

"Yes, Bob. Life's a bitch."

CHAPTER 56

A SURPRISE WITNESS

One rainy cold day, Carpenter was walking through the precinct speaking to store and shop owners to let them know that the police were not just law enforcers but people who had an interest in the welfare of the community. Many of the Black detectives were doing the same. He had just entered the Lion Food Market when he met Anne Soriano, one of the nuns in the LeMans church.

He stopped her inquiring, "Its Sister Anne, isn't it?"

Before answering she looked around to see who was close by. "It is," she said at last. "I heard from Ruth Johnson that you helped her learn about her daughter. We all knew she was dead but needed to know for sure."

"I'm sorry it could not have been with positive results," he responded.

"She also tells me that you need to have corroboration regarding her story to you. Is that right?" she asked.

"I hope that it was not a story but the truth. And yes, to take action on what she said, we need to have it supported by another independent source. That's the law."

"I can give you the corroboration you need," the nun said.

"Why would you do that?" Carpenter inquired of her.

"Why? To bring Doc down, that's why," she said surprised at his question.

"Why do you want to bring him down," he probed. "Is it because of Ruth? Has he done something to you?"

Looking about, she said, "Can we talk somewhere else? I'm afraid someone will see us together and I'll have a lot of explaining to do."

"If we can talk at the office, I will have someone there to take notes of your information, have it typed and you can sign it."

"Can we do it somewhere else beside your office?" she inquired. "I'm afraid of being seen."

"I can make arrangements," he said, "with St. Mary's Hospital to have a room where we can talk. You can go there soliciting alms."

"I'll be there in two days," Anne said. "Probably around 9:30 in the morning. Is that alright?"

"It will have to be. Thank you, Anne. Your help is critical." They parted. Carpenter thought, 'this is an interesting development.'

CHAPTER 57

CLANDESTINE INTERVIEW

Townsend, Carpenter and Gloria were waiting in the Emergency Room of St. Mary's Hospital. At 0930, Anne walked in the emergency room entrance going immediately to them. Carpenter noted that she looked resolute as she walked their way. Greetings were exchanged and the Lieutenant led the way to a small conference room on the ground floor.

"The hospital has been good enough to make this room available," he explained to the freighted nun. He introduced Sergeant Townsend and Gloria Philips informing her that Gloria would be taking stenographic notes of the conversation. They each sat and began the interview. He prefaced their remarks by introducing the people present, the time, date and location of the interview for the record.

"Where do you want to begin?" he asked.

"Do you know about the Bishop?" she countered clasping and unclasping her hands nervously.

"Bishop Brown?" he prompted. He knew that he was dealing with someone who wanted to tell someone about what was going on yet someone who was terrified of the possible consequences.

"Yes, that dear, sweet old man," she reminisced. "He cut his head off and showed it to us literally on a silver platter."

Gloria gasped audibly saying, "Sweet Mother of God!"

"Gloria!" Carpenter said as he turned toward her. "Are you alright? Are you able to go on?" She nodded and mouthed, "I'm sorry."

"Well, see," Anne Soriano continued, "the Bishop came back from his sabbatical—whatever that is—and he came to the church. Well, at supper time the Reverend opens the sliding doors in the dining room and there he is, rather there his head is. I damn near passed out; I wet my pants."

"When was this?" Carpenter asked.

"Years and years ago when the Reverend had been with the church for about a year," Anne explained, "the arrangements that had been made by the Bishop and

LeMans and it was at the end of that year that this happened." She sat there wringing her hands remembering.

"Go on, please," Carpenter urged.

"Let's see. We was bringing in money every day," she said stroking and wringing her hands, "and the Reverend said it wasn't enough. He had us stay out longer and bring in more money. When one of us didn't bring in enough, she, the nun, had to strip and he beat her with a piece of a fishing rod until she fainted. And see, he knew we couldn't always bring in so much money. Later, two more of us didn't have our quota and he was going to beat them too. Who's gonna argue with a fucker like that? But we had to do something, so I says, 'Why don't you beat us all?' he knew we couldn't meet those demands. Well, sir, he says politely as you please, 'bring in a light-skinned Black girl instead.' And when we did, he screwed these kids until they became pregnant."

"We have that information and now you have corroborated it. What did he do with the children produced?" Carpenter urged.

"He adopted them naming me or one of the others as the mother of the child or the mother of the child if she decided to stay. After the first couple of kids, he wasn't questioned anymore, but they was all adopted and became part of a family. They were assigned to one of the nuns, to bring up. See, we had seven families and these kids became part of one of those families."

Carpenter did not want to interrupt her but needed some clarification. "How many children are there?"

"See," she answered. "It's not that simple. When there were twelve or so, he made an application to open a day care center. When he got approval, he opened the school to the people in the community. After that came the pre-school, then a middle school. So our kids got mixed in with the others."

"What happened," he asked to encourage her along, "when one of the families was found guilty of some wrongdoing? Ruth told us her version; we would like to hear yours."

"You known about the basement set up and the table?" Not waiting for a reply, she went on. "If someone was accused by the Reverend or by one of his sons, that person and their family were called to the basement."

"I'm sorry, Anne for butting in like this, what do you mean 'or his sons'. What was their function in the family?"

"The Reverend has a queer notion about seven. The number means something mystical to him. He divided us up into seven families, he noticed the church on the seventh day of the month, I had seven boys by him and he thought they were a sign from God. My little boys were sent off to school to learn some sort of trade that he could use later on. Darryl the oldest, is his second in command and he does whatever his father tells him; Jeremiah was sent to school to learn how to butcher meat and he helps his father cut up the bodies; Marcus couldn't do much of anything so the Reverend sent him off and set him up in the city as a pimp with about ten of the girls that were brought in here; Shasta is a bricklayer, Gideon handle the books of the school and church; Yunki is an electrician, Jesse is a locksmith, an' Moses is a Carpenter and drives for his father and help out with the girls. In fact, they all became rutting studs. He has transformed my boys into something I don't like. My little girl, Femále, helps in the kitchen and in the chapel."

Townsend, a quizzical look on his face, interrupted, "Anne, you said your daughter Femále is that an ancestral name or an African name?"

"Oh no, that's the name the hospital give her when she was born," she replied earnestly.

Still confused, Carpenter asked, "Why did the hospital give your daughter a name?"

"Well, see, my last name is Soriano an' one day they bring in the baby for me to nurse and there on the cart is my daughter with the name the hospital gave her 'Female Soriano. It was a beautiful name so I kept it."

"Go on with your story," Carpenter said blowing his nose to keep from laughing out loud at this tension breaker.

"The basement is like an amphitheater and the family of the person accused sits in the bleachers, I guess you call 'em, and listens to the Reverend tell about what they did. Then he kills them in front of their family. He cuts them up or Jeremiah does and Yunki or Gideon packages them. The Reverend, Darryl or one of the others drives them up to White Sulphur Springs to the ranch he has there, to burn them and dump them in the lake. Then they come back like nothing has happened."

"Anne," Townsend asks, "where did the ranch come from, do you know?"

"Yeah," she answers, "at a board meeting here, somebody mentioned that this ranch could be picked up for taxes and as a religious organization he could get a break on its purchase at the foreclosure sale. I think that's how it went. Anyhow, he gets the property and he takes me up there for a look see. It's very quiet, surrounded by a lawns and woods and a lake right smack in the middle of the grounds. We would use it in the summer mostly as a retreat or to hold special meetings an' like that."

The trio took a meal break in the hospital cafeteria and got right back to the interview.

"The Reverend wanted each of us to know what was going on so that if we were to break one of his rules we would know what was in store for us. He would sometimes take us up there on retreat and while we were there, he would burn the body until it was just ashes. The smell was awful! Then he had it cool off before he took it out on the lake to dump the ashes. See, he took the ashes from the tub and put 'em in a bucket. He washed the tub down. Or he brought the smaller tub back and one of the boys washed them both out."

"Do you have any idea how many bodies were dumped in the lake?"

"No, there was no way to keep count 'cause sometimes he just took one of the families up on a retreat or an outing or whatever. He is a cold-hearted bastard and we're all scarred shitless around him."

"Is there anything else you want to tell us?"

Anne sat there shaking her head.

"Gloria will type up your statement and you need to sign it. We will also have it notarized. Do you have a problem with any of that?"

"Will he go to jail this time? It was tried many times in the past, here and upstate but nothing ever come of it."

"Nothing can be guaranteed. However, with what you and Ruth have given us, we stand a very good chance of putting him where he belongs; behind bars."

CHAPTER 58

BREAKING NEW GROUND

Deputy Commissioner Ruark was brought up to date on what had transpired since their last meeting. The corroboration was there, it was now a matter of how to move forward to take action that would not backfire. He scanned the papers before him then sat back looking searchingly at the Lieutenant.

"What do you see as your next step, Carpenter," Ruark asked?

"Another form of corroboration, Commissioner," he answered without hesitation. "We need to apply for a search warrant of the ranch based on these statements. Then, depending on what we find there, go for another to search the lake bottom."

"Search the lake bottom?! How in the name of God are you going to accomplish that?"

"I haven't thought that out completely. I'll come up with something after we have been over the ranch grounds."

"Get in touch with the Legal Bureau," he made a notation on one of the papers given him. "They should be able to help you out there. I'll give them a heads up before you call. Get it done, Carpenter and try not to step on too many toes in the process," Ruark warned. "Remember," he chided, "CYA and ours too."

"Commissioner, could you also have someone contact the ADA to make them aware of what we are doing? It would help."

"Yes, that should grease the skids somewhat. Better yet, ask someone in the Legal Bureau to give them a call. It will add more clout."

CHAPTER 59

SEARCH OF THE WESTCHESTER RANCH

Carpenter, armed with the appropriate search warrant, was accompanied by four detectives from the day; evening and late tours, as well as crime scene technicians, went to LeMans ranch in Westchester. They picked up Route 287 from Queens Boulevard then once through the Bronx changed to Route 87 to go north and upstate in New York. As they approached the ranch, they saw a sophisticated country home on about five acres of beautiful park-like property with a landscaped Japanese Garden, a new pool, about two acres of deer fence, stone walls, slate walkways, gated dog run, central air, vaulted ceilings, gourmet kitchen, two fireplaces, a large screened in Florida porch, a master bedroom with rolling ladder library, an outdoor Jacuzzi, there were large hedges, about twelve feet in height fronting the property, with an ornate gate blocking entry and a medium-sized lake in the rear yard. Once inside the grounds they were facing a wide gravel walkway, through a copse of trees, leading to a low one story house, with a driveway and garage off on the left side. Ivy covered most of the walls of the house giving it a rustic English look.

As they exited from the cars, one of the detectives observed, "I couldn't live up here for very long, too freakin' quiet." There was in fact, a hush about the place.

"You couldn't afford a place like this," another said.

The house was sedately furnished with what looked like the finest necessities. Each went about their assignment diligently, overlooking nothing but sticking within the parameters of the warrant. After some time and once the search had moved out doors, Carpenter was summoned to the north side of the house, the side facing the lake.

"Here's the tub, Lieu," one of the crime scene technicians called out. "It has been charred. Something was burned in it. We can run some tests here but we need to take it to the lab for more extensive testing. What do you want?"

"Run whatever preliminary tests you can here," Carpenter said. "Let's see what sort of results you come up with; if any. From there, we will decide where we go next. Have we found the boat yet?"

"Oh, yeah," another technician said. "It's over there in that make-shift boat house. We ain't gone over it yet. It's next on the list."

Several hours later while the detective were inside the house taking a lunch break, one of the technicians came into the kitchen. "Lieu, Patrolman Goodman."

"Yes, Goodman, come on in," Carpenter called out. "Have you had lunch?"

"Yeah, we ate out there," indicating the yard behind him. "I have some preliminary findings for you but keep in mind that they are preliminary."

"Lay it out for me, Goodman. You can send me a report later," he said as he stood.

"In the tub's drain we found traces of human origin. The tub is an old one with four legs and each of them has been scarred by scrapings from the boat or some other object. We took some samples and they will be compared with the wood of the boat. We also found traces of a number of burnings in the tub. The exact number may never be determined but they were done with a variety of accelerants. We have also taken rolls of tape, rope, and knives as evidence. We can compare them with the samples we already have from the dead girls back in Brooklyn. When we have gone over it all, we will get back with you. Is there anything else?"

"I think that's it for now, Goodman. Good work and tell the others we appreciate what they have done. We will probably see a lot more of you and your group."

"Thanks, Lieu. We'll be shoving off then. This place gives me a creepy feelin'."

"Thank your crew for us."

Carpenter sat back down to finish his lunch. Once they were all done, they planned their next approach.

"Sergeant Soriano," announced as the Lieutenant looked her way, "has had the foresight to bring a couple of cameras and film. Maria, pick someone to help you out and photograph everything that might be of evidentiary value. Photograph the way in here, the grounds themselves, inside the house, the tub and lake. Use up all the film."

"Georgie," Sergeant Soriano called out, "give me a hand. You take the 35mm camera and I'll take the other. Create a log of what shots you are taking along with the lens setting and film speed. Okay?" Marron got up, took up one of the cameras and walked out into the yard.

"Pete," Carpenter called to his sergeant, "You supervise the photography and be sure nothing is missed. But let them do their thing, just don't let them miss anything."

"Phil, Harv and Maureen, take different areas and begin constructing crime scene sketches. Let's get the dimensions as near as possible. Any evidence, get it photographed first then locate and identify it on the drawing. The pads and tape measures are there on the table. I'll climb into one of the upstairs beds and grab some shut eye."

"Oh, yeah," Maureen offered, "I'll just bet you will." They all laughed and got to their chores.

He walked from one detail to the other and was quite pleased with the performance of each one of them. These were good professionals and he liked working with them.

Several hours later, all gathered at the house brain-stormed what they had done and satisfied, moved to their vehicles for the trip back to the city.

When all the police personnel had moved off, Sergeant Soriano drove Carpenter back to the precinct in Brooklyn. Driving down I-87 Maria began asking her Lieutenant some personal questions.

"Lieu," she said tentatively, "is your last name Carpenter?"

"Yes," he responded, "you know that. Why do you ask?"

"I'm just curious. We know so little about you."

"And you feel you need to know more than that? I don't know that much about any of you either. You think we should get together and exchange personal profiles?"

"No, nothing like that, are you married?" she asked in one breath.

"Are you nuts? What has that got to do with anything?" She got the impression that he was being standoffish.

"I'm sorry," she said, "I didn't mean anything by it. I'll shut up."

They fell into silence and she gripped the steering wheel firmly until her knuckles turned white. She kept her eyes facing front.

After some time, as they approached the Bronx, he said, "Forget it, Maria. I was married but my wife divorced me without me knowing it. Divorce in Absentia! She had moved out leaving me with very little. She filed for divorce and had all the paperwork sent to her apartment. Three notices of Intent to Divorce were sent to her address in Florida, and when I didn't respond, the Final Decree was issued and we were divorced. Evidently in Florida you can be served by mail and it doesn't have to be signed for.

She is an alcoholic who refuses to take any proactive steps to change. We had no children and I guess I'm sensitive about it." After a pause, "I still live on Staten Island in an older house that belonged to my parents and sold to me."

"I'm sorry about your wife Lieu. I didn't know."

"There is no way you could. Listen, it's almost dinner time. Are you hungry?"

"I could eat." She responded quickly smiling. Her smile, he noticed, lit up her face. He smiled too.

"Well, then, you pick out the restaurant and we'll have some dinner."

In downtown Brooklyn she selected an Italian restaurant called the New Corner House. Carpenter had eaten here before, but that was some time ago. The place was beginning to fill up but they waited only a short time. They were seated at an outdoor table, under a Sabrett umbrella, the same as on frankfurter push carts. Dinner was begun with a bottle of Chianti wine followed by their salads, appetizers and later, their entrees. About an hour was filled with innocuous small talk and another thirty minutes over espresso coffee. Before either knew it, the meal was over.

She drove to the precinct where she dropped him off and after a few awkward moments, they said good night. He went into the building, checked his mail and he too went home.

CHAPTER 60

PRESENTING THE FACTS

The District Attorney Office is located in Brooklyn Criminal Court on Schermerhorn Street. The District Attorney, David V. Morgenthau, Esq., was an elderly distinguished gentleman who looked the part of the judicial system. He was tall, sparse, with long wavy white hair, a white goatee and he wore a starched shirt with a wing collar. When Carpenter was ushered in, the District Attorney was seated behind an ancient desk, smoking a pipe, the clouds of smoke hanging in the air. He had drawn the blinds and the room was lighted by several vintage lamps.

Lance quietly sat down while the DA read through some of the papers on his desk. Lance noticed that he wore no glasses unless he was wearing contact lenses. If the man knew he was there, he gave no indication. When he finally removed the pipe from his mouth, he laid it in a hand-carved rack. He placed the papers on the desk and turned his attention to Lance at last.

"Lance Carpenter. There used to be another Lance Carpenter who was a Deputy Chief Inspector in Manhattan North. Was he a relation of yours?"

"Yes, sir," Carpenter answered. "He was my grandfather. He passed away about eight years ago of a coronary thrombosis."

"He was a good man, one of the best."

"I would agree."

"Did you know that he was once accused of being part of the Irish Mafia in the Department?" Morgenthau asked.

"The Irish Mafia," Carpenter asked?

"Oh, yes, the top brass in the department were all Irishmen and they were accused of looking out for one another—thus—the Irish Mafia. It wasn't true of course, but it made for a good story.

"By the way, word has it that Chief Mannion is also a relation of yours. Is there any truth in that rumor?"

"I really don't know, I don't think so. He and his wife are very good friends with my parents for quite some time and, as a courtesy. I call him Uncle Frank. We walk our separate paths, however."

"Now, about these matters you bring to light," he said indicating the papers strewn about his desk.

"Well, sir," Lance began, "I want to go after the Reverend LeMans but I thought I had better check with your office to do that and do it properly, I didn't want there to be any possibility of a foul up with legal ramifications that would allow him to walk away from the horrors he has created and committed."

"And that's why you present your case here," again indicating the papers. "I'm glad that you did. We have to walk gently with this man who represents the Black interests in your part of the city, who is a credentialed religious man, who also happens—according to these documents—to be an outstanding citizen and a stone killer. A unique set of circumstances, would you not agree?"

"Oh yes, sir." Lance answered fervently. "And in addition, he is tall, handsome, and quite charismatic. His congregation loves him and his intimates think he is the devil personified. We have documented all of his heinous acts and our search of the premises in Westchester has turned up some highly incriminating evidence."

"What is it you want of us?"

"Well, sir, I need to get a search warrant for the Barstow Lake if possible," Lance clarified. "We feel the best way to go about searching the lake bottom is to have the Army Corps of Engineers drain the lake for us and we will lay in out in a grid pattern preparatory to any search."

"It's been some time since I was in the field and I am not familiar with the procedure. Drain the lake? What would that accomplish?" he probed.

"In the parlance of the trade, sir, we would create a grid pattern with horizontal and vertical lines dividing the lake bottom into small squares. Each square created in this fashion, would be numbered and become independent crime scenes. Since this was the dumping grounds for LeMans, we will use grates, screens, and sieves to run the mud through."

"And what is it you are hoping to find there?" the DA inquired.

"Well, this is not a fishing expedition. We have corroborated information that there are bones and teeth, and there is some jewelry. There may also be a cutting tool that was used to sever the fingers of his victims," Lance offered. "When we have the results of the search, we will compile our findings with what has been found before, along with relative reports and present it all to your office. Down the line we may have to call on the services of a pathologist and perhaps a forensic odontologist; bones and teeth."

"That sounds like a plan. What have you done with the authorities up in Westchester?" the DA asked. "They need to be brought in on this since it is in their backyard."

"Well, sir, I thought your office could work out the liaison with them since both jurisdictions might have similar prosecutions and interests. You know, people at your level contacting people at a similar level."

David Morgenthau pondered the ramifications of such an undertaking. "You know, Carpenter, the federal government must be notified and probably a federal warrant obtained as well. You will also need to contact the Army Corps of Engineers for this project unless you had some other way in mind?"

"I am out of my depth here, Mr. Morgenthau," Lance said as he brushed a strand of hair from his face. "With this proposal," he continued, "I will rely on your best judgment."

The District Attorney rose up from his desk and came around to shake hands with Carpenter. "It has taken quite a few years," he said "to bring this about but it looks like his house of cards might be tumbling down around him."

"We can only hope, sir," Lance answered. "We can only hope."

CHAPTER 61

SERVICE OF SEARCH WARRANT

Court Papers, consisting of a search warrant, were served on the Reverend Casius LeMans at the *Rehoboth Bethel Church of God*. Since Carpenter had rarely been inside the church, and had little conversation with the Reverend, he decided he should be one of the ones to serve the papers. He went there accompanied by Detective Marchand early one evening. It was after dinner and before his scheduled vespers. They were shown to the cleric's office. The rooms smelled on burnt candles and there was a hushed tone about the place, in part because of the austere surroundings and in part because some of the women knew what the visit was all about. They kept out of the way letting matters play out.

Casius had been seated behind his desk wearing a yellow Dashiki, working on some papers. He rose to greet his visitors. Carpenter was impressed by the bearing of the man. He would have been hard pressed to see any African ancestry.

"Lieutenant Carpenter," he said affably, "a pleasure to see you again. I was just going over the records of the Day Care Center, the Pre-School and our Middle School. The teacher's contracts are coming up for renewal and of course, they all want raises. You can't merely preach God's word nowadays; you must also wear many different hats."

Carpenter put out his hand and shook hands with the pastor. "The pleasure is mine, Pastor. Sorry for the interruption. This," indicating the detective, "is Detective Marchand of our detective squad." Neither man moved to exchange greetings.

"What is the nature of your visit, Lieutenant?"

Marchand moved forward handing the cleric folded papers.

The detective said, "These are Search Warrant papers for your property in White Sulphur Springs, specifically the lake thereon and the surrounding grounds."

"You've been over that ground before. Why this second search? Are you on a fishing expedition, you should excuse the pun?"

"You might say that, Reverend, since we will be looking into your lake." Carpenter looked to see what impact, if any, this news made on the cleric.

"My title is now Bishop, lieutenant and I have my doctorate in religious studies. The police seem to have a vendetta against me and the church because of my education.

I have made several trips to your precinct to answer one charge or another. Each time I was released for lack of sufficient evidence. Be assured that I will take these papers," waving the documents, "to our attorney. In the meantime, can I interest you gentlemen in a cup of tea?"

"No. Thank you, Bishop." The officers rose to leave. "Do you have a set of keys to the premises and grounds that we might borrow? We do not want to destroy church property unnecessarily."

"I will have one of my sons on site at all times. He will have any keys you might require. When are you planning your excursion, Lieutenant?"

"In two days," Carpenter replied.

Detective Marchand asked, "And which son would that be, Reverend?"

"Darryl, detective, my oldest son," he replied.

Walking out of the chapel, Marchand said Soto voce, "The son is an image of the old man."

"What do you mean?" Carpenter asked.

"A pit viper that one. He does the old man's dirty work and he has no moral conscience."

Carpenter made a mental note of his remark. "Listen, when we get back, get your partner to assist you in making all the notifications necessary. Let's start a running record of what we do, when we do it, and how it is done, with results. Specifically, get the names of people you speak with. Also include the work that we have already completed. We need a complete documented record from here on out."

"What would the department do without paperwork?" he asked no one in particular.

"The department and the courts," Carpenter included.

CHAPTER 62

SEARCH OF ESTATE AND LAKE

The Army Corps of Engineers used both a Floato-pump that pumped 30 gallons per minute along with three diesel pumps to remove lake water and incur the least adverse environmental impact. Drainage of the lake took over four weeks to accomplish. The streams and river outlets had to be widened and in some cases deepened, to accommodate the extra water and those relatively small amounts of water released at a time. Tanker trucks were also used to transport most of the lake water. The entire LeMans ranch had to be put under guard and a log record maintained of people in and out of the grounds. A temporary headquarters was established on the grounds and in a short period of time, the scene became a sort of governmental circus. The media were a constant problem demanding access to the grounds and inside the frozen zone. Television helicopters flew overhead almost on a daily basis and Carpenter was both pleased and annoyed at the media attention given to the project given the name Project Muddy Waters.

There were almost daily conflicts between the police, the military and the media. The military did not appreciate having to be checked in and out every day, the police objected to being shoved aside at the site of the dredging, while the media objected to being denied access. Supervisors from both services began to arrive to make themselves known to all present. Carpenter, in self-defense, organized limited sized access tours from afar that were supervised by police personnel to curtail them from trudging around the grounds destroying the scene.

At the end of the drainage phase, three weeks had to be given to dry out the lake bottom. When the ground was sufficiently dry, additional crime scene technicians were brought in to begin their work. Each numbered section becoming an independent crime scene and each had its own log. Dirt was sifted and run through screens and put to one side. To make their work easier, they photographed each item, located it on a crime scene sketch, packaged their findings on site and brought in the evidence to the house each night, if there were any, to document and catalog. Darryl LeMans was kept from the house which was also used to store equipment. Other personnel took the evidence, recorded its history and pedigree then placed it into appropriate containers or evidence bags; the bags were beginning to pile up. At long last, the search of the lake bottom was concluded, every square searched and everyone began packing up preparing to leave. Darryl voiced his objections to the removal of anything, claiming that it was not part of the warrant.

Carpenter answered him saying, "Your objections are noted, Darryl but we will take the packets."

Documenting the continuity of evidence, they rinsed the teeth and bone fragments. When completed, they were sent to a forensic odontologist, Doctor Paul Compton, in Brooklyn for reconstruction of unknown donor's jaws. The doctor was able to reconstruct four jaw fragments with partial teeth and jaw bone. He was assisted by Doctor Salaam Maumid, a forensic pathologist. Both men said that the other fragments were too inconclusive to do anything with. They also said that what they had constructed was sufficient to show proof of death. Photographs of their findings were sent to dentists within the metropolitan area. Six anxious months passed before there were four hits. These partials belonged to thirteen and fourteen year old Black females identified as Amelia Fuentes, Marcia Blackman, Charlese Williams, the daughter of Charlotte Williams, and Diane Riesgo. It was then an easy task to match these names with the names of complainants against Casius LeMans all of whom had disappeared prior to scheduled court appearances.

On learning of the discovery of her daughter's remains, Charlotte became an anxious witness for the prosecution.

Copies of the DD5s, the matching UF61 Complaint Forms, Police Laboratory reports, and the report of Doctors Compton and Maumid were sent to David Morgenthau for his review and follow up action. As a result, an Arrest Warrant was issued in the name of the Bishop Casius LeMans for the unlawful death of the four girls. Carpenter, Sergeant Soriano and Detective Jim Kelly went to the *Rehoboth Bethel Church of God* at five o'clock in the afternoon. They were there to affect the bishop's arrest. There was a large crowd in the street in front of the church, with many more gathered on both sides of the street. Somehow, someway word had gotten to the church congregation that an arrest was going to be made of their pastor.

As they exited the cars, Carpenter said to Detective Kelly, "Bring along the portable radio, just in case we might need them."

At the church, they had parked their unmarked police cruisers at the curb. They were admitted into the church by Sister Ruth who was told to go and get the Reverend. After a short wait, Casius Lemans came to the chapel. This time he was wearing a white dashiki with a large golden cross about his neck on a golden chain. He stood tall to demonstrate his authority over them.

"This inconvenience," he snarled, "is getting to be quite prejudicial."

"Casius LeMans," Sergeant Soriano said in a loud voice, "we have an arrest warrant in your name for the unlawful death of four females. You have the right to remain silent," she began, reading from an index card, "anything you say can and will be held against you; you have the right . . ."

"We've been through this before," Casius seethed. "I know my rights. Lieutenant, he asked, "Why are you persecuting me? I'm a good father and husband."

"Bishop," Carpenter replied, "You are amoral and a cold-blooded killer. That's why you are being arrested." He stepped forward. "Reverend, please turn around and put your hands behind your back. Also be advised that we have search warrants for your properties."

"Listen here, *Lieutenant,*" LeMans seethed all cordiality gone, "one word from me and you will have a riot on your hands. Is that what you are looking for?"

Carpenter stepped even closer. "You are leaving with us, LeMans. How you leave is up to you. I can have you manacled, chained and handcuffed and drag you out like the animal you are. Or, I can handcuff you and you can walk out with your head held high. However, *you will* be leaving with us. What is your choice?"

Casius LeMans turned around, placed his hands out in front of him and was immediately handcuffed. "You win this round in the bout, Carpenter but I will win the fight."

"We'll see, Bishop; we'll see," as he placed a coat over the handcuffs.

CHAPTER 63

CURSIOUSER AND CURSIOUSER

When Carpenter walked into the Brooklyn Criminal Court for the arraignment of the Bishop, he was flabbergasted to learn that Casius LeMans defense attorney was none other than Robert Tannenbaum, Esq., the former ADA in Brooklyn. He had heard that Tannenbuam had resigned but this turn of events was a surprise. Carpenter, Soriano and Kelly were seated in the hallway, waiting for the case to be called. Carpenter turned and asked, "Kelly would see if you can learn the circumstances that brought this curiosity of Tannenbuam and LeMans marriage about and get back to me on it?"

A short time later Detective Kelly returned. "Lieu," he began, "Mr. Tannenbuam left the DA's office about a year ago to enter private practice. He has offices in the seventy-seventh Precinct. He is the attorney of record for the bishop."

"This case gets Curiouser and Curiouser," he said. The State of New York versus Casius LeMans was called and the arraignment began. LeMans was held without bail and the trial date was set, sixty days hence. Within two weeks of the trial's beginning, the police had all testified and had undergone cross-examination. Next came the presentation of the forensic evidence, including forensic odontology and pathology which, they were informed might take a couple of weeks or more, after which the DA was going to have selected "family" members testify against the Bishop.

About forty-five days after the trial began; Carpenter was working an evening tour of duty in the squad office. A Mrs. Sharleen Evans came into the office to speak with a police officer or detective. Detective Gloria Aquila conducted the initial interview but after their conversation had begun, Detective Aquila came to the commander's office.

"Pardon me, Lieu. You said you wanted to be in the loop with anything dealing with the LeMans situation."

"I did, Gloria." Carpenter looked up. "What have you got?"

"A Mrs. Evans, the mother of Juanita Evans, one of the nuns, and the grandmother of Shalese Evans."

"Bring her in." Carpenter suggested. "Let's see what she has to say. Would you also turn on the overhead lights, please and bring in the recording equipment?"

Detective Aquila complied showing Mrs. Evans a seat by the Lieutenant's desk.

"Mrs. Evans," the detective said, "this is Lieutenant Carpenter, the detective squad commander. Lieu, this is Mrs. Evans, the grandmother of Shalese Evans children."

"Detective, would you please sit in on this interview? Mrs. Evans," Carpenter began, "how can we help you?"

Mrs. Evans is a very tall, almost emaciated older Black woman, who looks very tired. She wore a flimsy head scarf, a light jacket and has clenched in her hand a small white handkerchief that she keeps balling into a mass, opens it up only to ball it up again. Carpenter noticed that there are tears in her eyes.

"My daughter," she begins, "has always wanted to help people. That's why she became a nun with the *Rehoboth Bethel Church of God*. At first she was very happy. Then, the Reverend took her and she had five children by him, an older boy Darius, is 18 and girl Martha is 17, then two boys Joash age six and Carl age four. Then there's Esther age five. Shalese tells me that her three youngest children are being kept in a closet on the second floor, that they are bound with wire at their wrists and ankles and there is another wire around her head," she describes their location she demonstrates exactly where they are. "According to Shalese there is some kind of dowel in the wire that can be tightened and that cuts into their flesh."

"I'm sorry for the interruption, Mrs. Evans but I need to record the information you are giving us. It will become part of the case you are presenting. Do you consent to having your complaint recorded?"

Detective Aquida got up from her chair, went to the equipment closet and returned with a tape recorder and microphone. Carpenter broke the glassine covering on the tape and inserted it into the machine.

Carpenter recorded the required introduction; starting the interview anew. Mrs. Evans repeated the information she initially gave then waited for Carpenter to ask her his questions.

"What you are describing is torture," Carpenter interjects; Sergeant Aquila moved forward in her chair.

"That's not all. According to Shalese, they are naked, they are living in their own pee an' other stuff—that's shit you know."

Sgt. Aquila asked, "Why are the children being tortured? What have they done?"

Mrs. Evans turns to her before answering. "Their older brother and sister are testifying against their father. The children are being tortured to prevent them from continuing. It's also a message to the others to keep quiet."

Carpenter leans back in his chair, brushes a strand of hair from his brow, tents his hands and looks into her eyes. He wonders to himself how and why this case is becoming more complex. He thought initially of the little boy with his finger in the hole in the dike and what happens when he takes his finger away. Finally he says, "Why are they in the closet and how long have they been there?"

"Right after the Reverend was arrested and brought to trial. Those two of the LeMans children were testifying in court against him. The kids are there about five or six days. Shalese says they could hear the babies crying but not anymore. Can you get them out?" she pleads.

"Mrs. Evans," Carpenter informs her, "under the provisions of the Family Court Act, police are justified in breaking and entering a premises if the lives of children are endangered. So, the simple answer to your question is yes, we can get them out. Before we do that, however, your accusations must be verified by another source."

"What do you mean 'another source? Isn't my word good enough?"

"Under normal circumstances your word would be. But the courts say that you might have had an argument with your son-in-law; that you might be angry with him; or that you might want to seek revenge. That's why they require a separate source. Is there anyone else who can tell us the same story?"

"I do have arguments with him. I do want revenge for what he is doing to my grandchildren. I hate the miserable sonofabitch."

"Is there anyone who will testify and tell us the same story that you have?"

"No, sir there's no one. They are all scared to death about him!" The frustrated grandmother pleads further but finally resigns the children to their fate. Reluctantly she leaves and in her wake are equally frustrated detectives.

CHAPTER 64

ABSENTEE DIVORCE

For the next two weeks Carpenter thought about and agonized over those children in the closet and the conditions under which they were surviving, if they are surviving. That was the bad news, the good news was he had little time to his personal situation and the fact that he was now divorced.

A bone weary Lieutenant drove to his home on Staten Island. He entered the empty house only to find on the kitchen counter those four packets of documents from Florida. The first three are Notice of Intent to Divorce which he had never seen before. Scanning these papers anew, he noticed that he was required to respond by signing the document and returning; the fourth document was a Notice of Divorce that had been granted because of his failure to respond to the Notices of Intent. The particulars of their dissolution were spelled out.

Carpenter called his parents to inform them of what had happened. They came over immediately to commiserate with him. While his mother made them dinner, he and his father shared a glass of Bushmills. Over dinner they discussed the situation in general and the divorce. It was decided that the edict would not be contested and Carpenter would accept the finality of it.

The following day, Carpenter called the detectives into the Interview Room to go over the LeMans case and the information they had gathered so far. Taped to the wall was a quasi-organizational chart of the *Rehoboth Bethel Church of God* and the seven families. They sat for several minutes reviewing the chart.

Maria could see and sense that something had happened to her supervisor and she knew it had not been pleasant. She recognized her helplessness.

CHAPTER 65

PLAIN VIEW DOCTRINE

Carpenter and Townsend went to lunch one Friday afternoon, discussing the upcoming college football game between the University of Florida and Alabama. Townsend favored Alabama and Carpenter favored Florida. Their records and personnel were discussed and the coaching staff.

"Steve Spurrier," Carpenter was saying, "has turned the program around at Florida. He demands that his players be academically fit to play football."

"Academically fit," Townsend ranted, "what kind of bullshit is that? Alabama only wants people who can play the game of football. Academically fit . . ."

They were heading back to the station house, Townsend behind the wheel, their discussion still going strong. As they were passing the First National City Bank on the corner of Buffalo and Eastern Parkway, they both saw two men, apparently Puerto Rican, emerging from the bank ramming sawed-off shotguns into their waistbands. Townsend pulled to the curb and both men got out. They were spotted by the men from the bank and they took off running, Townsend and Carpenter in close pursuit. They ran up Buffalo to Sterling Place and turned toward Rochester Avenue. In the middle of the block, the two men ran up a stone stoop and burst through a door of number 320 Rochester. The officers were not far behind.

Carpenter was the first to enter as another male; Puerto Rican emerged from a side room. Townsend threw him against a wall and patted him down. Carpenter walking more deliberately moved down the hallway. He came to a door on his left. He paused, threw it open and there, sitting on a toilet bowl was one of the men from the bank, a shotgun across his lap. Carpenter removed the gun while motioning the man to stand up. Townsend had caught up with the first man in custody.

"Sergeant," Carpenter directed, "put that man in here with this one," indicating the man whose pants were down around his ankles. "Close the door." To the men he said, "If you come out before we tell you to, we will take that as a threat and shoot you. Do you understand?"

The men nodded sullenly.

Townsend and Carpenter continued down the hall of what they had determined was a railroad flat—one long narrow hallway with rooms off to the sides. As they moved to the rear of the apartment they observed one room filled with televisions, another filled with hifi and stereo equipment, another room was filled with movie, video and still cameras. At the end of the hall there was a large room filled with boxes and scrap newspaper. Carpenter pointed out to his partner—under a pile of papers, a pair of hightop sneakers were protruding. There was the second stick up man. They held their guns at the ready as each grabbed a foot pulling him out of the papers. As they did, the butt of a shotgun was on the floor beside him.

Carpenter handed Townsend his handcuffs. "You round up the others while I place a call for back up. We can seize this other property under plain view but I'd rather have a search warrant and really go over this place." He also placed a call to the Bank Squad giving them the location of the bank asking them to meet at the 77th Squad. The three men were initially frisked were placed into radio cars for transport to the station house.

The Lieutenant asked one of the patrol car crews to stand by and safeguard the apartment while a warrant was secured. He returned to the station house to place a call for the warrant and the processing of the bank robbery was started.

"Peter," we only frisked these men don't forget," the Lieutenant reminded the sergeant. "We need to search them to see what they are holding."

The Bank Squad arrived and the detectives let them take over. They had secured the cameras from the bank, dusted the counters and were turning their attention to the three men. Just then the door flew open and three suits entered in a flurry. The brashest of the trio flashed an open shield case announcing, "Federal Bureau of Investigation," he announced Loudly. "I am Special Agent in Charge, George Hocheiser. We'll take over from here." The detectives and officers from the Bank Squad took seats allowing the FBI 'take over from here.'

"Who's the ranking supervisor here?" Agent Hocheiser asked.

Carpenter had started toward his office and stopped. "I am," he responded.

"I'll use your office to question these men one at a time," he announced.

"Do they now teach manners at the FBI?" he asked. "The polite thing to do is to ask for the use of the office."

"Come on, quit the shit. Can I use your office?"

Carpenter bent at the waist, swept his right arm across his body toward the office. "Agent Carpenter, we have only frisked them . . ."

"I'll handle it, detective. Relax." He entered the office with one of the robbers. He had been in there only a matter of minutes when Carpenter heard the toilet being flushed. Instantly he knew what had happened. He hurried to the office.

As he entered he saw the agent seated at his desk. "Where is the prisoner?" he inquired but he already knew. He didn't wait for an answer but threw open the toilet door. Sure enough, floating on the surface of the toilet were bills, the seed money from the bank. "You," he exclaimed to the robber, "fetch those bills and be quick about it!" When that was done, he turned the prisoner over to Townsend and turned to the agent and closed the office door.

"You moron," he hissed. "That man just flushed most of the seed money down the toilet. Don't you know any better than that? I told you we had only frisked them." Again he did not wait for an answer. "Just you sit back and allow our Bank Squad to work and learn how *professionals* to it. Now, get out of my chair!"

"I'm new to this position," Agent Carpenter said in reply. "We haven't handled bank robberies before."

More serenely Carpenter said, "Let me recommend you and your men watch our bank squad. They really know what they are doing."

Patiently the agents were shown how to handle the film from the bank; how the dye packs were to be removed; they dusted for fingerprints on the countertops in the bank after learning they had scaled the counters to get to the teller enclosures; they counted the money seized and compared it with the amount reported stolen. Apparently almost three hundred dollars had gone down the drain.

In the meantime, other detectives, armed with a search warrant went back to the apartment and catalogued the property found. Serial numbers were obtained and compared with reports of burglaries and robberies. A good many open cases were closed by Exceptional Clearance as a result of their findings.

CHAPTER 66

SOUGHT AFTER CORROBORATION

Sunday evening two weeks before the end of the trial, Carpenter got a telephone call at home ["Lieu, Bart Adams,"] the caller identified himself.

"Good evening, Bart. Are you enjoying a quiet Sunday evening?"

["Lieu, everything is happening in bunches. Anne Soriano has been reported missing and she has been gone since Friday morning. Everyone at the church is assuming she's dead for coming forward to the police. Everyone suspects it was Darryl who got her."]

"What is the story on her? Was she taken from the church? Was she abducted somewhere else?"

["We don't know squat! What we do know is that we have one of the LeMans girls here in the squad office," Detective Adams said. "She has been beaten terribly and raped by her brother. The poor kid is in bad shape."]

"Does she need medical attention?"

["She has refused any attention at all. We can't talk her into any."]

"How old a girl is she?" he asked.

["How old are you kiddo?"] Bart asked the girl. ["She says she is eighteen."]

"Bart, when I get there, pick up on my lead; I'll be there in forty-five minutes."

Ninety minutes later Carpenter walked into the squad room. Sitting forlornly in a chair outside the Interview Room was a young Black girl. She was wearing dungarees that were torn at the knees, sneakers and a bloody New York Rangers t-shirt. The right side of her jaw was swollen, her lips puffed and her right eye was beginning to close. She looked quite dejected and was crying.

"Who did this to this poor young girl?" Carpenter inquired of no one in particular.

"Her brother, Shasta did this to her, Lieu. He's beaten the shit out of her," Detective Adams said.

"What's her name; what's your name, little girl?"

"B . . . Bobby," came her frightened reply.

"What do you want us to do about this attack on you?" Carpenter asked before she could give her last name?

"I want him arrested for hurting me. He hurt me bad."

"You want who arrested?" he asked.

"My brother, Shasta. Look! Look! He hurt me bad!"

"Okay then, that's what we will do!" Carpenter replied. "What's your last name?"

"LeMans, I'm Bobby LeMans."

"LeMans," he called out Loudly, a complete change of demeanor. He bent to look into the girl's eyes. "This isn't the first time you've had sex with your brother is it?"

The girl was shocked at this sudden outburst and turnabout. This man had been so kind just a few minutes ago, now he was changed. "No sir, but this time he hurt me. He hurt me real bad"

Carpenter turned toward his office. "Throw this little bitch out!" He stormed into the office as the girl began sobbing uncontrollably.

Adams picked up on the lead. He went to the girl explaining, "He's got a thing about your family. He knows about the cellar and the girls that are brought in. Let's leave him alone for a while then I will go and talk with him."

The detective walked to the commander's office, closing the door. The two men sat quietly for about five minutes. Carpenter got up from his seat announcing, "I guess she's stewed long enough. Let's go and talk with her and see if she can help us."

"Why do we have to do it this way, Lieu? Why did we have to have her think we abandoned her?"

"If we had asked her to help straight off, she would have shut her mouth and we would never have had our chance. She is too afraid of what goes on in that place in general and her brother in particular. This way, she is angry at her brother and, I hope will now be willing to help us."

They walked over to the girl. "Bobby," Carpenter said as they drew close, "Detective Adams has convinced me that we should help you. We will arrest Shasta and put him away. You know that you will have to testify against him in court? But before we do, I want you to answer a couple of questions for me; okay?"

As she dried her eyes, she nodded her head affirmatively.

"On the second floor, above the chapel," the girl took on a wary look, "in a closet at the back of the hallway," she put her left hand over her mouth, "there are three children being held there. Is that correct?"

She started crying again and again she nodded.

"These children are bound hand and foot with wire and a wooden dowel that is tightened every day. Is that correct?"

"Y . . . yes," she was crying now.

"Bobby, are those children in danger? You must tell me."

"Yes, they are in danger." She wept, sobbing with release of telling someone.

"Thank you, Bobby. We'll pick up Shasta. Let us get you some medical help. You really should be seen by a doctor." While they were waiting for the ambulance Carpenter had a statement prepared for her signature, which she signed.

Later that night Shasta LeMans was picked up and arrested for raping his sister. He could not understand that he had done anything wrong.

"We had sex before, what's she bitchin' 'bout now?"

"Women," Adams said mournfully. "Go figure."

CHAPTER 67

WHEN ALL ELSE FAILS . . . IMPROVISE

With the needed corroboration, on Monday morning Carpenter went to the Kings County Family Court on 330 Adams Street to petition for a warrant to enter the church and removed the three children known to be abused and in danger. After several hours of frustration and an unwillingness to issue such a warrant, Carpenter obtained the names of the judges sitting in the court. He contacted each one personally and each one turned him down on the grounds that he could not and would not interfere with church and its sanctuary protections.

"But no one has asked for sanctuary," Carpenter had countered.

"Regardless," was the meaningless retort.

While mulling over the situation, he remembered an officer, Hector Ramirez, who had been in the academy with him. Hector had later resigned from the department to study law and after several years, he was appointed a juvenile judge in the Bronx. It took some research but eventually he found his telephone number and called him for advice. He was passed through several functionaries but was finally connected with him.

"Hello, Hector. This is Lance Carpenter do you remember me?" he asked.

["Yes, of course Lance. How have you been, buddy?"]

"I'm fine, Hector. Congratulations on your appointment to the bench. Did you get my telegram?"

["Yes, thank you. Are you still with the department, compadre?"]

"Yes, still there. I became the whip in the 7-7 Squad in Brooklyn."

["That's great, Carpenter. I knew you would succeed. How can I help you?"]

"I've got a situation here I need help and or advice with." Carpenter told his friend all about the Reverend LeMans and the *Rehoboth Bethel Church of God.* "These three kids are in peril and we have had to sit on it for too long already. I petitioned the judges of the Kings County Family Court and the Court itself to no avail. No one wants to touch the church and sanctuary issues. The children, however, are being held in the living quarters and not in the church proper. Does that help our situation and where do I go from here?"

["You don't come to me with simple ones, do you? If you are sure you have corroboration and the residence is separate and apart from the church, you can break and enter, if necessary to secure the safety of the children."]

"I am sure, Hector. I'm hoping that the kids are still alive, it's that critical."

["Take the kids out Carpenter, today. Send someone to me in the morning and I'll have the warrant for you. I'll turn you over to my assistant and you can give her all the necessary information."]

"Thanks, Hector, I owe you a big one."

Carpenter called Brooklyn North Borough Command asking to have the surrounding precincts—73rd, 81st, 79th, 88th 84th, 78th and 71st send a Black officer on temporary two hour assignment, who are over six feet in height to assist in a raid about three o'clock in the morning to remove endangered children. It was explained that that hour of the morning was chosen because this was usually the time for sleep and the body's defenses were in the rest mode. The men were to report at 2:00 a.m. for briefing.

Detective Bingham was assigned the task of running down, on loan, ten sledge hammers and to have them ready for distribution by one o'clock. Sgt. Soriano said she would take care of the children once released.

At the designated hour, patrolmen from the various commands reported to the precinct and met in the muster room of the station house. The situation was explained to them and several of the men were issued sledge hammers.

Addressing the men, Carpenter explained, "We are about to break and enter a church, in particular the residence of the prelate of the *Rehoboth Bethel Church of God*. We are doing so to rescue from further harm, three children who are being held and tortured. We have selected three o'clock this morning because this is usually the time for sleep and the body's defenses are in the rest mode. We will give the occupants every chance to comply with our directives, if or when they do not, we will break and enter to save those children. We are supported in this effort by a properly executed warrant. Are any of you morally opposed to what we propose?" When no one objected, they set off to get the job done.

At the church Carpenter announced over a bull horn, that the occupants had five minutes to surrender alive, the children being in a closet on the second floor or the police break and enter to secure their release. At the end of that period of time, Carpenter picked up a sledge hammer and walked to the door of the residence. A huge Black officer, Jermaine McDonough, stopped the lieutenant.

"Can I be the first to enter, lieutenant," he asked?

Looking at the man's serious face, Carpenter handed over the hammer. The big man strode to the door, hefted the hammer and smashed the door in. There was a rush to enter. Once inside they saw Darryl coming down the stairs reaching to his back as though he had a weapon there. Carpenter and Townsend were at the bottom of the stairs, their hands on their weapons. Peter said, "Please, Darryl have a weapon and take it out. It will be the last thing you do." Darryl had a change of heart, no weapon was drawn. When he descended the stairs, the gun he was carrying was removed. He was placed in the rear of a patrol car.

Several of the big men went up the stairs two at a time. When they reached the closet door, they stopped to look at Carpenter for permission to open it; he nodded his approval. When they did, the stale rank odor of human waste assailed them. The emaciated children were brought out into the hallway. All those present saw that wires had cut into their flesh and had become infected. The children could hardly stand by themselves. There were angry red bands about their wrists, ankles and a wire with a dowel was around their heads

Carpenter had carried a wire cutter to free the bands but decided that the sudden release of pressure might prove too stressful to the children. Instead, he asked the officers to uncurl slowly releasing the pressure gradually. As they did so the children cried out. Carpenter looked about him. The department was currently undergoing allegations of brutality and corruption, he thought to himself. These weren't brutal and corrupt cops, with tears streaming down their hard bitten faces, gently helping these tortured children. They were like big brown teddy bears.

The nuns had been aroused by the thunderous noise were now clustered in the hallway. Carpenter asked them to clean up the children without causing too much pain and to have them dressed in order that they could be removed to the Children's Shelter. They were only too anxious to help. The next thirty minutes were agonizing to listen to; the urge to stop their pain had to be put aside. The men could only look down at their feet. Once cleaned, they were given a light snack and removed to the shelter.

Notifications had been made to the shelter and vehicles were on the street to transport them there. The patrolmen temporarily assigned were thanked for their assistance in this humanitarian undertaking. They were released to return to their commands. Carpenter, Townsend, Soriano, Adams and Tony Romano returned to the squad to begin the paperwork. The appropriate notifications were made to the Borough Command and at 0500, Carpenter received notification to report to the Big Building at 0800 that morning and report to the Police Commissioner himself.

"Maria," he called out, "would you and Adams pick up the children from the Shelter and meet me at the PCs office at or about eight o'clock this morning?"

Both officers agreed to be there.

CHAPTER 68

ACCOUNTING FOR ONE'S ACTIONS

Outside the Commissioner's Office was a large waiting room which is carpeted, well lighted, several upholstered chairs, a table with a large crystal lamp, and total silence. Carpenter was there at the appointed time and the Deputy Inspector that met him informed him that it would be a few minutes before the Commissioner could see him. The Deputy seated himself at his desk and resumed what he had been doing. Carpenter had brought with him several of the files on the case he anticipated he would have to brief the Commissioner on their contents.

Assistant Chief Inspector Peter Margolis, known throughout the department as 'Mister Clean' because of his shaved head, burst into the anteroom. He was tall, a powerfully built man, whose uniform didn't seem to fit properly. His presence was quite intimidating. He spotted Carpenter and walked over to him.

"What are you doing here," he demanded with no preamble?

"I'm waiting for the PC chief," Carpenter responded.

"What does he want with you?" he snarled again.

Carpenter played it dumb for this overbearing oaf. "Gosh, I don't really know, Chief."

Margolis moved forward until he was right in Carpenter's face. "Don't give me that bullshit," breathing his stale breath of coffee and cigars in Carpenter's face.

Carpenter took a backward step repeating, "Golly, I can't tell you what he wants."

The phone buzzed that was answered promptly. Looking up the Deputy said, "The Commissioner will see you now, Lieutenant."

Carpenter walked around the Assistant Chief to enter the rather large room noticing the plush carpeting, the antique desk behind which the Commissioner sat. There were several large windows, with heavy drapes and the blinds opened allowing sunlight to brighten the room. In the bright sunlight motes of dust were visible.

Slowly the Commissioner rose from his chair to come around the desk against which he leaned with folder arms. Commissioner Michael Todd was a cop's cop. He had come up through the ranks to earn the position he now held. He was a tall man with thick white hair, heavily built, with broad shoulders and slim waisted. He had a prodigious memory for people and names which were legendary throughout the department.

"Carpenter Carpenter," he began, "we met some time ago when you were in charge of the police detail at Gracey Mansion."

"Yes, sir we did. That *has* been some time ago."

"The reason I asked you here this morning is because of the Gestapo tactics you used in breaking and entering a church, for God's sake, in the middle of the night. Lieutenant, we are not the *Geheime Staatspolizei* from which the Gestapo derived their name and you are not Hermann Göring. Is that quite clear?"

"Yes, quite clear Commissioner. I never . . ."

Todd raised his right hand stopping Carpenter in mid-sentence. "Lieutenant, your actions early this morning are indefensible! I hear that thugs under your command smashed down the front door of a church and forced your way inside. What were you thinking, man?"

"Commissioner I was acting under the authority of a warrant, I directed that the residence be opened in advance of our entering, not the church. We broke and entered in order to safeguard the lives of three children that were being held captive there. They were being tortured and had been for some time. They were naked, unfed, with wires around the ankles, wrists and around their head, and they were confined in a closet, living in their own waste."

"Dammit Lieutenant, the media will have a field day with this. With all the bad publicity we are going through right now, you top it off with a caper like this. A church is a holy place, not some warehouse on the waterfront. You were way off base on this one. What warrant?"

"The warrant was out of the Bronx and one of my detectives is picking it up as we speak." As he said this, Carpenter heard a commotion outside the Commissioner's door. The children had arrived. "Are you finished, Commissioner?" Carpenter asked as he moved toward the door.

"Am I what?" the Commissioner, quite flabbergasted, said in a loud voice. "Where do you get off . . . ?"

Carpenter opened the door, motioned the children into the august office and once inside, they hugged one another and wet their pants, shivering. They had been cleaned, their injuries tended to, bandages in place about their ankles and wrists, the angry scars of their recent ordeal quite evident. The red, infested wound around their foreheads told of the torture they had endured. Carpenter turned to the Commissioner saying: "Now you tell me I did wrong, Commissioner."

Commissioner Todd sat back against his desk, his hands holding him upright. Waving his right arm toward the door, Commissioner Todd yelled, "Get the hell out of here and take them with you!"

Carpenter ushered the children out of the room content in the knowledge that the Commissioner would back his action. The children were returned to the Children's

Shelter for further medical treatment and attention. The officers returned to the precinct and the detective squad.

"How did it go, Lieu?" Sgt. Soriano asked concerned.

"He chewed me a new one, Maria but he will support us. Thanks for asking."

"Before you get comfortable," Maria said, "Commissioner Carole Perry, the Commissioner of Human Relations, or the Administrator for Children's Services, or whatever, has given you a forthwith to her office. The caller said she was quite pissed off.

"Into the breach again we go," Carpenter misquoted as he headed back out the door.

CHAPTER 69

COMMISSIONER OF HUMAN RELATIONS

W hen he entered the Commissioner's office, he thought he should have had someone bring the children here to support his actions this morning. He was met at the outer officer of Human Relations by an older Black man who stopped him.

"I'm the chief investigator for the Commissioner, Detective Clarence Wilson. I'm to take you to the Conference Room as soon as you got here."

"Lead the way Gaston. I hope Salome doesn't want me beheaded."

"What," asked the confused officer?

"Never mind." The Conference Room was an elongated affair with four occupied seats and two empty chairs. Along the back wall sat six or seven men and women with very somber faces, very somber indeed. Carpenter sat in one of the chairs as Commissioner Perry entered the room. The men stood. She motioned everyone to be seated.

"Good almost afternoon, Lieutenant," was her opening remark.

"And to you also," Carpenter responded.

"Earlier this morning you violated a number of human rights and a host of other violations. against a church of all things and its pastor! What have you got to say for yourself, hm? I've never run into anything like this before."

"Where would you like me to begin, Ma'am?"

"The beginning is always a good place to start."

Carpenter went into a lengthy explanation of the *Rehoboth Bethel Church of God* and its pastor, Casius LeMans. He described the raping of children taken from the streets, the beatings of nuns in his charge, the torture of three little children, the dismemberment of human beings, the forced audience at slaying and at the burning of their bodies and dismemberments and the beheading of the former pastor, Bishop Jonathan Brown.

"Lieutenant," Perry interrupted, "my chief investigator here," motioning to Clarence Wilson, "informs me that he has been there on a number of occasions and he has never seen any of the horrors you describe. How do you account for that?"

"Your chief investigator," Carpenter countered looking at the man, "has always met with the Reverend and/or his staff inside the chapel."

Perry turned toward the investigator, "Clarence?"

Wilson glared at Carpenter. "There was never a reason for me to go anywhere else."

"So, as I understand it, every time you went there to investigate the numerous complaints that we have had, you never went beyond the chapel, regardless of the circumstances of the complain. Is that correct?"

Wilson nodded his head sullenly.

Turning once again to Carpenter, Perry asked, "You said you acted under the authority of a warrant. Who issued such a warrant?"

Carpenter had recognized one or two of the people seated at the table as being judges, he boldly said, "I made contact with the Juvenile authorities to secure a warrant but every attempt was denied. The children had been subjected to unthinkable torture for some weeks and I felt it imperative that we enter as soon as we could. I secured a warrant out of the Bronx and acted under its authority," Carpenter explained.

"Those people along the back wall are attorneys attached to this office." Turning her attention to them she said: "I want that warrant emanating from this office. Are there any questions?" She waited for none. She turned to one of the judges, an elderly, matronly woman saying, "And you will sign it!" Turning back to Carpenter, she asked: "How many children are still in the clutches of the church and are they in danger?"

"There are twenty or more still there but I do not think they are in danger but that could change at any time." Carpenter offered.

"Regardless," she again turned her attention to be back of the room gang, "I want appropriate paperwork drawn up for the removal of the unspecified number of children today. If what the Lieutenant says is correct, they will all need psychological counseling." Turning back to Carpenter she asked, "Would you be willing to enforce such an order, Lieutenant?"

At last he breathed, saying to himself 'a woman with balls'. "Yes, ma'am I certainly would."

The commissioner again turned to the judge saying, "And you will sign it!" Commissioner Parry turned her attention to the Lieutenant once they were outside the conference room. "What you did, Lieutenant was most outrageous, impulsive."

"Yes, ma'am, it probably was but I felt it was necessary given the circumstances."

"In the future, if there is another situation, please feel free to contact me direct."

"It would be my pleasure."

"You are closer to this than we are obviously. With that in mind, do you think there is anything worth salvaging at the church and its facilities?"

"Commissioner, I am no expert but I would strongly recommend that someone more qualified be sent there to conduct a professional evaluation. He has operational schools, day care and other worthwhile activities. Let the professionals make that determination."

In discussing the ramifications of what the LeMans household had been forced to witness, Commissioner Parry suggested that the assault on their collective psyches had to have been incredible.

"Commissioner, that impact must be colossal, not only for the children but everyone in the household."

CHAPTER 70

NEW BEGINNINGS

Maria walked into the office at about 2330 hours to say goodnight to her lieutenant. She found Lance with his head on his desk. She could tell by the sound of his breathing he was sound asleep. She hated to wake him.

"Come on, Lance, it's time to call it a day."

"I'm alright, Maria, just let me splash some water on my face. Give me a minute."

"No, you're coming with me," she said assertively.

"Where are we going?" he asked drowsily.

"We're going to my apartment where you can get some shuteye."

"Maria, I can make it to my home," he protested.

"No, you'll fall asleep on the way. My place is not far and I've plenty of room. You will be safe with me and the price is right. Besides, I'll make you a great meal you will not forget. I happen to be a great chef!"

Without much argument, Lance allowed her to drive him to her apartment where she did, in fact, make him a meal worthy of a truly great gourmet. He had not realized how hungry he was until he had started eating.

Maria noticed though that he had nodded off several times, great meal or not. She took his fork away and led him to her bedroom.

"Crash here tonight. You look exhausted. Take off your clothes and crawl under the covers. You can sleep in your briefs. Let me know when you are in bed and I will come in and kiss you goodnight."

He began unbuttoning his shirt as she closed the door. When she reentered the room a short time later, he was covered up to his chin and quite asleep. She went back to the kitchen to clean up. When she returned to the bedroom, he hadn't moved. She removed her clothes, took a shower, turned off the lights and got in bed beside him. She nestled next to him quite content.

Later, Lance awoke with a strange sensation. He felt a naked body beside him generating heat. He could not fathom where he was or who was with him. He knew instinctively that he should not be here, wherever here was. He tried to move away but ended up waking his bed partner up. He saw that it was Maria and he found himself being aroused. To add to his dilemma, a warm hand took hold of him adding to his arousal. What followed were a release and an awakening; a release of the tensions he had been under for several weeks and an awakening to a bond that was there between these two. He moved toward her and both were grateful for the discovery. They surrendered to the discovery.

In the morning Lance lay on his back while Maria traced her finger down the front of his body exploring here and there.

"There is hardly a scar from that bullet wound in your shoulder. Do you still feel any pain there?" she asked.

"Only when it gets cold," he said drowsily, enjoying her gentle probing.

"Does it hurt here?" she asked wiggling her nail in his navel. "How about here?" she asked running her nails between his legs. He was instantly aroused.

"Yes, it hurts but I can't feel the pain."

"I'd better stop."

"You'd better not."

CHAPTER 71

HORROR IN THE COUNTRYSIDE

The trial was still going on in Brooklyn Criminal Court. Casius was being tried for the crimes of kidnapping, rape, unlawful imprisonment and murder.

Darryl received a telephone call from his father at about 4:30 on a Thursday afternoon. They had a lengthy conversation after which he was heard saying, "I understand, Bishop. I understand and I know what needs to be done." He then hung up the telephone. He went to the Reverend's study and office to make another call. Again, he spoke at length then hung up. His last call was to his brother, Marcus in Manhattan. They too had a conversation at length. After he had hung up, he left for the remainder of the day.

The following morning, as they were gathered at breakfast, Darryl stood up to make an announcement. "The Reverend called last night and told me that he thought that these last weeks have been very trying on everyone and that we needed a break from all that stuff. He wants me to take you all on a picnic up at the ranch in Westchester. The police aren't there any more so we will have the place to ourselves. We'll take a bus ride in a few minutes and a picnic lunch up there." Raising his voice, he asked: "Would you like that?"

A gleeful outburst met his question. A short time later they boarded a bus for the ride upstate. No one noticed the detour they had made to enter Manhattan. Darryl directed the driver to his brother Marcus's brothel. As they stopped at the curb a young Hispanic girl emerged from a building and entered the bus.

"Marcus said he was sendin' me on a picnic upstate, that right?" the girl announced as she climbed the short stairs.

"Sure is honey," Darryl assured her. "What's your name?"

"Bernadette but they call me 'Bernie.' You can call me anything you want darlin'"

The driver went up the East Side Highway to the Bronx, through the Bronx to the Parkway and up into White Sulphur Springs. From there Darryl directed him to the ranch. When they got there, he had the family get out at the front of the ranch house. It was a bright, sun shiny day without a cloud in the sky. He turned to the driver saying:

"Be back here in six hours for the trip back. Here's something extra for your trouble," he said handing the man a $50 bill.

The family moved into the house where there was a buffet luncheon spread out for them on a number of tables. A child's wading pool had been converted to a drink chiller on the patio deck filled with cans of soda, water and ice. For ninety minutes the family ate well and laughed at silly things.

Once lunch was over, Darryl directed the family to the rear of the house where portable bleachers had been erected. They had been erected so that the sun was at their backs. In front of the bleachers was a chain-linked fence attached to upright metal stanchions. He instructed the family to be seated in the bleachers but Bernie he asked to stay back. When everyone was seated, he took handcuffs and cuffed Bernie to the fence, placing a plastic sheet under her feet. A look of confusion covered the young girl's face.

Darryl began pacing back and forth as he spoke.

"Doc is on trial, as you know," he said as his voice grew louder, "and he has seen some of his family turn against him and testify against him. He also hears that some of you others are intending to do the same." He now walked to Bernie hanging from the fence and with a straight razor started to cut her clothing away. Darryl continued cutting, despite her screams of terror and continued his speech.

"He thinks you all need an object lesson and asked me to provide it." Bernie was now naked and more than a little terrified. She wet herself.

"Please, Darryl, don't do this. Please don't hurt me," she pleaded.

More intently now he said as he took hold of her left breast the cut it from her body ignoring her horrifying painful screams, "There will be no further testimony against the Bishop!" Mercifully Bernie had passed out, her blood running down her small body. He moved to her second breast. "Those that are testifying will stop and stop now!" Bernie was beyond feeling now and the family was the same as they watched wordlessly as Darryl methodically flayed her body as he concluded, "Anyone that defies the Bishop will meet the same fate as poor Bernie here," who was now quite dead.

Darryl folded up the plastic sheet with Bernie's body enclosed and carried it to another enamel tub that had been purchased for the occasion. He threw everything into the tub, doused it with kerosene and gasoline and set it ablaze. For the next four hours he kept replenishing the fuel when the flames died down but the acrid smoke spiraled upward. The stench of burning flesh made most of the onlookers quite ill. When it was finally completed, he emptied the tub's contents into a small bucket and put it in the rowboat. He rowed out on the replenished lake and dumped the ashes over board and rinsed the bucket.

That done, he cleaned up what needed cleaning and, with the others, went to the front of the house with the others to wait for the bus to return to them to the church. The group was morosely silent pondering the lesson they had learned. As the group entered the bus, the driver said, "What is that god awful smell?"

"Trash, we just burned some trash."

CHAPTER 72

WILL THE HORROR EVER STOP?

In the meantime, Marcus had been arrested on a charge of burglary in the 77th Precinct. He had been taken to the squad office when it was learned who he was and on the discovery that he was carrying a loaded automatic. His arrest was processed uneventfully and he was shipped to the Tombs for detention until his trial.

In 1902 a massive, gray building replaced the Tombs but its chateau-like appearance could not displace in common parlance the name of the original structure whose architectural style had been based on a steel engraving of an Egyptian tomb. Seven decades later that replacement was itself replaced by the present Manhattan Detention Complex but still "The Tombs" name persists.

The automatic Marcus had been carrying had been sent to the Police Department's Ballistics Section for examination. Carpenter was seated at his desk reading the result of that examination. He picked up the telephone and called the District Attorney's Office and spoke with ADA Charles Cohen explaining what he had. Cohen said he would be there shortly. In the meantime, Marcus was returned from detention and sat waiting in the squad office for the ADA's appearance. The ADA arrived and walked in and took a seat. As though rehearsed, Carpenter took up the lead in the meeting.

"Marcus, that burglary charge you have pending," he started, "is a trivial charge compared to the charge the District Attorney Cohen here will discuss with you." Carpenter picked up the report and quoted from it.

"A New York State Trooper, Philip Mohrman, was alerted by a 'hit' scored on a routine check of license plates. He pulled over the Reverend Casius LeMans who was driving, to the shoulder of the roadway. He suspected what the alarm had told him, but the family in the car and the clerical collar worn by its driver, put him off his guard and he became careless. As the car drove away, a short time later, they left behind a dead trooper, shot to death. The killing would remain unsolved for seven years. The weapon you were carrying was traced to that shooting death of a New York State Trooper in upstate New York. And in the State of New York, that calls for the death penalty. So, young man, you will fry for killing the State Trooper."

"Wait! Wait! That's not my gun, it's my father's!" he screamed at the two men. "You gotta listen to me, that ain't . . . that's not my gun!"

Cohen leaned toward Marcus, "The weapon was found in your possession and under the law that's constructive possession. It's your gun and you will be charged in the officer's death."

"Hold on. Suppose I gave you the nails for my father's coffin; could we make some kinda deal?"

"What kind of nails?" Cohen asked.

"Let's get 'em an' you'll see," Marcus pleaded. "Send someone with me to my pad an' I'll get 'em for you."

With the consent of the ADA, Marcus was manacled hand and foot and was sent in the company of Sergeant Townsend and Detective Bill Binghamton to Marcus' residence to pick up the nails for his father's coffin. The trio was gone about an hour before they returned. He was returned to the office carrying four paper bags. He said proudly:

"Here are the nails I promised you." He walked over to the desk, turned the bags upside down and spilled the contents onto Carpenter's desk top. Carpenter and Cohen reared back looking in horror at the nails lying there. They were twenty necklaces of ten human fingers wired together shriveled up and partially decayed. The men stared at them for some time before either could speak.

Finally, Carpenter broke the silence. "Put these back in the bags," he directed Marcus. "These . . . these," he said indicating the necklaces, "are not proof of death. They merely represent someone's morbid sense of the macabre. I'm afraid they will not help you much but that's up to the ADA Mr. Cohen. Before we get to that however, where did these necklaces come from?"

"I gotta think on that," Marcus hedged.

"It's now or never. Shit or get off the pot!" Cohen said annoyed.

"When a young girl was gonna make a complaint, or if she refused to have sex with any of us, she was given one last chance and if she broke one of the rules, well. After that, she was taken to the basement, put on the table and one of us, not me of course, killed her. Then and there Doc took these snips and cut off her fingers and Darryl usually strung wire through them to make these necklaces," he said indicating the fingers in the bag.

"Marcus," Cohen could finally speak, "you will be charged with the homicide of the officer along with the burglary. We may be able to work something out with your counsel but that remains to be seen. I'm going to have transcribed what you have just told us. When that is done, you will sign that statement. It will help you in sentencing."

"What choice do I have?" he asked.

CHAPTER 73

GUILTY! FOUR CONSECUTIVE LIFE TERMS

On July 7, 1977, the seventh day of the seventh month, of the seventy-seventh year, Bishop Casius LeMans was found guilty of four counts of first degree murder and was later sentenced to four life terms to run consecutively. He would never be a free man again. He was sent initially to Sullivan Correctional Facility, in Fallsburg and later transferred to Jefferson Correctional Facility in New York State to complete his sentencing.

Based on testimony of family members and trace evidence found on the ranch, along with unconsumed body parts recovered from the lake, Darryl was convicted of homicide and is serving a twenty year sentence in Sing-Sing Prison.

A deal was work out with Marcus' attorney and he served his prison sentence for burglary.

All of the children have deep rooted psychological problems and have undergone psychiatric counseling for some time. Some are still under care. The three children received medical attention and although their physical wounds have healed, their psychological wounds may never heal. The nuns have left the church, their whereabouts unknown. The schools have been taken over by the city, the church is closed; the other two buildings demolished.

Lieutenant Lance Carpenter and Sergeant Maria Soriano, celebrating the end of a long, tedious and gut-wrenching investigation, decided to have a quiet dinner before moving on to the next case.

THE ZEN OF
LISTENING

The ZEN of
LISTENING

MINDFUL COMMUNICATION IN THE AGE OF DISTRACTION

REBECCA Z. SHAFIR, M.A. CCC

A publication supported by
THE KERN FOUNDATION

Quest Books
Theosophical Publishing House

Wheaton, Illinois ◆ Chennai (Madras), India

A publication of the Theosophical Publishing House,
a department of the Theosophical Society in America

Library of Congress Cataloging-in-Publication Data

Shafir, Rebecca Z.
The zen of listening: mindful communication in the age of distraction /
Rebecca Z. Shafir. — 1ˢᵗ Quest books ed.
        p.   cm.
"Quest books."
Includes bibliographical references (p.   ).
ISBN 0-8356-0790-9
1. Listening.   I. Title.

BF323.L5 S53 2000
153.6'8—dc21

                                                                00-031759

        6   5   4   3   2   *   00   01   02   03   04   05

Printed in the United States of America

Table of Contents

Acknowledgments

I bow humbly to the people who taught me the power of mindful listening and helped bring this book into being. To Michelle Lucas, who taught me that a support group is for listening, not lecturing. To the staff and students at The Boston Center for Adult Education, who believed that a different approach to the teaching of listening could work! To my martial arts teachers who, through sweat and tears, taught me that the real strength lies in a focused mind. To Jane Sokol Shulman and my patients, who awakened in me the appreciation for the renewal that comes from loss.

To the physicians at Lahey Clinic, particularly Dr. Frank Scholz, Dr. Prather Palmer, and Dr. Stephen Kott, who continue to teach the meaning of a good bedside manner.

To the many supporters and nurturers, including Morty and Barbara Eagle, all my friends from the Greater Lowell Road Runners and Winchester Highlanders, who prove every day that listening is a part of good health.

A bow to Marcia Yudkin, writer, marketer, mentor, and friend, who gave shape to my writing and enthusiastic support throughout the process.

To Shaneet Thompson who shared valuable nuggets about listening from a mediator's standpoint. To Zen Master Bon Hyon who reviewed my manuscript and continues to clarify my understanding of Zen Buddhist philosophy and how it relates to communication.

I am especially grateful for the opportunity to have met so many people through the process of writing this book. To my agent, Susan Schulman, and to Christine Morin for their confidence in me. To Sharron Brown-Dorr, the publishing manager of Quest Books, who helped me focus my vision and bring it forward. To my editor, Jane Lawrence, a soul sister, whose patience and writing skills helped bring the final drafts to a new level of clarity and quality.

My loving appreciation to my mother, Iris, who has always been my inspiration for using my potential in all endeavors; and my father, Paul, who always encouraged me to look for the opportunities and take on the challenges.

To my sisters and brother, who listened tirelessly to me growing up. Now that I'm a bit wiser, I hope I can return the favor.

Thanks to my stepdaughter, Tal, who helps me see equanimity in all things.

To my loving husband, Sasha—soulmate, advisor, and technical guru—thank you for your unselfish support and guidance in making this book a reality.

And, finally, to my loyal friend and canine companion of thirteen years, Spud, who was the best listener a person could have. Spuddy, this book is for you.

Introduction

Welcome to the Age of Distraction! Never before has it been more difficult to get through an average day and feel a sense of accomplishment. According to Kirsten Downey Grimsely ("Message Overload Taking Toll on Workers," *The Washington Post*, May 20,1998), the average worker is interrupted six times every hour. David Shenk, author of *Data Smog* and *Why You Feel the Way You Do,* reports that Americans were exposed to six times as many advertising messages in 1991 as they were in 1971. Shenk claims, "Information overload has replaced information scarcity as an important new emotional, social, and political problem."

Unless we can arrange to live in a cave, there isn't much we can do to eliminate external distractions. In all fairness to the information explosion, it's exciting and convenient to have massive amounts of data accessible with a few keystrokes, and very educational to watch many of the cable TV channels. It's not just the noisy environments, megachoices at the mall, multitasking, information overload, or the intrepid remote control that challenge our ability to listen. It is the internal distractions that threaten our very existence and hopes for a better world—obsession with time, greed for speed and stuff, prejudice and aversion towards people and change, self-consciousness, ego gratification, negative self-talk, extreme preferences, dwelling in the past while obsessing about the future, and working so hard to sustain these beliefs. These are the delusions that endanger our ability to connect with each other, understand each other, and live in harmony.

The noise and distraction brought on by media hype and technology pale in comparison to our internal noise levels. If we could hardwire a speaker system to the brains of people we come in contact with every day, particularly as they try to listen to us, we'd be shocked at the blare of noise, chaos, and negative overtones of the signals emanating from their minds—critical judgments, visual evaluations, self-conscious comments, thoughts of the past or future, and fears of certain topics. Chances are, we might not want to be around a person who thinks such things about us and themselves.

One of the main reasons we listen poorly is because our internal noise levels are so turbulent and obtrusive that they mask most of what others are saying. Only bits and pieces of their message survive the barrage of our mental interference. Just as we have learned to manage external interference by tuning out, it has become somewhat of a challenge to tune in deeply enough to the messages we *need* to listen to—those of family, coworkers, and customers. Misunderstanding, not being heard, and missing key information due to poor listening are at the crux of societal ills. Traditional approaches to listening improvement are usually ineffective because they come from a point of view of altering surface features instead of reshaping the foundation. If we are to end the suffering associated with not listening, we need to dig deeper to get to the source so change can take place.

Many self-help books on personal relationships, negotiation, sales, and customer service tell us that good listening is essential to success in our personal and professional lives, but they do not explain *how* to listen. The available how-to approaches to better listening give you lists of new ways to behave, as if by magic you master techniques and stick with them. Just like after most self-improvement courses, you may try to force new behaviors for a few days, but gradually, because there is no foundation for these changes, your old tendencies to tune people out and repeat mistakes creep back.

Before you spend more time and money on more self-improvement endeavors, ask yourself what it is you hope to gain from reading this book. Here are some realistic expectations:

1) You can expect to start making some changes today in your ability to listen, changes that will outlive the most determined New Year's resolution and that will permeate other aspects of your life that need improvement.

2) You'll find out why, without heavy analysis, you have trouble communicating in some situations, and what you can do about it.

3) You'll find that these changes in the way you listen also *benefit others*.

This sounds like a tall order, but these expectations are not unreasonable. You hold in your hands *The Zen of Listening*, your thoughtful and practical guide to transforming your ability to listen.

I came to write this book for many reasons, and there was an interresting chain of events that led to my discovery of a mind-body link important in enhancing the ability to listen. I must mention here that most of the names of people whose stories I share in this book have been changed for purposes of confidentiality. Others have allowed me to share their identities with you. These people seemed to appear magically in my life as a way of teaching me the true meaning of listening.

As a speech/language pathologist for twenty years, I worked with adults with impaired ability to communicate due to stroke, head/neck cancer, head injuries, or degenerative diseases. I believed that in

3

order to consider myself a *communication specialist*, I would need to continually sharpen my communication skills. Therefore, I took every opportunity to enroll in workshops on listening and speaking. Since these were the same expensive communication classes being taught to companies and large corporations, I figured they had to be effective. To my dismay, all of the listening classes stressed only the *mechanics* of good listening, so as a conscientious student, I amassed a list of ideas in order to *behave* like a better listener. Whether I was truly listening was debatable. My fellow students also concluded these workshops feeling much the same way I did. As much as we took notes and role played good listening, few of us left the classes thinking that the experience had changed in any meaningful way our ability to listen. My desire to find a more effective way to get people to listen better to each other coincided with a string of events that suggested a possible solution.

At the hospital where I worked, managed care began placing severe restrictions on time spent with patients in order to drive down the cost of health care. For example, if you had a stroke, you would be granted a sixty-day therapy period in which to regain your ability to communicate. In addition, there were pressures to see more patients per day, and that meant more paperwork.

On the plus side, these measures forced me to take a closer look at how I could bring about progress in a shorter period of time with fewer resources. It was a challenge to my flexibility to find a way to keep quality in my work while meeting the economic goals of the hospital.

However, most of my colleagues and I were not eager to embrace a strategy that treated patients as mere statistics. In addition, patients began to feel alienated from their physicians. Could they trust someone who was paid to limit their care? And, from the physicians' point of view (most of whom were schooled in a nonmanaged-care philosophy), what could be considered adequate medical care? The fallout from this necessary evil was disgruntled, sicker patients, stressed-out physicians, and low morale among hospital personnel.

Due in large part to these drastic cost-cutting measures, I saw that I was losing my freshness and enthusiasm in treating patients. My cheerleader style had become dulled by the piles of paperwork and the pressure I had to place on my patients to meet their deadlines for recovery. Since saving money was paramount in this new healthcare environment, I was more reluctant to experiment with innovative methods of treatment, and this squelched my creativity. It was more conservative to stick with what methods usually worked and call it a day. I could sense that my responses were becoming more predictable, and after listening to a tape of myself working with a patient, I discovered that I was lapsing into a robotic response mode. As a means of conserving energy for my other job responsibilities, I found it easier to slot individuals based on age, background, and diagnosis. Aside from the few persons who did not conveniently fit these slots—those who presented some challenges for me—my satisfaction with my work life, once spectacular, had degenerated to merely fair.

Diligent efforts to keep up with the current research in my field and to apply occasional and less costly advances provided periodic sparks. Yet overall I felt frustrated, stagnant, and less fulfilled at the end of a workweek. This exposed an inflexible and self-absorbed side of me. That side fought to survive amid signals that change to a simpler path was imminent.

By my late thirties, I was starting to show the classic signs of burnout. Even my relationships with family were suffering. External amusements such as trendy activities, shopping, money-making endeavors, and competitive sports with the objective of winning became appealing to me. I had become vulnerable to impulsivity, excessive goal setting, accumulation of material things, competitiveness in sports, and advising my siblings instead of just being a good sister—attitudes and behaviors that disconnected me from myself and others. Despite all these self-inflating intentions, there I lay exhausted and unfulfilled after a day of trying to make myself a better person.

Seeking out new career opportunities held promise as a cure for my general malaise, but I had reservations. As many of you have already experienced, financial constraints tempered my impulse to make drastic changes. Instead, my intuition advised me to take a deeper look into myself and the way I related to others before abandoning a life's work for which my talent and personality were well suited. A major rethinking was necessary. I decided that it was worth going on a personal archeological dig to figure out what to do about my situation.

When I was a college student in the seventies, Transcendental Meditation had become a vehicle of self-discovery and a discipline that brought welcome clarity to eighteen credit hours of graduate work and two part-time jobs. Now, once again I began daily meditation. This enabled me to calm my mind and identify the inner obstacles that kept me from working *with* the system instead of against it.

During this renewal phase, I met my husband, Sasha. Aside from his job as a computer engineer, he was a third-degree black-belt martial arts instructor. Watching him, his students, and other instructors practicing various martial arts, I was mesmerized by their concentration and physical control. I admired their balanced state of mind and lack of self-consciousness in daily situations. These people were not monks or part of some spiritual cult, nor was their discipline violent or destructive. They were regular people, who owned businesses or were leaders in their communities. They too faced the same threats of layoff, crazy work schedules, and limited budgets, yet they were at peace with change and used their resources to find creative solutions.

After getting to know these people better, I asked myself, *Is the physical exertion of karate or kung fu the source of this concentration and serenity of spirit? Or is it the focus on quality of movement that improves the ability to attend completely and joyfully to the task at hand?* I believed it was the latter, since I had also observed this mind-body balance in artists, musicians, surgeons, and athletes. While painting, playing, dissecting, or diving, they were all willfully caught in the *flow* of their activities.

Looking back over the years, I recalled several such exhilarating periods of concentrated energy prior to my current burnout period. Many were memorable listening situations. I remember in college being totally absorbed physically and mentally in certain lectures, during medical rounds in my hospital training, or while being critiqued by someone whose opinion I highly valued. I recalled these moments of physical and mental readiness as a relaxed, balanced state, a connectedness between my mind and body. My next question was, *What if this zeal for quality and depth of concentration could be applied to one of our greatest needs, a gift so little used and so often taken for granted—the ability to listen?*

In my search to regain and perpetuate this feeling of connectedness, I enrolled in a martial arts class and studied everything I could find about the mind-body relationship. By getting to know myself painfully through the eyes of my instructors, my reasons for becoming disconnected from my world were made clear. I decided to start over fresh, not by focusing on the results or the outcome of my actions, but with the prospect of being in the moment and discovering the quality in every interaction.

I started to apply this new awareness to what occupied the bulk of my day—*my work as a therapist.* First, during this period of self-awareness, I noticed that when I interacted with patients and coworkers, I became distracted by my own agenda. Assumptions and periods of selective listening led me to miss valuable information. I had become closed within the walls of my routine protocols. In my eagerness to treat the patient, I found myself lecturing patients and their families much too often and asking way too many questions. If they did not comply with my recommendations or the advice of their physicians, I judged them quickly, dismissing their reasons for not following through. I could see how much time was wasted in rein-forcing practice, re-explaining, and revising treatment plans. What was at the heart of all this redoing? By not fully listening to the pa-tient or to my own spoken words, I was actually making more work for myself and stalling progress.

Because of my egocentric way of trying to help my patients, it was no wonder why I and so many others left the office exhausted and frustrated most days. I remembered the words of a favorite pro-fessor in graduate school that pointed to the importance of listening in a learning situation: "If you do not get to know where that patient is coming from (his background, expectations, etc.) you cannot un-derstand him, and he will not trust your advice."

Little did I guess that my next step toward enlightenment would come from a patient. Just as I was leaving work one day, a weary sixty-nine-year-old man, looking older than his age, stopped me as I closed my office door. He said effortfully, with a tight, twisted face, that he didn't have an appointment, but that he wanted to ask a question. "Sure," I said and brought him into my office. He awk-wardly introduced himself as Mr. Hennman; he already knew my name. Mr. Hennman sat down on the edge of his seat, visibly tired from seeing many other specialists that day. At that moment, I had a strange sense that this was not going to be a typical patient visit.

Mr. Hennman told me about his many medical problems and his difficulties expressing himself to others. He hoped that in coming to a communication specialist, I would "just listen." I was somewhat taken aback by his request. After all, wasn't that what I always did ? I put down my briefcase and jacket, sat with my hands on my lap, and looked Mr. Hennman in the eye. He spoke hesitantly, stuttering, looking away at first, and told me how the doctors put so much emphasis on his medical problems, but failed to ask him about *his* main concern, which was his speech. Because he found doctors intimidating (he sensed they were uncomfortable talking with him due to his stutter), he routinely answered in as few words as possible. It took so long to utter a sentence that his doctors often completed his sentences or interrupted him. Mr. Hennman was convinced that his years of indigestion and sleeping problems were in part due to his anxiety about communicating.

Mr. Hennman had a sixth-grade education, had never married, and had worked alone for forty-seven years as a metalsmith. He felt that now it was time to start living his life and learn how to interact with others despite his stutter. Interestingly, as I listened to his story, his speech gradually became less effortful with only an occasional word or sound repetition. His facial contortions eased. He appeared relieved and shocked at the same time as he realized that he had finally been able to express himself fully. Even though Mr. Hennman spoke for only about fifteen minutes, I felt as though I had been swept up in his life and in his remarkable transformation, even if it was only temporary. Now, as if by magic, I was back in my chair. Mr. Hennman thanked me profusely for listening. He felt he would be able to sleep well for once, because someone had taken the time to see his view of things. You can imagine how well I slept that night!

Several days later Mr. Hennman's physician, a doctor from another facility, phoned me and reported that his patient's overall condition had improved considerably following his visit with me. The doctor asked what I had done after years of unsuccessful treatment by his staff. I told him I had done nothing but listen. For the first time, I heard someone blush over the phone.

Mr. Hennman and others like him inspire me daily to extend this experience to others, to study it and teach it. I have had the pleasure of working with many physicians who have taught me the true meaning of the expression "bedside manner." With other doctors, however, I have seen how failure to listen to the patient adversely affects the accuracy of the diagnosis and subsequent treatment. Too often the patient is not given a chance to mention what's on his mind, to share his insight into his health problem. Just as often, due to various communication barriers, a patient does not understand his doctor's explanation of his illness.

Not only good medical practice, but *any* successful business requires optimal listening on both sides of the table. In all industries and, most importantly, in the home, a good bedside manner is the best medicine for solving disputes and getting along with others. Whether we are salespeople, parents, or provide some service, people come to us in need. Quite often they require assistance or are in distress, very much like someone who is ill or dying. They look to trust us in the same way that a patient looks to trust the judgment of a physician. We can all benefit from improving our bedside manner. It does not necessarily mean taking more time, but rather more *willingness to see a situation through the eyes of the speaker.* How can we achieve a positive outcome with each person we come in contact with if our scope is narrowed by self-interest?

My experience as a speech pathologist and my study of psychology, communication disorders, religion, and Eastern philosophy have produced a mindset for listening that I am pleased to share with my students. Judging from their responses, these ideas have been instrumental in shaping their attitudes towards others and their ability to understand and remember what they hear. Most students claim they are happier and more satisfied in their work and family relationships.

From a spiritual and social point of view, listening can be a powerful tool of change. Schoolteachers and counselors, prior to taking my listening class, report their jobs are getting more stressful because they cannot handle the listening needs of their students and clients. If children are not heard by their parents, if their emotional concerns are not taken seriously, they become behavioral problems at home and in the classroom. Hours of TV and video games splinter whatever remains of attention and concentration for schoolwork, and grades suffer. A lack of proper listening role models may lead to frustration, violent outbursts, and loss of self-control. Poor self-esteem cultivated over time leads to substandard performance in the workplace and unhappy family relationships as the ravages of poor listening are handed down to the next generation.

When a person is given a chance to tell his views without the threat of judgment or advice, even if his listener does not agree, that is the first step toward creating good feelings. A sense of openness on both sides allows for discussion and problem solving. Self-esteem grows from the respect that comes from being heard. People are better able to attend to school lessons, projects, and the responsibilities of the workplace when basic emotional needs, like being understood, have been met. Henry David Thoreau said, "The greatest compliment that was ever paid to me was when someone asked me what I thought, and attended to my answer." When confidence grows, we are better able to discover our potential and positively influence others. Mindful listening has the power to change the direction of our lives and those we come in contact with every day.

Listening is also a healthy activity. Studies show that when we listen, heart rate and oxygen consumption are reduced and blood pressure decreases. Contact with others promotes well-being and self-expression, both necessary for good physical health. By being good listeners, therefore, we promote the good health of others by allowing them to reduce their stress and empowering them to solve their own dilemmas. An empathetic listener provides helpful feedback that makes the speaker feel valued. This is a significant gift in a world where the human touch is a rare commodity.

Many of us would like to see an end to discrimination of all kinds, happier families, and a safer, more harmonious future for our children. But how can we as individuals make a difference? We can begin by learning to listen in a *mindful* way. Listening is the first step in making people feel valued. Mindful listening allows us to do more than take in people's words; it helps us better understand the how and why of their views. When understanding occurs, a sense of calm is achieved on both sides, even if no point of agreement is reached. From understanding, respect and trust for one another are possible; we are free to open our minds and widen the scope of potential solutions. Listening is also the first step in any negotiation, whether it means getting your teenager to clean the garage or arranging a cease-fire in the Middle East.

On New Year's Eve 1999, Larry King, on his nightly TV talk show, invited eminent spiritual leaders to share their hopes for the Third Millennium. The Dalai Lama looks to the twenty-first century as the "century of dialogue." Evangelist Billy Graham claims that "world peace can come only from the human heart. Something has to happen inside of man to *change our attitude.*"

How do we start changing our attitudes? By listening in a mindful way and becoming aware of what habits we can change today and what habits need to change over time. Sometimes all it takes is someone or something to come our way to make us stop and think about the need to be heard. By taking the ideas in this book to heart, not only will you accomplish more through communicating effectively, but you can begin to make a daily personal contribution to world peace.

Creating a Mindset for Good Listening

If every time we met with someone and
gave them our full and complete attention
for four minutes come hell or high water,
it could change our lives.

—Leonard and Natalie Zunin,
The First Four Minutes

*O*ur goal in becoming mindful listeners is to quiet the internal noise to allow the whole message and the messenger to be understood. In addition, when we listen mindfully to others, we help quiet down *their* internal noise. When they notice that we are totally with them, people feel freer to cut out the layers of pretense to say what's really on their minds. As you read on, you will see mindful listening is a gift not only to yourself, but to others.

It is maddening to think of the knowledge that went in one ear and out the other, the relationships that went sour, or the opportunities missed because we were not better listeners. Over the decades our ability to talk has dramatically surpassed our ability to *listen* to one another. We can easily give someone a piece of our mind, but we have much difficulty taking in another's point of view. We can talk for hours on a given subject, but most of us can retain only a small fraction of a professor's lecture. Research shows that at least 40 percent of our waking hours are spent listening. Within a few minutes following a discussion, the average listener is able to recall only 25 percent or less of what he heard. As the day goes on, even that percentage diminishes considerably.

In the corporate world, poor listening is responsible for the loss of billions of dollars due to unnecessary mistakes, lost opportunities, and minimal effectiveness. Faulty listening is often responsible for the letter that needs to be retyped time and again, the team that cannot produce results, or the physician who faces a malpractice suit. In our personal lives, low self-esteem, divorce, or family conflicts can be attributed to poor listening skills. If the need to listen better continues to be a recurrent theme in your work and home life, then this book is for you!

The mindful-listening approach is a mindset for connecting with people and information that stands up to the challenges of communicating in the twenty-first century. Look what you can gain:

- more fulfilling family, social, and professional relationships
- increased attention span
- better performance at interviews
- more cooperation from others
- improved productivity
- effective teamwork
- higher grades
- stronger knowledge base

- improved self-confidence

- better negotiation skills

Chances are, you have chosen this book because quick-fix attempts at achieving these personal and professional goals have been unsuccessful. Perhaps someone chose this book *for* you! Some of the students in my listening classes sign up, not because *their* listening skills are poor, but because they live or deal regularly with very poor listeners. The reasoning is, if these poor listeners won't change, maybe *they* can learn ways to get through to them. Even if only one party is at fault, both the poor listener *and* the speaker suffer, as do the managers *and* employees, husbands *and* wives, parents *and* children. In this book you will learn some ways in which you can be a good example for the other half. If indeed *you* are the one taking responsibility for improving a relationship by learning to enhance your listening skills, perhaps that incorrigible other may start to sense your desire to understand him better. Exercising fair listening encourages others to give us a turn at presenting our point of view. Often, by being better listeners ourselves, we can accomplish much more than by trying to change others.

Poor listening gets in the way of getting things done effectively. We are frantic to maximize our effectiveness in our daily must-do activities. It is important to spend time with our families, stay in shape, and be productive at work. But instead of achieving fulfillment through these endeavors, frequently just the opposite occurs. Many of us become disconnected from family, friends, and customers. The contradictions abound foremost in the workplace. Company downsizing has forced us to see our customers as mere statistics—a sales call, a medical procedure, a drop-in. "Customer satisfaction is our number one priority," says the boss, "but don't forget to keep the numbers up, be a team player, and maintain quality!" Reconciling these seemingly disparate demands is within your grasp!

It is by unleashing our powers of mindful listening that we can reconnect with others and be efficient as well. By changing our mindset toward listening, every interaction becomes a memorable one, each day an adventure. Best of all, by using our listening abilities to their fullest, we can set an example for others, particularly our children. Think about how much richer their lives will be if they learn the art of mindful listening when they're young. Many of us were conditioned to think that listening is a passive process, that it is the wiser person who does the talking.

Many learning specialists agree that a great number of children with learning disabilities have not been given adequate examples of good listening in the home. In 1995, the Carnegie Council on Adolescent Development completed a ten-year study that indicated that children are not getting enough interaction with parents or other adults. How can we expect our children to learn when we haven't taught them how to listen? The emphasis on computerized learning has been a boon to education in some respects. However, because of children's overexposure to fast-paced media (TV, video games, and computers) that reduce attention, listening, and concentration skills, educators are finding children more difficult to teach. One of the many challenges facing today's teachers is having to modify their teaching strategies to blend computer use with verbal interaction. Without a balanced approach, children may lose out on the development of interpersonal skills necessary to be successful in life. The personal interactions with teachers and other mentors throughout the years provide the groundwork for learning how to get along with adults other than our parents. In the classroom, students learn the give and take necessary to make and keep friends, how to successfully team up on projects—in short, *how to get along with others.* To allow technology to intrude upon that valuable education only furthers the growing trend of disconnectedness.

Growing up in the fifties and sixties, dinner-table talk was a staple activity in middle-class America. TV shows like *Father Knows Best* and *Leave It to Beaver* showed parents setting the stage for discussion about typical adolescent issues like peer pressures at school or jealousy between siblings. They showed children stating their feelings while parents listened with concern (they actually stopped eating!). The point was to illustrate how dinner-table discussions offered a family forum for character building. These forums addressed feelings and possible solutions—everyone participated. Of course, by the end of the program, everyone's problems were solved and all were happy again. The moral of these shows was to offer opportunities for caring discussion and put out the little fires before they get out of control.

Could schoolyard and family violence be mitigated by better listening? Researchers at the University of Minnesota and the University of North Carolina found that a parent's presence in the home at dinnertime was associated with a reduced incidence of drug use, sex, violence, and emotional distress among teens. Could we ever have imagined the Beaver getting to the point where he finds a gun and shoots Eddie for not giving him a ride in his new sports car?

Unlike most families on TV at that time, both my parents worked full time and all of my siblings were involved in extracurricular activities very much like families of today. My parents' friends would have labeled us a type-A family back in those days. Yet somehow my parents saw to it that every night the family sat down together for dinner for at least thirty minutes. Some of my family members came and went according to their schedules, but everybody got in on at least one topic of discussion or shared one event of the day with two or more family members. There, we developed our verbal and reasoning skills, learned how to argue a point, build ideas as a team, speak openly about our strengths and weaknesses, and listen. Now that we are all on our own, I believe that our lives were shaped by the magic that transpired around that table every night at six o'clock.

Many of us feel that if we do most of the talking, we will be perceived as knowledgeable and dynamic. Yet the communication situations we avoid are those in which one person, oblivious to the realities of others, does all the talking. A good listener is easy to spot—he is usually someone we look forward to talking with and being around. A good listener is not only one who processes the spoken word and the meaning behind the words accurately, but one who makes the speaker feel valued by encouraging him to expand on his ideas and feelings. A good listener touches the lives of those to whom he listens.

TV interviewers like Barbara Walters, Charlie Rose, Oprah Winfrey, and Larry King are examples of good listeners. It was said that Ernest Hemingway had a way of listening with such intensity that the person doing the speaking felt supremely complimented. Listening intently even for a minute is one of the nicest gifts we can give to another human being.

The lack of *self-listening* is often the cause of communication breakdown. If we could hear our words and comments through the ears of our listeners, we would be appalled at the overgeneralizations, the inaccuracies, and the insensitive, negative comments we make about ourselves and others. Learning to carefully select our words plays a major role in presenting ourselves in a favorable light, getting along well with others, and effectively getting the job done. When we make self-deprecating remarks about our looks, intelligence, or competence, we reveal an unhealthy mindset, chip away at our self-confidence, and create the wrong impressions, setting the stage for us not to be taken seriously.

We need to listen to ourselves to be sure we choose words that truly represent our meaning. Are our explanations concise and to the point? We may use words or a tone of voice that offend or turn people off to our message. These destructive communication behaviors push the listener's limits and discourage hopes of future interaction. No wonder we become confused and annoyed with others when they don't respond according to our expectations. The listening mindset you are about to develop will also enable you to better tune into yourself and what motivates you to act the way you do.

Listening abilities are put to the test in adverse conditions. Stressful interactions may include asking for directions, a first date, or an important interview. The stress factor increases when we must deal with hostile customers or coworkers. Further escalation of emotions ensues with an overly assertive personality or a potentially violent one. When ideas and points of view collide, how well do we process the whole message without building up our defenses? A list of tricks will not assist us when listening under stress. Our success in these situations depends on the strength of our foundation as listeners—this includes breath control, ability to concentrate, and awareness of our barriers to listening and how we work with them, among other factors. Knowing how to listen well in less than optimal conditions is a valuable and necessary survival skill.

In order to reap the benefits of listening, we must let ourselves develop and expand our ability to concentrate. We should be able to sustain our focus for several minutes or as long as we choose, depending on the nature of the listening task. If the topic of conversation is light and familiar, concentration is much easier to sustain than if the material presented is dry and technical. Intent and interest in the subject matter also play a role in our willingness to concentrate. Stress, depression, and self-doubt have the potential to cripple our ability to attend to, much less concentrate on what someone is saying.

Many of my students in their forties or fifties take my listening course because they feel they are starting to lose their memories; they forget names, lose concentration, or miss details. Because of this concern, they are hesitant to take on new challenges like learning to use a computer or obtaining advanced degrees. In most cases, they are not on the verge of dementia. Rather, they have lost touch with the ability to focus for long periods of time. Other students wonder whether they have ADD (attention deficit disorder). These difficulties with concentration can affect our confidence for learning new tasks. The relationship between listening and memory is complex and beyond the scope of this book. However, a basic understanding of this relationship will better motivate us to apply some of the upcoming strategies.

Memory comprises three basic processes: encoding, storage, and retrieval. Encoding requires us to pay attention. During the encoding process, sensory information (words, pictures, music, etc.) is perceived. This information enters our *sensory memory*, where it is held for about one second. (Think of sensory memory as surface memory.) If we choose to further preserve this bit of information—directions to a new restaurant, for example—we need to take it to the next level of processing called *short-term memory* (STM). For the direction "left on Lehman and right on Hathaway" to enter STM, we need to repeat or rehearse it aloud to ourselves for about fifteen seconds. Our STM is able to hold on to plus or minus seven bits of information at a time, equal to the average phone number. If we want to retain these directions for use again in the future, we need to take this direction to a even deeper level of memory called *long-term memory* (LTM). There are various methods for the transfer of information to LTM. Drawing a map, picturing familiar landmarks (the Dunkin' Donuts will be on your right), or associating the street names with the names of familiar people, among other methods, can move those directions into long-term storage.

If we choose to *remember* or deeply process a phone number and put it in long-term memory, it may be necessary to make associations with other familiar numerical sequences. Do the four digits in a particular phone number (222-1812) remind us of an important year (the War of 1812), or is the pattern a visual one like 1-800-8008? Linking the memory of the interaction with the phone number is often helpful. If the discussion with this particular individual was a stormy one, then 1812 is a natural link. The process of associating new information with prior knowledge enables us to retrieve that information months or years later. We do not have to spend a lot of time to efficiently encode, store, and retrieve information (processing the directions to the restaurant from sensory memory to LTM took fewer than sixty seconds), but you must be able to concentrate.

Concentration is like a river. The stimulus or object of our attention may trickle into consciousness. Our interest heightens and other ideas (associations) enter our minds, similar to a stream fed by other streams. Unflustered by the obstacles in its path, the larger stream picks up strength and speed just as our enthusiasm hones our focus on the topic. As the stream becomes a river, the mind remains focused on the development of the thought or idea. That mental energy can be as powerful and sustaining as the undercurrent of a raging river. When someone speaks we can ignore the message, simply skim the surface, or follow the way of the river and concentrate.

The reality is that television, with its frequent commercial breaks, numerous choices (no thanks to the remote control), open-door policies, and our hectic, multifaceted lifestyles, has shortened our attention span and limited our opportunities for concentration. Fortunately, since most of our brains are still intact, it is possible to regain (or for many of us, uncover for the first time) the ability to focus our attention, concentrate, and restore confidence in our ability to learn.

I do not suggest that effective listening is a form of acting or a technique to be learned. On the contrary, we innately possess the ability to concentrate on verbal messages and deeply process information. Listening is one of our greatest personal natural resources, yet it is by far one of our most undeveloped abilities. Our education has emphasized speaking, reading, and writing, yet the activity that takes up a big hunk of our day—listening—is the one for which we receive the least training.

This book does not approach listening as a technique or group of skills to be learned. I even resist the phrase *active listening*. If we get hung up on a laundry list of listening to-dos, we can miss the speaker's message altogether. We do not need to manipulate our speakers by acting like we are listening, nor do we want to have to work at having a conversation. That is fake listening. Instead, let's take a look at what happens when our natural ability to listen catches us off guard.

Think of situations when you were particularly interested in a topic or when you were startled by an alarming news broadcast, say the Kennedy assassination or the Oklahoma City bombing. Many of us can recall experiencing the tragic thrill of being completely absorbed with the spoken words; we might even be able to recall where we were at the time or what we were doing. No skill set or technique came to mind as to how to listen—our inborn, *listening reflex* kicked in. But how can we achieve and maintain a similar level of absorption during everyday conversation, at a lecture, or during a heated discussion?

To accomplish this does not require extensive course work. It does require a change in our mindset toward listening. It begins by opening our minds to accept the notion that any verbal encounter could contain a golden nugget of experience, information, or insight, quite often when we least expect it.

Sometimes, the greatest insight of my day comes from the person who cleans my office. The commitment to a change in attitude or mindset toward listening allows our innate listening abilities kick in. This leads to a change in behavior. People's positive reactions toward us and our improved efficiency will perpetuate our new listening outlook!

Mindful listening is presented here as a synergy of three factors—*relaxation, focus,* and a *desire to learn* or gain another's perspective. This mindset involves becoming aware of the barriers we have built toward others, our inner obstacles, and how to put them aside. For every tiny change we make each day in our listening the rewards are tenfold. My students report feeling more positive about themselves and their relationships. They notice how their business interactions are more successful, and they feel more fulfilled at day's end.

Most of the ideas expressed in this book have roots in Eastern philosophy and Zen Buddhism, yet they are not intended to convey or conflict with any religious point of view, nor are these approaches mystical or occult. Contrary to what some people think about Zen and Buddhism—that these concepts are strictly contemplative and intellectual—the philosophy and mindset presented in this book are very practical and easily understood. The Zen Buddhist philosophy gives us ways of dealing with everyday challenges. It teaches us how focus, concentration, and compassion keep our everyday lives healthy, peaceful, and productive. Zen is a process of undoing rote behaviors rather than learning new ones. Zen helps to dissolve the habits destructive to effective communication—prejudice, negativism, closed-mindedness, and preoccupation with the self—and cultivate their opposites. I do not profess to be an expert in Eastern thought, nor have I attained enlightenment. Nevertheless, what I have studied and applied assists me with many of life's challenges. Listening effectively is one of those challenges. My students, patients, and I have found that these simple concepts have the power to transform the average listening situation into an opportunity for self-development and relationship building.

We may look at Zen Buddhism as a psychology or philosophy about life. Listening with the heart, body, and mind requires a change in our attitude toward how we relate to the speaker. It involves focusing on the *process* of listening versus the *payoff.* The Zen approach to listening offers us insight into our true nature, or *kensho*. This heightened awareness frees us from the confinement of self-interest and self-consciousness that bars us from connecting with the minds of others.

The origins of Zen Buddhism go back about twenty-five hundred years to northern India, when Gautama Siddhartha, a humble prince, left his cushy life to better understand the nature of existence. He lived like a beggar and watched the suffering brought on by old age, famine, and loneliness. After meditating for six years, he became enlightened to the truth of existence and became known as the Buddha—the Awakened One. Buddhism took two directions after the death of Gautama Buddha, the Theravada tradition that spread to southwest Asia, and the Mahayana tradition that mingled with Taoism in China and then spread to Japan where it was called Zen. The Mahayana way emphasized spiritual development and meditation as the vehicle to awakening to the true reality of life. Both branches of Buddhism share many of the same beliefs, but Zen Buddhism is known for its simple and straightforward application to everyday life. Gautama Buddha realized that discontent in life is the result of attachment to things and the way we think things should be. Nonsentient, or unenlightened human beings (most of us, that is) are distracted to the point of being deluded by egocentric thinking, self-consciousness, yearning for what we don't have, and wishing we were somewhere else. The torment in our lives is brought about by working so hard to be separate from everyone else. Therefore, we continually grasp for status, material possessions, speed, and extraneous preoccupations to be one up against the competition—our neighbors. These attempts to work against ourselves and others serve only to bring on more distress in the form of anxiety, illness, depression, and other more serious tragedies in our society.

These are exactly the reasons why poor listeners make life so much more difficult for themselves. They crave attention as the speaker, think about what to say next while others are still talking, interrupt to take control of the conversation, hold fast to opinions, constantly dwell on the past or dream about the future, and other self-defeating behaviors. The purpose of *The Zen of Listening* is to help you reverse these trends so as to make your life and the lives of those around you more satisfying and effective. Also, by exercising mindful listening a little bit every day, others will start to respond to you more favorably, even difficult people.

The distractions and human concerns of the twenty-first century require mindful listening more than ever before. If we want to put an end to prejudice, racism, conflict, and suffering it won't happen with a just-do-it attitude or an active-listening approach. As long as we think about trying to listen, we will not be able to hear clearly. Altering our mental foundation for better listening must come first. It is like giving a beggar a cookbook and saying, "Here, enjoy your meal!" He has no heat, no pots and pans, no cooking skills, just the will to eat but little means to accomplish it. He might also lack the vigilance and patience to cook the food correctly. However, once he is given the basic necessities, sees the value in being able to cook, and gets some practice at it, the cookbook will serve him well. Eventually he will be able to cook without the book, as long as he cooks a little bit every day. Despite the fact that many of the listening discoveries that I describe in this book are derived from my experience as a speech therapist in a medical setting, they have universal application. The methods I propose have been tried and tested not only by hundreds of my workshop participants in the last few years, but for centuries by scientists, Zen masters, and their students. Over 90 percent of my students have found at least one of the strategies for attaining mindful listening key to making their lives happier and more productive. The success of mindful listening is due to its simplicity and applicability to everyday life.

Just as each reader sees life from a different angle, different approaches to mindful listening are presented here. We all have different listening needs and concerns. Some of us take classes or read books about listening in hopes of improving our interpersonal or marital relationships; others, because we want to do better in school. Some of us seek new careers or look for ways to improve ourselves or make happier customers. Therefore, I have approached the subject of listening from a few different angles. One main theme supports them all: the best listeners see listening as a process rather than a goal.

You may find a few chapters key to your ability to listen better, or you may need to spend more time on the reflection and relaxation sections before you can apply some of the other ideas. Read through each chapter thoughtfully. Once you have digested these thoughts, take a few days or weeks to apply the exercises at the end of each chapter. The rewards of good listening will happen without working for them. Judging from the comments and letters I have received from former students, this approach to listening has been very helpful.

Make your new behaviors habits by using the buddy system or creating visual reminders in your home or office. Once you have established a new awareness in your daily routine, notice how you become more attentive to people and things. Move on to the next chapter and incorporate another step. At the end of each day reflect for a few moments on how well you did, how differently and positively people responded to you, or how much more information you were able to recall.

Using this cumulative approach of reflection and application, you will, by the time you are finished with this book, have abandoned any narrow and self-limiting views about listening. You will be free to experience the vast richness of each person you meet and be able to absorb the wealth of knowledge and opportunity that exists with every waking breath.

Chapter Two

How Well Are You Listening Now?

Why not go out on a limb?
That's where the fruit is.

—Will Rogers

How tiresome it is to leave a performance review with the comment written in bold print: **"Your listening skills need work."** It is a déjà vu experience for many of us, one that we can easily recall from numerous early sources: our parents, scout leaders, coaches, and teachers. Since our youth these words of wisdom have come in various forms. For example: "Stop talking and pay attention," as if when we stop talking we somehow start paying attention, or more indirectly, "Maybe you should get your hearing checked." When we are told to listen up, what exactly does that mean? How do we know if we are really listening (and paying attention) or just acting like we are? How can we convince others, like the boss, that our listening skills are deserving of a promotion? Would we know a good listener if we met one? How far are we from being considered a good listener?

Self-knowledge is the first step toward self-improvement. Let's take a look at how well you listen today. This pretest will also make you aware of the wide spectrum of listening behaviors we intend to discuss. Carefully consider each question and indicate whether or not you consistently demonstrate each behavior. Then check your responses with the answer key on the next page and total your score.

Do you:

1. Think about what *you* are going to say while the speaker is talking?
❑ Yes, consistently ❑ No, almost never ❑ Sometimes

2. Tune out people who say things you don't agree with or don't want to hear?
❑ Yes, consistently ❑ No, almost never ❑ Sometimes

3. Learn something from each person you meet, even if it is ever so slight?
❑ Yes, consistently ❑ No, almost never ❑ Sometimes

4. Keep eye contact with the person who is speaking?
❑ Yes, consistently ❑ No, almost never ❑ Sometimes

5. Become self-conscious in one-to-one or small group conversations?
❑ Yes, consistently ❑ No, almost never ❑ Sometimes

6. Often interrupt the speaker?
❑ Yes, consistently ❑ No, almost never ❑ Sometimes

7. Fall asleep or daydream during meetings or presentations?
❑ Yes, consistently ❑ No, almost never ❑ Sometimes

8. Restate instructions or messages to be sure you understood correctly?
❑ Yes, consistently ❑ No, almost never ❑ Sometimes

9. Allow the speaker to vent negative feelings towards you without becoming defensive or physically tense?
❑ Yes, consistently ❑ No, almost never ❑ Sometimes

10. Listen for the meaning behind the speaker's words through gestures and facial expressions?
❑ Yes, consistently ❑ No, almost never ❑ Sometimes

11. Feel frustrated or impatient when communicating with persons from other cultures?
❑ Yes, consistently ❑ No, almost never ❑ Sometimes

12. Inquire about the meaning of unfamiliar words or jargon?
❑ Yes, consistently ❑ No, almost never ❑ Sometimes

13. Give the appearance of listening when you are not?
❑ Yes, consistently ❑ No, almost never ❑ Sometimes

14. Listen to the speaker without judging or criticizing ?
❑ Yes, consistently ❑ No, almost never ❑ Sometimes

15. Start giving advice before you are asked?
❏ Yes, consistently ❏ No, almost never ❏ Sometimes

16. Ramble on before getting to the point?
❏ Yes, consistently ❏ No, almost never ❏ Sometimes

17. Take notes when necessary to help you remember?
❏ Yes, consistently ❏ No, almost never ❏ Sometimes

18. Consider the state of the person you are talking to (nervous, rushed, hearing impaired, etc.)?
❏ Yes, consistently ❏ No, almost never ❏ Sometimes

19. Let a speaker's physical appearance or mannerisms distract you from listening?
❏ Yes, consistently ❏ No, almost never ❏ Sometimes

20. Remember a person's name after you have been introduced?
❏ Yes, consistently ❏ No, almost never ❏ Sometimes

21. Assume you know what the speaker is going to say and stop listening?
❏ Yes, consistently ❏ No, almost never ❏ Sometimes

22. Feel uncomfortable allowing silence between you and your conversation partner?
❏ Yes, consistently ❏ No, almost never ❏ Sometimes

23. Ask for feedback to make sure you are getting across to the other person?

❑ Yes, consistently ❑ No, almost never ❑ Sometimes

24. Preface your statements with unflattering remarks about yourself?

❑ Yes, consistently ❑ No, almost never ❑ Sometimes

25. Think more about building warm working relationships with team members and customers than about bringing in revenue?

❑ Yes, consistently ❑ No, almost never ❑ Sometimes

SCORING: Compare your answers with those on the chart below. For every answer that matches the key, give yourself one point. If you answered "Sometimes" to any of the questions, score half a point. Total the number of points.

1 N	6 N	11 N	16 N	21 N
2 N	7 N	12 Y	17 Y	22 N
3 Y	8 Y	13 N	18 Y	23 Y
4 Y	9 Y	14 Y	19 N	24 N
5 N	10 Y	15 N	20 Y	25 Y

Total points: _____

If you scored twenty-one or more points, congratulations! Continue to read on and reinforce what you already are doing well. Note which areas could use further improvement. Are there any listening behaviors that require more consistency? Chapters four, six, and nine will be particularly helpful in strengthening your listening ability. Good listeners can fine-tune listening under stress (chapter nine) and help others listen better.

A score of sixteen to twenty suggests that you usually absorb most of the main ideas, but often miss a good portion of the rest of the message due to difficulties with sustaining attention. You may feel detached from the speaker and start thinking about other things or about what you are going to say next. Students who score at this level frequently comment that rechecking details is often needed. Chapters six and ten will be particularly helpful in this regard. Examine typical response styles (chapter seven) that may prevent you from receiving that extra information.

If you scored between ten and fifteen points, you may be focusing more on your own agenda than the speaker's needs. You easily become distracted and perceive listening as a task. Perhaps personal biases get in the way of fully understanding the speaker. Chapter four will help you work through many of the obstacles that prevent you from receiving the whole message. Pay special attention to chapters five and six, which set the foundation for sustaining your focus on the spoken message. If you find it particularly difficult to process spoken information in stressful listening situations, a few basics from the earlier chapters will help you benefit from the information in chapter nine.

Those of you who scored fewer than nine points will notice the most dramatic improvement in your communication by applying the suggestions given in this book. Most of the time you experience listening as a boring activity. You might complain often that your memory is poor and feel great frustration when trying to retain information from presentations and succeed in a classroom situation.

If you answered "Sometimes" to many of the questions, then obviously you are a sometimes listener. Chances are your ability to concentrate may be at fault and/or you are a highly critical individual and quick to judge whether a listening opportunity is worthwhile. However, there have been times when you have experienced the satisfaction of being fully absorbed in what someone has to say. Imagine how successful and effective you could be if you would let yourself experience that sense of total absorption in every listening opportunity.

Now that we have a taste of some of the ingredients for good listening, let's come up with a good working definition. If you were to poll various individuals and ask what it means to be a good listener, you would hear several versions. Here are some examples. Sales consultant Michael Leppo describes good listening as the ability to hear attentively. Michelle Lucas, a psychotherapist, says that good listening is a process of showing respect and validating a person's worth. The International Listening Association defines listening as "the process of receiving, constructing meaning from, and responding to spoken and/or nonverbal messages." Others say it is simply the ability to understand and remember what was said. Ralph G. Nichols, one of the founding fathers of listening studies, said, "Listening is an inside job—inside action on the part of the listener." This suggests that good listening is the ability to get into the shoes of the speaker in order to see his side of the issue.

As you can see, a practical definition of listening must take into account its many aspects. For the purpose of this book, I will define a good listener as one who is *mindful* of the wide spectrum of listening skills. These include the ability to

- receive the spoken word accurately, interpret the whole message (the words, gestures and facial expressions) in an unbiased manner;

- retain the information for future use;

- sustain attention to the spoken word at will; listening is a process that occurs *over time;*

- attend to *your* speech and be sensitive to the accuracy of the message and the possible interpretations that could be derived from it;

- encourage a speaker to speak from his heart and expound on his or her ideas without censure. This makes your speaker feel valued and respected.

This book teaches you that the real power in communication lies in using your natural ability to listen: to process information, gain insight, and retain information so you can put it to work. Mindful listening is already a part of you. However, it does require a desire to listen. A desire to listen involves a curiosity for new information and a willingness to pay more respect to your speaker. If your desire is to build stronger personal and professional relationships, a degree of compassion is a basic requirement to becoming a better listener.

Mindful listening is the mind and body working together to communicate. Furthermore, it does not require two functioning ears to listen in a mindful way. Mindful listening requires you to see, hear, and feel with your whole being. To attend mindfully to the message, whether the message is spoken or signed, is to perceive as closely as possible the intent and experience of the speaker.

Mindful listening can be applied to the wide continuum of listening types:

- information processing

- information seeking

- critical or evaluative listening

- therapeutic listening

- empathetic or compassionate listening

- small-talk listening

In any given situation there is much overlap between the various kinds of listening. For example, when meeting someone for the first time, small talk may spark a discussion about a shared topic of interest. That may lead one of the partners to relate some controversial information learned on the Internet. The listener may have doubts about the information based on her prior knowledge; a friendly debate on that topic could ensue. Various other combinations may occur depending upon whether the discussion takes place in a classroom, a service center, a bus stop, or a party. In all of these settings, mindful listening is effective.

Now that we have surveyed the vast landscape of good listening, let's begin our journey through the brush and start clearing a path towards realizing our listening goals.

Chapter Three

Awakening Your Sense of Listening

Toto, I don't think we're in Kansas anymore.
—Dorothy, *The Wizard of Oz*

*M*ost of us with good hearing cannot imagine a world of silence, just as those of us with the ability to taste cannot imagine a life of not tasting. Unfortunately, it is when we lose these precious gifts that we realize how we took them for granted. If lost and then found, we savor their presence like never before.

A photo album, thought long gone, reappears beneath a pile of baby clothes and thirty-year-old toys. The sweet-sick smell of slightly molding leather and paper rises as you lift it reverently from its forgotten spot. You open the cover and gaze at the faces looking back at you. Feelings of joy and melancholy make you ache a bit all over. The sticky, dusty edges of the photos catch on your fingers as you turn the pages. Would you have treated that album with the same respect and appreciation if it had been kept on your coffee table day after day? Probably not.

Hearing is the sense that allows you to listen to your world. It is the sense that perceives and discriminates between sounds. Listening is the process of making sense out of these signals and translating them into meaning. The gift of hearing and our magnificent ability to listen are often taken for granted. Our lives change considerably when we develop a hearing problem or lose our acuity for the sound of a bird or a whisper.

A hearing problem can be due to wax, fluid, or infection. It can be noise or drug induced, accompanied by age or damage to the auditory nerves. In many cases it can be treated or assisted. These impediments to listening are often not under our control; they are a function of age or environment. Sometimes this vast array of sounds bombarding our ears is so complex that, in order for us to survive this information overload, we need to exert some control over what we listen to. Listening predicaments arise when

- your self-interest keeps some voices permanently in the background when they should be in the foreground, or

- your attention is so scattered that you have a hard time keeping selected information in the foreground.

Later in the book we will address these listening problems that stem from self-imposed filtering and poor concentration. But before we tackle the problems, let's take a few minutes to explore the wonders of our hearing and listening abilities.

Begin by closing your eyes wherever you are right now. Listen to the different sounds around you. Notice how the textures of the sounds vary. Hear the whir of the overhead fan as it resists the air. Contrast that with the featherlike flutter of a gentle breeze outside your window. Now count the sounds you can perceive all at once—for instance, the ticking of the clock, the car turning the corner, the sound of pouring coffee, and many others.

Do you hear how some sounds are fainter or louder than others? Marvel at your ability to direct your attention to one sound and shift to another at will, remaining well aware of the sounds you have left behind. You have names for all these sounds and have experienced them at different levels. You've tasted some, ridden in others, held some in your hand. Many of these sounds you have judged and categorized according to their desirability. It is a wonder how these sounds have worked their way into your consciousness.

Right now I am sitting in front of my computer, and I can hear several layers of sound around me. If I take a minute to pay attention to this little symphony, it is interesting to note that, while a small part of my brain is processing this auditory information, it is also reminding me that it is about seven-thirty on a Saturday night. I hear the dishwasher on the rinse cycle (the rinse cycle is a higher pitch than the wash cycle). Someone is watching CNN in the living room (the news anchor's voice is very familiar to me), and my dog, Spud, is snoring at my feet in concert with the steady hum emanating from my computer. Occasionally a car drives down the street or the phone rings and interrupts these steady rhythms. If an unusual noise, however soft, would creep into this mosaic of sound, I would question it immediately. A gentle tinkling of the chandelier or a whisper through my window would stand out like an alarm and claim my attention.

All sounds, no matter what their source, are vibrations at various pitches. The vibrations are gathered by the outer ear (those odd-shaped receptacles on either side of our heads) and travel into the middle ear where the sound waves cause the eardrum to vibrate. That in turn causes the three tiny bones in the inner ear, called *ossicles*, to vibrate. The quality, loudness, volume, and resonance differentiate one set of vibrations from another. The light raining sound of my dishwasher contrasts substantially with the wider range of pitches and timbre flowing from my dog's nostrils.

The vibrations move from the middle ear through the snail-shaped, fluid-filled inner ear called the *cochlea*. The microscopic hair cells in the cochlea convert the fluid movement into electrical energy. This energy is transmitted by the hair cells to the hearing or *auditory nerve*. The auditory nerve automatically sends electrical signals to our brains to let us know that a woman versus a man is speaking on TV right now. Women's voices tend to lie within a pitch range of 139 to 1108 Hz while men's voice have a pitch range between 78 and 698 Hz. From the vast catalogue of female characters logged in our memory banks, we can discern which woman is talking by the degree of nasality in her voice, any accent that may be present, and the rhythm and inflection of her words. We can determine the emotion behind the words based on volume, pitch, and rate of speech. We know whether we like her or find her worth listening to.

The words themselves—stock prices, political analyses, sports scores—supply information, but primarily serve to reinforce our hunches about who's talking based on voice characteristics alone. Simultaneously, the brain is also receiving sounds from the dog, the dishwasher, and the street without causing mass confusion, only calm acceptance that, yes, this is a typical Saturday night.

A patient at the clinic, Jane Sokol Shulman, gradually began losing her hearing in elementary school. At age seventeen, she started to notice difficulty hearing the fine differences between speech sounds. Over the next two decades, Jane lost more and more of her hearing. Despite excellent lip-reading skills, she had become dependent on hearing aids while completing her education. By age thirty-seven, Jane could no longer use a telephone, even with the most powerful amplification. At that point, she accepted her deafness and eventually became president of the Boston chapter of the Association of Late-Deafened Adults (ALDA).

Even though Jane had accepted her new life, she still longed for the world of sound. She had learned about a surgical procedure called a cochlear implant and began researching the possibility of restoring some of her hearing. Jane had learned about the mixed results among other latent-deaf persons and was aware of the possibly rigorous rehabilitation period that would follow implantation of the device. But lip-reading was exhausting and it limited her job options. The sense of isolation and exclusion among her hearing friends had become intolerable. In 1997, Jane decided to have the implant procedure.

A few weeks after her surgery I had the opportunity to sit in on one of her rehabilitation sessions. Listening to Jane describe the awakening of her hearing ability had me nailed to my seat. Jane goes on to tell her story:

> So what is it like to hear again? The first word that comes to mind is *weird* and the second one is *miraculous*. . . . The biggest surprise was my auditory acuity. Nothing had prepared me for the shock of hearing soft sounds. Knowing that I could hear footsteps behind me and the chime when I leave my headlights on made me feel safer and more secure. Birds chirping, rain, rustling papers— I became reacquainted with the subliminal sounds that anchor us in the environment. I discovered new sounds, such as the beeps of ATM keys. And I rediscovered how supremely annoying other sounds are, such as laugh tracks on television. . . . I constantly found myself wishing I could focus on developing my new hearing without also having to manage my job, family, and household responsibilities as well. The amazement and wonder were overwhelming at times. I could hear people behind me saying "excuse me." Casual chitchat with strangers was no longer a Herculean effort. I could once again participate in these nonevents that hearing people take for granted, the social glue that holds us together.

A few times over the next several days, try this listening exercise. Even if you are not a music lover, try to listen objectively. Find a concert on the radio and see if you can pick out the different voices, instruments, and harmonies. Try isolating one particular voice or instrument for as many seconds as possible. Then return your attention to the blending of all the instruments and take in the whole piece. Notice how each voice is necessary to carry this performance, but that each voice alone is just a fragment of the whole. Now, without analyzing or dissecting the musical performance, sit for a few minutes and take in the music. Simply be witness to it. When we listen to music in this way, we get a taste of the Zen approach to listening. You are not thinking about the notes that came before the ones you are listening to now, nor are you anticipating the next passage. You are not judging the piece nor worrying about how long it is. You are just absorbing the music with your whole being as the music moves and changes. This is the interval of mental space that needs to be present when listening to another human being. To widen the gap of time between perceiving a message and interpreting its content is the essence of mindful listening.

In Chinese, characters or pictograms communicate ideas and situations. The character for *listening attentively* consists of the characters for Ear, Standing Still, Ten, Eye, and Heart and Mind. According to Zen Master Dae Gak, this pictogram for listening attentively means, "When in stillness, one listens with the heart. The ear is worth ten eyes." When we listen for the whole message, our senses need to be poised and focused, like a deer that freezes its gaze in the direction of a lurking predator.

Wherever you are, listen to how sounds, great and barely perceivable, come from all directions. At all times, a 360-degree vista of sound fills our ears. Ping-pong in the basement, steam from the iron, Bach down the hall, and the sweeping sound of the rowing machine upstairs makes us feel as if we are in a constant bubble of sound. Many noises bring out feelings and emotions more than words. The rustle of falling leaves and birds chirping in the woods spark thoughts about the seasons. The sound of waves is mesmerizing and soothes an unquiet mind. For decades, sounds and their effects on us have been the object of scientific research for the purposes of treating stress-related disorders. It is the process of listening over time to the sound of the loons on a lake or a spring rain that gradually calms our minds. It is not an instantaneous effect, nor would we want those sounds to be fleeting. We prefer to luxuriate for minutes and hours in the call of the seagulls or the pop and sizzle of a crackling hearth. Some say that we can become smarter listening to Mozart.

Even a single sound can release a flood of thoughts and sensations held captive in our memory's lost-and-found. The sound of a marching band in the distance reminds us of the football games and parades we experienced while growing up. The rush of a train overhead recalls commuting to the city for our first job. We all have moments when sound takes us back to another time and place.

Almost against my will, a familiar song from the sixties will sweep me back in time to my school cafeteria along with the mouthwatering smell of the chocolate chip cookies famous at Homewood-Flossmoor high school. The tune of "Hey, Jude" by the Beatles, a frequently played selection on the jukebox around lunch time, is accompanied by feelings of hunger and exhaustion after emerging from gym class across the hall. How strange and powerful is our sense of hearing to be able to transfer our consciousness at lightning speed to another time and place.

Indeed, some sounds are more pleasant than others. But these less melodious noises, like a smoke alarm or a jackhammer, connect with our survival or quality of life. Despite their unpleasing characteristics we are grateful for what they represent, in this case, preventing a fire and mending a broken water main. They draw our attention to issues concerning our well-being. In fact, many sounds are so necessary to our existence that despite their pleasant or unpleasant qualities, we accept them unconditionally. All sounds play a role in balancing our environment; each sound plays a role in the big picture. Can you imagine having equal tolerance for listening to your best friend tell about her new job and your most agitated customer complaining about his late order?

Yet to attend to every sound equally would be chaotic and possibly life-threatening. In our information-rich society the ability to tune into selected auditory information and sustain our attention to it while tuning out background noise is becoming more of a challenge. When we spread our listening too thin, we run the risk of making hasty decisions based on processing only bits and pieces of major issues. On the other hand, if we are too selective with the people or the programs we listen to, we run the risk of becoming so judgmental and critical that we become closed-minded. The goal in listening is to find the balance between focusing our attention and remaining open-minded and tolerant of different views.

The most negative and sometimes heartless forces working against our good intentions to strike that balance are our *mental barriers*. Let's continue along our course of self-discovery to prepare for a close encounter with the enemy.

Chapter Four

The Great Walls of Misunderstanding

May we open to a deeper understanding
And a genuine love and caring
For the multitude of faces
Who are none other than ourself.

—Wendy Egyoku Nakao

*B*arriers are the distractions, prejudices, judgment calls, and preconceived notions about a person and the value of his message. Zen Masters refer to these barriers as *unwholesome mental formations, mental obscurations,* and *ignorance.* They believe that the people who are most unhappy in this world are those with irrational perceptions of people and ideas. Many of us think that the more toys, stocks, and houses we accumulate, the happier and more serene we will be. Some of us strive to identify with prestigious people and hang out at the right clubs in hope that some of that prestige will rub off on us and make us feel better about ourselves. We can be deluded into thinking that if we lose what we have, we'll be miserable. In terms of listening, such delusional thinking can block new ideas—

ideas with the potential for creativity and innovation. We can be frightened by what looks like a snake in the water, only to find upon closer inspection that it is just a piece of rope resting in a puddle. These perceptions are not just the product of our collective consciousness passed down through the generations; we manage to add our own special twist to further contort the perception. Instead of just an ordinary snake in the water, we now see a deadly viper.

To see into our own nature, to become aware of the barriers we create between ourselves and others, is the first step in creating a mindset conducive to becoming a good listener. Awareness of our actions, noting our programmed tendencies to unfairly judge others, is the goal of Zen.

These barriers may take the form of filters that allow only selected words and ideas into our consciousness and screen out the less familiar and uncomfortable messages. Therefore, only *pieces* of the message are received—the comfortable pieces that fit our stereotypes. Clinging to unsubstantiated biases and misperceptions brings pain and unhappiness to our lives. It is not so much the barriers themselves that create communication disasters but the emotions associated with them—jealousy, hatred, and desire. Moreover, like weeds in a garden, these barriers choke our potential for developing fruitful relationships and fresh ideas. The good news is that you can escape these great walls—if you choose.

As an example, let's create a fictitious group of people toward whom you are prejudiced. Let's say they come from a country called Batamia. Imagine that you grew up in a Batamian neighborhood and accumulated a wealth of information about Batamians. Your family, of strictly Losmanian ancestry, always disliked Batamians. In fact, your parents pointed out aspects of Batamian women's personalities that you never even noticed before. You got to be such an expert at disliking Batamian women that you started to notice even more undesirable traits as these women began to appear in your workplace.

Even though you may have had a few pleasant Batamian neighbors, they were the minority. Now your dislike is so well honed that you have developed a dislike for anyone who even *looks* Batamian. Your recollection of the women in your neighborhood is, among other things, that they are lazy and complain a lot. Therefore, when Mrs. Jones, a Batamian woman in your office, complains about the lack of adequate support staff, you simply disregard her comment. It is easy for you to brush her off and close your mind to her very real problem. However, if a male coworker, someone who easily intimidates you, makes the same complaint and you act on it, you may find yourself penalized by your own barriers in the form of a sex discrimination suit. Barriers, at the very least, can cost money, reputations, and careers.

Some barriers are so impenetrable that they may totally restrict certain persons from entering our ear space. If you are fervently religious or totally committed to a cause, you may be unwilling to give any serious attention to the views of someone with different beliefs. Let's ask ourselves: Why shut our ears to this new information? Is a different take on a topic something to be feared? Is it unsettling to think that a different viewpoint might force us to change the way we think? Does our ability to say no evaporate if we give someone a few minutes to describe his point of view?

If you are a negative thinker to begin with, you may fear change because it can disrupt the status quo. Your boss and your marriage partner may not agree, your friends might leave you. If you see the cup as half full, however, change could mean a more challenging job, a more compatible spouse, or friends who are supportive instead of competitive. These blocks to listening can stifle our creativity and limit our knowledge base. In addition, they can become so obtrusive that they affect our ability to pay attention and concentrate.

If we look at all the listening opportunities that present themselves, they generally fall into two categories—events (shows, lectures) and people. People fall into further categories: those we want to listen to and those we don't—even if we know we should. When we *want* to listen, there are few obstacles to receiving the message. We easily welcome good music, a funny joke, or a discussion on our favorite hobby. It serves us well also to *want* to listen to what we *should* listen to—a loved one or a lecture we signed up for. If we choose not to listen to someone or something, we may have some very good reasons for that. Perhaps their voice hurts our ears, the message is offensive or of no interest. Our barriers become clearer to us when we feel we *should* listen to someone or something that we *don't* want to listen to: a disgruntled employee, our teenager's plea for a new wardrobe, our company's new quality-assurance standards. However, there may be unpleasant consequences for not listening in these situations. If we cannot disregard the consequences, then we have to listen.

What are the obstacles that keep us from getting the whole message in these should-listen activities, and why can't we let ourselves accept a differing point of view? Barriers that appear very logical to us may prevent us from being receptive to what our speaker has to say. If you are having marital problems, why, for heaven's sake, would you listen to the advice of a counselor who is a recovered alcoholic and twice married? Before heading for the nearest exit, though, take a moment to consider: Maybe he's got more common sense about relationships than someone who stays in an unhappy marriage. Did his rehabilitation give him more insight into working through problems than someone who never had to overcome an addiction? Maybe he lost his spouse to unfortunate circumstances beyond his control? Perhaps you'll give him a chance after all.

Getting through the fog of distractions and personal biases to allow the message to be heard is a challenge to the listener. When we are aware of our obstacles, we are then better able to deal with them. We may not be able to eliminate these barriers—many of them were programmed into our psyches in childhood. However, if we face our barriers and witness their pervasive power to shut out opportunities for personal growth, we can allow them to be more transparent. After that point, we can get on with the business of listening. Some of the great walls that prevent us from getting the full message include:

- background noise

- status

- gender, race, and age prejudice

- physical appearance

- past experiences

- personal agendas

- focusing on the outcome versus the process of listening

- negative self-talk

Many of these obstacles to better listening are learned from our parents, our culture, and the media. They begin as preferences (what do we like better, apples or oranges?) and evolve to steadfast points of view.

It is only human to have preferences and opinions. The difficulty begins when we feel compelled to defend our opinions and ignore evidence to the contrary. This leads to argumentative and aggressive behavior. According to Voltaire, "Opinion has caused more trouble in this earth than all the plagues and earthquakes."

Some of our barriers are the product of minibrainwashings that have now become our reality. These biases learned from TV, movies, and our parents seep into the subconscious and create much needless suffering. For example, most of us dread Monday morning because of its bad reputation. We've worked hard to perpetuate that reputation by using our Sunday nights to agonize over our most undesirable work tasks and dream up disastrous circumstances that could make Monday miserable. Monday arrives and we almost reflexively moan at the sound of the alarm and snap at the driver who took our parking space. Mondays have become problem days because we see to it on a regular basis that the prophecy is fulfilled. These delusions are all learned and selectively programmed biases in our minds. The truth may be that Monday is no different than another day; as a matter of fact, we're rested after a weekend, and on Wednesday or Thursday we've probably met with different but equally daunting challenges. The only difference is that we haven't inherited or developed a distorted mindset for Wednesday or Thursday.

Fortunately, the fact that we enjoy certain preferences does not mean that we have to despise their alternatives. Our hands are a good example. We may be right-handed, yet we do not ignore or reject our left hand because we don't use it to write, swing a tennis racket, or hammer a nail. For most activities, in fact, we need both hands. When I feel that a certain preference is overtaking my ability to listen, I think of my hands and how I depend on both of them to get me through my day. We need to develop the same ambidexterity when it comes to listening.

Dr. Marshall Rosenberg, in his book *Nonviolent Communication,* tells how we find it difficult to separate *observation* of a situation, person, or thing from an *evaluation.* Rosenberg calls our tendencies to observe and judge at the same time "life-alienating communication."

For example, when we start listening to someone talk about the economy, we immediately observe her looks, mannerisms, voice, sex, and age, and sift these observations through our personal filters. After only seconds we have judged whether she is worth listening to (the chances of continuing to listen are much greater, by the way, if her opinions agree with ours). Can you imagine what it would be like to just listen to someone without jumping to judge or evaluate? According to Indian philosopher J. Krishnamurti, "To observe without evaluating is the highest form of intelligence."

We may not be able to rid ourselves entirely of these great walls, but we can get a better understanding of why we don't connect with certain individuals and why some persons have trouble connecting with us. Furthermore, mental barriers interfere with our ability to be flexible in our thinking. The ability to accept change and adapt to change either at home or the workplace is directly related to our ability to be flexible with different ways of seeing the world. Some of these walls will yield more easily than others. As you go through the list on page 49, start by thinking about the people you don't want to listen to, but *should* listen to. Try to identify the obstacles that are your most frequent barriers to listening.

First consider the obvious. How can we expect to "mind-meld," as Mr. Spock would say, with our speaker if the TV or radio is too loud or if the office is full of **background noise**? We generally speak at a volume level of about sixty to seventy decibels. Office noise—people talking in the next cubicle, the rustle of papers, the hum of equipment—can compete with and exceed those volume levels, masking the speaker's voice. We know how difficult it is to have decent conversation at a noisy bar or a wedding reception where everyone ends up screaming across the table just to be heard over the band. One of the simplest courtesies we can extend to our speaker is to eliminate these distractions. If we want to have a meaningful conversation in these situations, go to a quieter place or eliminate the noise source. Even though we have two ears we can listen to only one thing at a time.

By the way, how is your hearing? The American Speech and Hearing Association estimates that over thirty million people in this country have a hearing loss that could be treated. A great way to discourage others from sharing information with you is to ignore a perceptual hearing problem that could be improved with wax removal, a hearing aid, or an assistive listening device (ALD). Hearing aids cannot restore hearing, but they can maximize whatever hearing capacity is still present. Approximately six million Americans wear hearing aids. Seven to eight million people would benefit from them but are not wearing them. Technological advances in hearing aids (digital hearing aids) in the last few years provide better sound quality than ever before. Many others would be helped by ALDs, such as phone adapters, speech amplifiers, FM systems in movie theaters, TV closed-captioning, and various alerting devices. Lip-reading courses, generally taught by audiologists or speech pathologists, are another option to enhancing one-to-one communication.

Many children and adults with acquired nerve deafness can benefit from cochlear implants. As I mentioned earlier in Jane's story, it is a surgically implanted device with an externally worn speech processor that stimulates the surviving auditory fibers in the inner ear. Although there are risks to consider (as in any surgical procedure), cochlear implant is recognized by the American Medical Association as standard treatment for profound hearing loss.

Ringing in the ears and head noises, or *tinnitus,* is believed to be brought on by noise and stress. Persons with tinnitus describe the constant presence of noises like buzzing, roaring, hissing, and whistling. To some, it can even take the form of a high-pitched screech. This nerve-racking condition can significantly impair the ability to concentrate on the spoken message. The American Tinnitus Association (ATA) claims that over twelve million Americans suffer from this malady in its severe form, and others experience it to a lesser degree. There is no cure at this time, but some medications and tinnitus retraining can significantly improve the ability to cope with the disorder.

If you or others suspect you have a hearing problem, or if you experience tinnitus or a progressive hearing loss, see an ear doctor and an audiologist. They can best help you determine what treatment would be most beneficial. Until then, turn down the TV, close the door, or find a quiet place so you can *hear* what is being said. If you are hearing impaired, don't be shy about asking your conversation partner to speak clearly and a bit louder. Particularly on the telephone, distinct pronunciation is often more helpful to the hearing-impaired person than increasing the volume, which may only distort the message. If you have hearing-impaired family or friends, speaking clearly and facing your listener saves you from repeating and straining your voice. Best of all, this gesture creates a communication link that may be otherwise lost.

One of the most obstinate barriers to listening and one that virtually slams the door on the speaker is the issue of **status**. This reminds me of a story about job titles. One day the Governor of Kyoto paid a visit to Zen Master Keichu. The governor's visit was announced by an attendant who presented the master with a card that read, "Kitagaki, Governor of Kyoto." "I have no business with such a fellow," Keichu snapped. When the attendant relayed Keichu's response to the governor, the governor took a pen and scratched out the words *Governor of Kyoto* and handed the card back. When Keichu saw the card, he exclaimed, "Oh—Kitagaki! I'd love to see him!"

Status gets in the way of listening between rich and poor, doctors and patients, and managers and staff. I once knew a manager of a large department who, as part of his power trip, ordered his staff to follow him down the hall as they asked questions or presented ideas. He rarely made eye contact with his subordinates and walked past them as they spoke. Yet, when conversing with his peers or those higher on the administrative ladder, a dramatic change in his voice and body language took place. He looked them in the eye and smiled, nodding his head at any comment or suggestion. He laughed uproariously at their jokes and thanked them profusely for their unique insights (many of which his staff had voiced earlier and which he had ignored or dismissed). Unfortunately, this manager's transformation was most evident to his staff. His method of managing people was control and the assertion of *status* as a way to force cooperation. As a result, staff turnover was high and morale was low.

If we want to encourage loyalty, creative input, and positive attitudes from our employees, our kids, or our customers, we need to treat each individual with courtesy and respect. We do that by acknowledging that every person, by virtue of sheer life experience, has valuable insight to share. We all need to know that our opinions are valued.

Listening to what motivates employees helps them to excel in what they do best, thus creating a happier, more fulfilling work environment. By sitting down and facing our speakers, we value them. Not interrupting and keeping eye contact shows our respect. Reinforcing their contribution produces a feeling of idea sharing. Sam Walton, the late retail business tycoon and founder of Wal-Mart stores, said, "The key to success is to get out into the store and listen to what the associates have to say. It's terribly important for everyone to get involved. Our best ideas come from clerks and stock boys." By neutralizing the status discrepancy in this manner, we foster an atmosphere of communal vested interest and positive morale.

Many of us feel inferior to our doctors. Dr. Bernard Lown, in his wonderful book, *The Lost Art of Healing*, says, "To heal requires a relationship marked by equality." Can you imagine a situation more crucial to listening than talking with your physician about your health? Some of us feel belittled by a physician's status, and we often feel too intimidated to ask for an explanation or share concerns about our health. Other times, it is the fault of an individual doctor's poor bedside manner that makes us, as patients, feel insignificant. We may perceive that we're being looked down upon and may not feel comfortable sharing pertinent information that could lead to a diagnosis. In a litigation-prone system such as healthcare, health professionals in particular must practice good listening. Patients are less likely to sue when they feel that the doctor's treatment decision was motivated by concern for them. Any competitive healthcare organization is well aware of this need to be sensitive to the communication needs of its employees and patients.

At a recent gathering, I overheard the following remarks from a pleased customer: "Wow, that service manager at X Company was terrific! I wish I had started with them in the first place. She actually listened to me without interrupting! It took her ten minutes to fix the problem and I was on my way!" X Company has learned that listening shows respect and, even more than a free cup of coffee or a clean bathroom, respect for the customer leads to repeat business. The feeling of being appreciated as a customer stands out in stark contrast to the impersonal, give-me-a-break service attitude that dominates the marketplace today. In business, the more distance we put between us and our customers, the more they will stray towards the feel-good businesses and services. They may choose our business because we're faster, but resent the way we treat them. All it takes is for somebody to come around the corner who is faster—and friendly—and you're toast.

Some of us are uncomfortable with the idea of putting aside our egos to really listen and experience another's perspective. It may make us vulnerable to step out of the role we have learned to play. We may feel it is too risky to get close to our subordinates, clients, or family members. Or perhaps we fear losing our objectivity. It is the self-actualized individual, however, according to psychologist Abraham Maslow, who is secure enough with herself to demonstrate her wide potential as a communicator. The person on her way to becoming self-actualized is comfortable enough to mind-meld with others without fear of losing her sense of self. This ability springs, not from applying techniques learned in some seminar, but from a stable self-image and genuine respect for another's perspective. (I will discuss more about self-actualization later.)

Listening to ourselves, choosing words and tone of voice that facilitate an understanding with our conversation partner, can help break down the status barrier. For example, do you frequently use professional jargon or vocabulary with clients who are not in your line of work? Might anyone perceive your tone as condescending or cold? Intentionally "swinging the lingo" is the ultimate tool of information control that alienates the consultant from the customer. Using unfamiliar words on purpose is the opposite of communicating. It can be a major barrier to a satisfying customer interaction. Unfortunately, the receivers of shop talk, when they are not from the same shop, frequently nod their heads, not wanting to appear ignorant, and leave the office with a sense of helplessness. The insensitive consultant, on the other hand, may be totally convinced that he has not only impressed the customer, but that the customer actually understood what he had to say.

As a rule of thumb, if you are spoken to in this manner, say to the consultant, "Excuse me, but I am not a lawyer (accountant, doctor). Please use laymen's terms so I can understand what you are talking about." Whenever I do this, I usually get a translation that makes me more knowledgeable and satisfied with the service. It also saves time. (Coincidentally, it can be a wake-up call to the consultant. He gets the message that you're there to get your money's worth, not to be impressed. He may guard his words more carefully with the next client.)

Public speakers looking to promote their services or educate the public need to avoid this communication pitfall. Prior to the engagement find out about your audience. How well do they know your topic? Chances are, they would not be coming to listen to you speak if they already knew your buzz words as well as you. Be sure to at least define the jargon in simple terms before you get too deep into your lecture.

If any of these status barriers get in the way of your understanding the message and getting the message across to others, begin by applying the golden rule of listening: listen to others as you would have others to listen to you. And, if you are a consultant, please speak to others as you would like to be spoken to.

As soon as we meet someone for the first time, we start to evaluate whether or not they are worth listening to. If she doesn't meet certain personal criteria, her words become fainter and fainter until only our thoughts fill our attention. Some people's checklists include **race, gender, and age prejudice.** Some of us judge according to dress or **physical appearance.** Many a fund-raiser can attest to the fact that, at times, the least best dressed is often the inconspicuous donor for the new children's cancer center. Preferential listening based on such shallow biases can cost millions in mistaken identities and sex-discrimination law suits.

One of the most common obstacles to listening comes in the form of physical handicaps. As children we may have been taught to feel sorry for those who were lame, disfigured, or blind. It was impolite to stare at such people, a courtesy we resisted because of fear or curiosity. Interaction with a handicapped person with communication deficits may have caused us to assume that a disabled body means a disabled mind. Such stereotypes can persist into adulthood. Those of us in the healthcare field are fortunate to have broken through this barrier to some extent, although many disabled people would agree that their physical condition often discourages even healthcare professionals from taking other medical concerns seriously. As handicapped access becomes more common in public places, our opportunities for interaction with disabled persons are on the rise. More people with disabilities are overcoming these stereotypes by speaking out in the media. Christopher Reeves, the actor who sustained a spinal cord injury following a fall from a horse, and Stephen Hawking, physicist and author of *A Brief History of Time,* wheelchair bound by Lou

Gehrig's disease, have not allowed their disabilities to be sheltered from the public eye. They have helped to dispel faulty notions about the physically handicapped population. My experience is that there are more able-bodied people with communication handicaps than there are people with physical handicaps. The true handicap lies in our perception of the individual. This applies to all the barriers to better listening.

. Other times we allow negative **past experiences** with a person to interfere, or we might experience a feeling of immediate dislike for no apparent reason. (Maybe, we tell ourselves, she was our worst enemy in a past life!) Try not to let past experience contaminate the present. Use past experience to help you learn about the world and how to avoid repeating your mistakes. Do not, however, rely blindly on previous experience to evaluate a present situation. This builds barriers between us and our speakers. We assume, for example, that we know what this person is going to say, so we really don't have to listen. Parents and spouses frequently complain of this phenomenon. We tune out familiar messages, particularly those associated with criticism and household chores, and attend only the novel and desirable messages. Expanding our response styles (chapter five) will help to decrease the selective listening in our household and at the workplace.

Some of the most crucial information to be gained as listeners—like people's names—gets lost while we are in the midst of acceptability checklists. It is essential for us to become aware of the extent to which these obstacles interfere. Our challenge is to drive that discriminating force toward a positive end. See these differences between people as invitations to broaden our spectrum of possible points of view. Every time we truly listen to people different from ourselves, they give us an opportunity to see a view through another window. This mindset expands our creative potential. An overly judgmental and critical approach diminishes our scope of possibilities.

Let me say a few words about being judgmental. Of course we are judgmental when we listen to others. We may be able to put our biases aside, but we still evaluate to some extent, especially when decisions have to be made. In fact, our survival depends on such critical evaluation. If we were not selective to some extent, we wouldn't think twice about picking up a stranger on the highway, ingesting certain substances, or engaging in risky or unethical activities. Learning from past experience also saves us from wasting time. Our ability to get to work and back in one piece, hold onto our jobs, and be responsible parents depends on our ability to judge situations and act accordingly. But at what point does survival judgment stop and our biases and closed-mindedness begin? When does the healthy instinct to discriminate become self-limiting and unfair to others?

In studying the descriptions of my students' thought processes when listening, it appears that judgment evolves through different stages. The first stage is general recognition of the person talking (Do I know—or know of—this person?). This observation may be related to the first-fifteen-seconds phenomenon reported by image consultants. According to these experts, we make hard and fast decisions about people during the first fifteen seconds of contact. These first fifteen seconds may be part of our normal, healthy survival judgment. With some, however, this brief period of evaluation is reflexive. Thus, we may have great difficulty in eliminating this knee-jerk response.

When we are deciding whether to listen, however, our barriers kick in fairly early. Immediately, a person's physical appearance triggers a whole list of possible judgment calls, good and bad. The speaker's voice and mannerisms may set off another chain of prejudices. If we cling to any one of these biases in depth, we run the risk of missing the content of the person's message.

My theory is that the extraordinary listener does not allow her attention to be consumed by any bias. She acknowledges the presence of certain learned barriers, but turns her attention to what that person has to say and the feelings behind the message. A student said it best, "Putting aside your biases and tuning into the speaker are like tuning in a radio station to receive a clear signal with no distortion."

Judgments and criticisms, if allowed to overtake the interaction, are destructive to the relationship and the potential opportunities that exist between speaker and listener. Judgment creeps into our psyches at an early age. We show preferences for certain toys, learn to be picky about food, select TV over homework. As adults, certain activities are earmarked as enjoyable or distasteful with varying degrees of acceptance in between. Procrastination, another self-limiting behavior, is in large part due to the relentless discrimination between what we need to get done and what we want to do at the moment. The habits of harsh judgment and negative discrimination are at the heart of our inability to genuinely listen to people. How can we begin to break down these barriers?

Les Kaye, the author of *Zen at Work,* a teacher of Zen, and a former IBM executive, writes about seeing each activity of the day as equally necessary and important. This is the Zen concept of equanimity or even-mindedness. To cling to the mindset that there are distinctly desirable and undesirable activities and people creates distress and anxiety. We go through life trying to decide in which mental box a particular person or activity belongs—good or bad, right or wrong, interesting or boring. This attitude puts limits on our flexibility of thought and openness to new ideas.

Alan Watts said, "Good without evil is like up without down, and . . . to make an ideal of pursuing the good is like trying to get rid of the left by turning constantly to the right. One is therefore compelled to go round in circles." In a footnote, Watts mentioned that there was a politician in San Francisco who so detested the political left that he would go to great inconvenience when driving to avoid making a left turn.

Accepting the notion that our daily activities are interrelated, no matter how trivial, is one way to dissolve some of the barriers to listening. Kaye says that concern for efficiency in each activity (versus concern for achieving goals) facilitates the flowing nature of work. In this approach, he says, "Work became like a garden, with new and interesting shapes, textures, and fragrances at each turn. Problems and difficulties did not go away, but my relationship with work was different."

One recent autumn, my father and I took a weekday vacation and went mountain biking in Franconia Notch, New Hampshire. The weather was beautiful, and along our path were waterfalls, natural rock formations, and a forest full of color. The air was clear and fresh. I returned from that day trip suffused with a sense of peaceful satisfaction. As I reflected recently on this experience, I realized how I have changed as a result of dissolving some of my barriers. The sense of satisfaction I experience when making a connection with a patient or coworker is similar to the sense of connection with nature that I experienced biking through that mountain paradise.

In the past, I might have seen this day trip as getting away from the rat race and leaving it all behind. Now my sense is that work and nonwork activities are both deserving of time and attention. To realize the equality of satisfaction between two formerly disparate activities was a taste of enlightenment. Instead of critiquing and comparing, I now see the slender thread of connection between all activities. It has made me less judgmental and critical, and has made me a more balanced and positive person.

If we can dissolve our hard and fast judgments of people based on their attitudes, styles, and points of view, we can then begin to see each person as equally essential to the workings of life: the guy who dumps your garbage is as integral to the process of living as the brain surgeon who eliminates your dizziness.

A few years back I had a patient with an extreme case of people discrimination. John was a middle-aged administrative assistant for a computer firm. He was referred to me by a psychologist. He had a history of depression associated with attention deficit disorder since childhood. John was extremely knowledgeable and intelligent despite test results that showed marked difficulties with listening and memory. He had benefited significantly from a combination of counseling and medication, but still had major difficulties with his coworkers.

Aside from being a poor listener, he showed little ability to hear himself. He spoke endlessly and appeared totally unaware when others tried to join in. He did not perceive his interminable monologues as rude and showed no interest in letting anyone else speak. In addition, he often drifted from the subject and rarely answered a question directly. I could see why John was never invited to participate on a team or given advancement opportunities at work, or why, despite his vast technical knowledge, his job was at stake.

After some discussion and a few roleplaying activities directed towards heightening his awareness, John admitted that he was torn between having to get along with people to make a salary and his unyielding perception that *no one else at his workplace was worth listening to.* No one there knew as much as he knew, and it was a "waste of time" to hear from the others. It was clear that for John to improve his listening skills, he would have to curb his ego and learn to value the opinions of his coworkers.

John is a dramatic example of how even the most sophisticated skills and strategies are doomed to failure unless we can develop the attitude of openness essential to mindful listening. Choosing to see our conversation partners as equals is the mindset needed to be an effective listener.

Another major impediment to listening is the emphasis we place on getting to **our personal agendas.** Let's say you have just been introduced to the new CEO of the company. As she tells you about herself and her intentions for the company, you may find yourself formulating your mission statement and chomping at the bit to introduce yourself and your interests. You want her to like you, so you wear your best smile, straighten your collar, nod frequently, and try to act in a professional manner. Finally, when it is your time to speak, your content bears little or no relationship to the new CEO's agenda. Because the only thing you paid attention to was your own agenda, you leave the meeting having learned nothing.

This approach to accomplishing goals leads only to frustration and low self-esteem. The more productive method of communicating our interests would be to sit back and make an effort to listen. Learn about this person and be alert to commonalties or differences between her plans and your concerns. Notice her manner, pace, and style. What are her priorities? Are yours in there somewhere? Make her agenda your agenda. When it is your turn to speak, indicate that you have carefully considered her message by making a connection between her interests and yours. Stick to the need-to-know facts and keep it short. Let her ask for more information. When she learns that you are a thoughtful listener, chances are that she will be open to you in the future. A reputation for emphasizing your own agenda above the interests of the group makes you an unlikely pick for team projects or positions that require flexibility, vision, and leadership.

When meeting a new customer, you may feel pressed to take control of the meeting and start out by telling the customer what you can do for him. You are **focused on the outcome** of the meeting—usually the sale—instead of the process of cultivating a relationship. Instead, if you recall from your Business 101 course, let the customer tell you his needs and concerns; let him focus on his agenda first. Then you will be better able to use your agenda to make a happy customer. Why is it important to put aside your agenda when listening to someone else? So that you can hear what the other party is saying. This requires mental flexibility. If you focus only on your own needs, you'll miss opportunities for a successful outcome.

Harvey Mackay, the legendary salesman, best-selling author, and motivational speaker, believes that the strong personal relationships that he developed over the years transformed an ailing manufacturing company into a revenue-generating workhorse. At a speakers' seminar a few years back in Boston, I recall standing in line to get some advice from Mr. Mackay. Before I could ask my question, he got me to talk about myself. He had such an intense way of listening that I found myself divulging personal information quite voluntarily. He made note of this information and succinctly answered my question, which was well worth the twenty minutes I spent standing in line. He not only answered my question, he linked the answer to how I could use the information in a creative way given *my* circumstances. In a matter of a few minutes I felt indebted to him because of the effort he made to get to know me and solve my problem in a personal way. Wouldn't we like all our clients to feel that way about us?

In *Success* magazine (February 1999), Mackay reveals how he acquired the skill to establish relationships through listening. He says, "My father handed me a Rolodex when I was eighteen and said, 'Every person you meet for the rest of your life goes into this. You add a little something about them on the back of the card—family, hobbies, et cetera. And you cultivate that Rolodex like a garden.'" Mackay says this information is essential to sales work, because "people buy from people, and the more you know about them, the more they're flattered, the more they're at ease—and the more they buy."

This advice was clearly unknown to the customer relations manager at my car dealership from whom I received a form letter. Keep in mind that I only service my car there, I have never *purchased* a car from them. It opened by thanking me for servicing my car there a few weeks earlier, which was fine. It went on in the second paragraph to tell how only 100 percent customer satisfaction with their technical service is acceptable. That was standard fare also. But the closing paragraph said, "Our relationships really do begin *after* the sale is made. We value *those* relationships and look forward to your allowing us to continue to serve you." If that's what they really believe, I can bet that when I walk in there to have my car serviced or to shop for a new car, I'll be treated like a number or worse, like a steak—until, of course, *after* the sale.

Listening to establish a relationship with anyone, whether customer, friend, or family member, requires that our concentration be flexible enough to shift into receiver mode and stay there, instead of being distracted by our agendas. (We will discuss in chapter five a way to do that.)

Stephen Covey, in a commentary in his book, *The Seven Habits of Highly Effective People,* calls listening "the magical habit." He suggests our goal should be to "listen first to understand." A good listener sees himself as the receiver rather than the taker. He must not impose himself on the speaker, but instead let the speaker's words flow in on him. Otherwise, the listener's prejudices and expectations will interfere and cloud the message and intent of the messenger. This is the difference between self-serving, egocentric listening and patient, selfless listening. It doesn't take a smart person to sense the difference between someone who listens in order to gain something and one who listens to build a relationship.

If you are a goal-oriented individual, then consider a loftier goal than just making the sale. Strive to build a strong working relationship with customers or coworkers by listening. The sale may not be immediate, but if and when it does occur, it will yield greater satisfaction for all parties and greater potential for profits. You become more flexible in your thinking because you are less discriminating, and therefore open to the opportunities and ideas that may present themselves.

Efforts to put aside our self-interest to really listen to someone else are often thwarted by other thoughts. At any given moment our attention is focused on thoughts external to the self, such as "It's raining again today," or "Interest rates are dropping." Internal thoughts may sound like "I'm thirsty," "I'm really out of shape," or "I hope the boss likes this report." A steady stream of internal focusing blocks our ability to listen. It is very easy to nod our heads and *act* like we are listening when actually we are consumed by our internal jabber.

A constructive dose of self-awareness is a good thing. Thinking about ourselves, analyzing our actions, and planning our behavior have helped us achieve personal success. This book encourages close self-study in order to make changes that enhance personal growth. But this positive initiative can become a negative force if our attention shifts from developing our potential to the discrepancy between standards set by others (how we should look, act, and achieve) and what we see in the mirror.

Numerous reports suggest that self-awareness can be a negative experience. Internal brooding interferes with creativity, the ability to relax, and openness to experience. In 1982, a study by Mihaly Csikszentmihalyi of the University of Chicago, *Self-Awareness and Aversive Experience,* sought to explore the effect of self-awareness in natural settings. One hundred and seven employees from five large companies, ranging from assembly line workers to managers and engineers, volunteered to participate in the study. Volunteers were given electronic pagers to carry all day. The pagers emitted signals randomly seven to nine times a day during regular waking hours. When subjects were beeped, they were required to fill out a short questionnaire regarding their activity, thoughts, and moods at the moment. Responses were ranked according to whether these thoughts dealt with self-concerns or external concerns like food and work. Subjects were also asked about the quality of the experience at the given moment: feeling 1) happy and cheerful, 2) alert and active, or 3) involved. The results showed that internal thinking is a particularly unpleasant experience, since focusing on the self was ranked lowest across all three aspects of quality. Thoughts about other people and conversation were reported to be significantly more pleasant and active. It is fair to conclude that instead of dwelling on self-assessment (usually filled with negative self-talk), we might be happier listening to someone else.

How many times a day do you find yourself thinking, "I don't believe I said that!", "How stupid!", "What an idiot!", "I look terrible today," or "I know I will not be able to remember all that he's telling me." Sound familiar? By proclaiming our deficiencies in **negative self-talk,** even silently to ourselves, we chip away at our self-confidence. Negative self-talk attacks our feelings of self-worth. By increasing our anxiety, these internal distractions prevent us from focusing our attention on the message and the messenger.

Anxiety breeds fatigue and depression, both of which deter effective listening. Negative self-talk saps our energy and weakens our enthusiasm for initiating and completing tasks, whether they be cold-calling, solving a problem, or arranging for that interview. Perpetuation of self-directed put-downs limits the range of opportunities we allow ourselves to experience.

Chances are, if we tally our ratio of negative comments to positive comments, it will be strikingly skewed to the negative side. One way to rid yourself of this self-defeating behavior is to balance out a negative comment with a positive one. Every time you say something like, "Gee, that was a dumb thing I said," counter it *immediately* with something positive like, "Next time I'll choose my words more carefully. Perhaps I could have said it another way," or "My presentation on Thursday really went well; I was very concise."

In our efforts to improve our listening, it is important that we examine our behavior as objectively as possible. Only then can we make changes that are welcome to ourselves and those around us. Negative self-talk starts to take over when we lose objectivity about our weak points. We dwell on the weak points and neglect the positive ones. A negative self-image sprouts from attaching too much importance to occasional lapses like forgetting our keys or making a careless error on a test. Instead of calling yourself stupid or an idiot, take a deep breath, accept the mistake as part of the human experience, and resolve to learn from it. Then feel the disgust and irritation fade.

The more lengthy and severe a beating we give ourselves, the less time we have for listening to constructive and rational input. That negative inner voice is not a helpful guide, but a self-destructive force that can lead to tragic ends. It is useful to ask who that negative voice sounds like. Could it be the voice of a verbally abusive parent or an overly condemning spouse we could never please? Negative self-talk can be so pervasive that it distracts us from processing the spoken message. Instead of taking in words and meaning, we think, "I wonder if I have bad breath?" or "What will I say if he asks me about that project I haven't started yet?" Others perceive our lack of confidence through our posture, eye contact, and vocal characteristics. Negative self-talk sets us up for negative treatment by others. Remember the words of the famous motivational speaker, Zig Ziglar: "No one on the face of this earth can make you feel inferior without your permission."

Getting to know our personal barriers and the energy we waste trying to reinforce them is the next step in becoming better listeners. When I encounter a barrier, I discuss it aloud with myself. I also voice any supporting arguments that contribute to this way of thinking. Often, hearing my weak argument for upholding a barrier is enough to dispel it. Sometimes my reasons make me laugh. Other times, I'm disappointed with how selfish I sound. In every instance, however, I at least try to acknowledge my resistance, and over time, resolve to work through it whenever it comes up.

Sometimes we have to be satisfied with a slow chiseling away of obstacles to better communication. After all, it took a lifetime to create them. Cleaning house of these unhelpful judgments, however, makes room for new learning and personal growth. It is also one of the best ways to get to know ourselves.

Becoming aware of our barriers to the message or the messenger helps us to better understand, and in some cases, accept the barriers of others toward us. Many of the barriers discussed in this chapter reflect the diversity present in our culture. Beliefs, customs, and behaviors vary not only between persons from different countries but between persons from the same country. If you have ever worked at a job where employees in one department were very easygoing and team oriented, but in another department were more rigid and less interactive, you have experienced minicultures within a larger culture. To further complicate the variety, there can be people of twenty or more different nationalities working together in one corporation. They also have their unique biases towards gender, seniority, race, and work ethic.

Identifying our barriers is easy. Conquering them is another matter. Trying to eliminate our barriers one by one is a painstakingly difficult process. We cannot expect ourselves to reprogram reflexive ways of thinking that have been ingrained since childhood. Applying mindful listening every day, however, can diminish their potency and open our minds.

A global approach to softening our barriers is to think of listening as a way of building a sense of community. According to Zen tradition, we are all connected as living beings; we are cousins with every living thing in the universe. This concept is called *sangha.* If we listen with *sangha,* in the belief that we are all connected, it is easier to be respectful and patient. When we honor our speakers in this way, we also show respect and tolerance for ourselves. Conversely, when we shut out others due to our biases, we also hurt ourselves.

Networking is a modern application of *sangha.* We make contacts with others in our professional communities and, because we share similar interests, listen to them in a special way. Networking sessions or support groups are usually positive exchanges, not a setting for putting down one another. Town meetings, fund-raising activities, and religious services take place in the spirit of connecting with one another toward some positive end. It is heartening to see an increase of interfaith and cross-cultural celebrations designed to enhance understanding and respect for the beliefs and heritages of others in our local communities. Participation in such events can expedite the mental housecleaning necessary in order to become mindful listeners. This global mindset will calm an overly critical ear, particularly in situations when it is necessary for us to listen.

Crack a Few Walls

1. Noise is ever present in our environment. Hone your auditory discrimination skills by purposely turning down the volume on the TV just when you want to turn it up. Leave the sound of the dishwasher and the dog barking in the background and put all your attention on what the person on TV is saying. This also challenges your ability to concentrate in noisy situations that are not under your control.

2. Two or three times a week, open your mind to something you've previously opposed and don't know much about. For example, I used to dislike football, based on preconceived notions about the type of people who play football and those who watch it. But I had never taken the time to really watch a game and look for the good in it. So one day I said to myself, "If football is so popular, maybe I'm not giving it a chance." I turned on a Buffalo Bills game for about thirty minutes, and I discovered at least three things that make football interesting and entertaining. Even though it may never be my favorite sport, I now understand the attraction to football and I am less critical about the sport. Try this approach with your not-so-favorite things or people. Be open to their views and listen to them from the standpoint that there is, at least, something to learn from them. As you widen your knowledge base, you will grow to appreciate these various perspectives as valid as your own.

3. Here's one of my favorite listening activities. Try this at a company outing or some large gathering. When you get into a conversation with someone, keep the conversation away from *your* agenda. Ask a few open-ended questions that begin with *why, what,* or *how* to get the other person talking, for example, "How did you get interested in fly-fishing?" or "What do you think is a wise investment?" Your aim is not to see how many questions you can ask, but to let others do more of the talking and you, more of the listening. At the end of the day, notice how much you learned and how many new acquaintances you made simply by giving others the spotlight.

4. Identify people in your life whom you dislike. Facing your prejudices or strong dislikes, whatever they may be and for whatever reason they exist, is an unpleasant task for most of us. Now, find one thing you like or respect about that person or activity. The next time you interact with him, focus on that one thing. Most likely, your negative judgment will also compete for your attention. Acknowledge its presence and refocus your thoughts back to the positive aspect.

5. Over the next few days, notice how often negative thoughts about yourself or others creep into your mind. The longer you dwell on negative thoughts, the more deeply they become ingrained. Counteract these negative thoughts with positive ones.

6. To broaden your perspective on any given topic, try this eye-opening activity. Pick up a popular magazine with a wide readership, like *Time* or *Newsweek*. Read the featured article, which is usually several pages. Think about your opinion of the article: the writer's point of view, the tone, the accuracy or credibility of named sources. Were the points well supported? Get the next issue of the same magazine and read the letters from readers. Even if the article was not particularly controversial you will read at least four points of view different from yours. If you have time, go back and reread the article, keeping other readers' comments in mind. It may be startling to see something you missed or interpreted differently. Whether you agree or disagree is not the point. What's important is to accept these observations as valid perceptions.

7. You cannot will yourself to stop judging and criticizing others, but you can stop and analyze it when it occurs. Examine the foundation for not wanting to listen to

a particular person or idea. Which barriers are operating? Perhaps you adopted these responses from a TV personality, a parent, or a mentor. If you trace it back to the source you may find it has no reasonable basis. You may start laughing when you try to reason it out loud, "Well, my mother would never have permitted me to talk about those things," or "It's not respectful to question my doctor's opinion or ask for an explanation." The origins of our barriers are usually flimsy and out of context. Other times, the basis for our reactions has more substance, but is still from another time and place. For example, if an old boss with whom you had some difficult times in the past visits your office to discuss a new project, notice how instantaneously those memories come back to haunt you. You may find yourself prejudging what she is going to say and criticizing the timing of her visit. Tell yourself, "I see how I am thinking of those past experiences with Amy right now. I will put them aside and listen openly to what she has to say. This time may be different." In this way you take control of your barriers instead of letting them interfere with a potential opportunity for growth or reconciliation.

8. At least once a day when you're listening to a co-worker relate a story, set aside your evaluative self. Be a witness to his ideas. Notice how your barriers want to kick in and start judging. When this happens, put your mind in neutral and simply observe.

9. As a way of re-examining some of the snap decisions and judgments we make during the day, Zen Master

Thich Nhat Hanh suggests copying the question, "Are you sure?" on a piece of paper and taping it to a wall. Great opportunities are often lost to the snap-decision maker who failed to open his mind to find the golden nugget of potential in an idea.

Mindful Listening

Zen Master Seung Sahn said it best in a poem: "If in this lifetime/ You do not open your mind/You cannot digest/Even one drop of water."

The best way I know to open the mind and clean house of the noise and barriers that sabotage our capacity to listen is meditation. Zen means "meditation practice." There are several different ways to meditate, but here I will describe Zen meditation, also known as *zazen*. I also refer to meditation as *breathing practice*.

Meditation does not cause us to be dull, listless, or emotionally detached. On the contrary, it unleashes positive physical and mental energy held captive by stress and anxiety. It brings us to a level of relaxed awareness, which is the first step in harnessing the destructive tendencies of the barriers to listening.

After even a few weeks of meditation practice, you will find that your tendency to overreact in the face of your barriers is less. If your spouse starts complaining about money, you'll be less apt to shout back or use hurtful words. Instead of creating more negative energy you'll be able to rechannel that energy in a more positive way— talking through solutions, feelings, and other needs that may be at the root of the complaint. If you make a mistake or a bad decision, you can simply acknowledge it, learn what you can about it, resolve to avoid repeating it, and put it aside. This more constructive use of energy stimulates personal growth. Dwelling ad nauseum on mistakes and past experiences drains your energy and perpetuates low self-esteem.

Every person is born with a mental space, in inner area of the mind reserved for peaceful contemplation. However, over time this space becomes like a closet where we've thrown outworn clothes, warped records, and broken tools. We may want to hang something new and beautiful there, but there's simply no more room.

The Zen masters promote meditation as a way of emptying the mind of clutter and unproductive thoughts to make space for personal growth. As it pertains to listening, meditation allows our minds to hear with less distortion new ideas and points of view. After a few weeks of practice you will notice that you are less anxious when hearing ideas that differ from your point of view. Your ability to concentrate is deeper and more enduring, and with anxiety under control, you can better focus your attention on getting and retaining the message. Moreover, regular meditation practice improves your attitude, the ability to deploy attention, and sets the stage for mindful listening.

Meditation costs no money and is free of religious bias. It is simply the most natural way to connect your new way of thinking with the way you listen. Calmness, an open mind, and focused attention are the foundation for mindful listening. Here and in subsequent chapters I will describe a few different ways to meditate. For some of you, this first step, as simple as it seems, will be the greatest challenge to your commitment to become a better listener.

Here is a basic method I use for daily practice. I prefer to meditate for thirty to forty minutes at a time, twice a day. When you are just starting out, ten minutes is fine. It is best to practice daily, even for short periods. As you start to experience the benefits of meditation, you may want to extend your meditation time. To avoid falling asleep during practice, do not meditate right after eating. Therefore, early in the morning and before dinnertime are ideal.

Choose a quiet spot free of distractions. Sit in a solid but comfortable chair or get a cushion for sitting cross-legged on the floor. A firm cushion called a *zafu* is traditionally used during Zen meditation. As a meditation teacher once told me, "Sit up straight, dignified like a tree, but with shoulders and arms soft at your side." Rest your hands on your thighs with palms up or down. There are several hand positions. When I began meditating, I preferred to sit in a half-lotus position with my hands on my knees, palms up. I liked to think that this position inspired me to be more open-minded and receptive to different perspectives.

Begin your meditation by keeping your eyes slightly open and gaze down at a forty-five-degree angle. You may keep your eyes closed, but you risk daydreaming and falling asleep. Breathe in and out through your nose, deeply and slowly. Feel your breath move in and out of your body. To check your pace, count slowly up to three seconds as you inhale and exhale for three seconds or more. Do not hold your breath. Keep your mind's eye and ear on the breath. Other thoughts will sneak into your mind. You may start thinking about your grocery list, an upcoming meeting, or a hundred other concerns. As soon as you notice these intrusions, acknowledge their presence, let them pass, and get back to watching your breath. Do not become impatient with yourself for straying from the focus on the breath, this happens to everyone. Simply guide your focus back to the breath. If you find it difficult to stay focused at first, try counting your breaths silently. Inhale on one, exhale on one; inhale on two, exhale on two, and so on. When you get to ten, start over again at one. If you find yourself sneaking peeks at your clock to check the time, set a timer with a gentle alarm or ask someone to softly knock on the door to let you know it is time to stop. When you are finished with your practice, gradually open your eyes completely and stay seated for a minute or two. Slowly stand up and continue with your regular activities.

Another popular way to stay with the breath utilizes visual imagery. As you inhale slowly through your nose, picture inhaling positive energy from a glowing star overhead. As you fill your lungs with air, see this star filling your mind with goodwill and happy feelings. As you exhale slowly, think of cleansing your mind and your body of the wasted energy that supports petty jealousies, irrational biases toward others, and negative self-talk. Allow only goodwill and self-confidence to remain.

Start to open your mind to your *sangha*, the community of people you come in contact with every day. This helps to neutralize your barriers or bad feelings toward those to whom you have the greatest difficulty listening. Toward the end of your meditation, as your breathing becomes shallow, think of wishing your friends and family well. For the moment, let go of any negative feelings between you and them. Go on to wish your coworkers and customers well. Finally, think of the people you are uneasy with and wish them well too, in the spirit that we are all members of a very large family put here to help each other.

Breathing practice or meditation can be more contemplative at times, particularly when we are in conflict of some sort. These are the moments when we can begin to dissolve barriers. I liken this process to a solid block of sandstone sitting in a pool of water. Slowly over time, that block begins to break apart in chunks and ultimately, particle by particle. Contemplative meditation allows us to detoxify some of our most powerful negative emotions.

For example, if you have been working diligently on a project for a long time without success and a friend, Max, experiences overnight success with something that took him only a few days to put together, you may feel disappointment at first. The status barrier may make it very hard to listen to him talk about his success. Then the negative self-talk barrier kicks in, and from these two come resentment and jealousy. During a contemplative meditation, you might go back to the feelings of disappointment you felt when you heard the news: *What is at the root of my disappointment? Jealousy over money? His better house? His fame? Are these the reasons I started my project? Are these things necessities for me and my family? Would I really be happier with those things? Why would I deny Max his success and happiness? If the tables were turned, how would I want him to feel? Defeated? Cheated? Would that make me feel prouder of my accomplishment? Is there any good that can come from Max's success? How can I learn from his experience? If I never achieve success, will anything bad happen to me? Can I listen to Max and other successful people any easier now?*

In this way, meditation can transform your barriers into open doors to self-transformation, creativity, and wisdom. Negative emotions stemming from these barriers only impede personal growth. Breaking down barriers can be an uncomfortable process, but a process you must go through to become a better listener. As a Zen monk and coauthor of *The Monk and the Philosopher*, Matthieu Ricard, said, "Actions are born from thoughts. Without mastering your thoughts, you cannot master your actions."

Make a habit of several minutes of quiet meditation every day. To listen well, you have to first settle down the internal noise. Think of your mind as a glassful of water and sand. Shake up this container and notice how the mix of sand and water makes it difficult to see through. Let the container sit for several minutes and watch how, as the sand settles to the bottom, the water clears. This is essentially what happens in our bodies during breathing practice. After a few sessions, you will emerge from your meditation feeling more mentally balanced. This settled feeling state, free of internal clutter, is the ideal state for new learning. You will start to notice this sense of relaxation extending to several minutes and eventually to hours. Your threshold for becoming annoyed will increase. As you become more consistent in meditation practice, this state of balance can be maintained for longer periods, enabling you to focus and listen better.

Contrary to meditation myths, this practice will not make you apathetic or indifferent, nor will it alienate you from your environment and the people around you. It will, however, help you to become detached from the excess emotional upheaval and interference generated by your barriers.

Chapter Five
What's Their Movie?

To study the way of the Buddha is to study your own self.
To study your own self is to forget yourself.
To forget yourself is to have the objective world prevail in you.
— Master Dogen (1200-1253)

There are many reasons we find movies entertaining. We get a chance to escape our mundane, predictable lives and get into someone else's shoes. Good movies have a way of drawing us into the characters' consciousness, values, and lifestyle. We, the audience, empathize with the characters, often to the point of feeling their fear or sadness. We leave the theater with the thought that our connection with the characters, at least in a small way, has changed our lives. Our mood and our scope of understanding have been altered by forgetting ourselves for a while to view another's perspective. In real life, speakers often invite us to get into their movies with comments like, "Do you see it my way?" or "Put yourself in my place." If we approach a listening opportunity with the same self-abandonment as we do at the movies, think of how much more we stand to gain from those encounters.

The movie mindset is opposite to the act-like-you-are-listening approach, in which you mimick a listening posture, nod often, say "Mm-hmm," and maintain eye contact. How can you possibly make all these adjustments and still concentrate on the speaker? It is not that these actions are contrary to what you do when you really listen. But to focus on this list of body language to-dos risks appearing artificial to the speaker. Just like at the movies, when you forget yourself and get into the shoes of the speaker, your body *naturally* relaxes into listening posture. When you truly listen, you don't need to think about your posture or what you should be doing with your hands. Your gestures and expressions effortlessly reflect your interest. All you have to do is enjoy the adventure!

You take time to listen for many of the same reasons that you go to the movies—to satisfy your curiosity, to be informed, to be entertained, to get another point of view, to experience something outside yourself. Therefore, when you listen to another person, how simple it is to do nothing more than get into his movie!

My effectiveness as a clinician has improved much since I made it a habit to get into my patients' movies before delving into the test or treatment of the day. The movie mindset gives me a third ear to fully grasp the patient's reasons for coming to see me. A few minutes of listening to the patient or a family member tell me about himself, the patient's interests, and lifestyle give me that extra insight into their world that may make all the difference in our success as a team. They may volunteer their feelings about their physical handicaps or describe some of the other challenges they face. These comments are very helpful and save time in the treatment planning process. After getting into their movies and understanding how they see the world, I know better how to structure my therapy sessions. For example, if my patient has a history of being extremely organized and precise, I will present the information and his performance results in an outline format or graph. This way I remain flexible in my craft, the patient appreciates my sensitivity to his way of seeing the world, is more motivated to practice and comply with the recommendations, and will show faster improvement. Similar results can be achieved if I know my patient is an avid golfer. I will select articles on golfing and use golf lingo to make analogies between golf and the patient's performance on various therapy tasks. Getting into their movie not only makes people feel comfortable disclosing information that can affect the outcome, but also adds sparkle to what could otherwise be an ordinarily dull and less effective interaction. For this reason, the movie mindset is a win-win listening approach.

The movie mindset may be most needed with the people we have the hardest time relating to—our children. For example, your teenage daughter comes home after school, mumbles a few choice phrases about the basketball coach, rushes upstairs and slams the door to her room. You have two alternatives: 1) You could make matters worse by scolding her—after all, that particular show of disgust is not appropriate for a young lady; or 2) you could offer to share her movie and listen to her tell about her day. If you choose the latter action, you'll forget about the swearing and door slamming for awhile and put yourself in her place while she relives the day's miserable events. Just like at the movies, you put yourself aside and lock into the drama. What your teenager really needs is for you to relate to her perspective, her stage of maturity, her needs. If you stay tuned to her predicament and remain silent but attentive, she may reveal that her outburst was the result of the upcoming SAT test or not being asked to the homecoming dance.

Getting into the movie gives you the chance to identify with her frustration and disappointment. You empathize with your daughter. You look back at your own high-school days and recall a similar frustration after being chastised for arriving late at swim practice because of a big science project or an argument with your boyfriend. Your teenager senses your attempt to identify with her and breathes a sigh of relief. By withholding your usual parenting approach of scolding and advice, which would have alienated your daughter, you chose to strengthen your relationship by just being a good friend. (I will talk more in chapter seven about specific response styles that cut these valuable movies short.)

As mentioned in chapter two, your barriers are most resistant to change when you are self-absorbed. Getting into the movie of the speaker as she relates her troubles, predicaments, or triumphs is an easy and familiar way to give your barriers a back seat. But for some of us, the preoccupation with personal agenda and status gets in the way of connecting with others.

At work, it may be difficult to shed your armor and feel that you are doing your job. You may even think that some degree of coolness is needed to get the client to cooperate with you. We have been conditioned by our teachers to act superior or distance ourselves from our clients in order to gain their respect. It is, of course, important to communicate that you are experienced and knowledgeable. After all, your skill is what got you this job. Customers, like yourself, overwhelmingly prefer to connect in a symmetrical manner where people speak to each other as human being to human being, not top dog to underdog.

A good way to connect with customers and establish their trust is to reveal some information about yourself. As awkward as this may feel (self-disclosure may be regarded as unprofessional), telling your clients a bit about yourself sets the stage for a cooperative effort. For example, if I have a singer who is coming to me for voice therapy, I feel comfortable letting him know that I was an aspiring opera singer in college, and I can understand how difficult it is to pass up an important audition when you have laryngitis. I don't need to go into details; I just make a statement that indicates I can fully understand her predicament.

I have interviewed many singers and athletes who resist sound medical advice because they don't believe medical people can relate to their passion for singing or sport. They are more likely to accept the advice of a coach or mentor who may have less medical background but more empathy and experience with their problem. For example, runners prefer to take their injuries to runner-friendly doctors. Even though the recommendation may be to stop running and start swimming, most runners take such advice more seriously if given by a doctor who also runs versus a doctor who has never experienced the pleasures of running. Just a detail or two about yourself in the context of your client's dilemma can inspire a trusting relationship. Your client then sees that you relate to his problem and, since you have also experienced a similar predicament, will probably have much more to offer him. Your client feels connected to the process of solving the problem, rather than manipulated by some specialist who lectures with a memorized list of shoulds and shouldn'ts.

Your intent is not to steal the show and become the center of attention. Instead, you want to connect with your client's experience in order to influence a positive outcome. It is the customer's movie that takes priority here, so unless you can shift your focus to the speaker's movie and steer clear of your own, sharing information about yourself is not advised. Many of us have had the experience of paying a consultant big bucks only to have most of the session taken up by the consultant's monologue about his own problems.

Some of the most effective therapists, doctors, and salespeople I have known are those who focus on connecting with their clients. Their good results with patients and customers stem from their ability to use the movie mindset. Jack Carew, a well-known sales trainer and author of *The Mentor: 15 Ways to Success in Sales, Business and Life,* supports the movie mindset as a way to understand the speaker. Only through understanding does a salesperson have the power to influence a customer:

You really don't discover what the customer wants until you deliberately listen to him. . . . If you don't really understand what's important to the customer, preparing your sales proposal will be as futile as mowing your lawn at midnight. You will not know where you've been or where you are going. You will be inviting stiff resistance to your solution because you didn't give the customer a role in helping you discover the problem. Only when you understand your customer's needs will you be in a position to resolve the customer's problem and ultimately win the business. . . . You will get and hold your customer's interest in you by staying in his operating reality or area of interest.

You have all heard about getting into the shoes of the speaker, but getting into his movie is a more powerful mental shift: you are not trying merely to see into the personality of the speaker, but rather the circumstances and motivations that make that person tick. A mediator friend told me about a concept in conflict management called *attribution* and the way it interferes with resolving conflict. We tend to justify our shortcomings, such as tardiness or disorganization, as the result of environmental conditions. We are late because the train was late; we are disorganized today because we have a new secretary. Yet when someone else is late for a meeting or appears disorganized, we do not take into account the possible mishaps she may have encountered that day. Instead, we attribute her lateness to a personality flaw—"She's lazy" or "He's not reliable." Getting into the movie helps you to be less critical and realize that circumstances beyond our control can occur to anyone at any time.

One of my best experiences in witnessing the power of the movie mindset was in graduate school. A very experienced speech pathologist and researcher, Dr. Blom, at the Indianapolis Medical Center, was counseling a patient who had had his voice box removed due to cancer. Dr. Blom encouraged the man to try a voice restoration device so that he could communicate easier on the job. The patient was a sixty-eight-year-old farmer from a small town in Indiana. It was only his second time in twenty-six years in a big city; the first time had been his surgery two weeks earlier. It was obvious that the man was feeling low. He was unable to speak (except with the aid of an electronic device called an electrolarynx), and he was quite anxious about having to deal with yet another medical procedure. His well-weathered overalls, ruddy complexion, and callused fingers stood out in stark contrast with the gleaming, sterile background of the examination room.

The patient sat rigidly in his chair, nervously awaiting his examination and—most probably—a painful procedure. Sensing the farmer's nervousness and apprehension, Dr. Blom put down his instruments and pulled up a chair across from the patient. He had noticed a tiny ornament in the shape of a fishing hook pinned to the farmer's overalls. Dr. Blom sat back in his chair and asked him about the pin. The farmer started talking about fishing in nearby Lake Munroe. He visibly relaxed as he began, using his electronic voice, to share a fishing story. The farmer's eyes lit up as he relived the day he hooked the biggest bluefish ever caught in the county!

Everyone in the room, including those of us who had never gone fishing in our lives, was glued to his seat. For about ten minutes, he told us about the joys of fishing in Indiana. Then, with a big smile on his face and tears in his eyes, he thanked us for listening. Then he turned to Dr. Blom and said, "Let's see if that fancy gadget works!" With a willing and relaxed patient, Dr. Blom carried out the necessary procedure in less than five minutes. The farmer left, relieved and satisfied, with the sense that he had just made a friend.

Applying the movie mindset when listening opportunities arise teaches us to be sensitive to the speaker's needs and feelings. Even though the farmer's words denied fear and nervousness, the doctor sensed his worry and chose to be sensitive to his client's needs. Dr.

Blom knew that if he exposed his patient's apprehension directly, the farmer would have been embarrassed and ultimately resentful.

By forgetting about yourself for a few minutes, you glimpse how your speaker feels about his situation. He may not come out and say, "I feel so frustrated right now," or "I'm very pleased with your service," but because the movie mindset takes you to a level of communication that is deeper than words, you can get a pretty good sense of his view of the situation. The speaker's views may shock, embarrass, aggravate, or hurt you, but you have been truthful with yourself in accepting the existence of another's reality. As a mindful listener, you strive to relate to the needs—positive or negative—of the speaker. This is reflected in words, body language, and tone of voice. If this seems difficult, try to imagine how you would like people to respond to you in a similar situation. (I will delve more into self-listening in chapters seven and eight.)

Before you picked up this book you may have approached your daily conversation partners as one-dimensional characters, merely talking heads with different hairdos. As you learned in chapter three, part of the reason we have such difficulties remembering what was said is that our barriers distance us from the speaker. We may hear the words, but not fully understand or let ourselves accept the meaning behind the words. Your friend, for example, may tell you about her problems with her new boss, yet you are not aware of how serious her concerns are unless you share her movie.

Let's say your vice-president stops you in the hall to discuss a new project. Instead of processing the key ideas in order to make a mental record for the upcoming meeting, you focus instead on a negative experience you had on a past project. By letting that past experience snatch your attention, you set yourself apart and remain outside the theater, so to speak. Failed business and social relationships and lost opportunities result from letting our barriers distance us from the speaker and his views. Instead, when you encounter a situation in which you need to listen well, ask yourself, "What's his movie? What's her reality? How does he see things right now?" This gives you a window into that person's world and a chance to give your own agenda a rest. When you are absorbed in the speaker's movie, not only do his words take on a deeper meaning, but even his gestures and facial expressions add another layer to your understanding.

According to Albert Mehrabian, author of *Silent Messages,* the listener perceives 55 percent of the meaning of the spoken message through gestures and facial expressions; 38 percent is interpreted through tone of voice, speech rate, rhythm, and emphasis; and words transmit approximately 7 percent of the message. In other words, nonverbal cues communicate the bulk of the message. This supports the notion that indeed actions speak louder than words. Yet it is up to the listener to synthesize words, actions, and vocal cues to arrive at the whole message the speaker intends to convey. The movie mindset facilitates this synthesis.

Richard Ben Cramer, in his book *What It Takes,* compares communication styles of various presidential candidates. He speaks highly of Senator Richard Gephardt's ability to get into the movie of the speaker:

> When Gephardt started to listen, his whole person went into receive mode. He locked his sky-blue eyes on your face, and they didn't wiggle around between your eyes and your mouth and the guy who walked in the door behind you, they were just on you, still and absorptive, like a couple of small blotters. . . . If it was just you and your problem, he'd stay on receive until you were weak from being listened to.

Our powerful self-interests set limits on what we permit ourselves to experience. Why not turn those self interests into an interested self? Mahatma Gandhi described the rewards of getting into the speaker's movie when he said, "Three-fourths of the miseries and misunderstandings in the world will disappear if we step in the shoes of our adversaries and understand their viewpoint."

The movie mindset confers the gift of another's vision of life. Everyone's movie is an adventure. Granted, some movies may not be as adventurous as others, but at least if you give the speaker a chance, you run the risk only of learning something new.

Another benefit of getting into someone else's movie is how good it makes the speaker feel. Can you recall the exuberance you felt the last time you had a captive audience? Telling that story or joke was like experiencing it for the first time—even *you* became immersed in the plot again. The audience were willing hostages, bound to your experience. You also know the lonely feeling of inviting someone to share your movie and getting no response, or worse, hearing that person belittle or devalue your experience. When that happens, it's easy to let negative self-talk intervene and convince you that your experience wasn't that great after all. You can see how not truly being heard can affect self-esteem.

I frequently ask students, "When you are the speaker, how do you know that you have been heard?" The majority say that they feel they have been heard when their concerns become the concerns of the listener, when their needs or feelings have been understood or interpreted correctly, and when the listener responds appropriately. Other responses include:

- When they don't keep asking me the same questions.

- When they look at me and do nothing else while I speak.

- When they don't start talking about themselves or something totally different.

- When I see them days or weeks later and they ask about something I said days or weeks ago, as though it was important enough to stay on their minds.

- When they act on what I said.

When I ask, "How do you feel when you have been listened to?", responses are quite varied:

- A feeling of relief.

- Guilty, like I'm dumping on them.

- That my opinion counts.

- Like someone cares about me and my point of view.

- Appreciative and a little guilty for feeling so good afterward.

- It makes me feel important.

By getting into the movie of your speakers, you not only benefit in the sense of understanding them better, but, as you can see from the responses, speakers feel respected, even apologetic for taking your time.

I find the guilty reaction difficult to explain, except that perhaps because there are so few moments in our lives when we are truly heard, it is like receiving a rare gift for which we can offer no equal. Listening is a very inexpensive way to give to others. It is unfortunate that we feel the need to give money or material things to make others feel valued. Several studies have shown that workers prefer nonmaterial reinforcement and recognition for a job well done rather than money. Truly listening, forgetting yourself for a short time, and getting into the speaker's movie can be the kindest gift you can give to another. It is emotionally uplifting to speak to a person instead of a wall or a TV. As the listener, it doesn't matter if you cannot offer the solution to the problem; at least you can be the sounding board, which is frequently all it takes for the speaker to determine her own solution. As speakers, we develop the trust of mindful listeners and look forward to interacting with them again.

Trust does not develop when the other party merely acts like he is listening. A study by Ramsey and Sohi in 1997 shows that ". . . when customers feel that a salesperson is listening to what they are saying, it enhances their trust in that salesperson." The results also show that when customers feel that a salesperson is honest and sincere they are likely to be satisfied in their dealings with him or her. Similarly, trust in the salesperson increases customers' anticipation of future interaction with that salesperson.

Isn't this the same trust you want to build with your spouse, children, and friends? The movie mindset is a shift to the reality of the speaker, not a list of dos and don'ts or tricks to demonstrate that you are listening. Your aim is not to make speakers perceive you as working hard to listen. False listening is worse than no listening at all. The harder you work at listening, at getting people to like you, to meet your customer quota, or make money, the more you work against yourself. It's like golf. The harder you try to hit the ball, the greater the chance that you'll miss it. The movie mindset is the path of less resistance to achieving the success that comes from good listening. This is because your aim is simply to understand the speaker. Everything else falls into place if you get into the speaker's movie.

Coincidentally, the movie experience gradually results in other needed changes in your communication behavior. You begin to find *your* movies less pressing, and therefore you are less prone to talk so much about yourself. Your movie, despite a great story line, gets to be boring, and you learn nothing from playing it over and over again.

As I apply the movie mindset to listening situations, I have become more reluctant to talk about myself and my knowledge of a subject. I am happy to share what I know, but I would much rather delve into another's scenery and get a fresh perspective. Forgetting yourself and getting into the speaker's movie is like going on a vacation from your ego.

One of my students described his experience using the movie mindset:

> Every customer takes me on a journey to his land of problems and concerns. If I let myself become preoccupied with my problems and concerns while listening to his, my day turns out to be a drain on my energy. If, on the other hand, I enter into his situation and forget myself, my day turns into a Technicolor experience! My customers seem less difficult to deal with, I get the job done, and I go home at night telling my wife stories about my fascinating clients. I see my job now in a very different light. I look forward to each workday as a new adventure. Who would ever think that the job of a repo man would be an enlightening experience?

Another plus to the movie frame of mind, just like at the movies, is that except for an occasional exclamation, our tendency to interrupt significantly decreases. Speakers rate interrupting as the number-one most annoying conversational trait. Wanting to interrupt is a struggle for power in conversation. If you are an interrupter, notice how attached you are to controlling the topic and getting across your point of view, how immersed you are in *your* movie, how you are distancing yourself from the listener. (There will be more about interrupting in chapter 8.)

The more you practice getting into other people's movies, the more you will notice how much better people respond to you. We all appreciate a nonjudgmental ear. When listening in the movie, our barriers do not interfere. Because we are seeing from the speaker's perspective, we are not in a position to judge. Instead, the motivation of the speaker's actions are revealed to us. In the end, we may agree or disagree with her views, but we have allowed ourselves to understand why our speaker feels the way she does. In turn, speakers will naturally want to hear from you. You can only hope that when it is your turn to talk, you can contribute to your listeners' knowledge in a worthwhile way.

There are some situations in which getting too deeply immersed in another's movie is not advisable. Doctors working in a emergency room in a big city hospital, for example, may find the movie mindset exhausting and unproductive. Emotions continually run high and many patients' movies are of epic proportions. In a life-or-death situation, listening to how the patient ended up in the ER is not a priority. A physician needs to act quickly and maintain concentration in order to save lives. Yet a social worker, a lawyer, or a policeman may find it necessary to get into the movie of the victim to take the appropriate legal action.

For patients and their families, it is necessary for the physician and staff to acknowledge their feelings and help them find a way to cope. I tip my hat to the physician who, faced with a critically ill patient, can walk that tightrope between sharing the patient's feelings and preserving the necessary objectivity to see that patient and his family through treatment.

Crisis counselors who offer telephone support to the distressed and potentially suicidal are at high risk for burnout. For purposes of safety and openness, these sainted volunteers can offer only phone support and must remain anonymous. Due to the magnitude of callers' difficulties, sometimes these discussions can go on for an hour or more. In addition, counselors have to choose their words carefully and are frequently subjected to harassment or manipulation by the caller. To become too deeply entrenched in the emotional problems of these needy persons puts a counselor at risk for not being able to offer constructive advice in a time of crisis.

Listening to a stroke patient trying to communicate with one good hand, a myriad of facial expressions, and incomprehensible words is a particular challenge. You have to focus on finding the patient's intent and facilitate the release of his thought through some medium—a picture board, spellboard, or writing. This requires you to feel and try to imagine what could be on his mind. Most times, it is neither a bedpan nor a blanket that the patient wants. Instead, it may be his need to hear that his frozen speech is only temporary. Unhappily, this prognosis is not always the case. Equally difficult is dealing with family members who cannot communicate with a loved one victimized by a stroke or head injury. In these situations, distance is not required, and the movie mindset can help you try to understand their pain. It is a way of lightening their burden. They do not need you to cry with them; they need you to listen as they voice their fears and remorse. Only then can they discuss treatment alternatives and make rational decisions about rehabilitative strategies. If patients and families are not genuinely heard during these difficult times, their ability to cope with their situation and accept help will be greatly compromised.

Those of you who complain about poor attention span will probably say that you rarely have a problem concentrating at the movies. In a movie theater there are no other distractions. It is dark and you are so involved with what's happening on the screen that you don't even pay attention to the strangers sitting only inches away to the left and right. Your ability to concentrate is magnificent! However, it is the everyday stuff, like meetings and lectures, that challenge your ability to concentrate.

Most of us have had the experience of becoming absorbed in a movie, so we know how it feels. It is not something we have to *learn* how to do. Yet why is it difficult to get into a conversation partner's movie?

Perhaps the problem lies in your ability to connect with the speaker. How can you step out of your reality and into another's if you have deeper self-concerns competing for attention? Getting out of your own movie and becoming a mindful listener requires three things: 1) the desire to get the whole message, 2) the ability to eliminate the noisy barriers discussed in chapter two, and 3) the willingness to place your agenda lower on the priority list. A mindful listener is not a jealous listener. For example, when a friend or coworker returns from vacation exuberant about his adventures, do you wonder resentfully where he got the money or ruminate on how you wish you had gone somewhere equally exciting? As if there are only a finite number of good vacations to be had or a limited number of promotions to be earned, you may not feel compelled to lend a generous ear. Would you then be satisfied if you could hoard all the great experiences that exist?

On the other hand, if your conversation partner is just plain boring you—like a bad movie—it's a challenge to look for the golden nugget of information or opportunity. You will not find it shuffling along with your eyes focused on the horizon. (Chapter ten will be helpful with these more challenging listening conditions.)

Opening your mind to another's point of view may make you uncomfortable, but your willingness to bend by putting yourself aside to get into your partner's movie is a powerful force in forming stable marital relationships. John Gottman, a psychology professor and marriage-therapy guru at the University of Washington, claims that "only those newlywed men who are accepting of influence from their wives are winding up in happy, stable marriages." He goes on to say that by "getting husbands to share power with their wives by accepting some of the demands they make is critical in helping to resolve conflict." This new approach to marriage counseling may prove more effective than the traditional method of teaching couples mechanical listening approaches like active listening.

Let's examine another path to learning more about our nature. According to Abraham Maslow, the eminent psychologist, the goal of self-development is to achieve self-actualization. If you are self-actualized, you are eager to reach a level of understanding that eventually frees you from focusing on yourself and allows you to focus on others instead. You lack self-consciousness and are psychologically free to explore others' insights. You can turn everyday routines into peak experiences. Each conversation can be as exhilarating as standing breathless before a magnificent sunrise or reveling in the warmth and scent of a crackling hearth on a frigid afternoon.

Eleanor Roosevelt and Henry David Thoreau were among the people Maslow characterized as self-actualized. They accepted themselves and others for what they were. They did not wait for the approval of others before taking action. Self-actualizers listen as though no one else on earth exists at that moment. Isn't that how you want your customers, friends, and family to feel after speaking to you?

Getting into someone else's movie is a natural way of listening. There is no step-by-step approach, nor is it contrived. It is an extension of your curiosity about what it's like to be in their shoes. As a result, people respond to you better because they notice that you are less judgmental and less critical. Dr. Maslow says, "The most efficient way to perceive the intrinsic nature of the world is to be more receptive than active."

Where are you on the road to self-actualization? How secure is your foundation for *listening readiness*? According to Maslow's hierarchy of needs, there are four levels of needs to be satisfied before you are ready to seek self-actualization. The order of needs described below is not fixed, and may vary among individuals. The degree of satisfaction may also differ.

Level 1 involves the basic physiological needs, such as hunger, thirst, sex, and sleep. Once these needs are met, a new set of needs emerges. Level 2 requires a sense of safety. If you have not satisfied your needs at this level, you will mistrust others and be overly cautious in new situations. Next come the needs for affection from others and feeling like part of a group. Maslow refers to these needs as *love* and *belongingness*. Level 4 includes the desire for self-esteem and the ability to achieve goals, to be independent and competent. You are then said to be growth oriented, extending beyond yourself and your ego to become receptive to a wide vista of perception. A self-actualized person becomes, in essence, receptive to seeing life from someone else's perspective.

How to satisfy your basic needs toward becoming self-actualized is beyond the scope of this book, but if you are having difficulty letting yourself listen or if you find it difficult to work through your barriers, there may be other unmet personal needs that require attention and perhaps professional counseling. Attending to some of your unmet basic needs and working your way up the ladder, you can look forward to listening becoming a peak experience.

When you routinely substitute artificial means of communication (e-mail, Internet chat rooms, form letters), you reduce your opportunities for peak experiences that can change your life. Perhaps the attraction of these media is to establish the connections we crave without the hassles of face-to-face contact. Occasionally, my students complain about the inefficiency and dissatisfaction they experience with direct contact with family, friends, or customers. According to them, people don't say what's on their minds; they act foolishly, laugh too much, and beat around the bush. They interrupt, judge, give unrequested advice, and talk too much.

Being drawn into an interesting movie is a spontaneous experience; you do not have to work hard to listen or rely on technique to get into the character's shoes. It is only when we block the spontaneity of listening by focusing on outcome rather than process that listening becomes stilted. Posing, head nodding, and other mechanical listening tricks are unnatural and actually interfere with listening. In *The Way of Zen,* Alan Watts illustrates the virtues of unself-conscious action by describing a centipede's skill in using a hundred legs at once:

> The centipede was happy, quite
> Until a toad in fun
> said, "Pray, which leg goes after which?"
> This worked his mind to such a pitch,
> He lay distracted in a ditch
> Considering how to run.

One of the most interesting listening situations I ever experienced was with my Russian mother-in-law a few summers ago. Unable to speak more than five words of English (four of them dealt with shopping), Etel came to Boston for a visit. My Russian, limited to very basic conversation, contributed nothing but small talk to our relationship. Fortunately, my husband, fluent in English and Russian, was usually around to help with the translation. One night, however, he had to go to a meeting. Earlier in the day he had told me that Etel was tired of watching American TV and preferred to spend the evening talking with me. How, I asked, could she possibly find my limited Russian more entertaining than *Wheel of Fortune?* I pleaded with him to reschedule his meeting! Alas, there was no way out.

After my husband left, I boldly brought out tea and cookies, a Russian dictionary tucked discreetly under my arm, while Etel sat patiently at the dining room table. This, I thought, is going to be the Russian crash course from hell. I poured the tea, hoping that the grammar rules would kick in sometime within the next couple of hours. Etel smiled and looked at me as though I were an old friend and began talking slowly. From the few words and names I could pick up, I deduced that she was talking about life in the old Soviet Union. Gradually, she began to pick up speed, and she became somewhat melancholy. Although I could barely pick out a familiar word, it was obvious that Etel was reliving the past and having a great time telling me about it.

Etel did not sense that I was lost. How could she keep talking without checking to see if I was following her story? At that point, I could have stopped trying and merely nodded every so often to be polite. But I decided to persist. If I couldn't understand her words, I could still listen to the expression in her voice and watch her face. I could also have switched to an overly active approach to listening, interrupting to look up unfamiliar words, asking for repetitions, but I knew instinctively that was not what my mother-in-law needed at the time. Etel needed me to just *listen.* I stayed vigilant; if I surrendered my attention for even a moment, I would lose what fragments of the message I had understood.

An hour went by and I was right there with her *as the KGB officer searched her belongings looking for black-market goods. He reached deep into the side pockets where she had hidden the American blue jeans and the Beatles tapes she had purchased for her son! As she broke out in a cold sweat, the officer glanced up, first with a glare and then with a wink, shut her suitcase and let her go!*

Later, I began to think that my interpretation of what Etel said was off the mark, but it didn't matter—Etel was having the time of her life! My ego, initially obsessed with getting every word and verb tense correct, decided to take an aisle seat and enjoy the show.

An hour later when my husband finally came home, I was sorry to see these stories come to an end. Prior to this night, I had never seen Etel laugh out loud or show so much emotion. I'll probably never know the real stories she shared, but that night changed our relationship. Listening to her did more to establish closeness between us than a hundred shopping trips.

Let's go to the movies

1. Go to the movies or rent a video if you don't have too many distractions at home. An action film or thriller increases your chances of getting involved. Notice how caught up you become and how your body language reflects your involvement in the drama. (I'll bet you didn't plan to lean forward, eyes glued to the screen, when the spy whispers the secret code to his lover prior to falling into shark-infested waters!) When someone leans forward and keeps eye contact while you speak, you know she is truly listening. Also notice how, during the less exciting parts, your mind wanders and how often you have to remind yourself to *get back into the movie.* Are you able to follow the plot or do you easily get lost? Think about how often you drift in and out of conversations and miss out on the plot or the main ideas. Some TV talk shows and sitcoms also lend themselves to this exercise. Using movies or TV shows to sharpen your ability to concentrate is effortless and enjoyable. Afterward, you can reflect on how you were able to put aside your to-do list and forget your own agenda for a while.

2. Plan to get into at least one person's movie a day. It could be a client, a child, or the person who cleans your office. Look forward to a great miniadventure! It might be the cab driver telling you about her busy day, a coworker describing his weekend, or a child relating a funny thing that happened in school. *Live it with them—just like in the* *movies.* Experience the sensation of being in two places at once—in your chair *and* in the speaker's situation. Notice how time stops.

3. Cultural differences pose special challenges to even the best listeners. To get into the movies of people from other countries, you need to be somewhat knowledgeable of their culture and how they feel comfortable relating to others. If your new job or community is made up of foreign-born people, find some literature on their social customs. Pay attention to the kinds of questions, comments, or nonverbal clues that are unique to them. It even makes good business sense to study these differences. Remember, a good listener seeks to understand the speaker.

4. Next, you need to apply this listening mindset to less thrilling but more realistic settings like lectures or meetings. Each speaker has a movie to share. Choose an audiocassette or a radio talk show (like public radio) with few interruptions to practice your concentration powers. Notice how many of the main points you were able to remember. What was the golden nugget of that interview about quantum mechanics? If the topic was not of particular interest, perhaps it was the way the speaker argued his point and handled the criticisms of the interviewer. Go for the gold during these listening opportunities; there's always *something* to be gained. But please, don't get too involved in the debate when you are driving—you may miss your exit!

Mindfulness: Listening in the Moment

If you cannot find the truth where you are,
Where do you expect to find it?

—Master Dogen

In my search for a decent pair of ski pants in a perfectly yuppie ski store, my attention was momentarily snatched by a video advertisement for upscale ski gear. There I was, surfing the racks of jackets and pants, and suddenly the whoosh of skis and a beguiling male chuckle stole my glance. On a large TV monitor was a mountain climber scaling a jagged wall of sunlit ice. The next shot showed a skier being dropped from a helicopter into a powdery bed of snow high above a no-name mountain range (it had to be the Himalayas, I thought!). The sights were spectacular and the athletes courageous, and it was all designed to make the average person like me feel like we were missing out on something—big time.

In between these breath-taking escapades flashed the words that made me sad for those who would take them to heart: "I am not alive when I'm in the office . . . I am not alive when I'm in a taxi . . ." This was clearly code for *I feel alive only when I'm doing something exciting, like risking my life.* Our innate power to stay focused in the present moment, no matter what the task, lies smoldering under the ashes of wishing and dreaming to be anywhere else except where we are right now.

This experience made me think about how extremes of preference and denying the worth of our daily activities and the people in them, for that matter, set us up to feel depressed, stressed, and resentful. For example, cafeteria talk abounds with the following sentiments: *Work is a drag. . . . I live for the weekend. . . . Is it Friday yet? . . . I hate Mondays. . . . It's just a job. . . .* We spend so much energy and thought hardwiring these preferences into our brains that there is little room for seeing our work or our weekends any other way.

The Zen masters claim that it is this constant judgment of people and things, plus our critical self-judgments, that bring on suffering. The barriers to listening discussed in chapter four are some of the ways that we punish ourselves every day. Since we are so attached to our weekends, we rush through work in order to get out of work. We make mistakes, scrimp on quality, and feel guilty, knowing we could have done better. Attachment to these barriers stifles creativity and limits our receptivity to new ideas. Furthermore, this internal strife breeds distractibility and discontent, which in turn weaken concentration and memory. It will take a mighty big raise or a catastrophic event to see our work in another light.

So it is with listening to others. Either the speaker's comments jibe with our way of seeing the world or they do not. Judging and attacking ideas that are contrary to our frame of reference is a form of suffering. It is energy depleting, both internally (makes you frustrated and tense) and externally (creates tension between you and the speaker). The result is poor relationships with others, lost opportunities, and low self-esteem, which are the *real* suffering.

In previous chapters I have described meditation—watching

the breath—as the most natural and effective way to calm the cacophony of the mind. Improved concentration allows you to connect better with the task at hand, regardless of its desirable or undesirable qualities, by producing a deep state of calm accompanied (over time) by a broader and more balanced view of everyday tasks. You see the different features of a task as interdependent and complementary. You may still have preferences, but they remain flexible in your mind—you become less fearful of change.

This more balanced attitude relates directly to listening. If you recall from chapter two, the working definition of mindful listening includes the ability to sustain attention to the spoken word over time. Your ability to concentrate on the message allows you to process and retain the information and determines how well you will remember it minutes and years later.

Concentration is the key to performing *any* meaningful activity well. It is heartening to know that we innately possess the ability to concentrate. It does not require any special training, just frequent application. Think of an activity that requires complete, sustained attention, such as taking an important test, driving in a snowstorm, or playing chess. Your focus on these tasks is propelled by a strong intent to assure a positive outcome—to excel in school, get home safely, or choose the best move. However, the more you concentrate on the *process*, the more positive will be the outcome. Reading each test item carefully, looking for tricky wordings, and rechecking your answers increases your chance of scoring a high grade. If you were to think of nothing but getting an A, the end result would not be so positive.

On the other hand, there are activities that once required a similar level of concentration, but have now become mindless, like sweeping the floor or grocery shopping. These rote activities give the brain a chance to unwind and relax. You can think about other things and even perform other tasks simultaneously: you can eat *and* read, surf the Internet *and* listen to music. These combinations can be very enjoyable. However, you may tend to overuse this ability to multitask and misuse it when it is necessary to focus your attention on a single activity, such as listening. Our environment with its constant bombardment of stimuli challenges your innate ability to relax and focus completely on one task at a time.

Not long ago, I was in an airport with an hour wait for my plane, and I met a former high-school classmate whom I hadn't seen in more than twenty years. We decided to go across the street to a nice hotel for something to drink while we caught up on each other's lives. Outside the bar was a sign that invited us to COME IN AND RELAX. As soon as we were inside, we noticed five TVs, all tuned to different channels! In addition, there was noise from the nearby kitchen and a radio playing behind the bar. Some patrons at tables tried to maintain conversation-like activities while their eyes shifted from TV to TV. It was dizzying! It took every bit of our concentration to hear each other and even more effort to discuss anything in depth. It occurred to me that an intensely distracting environment is regarded by many people as "relaxing."

You lull yourself into a false sense of competency when you think you can make dinner, plan that sales meeting, and help your son with his homework, all at the same time. You may finish all these tasks in thirty minutes or less, but how is the quality? When you look closely, dinner was just edible, you overlooked two of the seven main points for the meeting, and your son is able to spell only six of the ten words on his vocabulary homework. Since the goal is to *finish* these tasks so that you can rush onto the next one, the results are less than satisfactory. You feel depleted and inadequate.

Such mindlessness becomes a habit and begins to creep into tasks that require your full concentration. How often do you look back at the week, the month, the year, and wonder where the time went? Many of us can't remember because most of the time we were in a fog of preoccupation with the past or planning the future. Our attention was scattered all over the place, and the quality of our actions was just good enough to get by. Substandard performance on any task results in low self-esteem and lack of fulfillment.

Eknath Easwaran, author of *Words to Live By: Inspiration for Every Day,* speaks of the dangers of mindlessness: "There is no joy in work which is hurried, which is done when we are at the mercy of pressures from outside, because such work is compulsive. All too often hurry clouds judgment. More and more, to save time, a person tends to think in terms of pat solutions and to take shortcuts and give uninspired performances."

When mindlessness teams up with personal barriers, our ability to concentrate on the message is out of reach. The antidote is to challenge those distractions and focus on the process—establishing a warm relationship with another person, seeing the other's view, and accepting it as valid whether you agree with it or not. Focus on process ensures the favorable outcome you hope for—repeat sales, cooperation from difficult people, better recall. When you listen in a state of mindfulness, your thinking does not yield to the negative barriers described in chapter four. If, however, you still find that your barriers overpower your ability to focus, then you need to spend a bit more time thinking them through.

In my search for a practical means of improving the ability to concentrate and listen more effectively, I came across the writings of Thich Nhat Hanh, a Zen Buddhist monk. After studying his book, *The Miracle of Mindfulness,* I found that my ability to listen had become richer. The essence of Zen is to be in the present. Thich Nhat Hanh describes mindfulness as keeping your consciousness alive to the present reality. Living the present moment of any activity, paying attention to the process, lend themselves to a quality outcome.

A good way to experience mindfulness is to choose a task you typically rush through, like washing the dishes. According to Thich

Nhat Hanh, "There are two ways to wash the dishes. The first is to wash the dishes in order to have clean dishes and the second is to wash the dishes in order to wash the dishes." He says that if we hurry through the dishes, thinking only about the cup of tea that awaits us, then we are not washing the dishes to wash the dishes; we are not alive during the time we are washing the dishes. In fact, we are completely incapable of realizing the miracle of life while standing at the sink. "If we can't wash the dishes," he continues, "the chances are we won't be able to drink our tea either. While drinking the cup of tea, we will only be thinking of other things, barely aware of the cup in our hands."

When you are listening to another but planning your own agenda at the same time, you are really talking to yourself and therefore not truly listening. You have escaped the present in order to be in the future. You may be physically present, but mentally you are bouncing back and forth between past events and future expectations.

Another challenge to mindful listening is that the average person speaks at a rate of 125 words per minute, yet we can process up to 500 words per minute. During that lag time, you can think about your to-do list or you can listen mindfully by using that time to summarize what the speaker has said so far or see the possibilities in what the speaker is proposing. You can also note the emphasis in his voice or the degree of concern in his gestures and facial expressions. When you are in the speaker's movie, you use your resources to be a competent, intelligent listener.

If you have difficulty putting your thoughts, judgments, and other noise aside while you are trying to get into the speaker's movie, you may need some practice staying in the present. Poor listeners have little patience for the present. Thoughts of yesterday and tomorrow are more enticing. Your barriers have little tolerance for information or ideas that are contrary or too lengthy. Impatience shows itself when you fall out of the speaker's movie or want to interrupt.

This is where your daily meditation practice can help. Watching the breath for twenty minutes or more, once or twice a day, is the most effective way to cultivate a sense of comfort with the present. During your practice, do not work at avoiding thoughts of past and future; this is impatience creeping in. Simply recognize the presence of those thoughts and let them pass. Gently steer your focus back to the breath, back to the present. Feel and listen to your breath as it moves in and out. After a while you can breathe less consciously, and eventually you will be able to step back and let the breath move on its own. The same automatic focus will persist when listening. You will be able to step back from your barriers and, without much work, take in the whole message.

Time spent listening, consulting, teaching, or working in the present can be just as memorable as those moments in your life when time appeared to stand still. When listening mindfully, however, your perception is heightened and you experience multilevel awareness. You are able to delve into what makes the speaker tick, how well his body language matches or contradicts his spoken message, his mood, energy level, and other subtle nuances. When you are fully absorbed in the speaker's movie, you are in the present; time appears to stand still. Mindful listening is not a trance or a hypnotic state. You are aware of your surroundings, but they are not a distraction.

The first-century Buddhist philosopher Ashvagosha gives a humorous account of mindful listening:

> If we are listening to a friend, even if a parrot flies down and perches on his head, we should not get excited, point to the parrot, and burst out, "Excuse me for interrupting, but there's a parrot on your head." We should be able to concentrate so hard on what our friend is saying that we can tell this urge, "Keep quiet and don't distract me. Afterwards I'll tell him about the bird."

He goes on to describe mindfulness as "one-pointedness." This means to focus the attention completely on one task at a time. By applying this approach to your daily tasks, you can complete the same number of tasks, only with better quality, and hence, better outcomes. Many of my students tell me they are better able to prioritize activities and eliminate the time wasters. When being mindful appears daunting, remember that one minute of mindfulness makes up for many minutes of mindlessness.

My first experience with mindful listening came on the wings of a martial arts class a few years ago. (Whenever I share this story in my class, there are always a few students who have also studied martial arts who will smile and nod their heads.) In my first martial arts class, after a short breathing meditation, my instructor demonstrated a series of three movements for me to practice by myself. He assigned me to a corner of the room and turned his attention to the higher belts. I couldn't help but notice the black-belt student only inches from my space whirling, with what appeared to be complete control, a jong bong (a six-foot wooden stick). In front of me were a couple of students practicing knife defenses. The instructor noticed my lapses of concentration as I repeated the three-step exercise. After a few reminders, I was punished with a series of fifty pushups that quickly helped me to focus. Never, since grade school, was I so humiliated and humbled by having a weakness exposed publicly. With every class my concentration improved, but not because of the threat of fifty pushups. Rather, it was the sheer pleasure of feeling focused and centered on my task, which was to carry out each movement to the best of my understanding. Eventually, I went beyond what I thought to be my physical limits. What I had always blamed on poor coordination turned out to be the fault of poor concentration and delinquent listening.

Through three years of tears and tests, the mind-body connection began to seem attainable. Mindfulness would stay with me longer and longer after each class, at first just until I reached my doorstep, then for days and ultimately weeks. My work and my personal life reflected this conscientiousness. Even cleaning the martial arts studio after each class along with the other students (originally I judged this as degrading) gave me a sense of contributing to the well-being of my fellow students and the school. After awhile, I noticed it was the higher belts who offered to clean the toilets and scrub the corners. No task was too menial; every task was completed with concentration and care. Now I could better understand how the monks in a monastery take special joy in repeating the same chores day after day.

A similar mind-body connection was described by Mihaly Czikszentmihalyi, author of *Flow*. He defines a flow experience as the pleasant state of concentration or total absorption in a task. Those he interviewed—painters, dancers, and athletes—said that when they were in the midst of their art or hobby, their state of focused energy was like "floating" or "being carried by the flow." When you experience flow often, the quality of your life improves. The opposite of flow is mindlessness. During mindless listening, your barriers create resistance to the message; your mind is scattered.

During my most gratifying listening moments, when my interest and concern about what someone is saying overwhelm my barriers, the sense of flow or timelessness is striking. Sometimes, running with my predawn companions, for example, I become so involved in what my friend says that I don't become breathless climbing a steep incline, nor do I care that it is only ten degrees outside. The run is effortless, and I feel smooth and light and extremely happy.

Take a minute to think of times when you have experienced being in the flow of an activity. It may have been as simple as frosting a cake or as complex as solving a quantum physics equation. How can we summon that sense of flow as we listen to someone?

In my listening classes, we begin to practice mindfulness in gentler doses. We begin by experiencing orange juice as I narrate. Students watch the rush of the deep orange color as the juice is poured into their cups. Together, we smell the citrus perfume and notice how our mouths begin to water. We sip and savor the tartness. We consider the work that went into producing this cup of juice and imagine the beauty of the tree from which it came. We think about the people who made it possible to get the juice to our table. This full experience endures until the last sip. As they listen and ponder the juice, it's always interesting to note that no one looks around the room; each one's gaze and mental focus are centered on the juice.

The point of the exercise is to take a simple human act, something that we typically take for granted, and make it come alive. So often we sleep through life, attributing little or no meaning to our daily activities. Imagine if you lent that same zest to sipping your coffee, conducting a meeting, or cleaning out the refrigerator; how much more satisfied would you feel at the end of the day? I can be sure my students will never again drink orange juice the old way. And if they need a mindfulness refresher, they will simply pour themselves a glass of orange juice.

Mindfulness connects us with the experience of the moment, no matter what the activity. With listening, mindfulness connects us to the listener. *Mindlessness,* on the other hand, means letting the ego-dominated self—concerns with status, past experiences, and other barriers—separate us from the listener. The mindful listener lacks this obsessive self-consciousness that interferes with the ability to concentrate. We feel happier and more positive when we are not focusing on the self.

The most direct way to improve your concentration and become mindful of the present is to practice daily meditation. Meditation helps you to experience a sense of here-and-nowness so that it becomes easier to transfer that state to the act of listening. Quiet, undisturbed deep breathing instills a sense of calm that is conducive to focus. Those who practice meditation know that after even a few days, the ability to stay focused is noticeable. Simply stated, if you cannot keep your mind centered on your breath, how can you expect to concentrate effectively on anything else?

Regular meditation practice has a way of neutralizing your personal prejudices and negative self-talk. These barriers may still pop up from time to time, but they become easier to set aside and impinge less upon your ability to listen selflessly. Because your mind is free of self-conscious noise, you have space to make room for the concerns of others. This is where compassionate or empathetic listening begins.

When you are calm, you can eliminate the noise and pay attention to many different layers of the message simultaneously. Just as a wave is a manifestation of wind, speech is the manifestation of thought. As the wave stirs particles of sand and algae, gesture, facial expression, and vocalization reflect the spoken word. We can appreciate the beauty of the wave with its many life-sustaining elements or we can choose to see only water crashing on the shore and spewing debris. Which do you prefer—watching a talking head or living the moment with the speaker and sharing the riches he has to offer?

Students ask, "Do I have to be mindful all the time? Isn't that exhausting? Doesn't it take too much time?" Ideally, to make mindfulness a habit, we should perform as many acts as possible carefully and with thought. Begin by noticing how often you act mindlessly—driving through a stoplight, leaving the house without your keys, taking down the wrong phone number. That kind of wasted energy is exhausting and time consuming. Mindfulness saves time because you think as you act. Slowing down and carrying out the task with mindfulness significantly reduces the chances of error and mishap.

Whenever I catch myself performing a task mindlessly, I notice that it usually takes about three times longer. For example, today I made a pitcher of grape drink from a can of concentrate. Instead of gently scooping out the contents of the can in a mindful manner, I hurriedly dumped the concentrate into the pitcher. It splashed out all over my white cabinets and sprayed specks of purple on my yellow sweater. Immediately, I had to find spot remover and a white cloth to remove the stains from my sweater. That took five minutes. Another two minutes were needed to clean off the cabinets with bleach, rinse out the rag, and wash my hands. Finishing up the grape drink required another two minutes. It took me nine minutes to complete a task that, if I had performed it in a mindful manner to start with, would have taken three minutes.

On another day, I handed my secretary a hand-written letter to type. I had composed it using a few abbreviations to save time and proofread my rough draft from my perspective only. Instead of taking thirty seconds to review the letter with my secretary or write out some of the ambiguous abbreviations, a two-paragraph letter that would have ordinarily taken five minutes to type required fifteen minutes of revisions—her time and mine.

Recently, a coworker who was about to leave for her vacation told me three vital points to include on an upcoming financial report. Feeling cocky (after all I was writing a book on listening!), I did not take that mindful twenty seconds to repeat what she had said or write it down. Two days later when writing the report, I was able to recall only about 90 percent of the information. To get that forgotten 10 percent, I had to spend another hour tracking down another source.

I'm sure you can think of a dozen examples in your own life of mindless behavior that cost you time, money, or worse. Clearly, the time spent each day cultivating mindfulness through meditation is more than compensated by increased efficiency in all your activities.

Instead of insulting yourself when mindlessness strikes, consider it a wake-up call to become mindful. Make it a point to commend yourself for the moments of mindfulness that make up your day.

Initially, it may seem like you are taking more time to carry out your tasks. You are used to doing everything in haste, so even a minute more will seem like days. Yet as your ability to concentrate improves, you will become more efficient. Tasks done mindfully are done right the first time. There is no need to recheck or redo. Mindfulness saves time.

Get Mindful

1. Choose a few activities that you normally rush through, like washing the dishes, eating your breakfast, or walking to the train. Apply mindfulness by getting all your senses involved. At first, avoid combining activities like eating and reading. Take each activity and experience every aspect for as many minutes as it takes to complete the task. While walking, feel the solidness of the earth on the soles of your shoes, notice your breathing rhythm, sense the air temperature, the breeze against your face. Offer a silent commentary as you walk: "I feel the solid earth under the soles of my feet. My breath is slow and steady. The air is cool with a hint of chimney smoke, and the wind causes the leaves to race against my feet." According to the Buddhist literature, this is called *mental noting*. By thinking or speaking aloud as you perform a task in mindfulness, your concentration stays in the present, centered on the activity. Stray thoughts of the past and future may try to intrude. Acknowledge their trespass (they may be important, like "Whoops! I forgot my umbrella!"), but get back to the present. Notice how you are completely in the present reality, totally focused on the experience of walking. Your initial experiences with mindfulness may seem like they take more time. You'll catch yourself often

thinking about other things. But as your concentration improves, you will be able to derive as much pleasure from your daily ten-minute walk as you would skiing the Rockies.

2. Do a mindfulness check periodically throughout the day. These checks can be very helpful in sharpening concentration. For instance, when I am practicing piano or playing tennis and I start to make careless mistakes, I realize that for those few seconds I imagined myself in Carnegie Hall or I was focused on winning the tennis game rather than playing my best. When I catch myself, I immediately refocus and get back to thinking about being the music or moving with the ball. In an instant, my performance improves dramatically. These slips of the mind can occur during listening too. When you notice it, refocus on your speaker. It's the same with meditation. Ideas seep into consciousness while you are trying to stay with your breath. Let them leave as gracefully as they entered. Get back to following your breath.

3. After you have made a habit staying mindful in a few simple tasks every day, apply mindfulness to listening. Begin by listening to a coworker describe a weekend or a child tell you about a baseball game. Let yourself become part of their experience from start to finish. This is very much like getting into their movie. Notice how much more of the message you absorb when you feel their delight, embarrassment, or other emotions. You'll be surprised at your ability to recall more information, including subtleties like the feeling behind the message. Notice how your thoughts do not stray and how you stay connected with your listener. Next, apply mindful listening to more factual, less engaging discussions, like your boss presenting sales objectives for the month or a lecture on quality assurance. Hear the words, but let yourself savor the motivation behind the words. Think of how these objectives or issues apply to your position and creative ways to implement them. How can you make achieving those objectives fun or more interesting?

4. We are able to listen to information at three to four times the average speaking rate. It is easy for your brain to spend that down time on other things, particularly if the information being presented is rather dry. Look for the golden nugget of opportunity by staying in the present. Instead of thinking about your shopping list or upcoming weekend activities, use that extra brainpower to review what the speaker has said thus far. Look for the possibilities associated with the topic. (We will talk more about how to pay attention in boring meetings later in the book.)

5. A simpler way to set your foundation for mindful listening is to put aside sixty seconds every day for a mindfulness minute. Plan every day, let's say at noon, to become totally immersed in the task at hand. The pleasure from that one minute spent luxuriating in the fullness of the moment, void of negativity, judgment, past, or future, will inspire more mindful minutes down the road.

Chapter Seven

Listening to Ourselves

Part 1: Our Response Is Key

There is a way between voice and presence
Where information flows
In disciplined silence it opens
With wandering talk it closes.

—Rumi

A mindful listener is one who allows the speaker to express her heart and mind and expound on her ideas without censure. If we continually cut people off or refuse to get into their movies, we ultimately discourage them from trying to connect with us.

I recall listening to several radio talk shows following the shooting deaths of twelve students and a teacher at Columbine School in Littleton, Colorado, in April 1999. Some of the talk shows consisted of high-school students discussing the possible motivations behind those who planned the assault. Inevitably, the subject of poor communication with parents or mentors emerged. Several students mentioned that they could not talk easily with their parents. Further probing by interviewers revealed that kids are put off by the *kinds of responses* they are likely to get from parents, especially if they bring up subjects like peer pressure, sex, drugs, or grades. The most dreaded responses reported by these teens were denial and advice giving. Several students said they feared negative judgment by their parents; therefore, they kept to themselves or preferred the company of peers who were less likely to pass judgment.

You can change your way of responding, not by memorizing a new list of tricks or acting differently, but by listening to yourself and becoming aware of the impact of your behavior. When you speak, notice how your words and thoughts consume your attention. The content will most likely be forgotten days or weeks after the interaction. What listeners do remember, however, is the core message of your remarks—that you were intense, full of yourself, naïve, insecure, or upbeat. This chapter introduces you to the insight of self-listening.

The first exercise for this chapter is to eavesdrop (Let's face it— we all do it!) on conversations in a restaurant or at a party, and to note the ways people respond to statements by others. Some people react by giving their point of view, adding information, or simply nodding their heads. The way you respond tells a great deal about you as a listener and the kind of person you are. Think about the people you easily open up to; think about what makes that happen. Then think about a person you find frustrating to speak with. In both cases, you will discover that their manner of responding is a major factor.

If you want to know why your kids don't talk to you, why people avoid striking up a conversation with you, start by identifying your most frequent response types.

Listed below are three statements. After reading each one, jot down on a separate sheet of paper your knee-jerk response. If you have no response, leave a blank. There are no wrong answers here.

1. A coworker says, "If my boss doesn't stop criticizing every suggestion I make, I'm going to quit and go with another group."
Your response: _____
_____
_____

2. A friend at your health club says, "I'm having a real struggle getting myself to come and work out. Between my job and the kids I have no energy for myself. Plus, I feel guilty when Janet has to stay home with the kids while I work out."
Your response:_____
_____
_____

3. Your husband says, "This is the best job offer so far! I wonder whether it's work I'll really enjoy, or do I want it for the money?"
Your response:_____
_____
_____

4. Your teenager announces, "Mr. Atkins will probably be calling you. He said I didn't write that essay—you know, the one I worked so hard on? He thinks I stole it off the Internet."

Your response:_____

_____

_____

During real interactions, notice how often your responses are more like *reactions*. When someone complains, criticizes, or states a feeling, notice how automatically statements of certain types flow from your lips. These are programmed responses, your barriers exposing themselves for the world to hear. If friends, family, and coworkers avoid connecting with you, it may be that you have allowed self-interest, prejudice, negativism, and status to take control of the conversation. On the other hand, the people you like being around forget themselves and their judgments while listening to you. Their responses reflect a selfless sensitivity to your predicament—they get into your movie!

We will now examine some response types that I call *listening stoppers*:

- Denial

- Interrogation

- Advice giving

- Psychoanalysis (without a license)

Then we'll take a look at some *listening encouragers:*

- **Silence**

- **Reassurance**

- **Paraphrasing**

Keep in mind that none of these response modes in isolation is wrong. It is just that some ways of responding are more conducive than others to enriching the conversational connection. Your challenge is to see how your comments reflect your barriers to listening. As you ease the barriers, you will notice greater flexibility in your responses; you will spontaneously be more sensitive to the perceptions of others. A forced or unnatural change in your response style is neither effective nor advised. If, however, you listen in mindfulness with a nonjudgmental ear, you will naturally respond in a way that encourages open and satisfying communication.

Denial in its pure state ("No, I didn't do it," or "No, it is not true,") has its place in the courtroom or in a confrontative situation when the facts are at stake. In these situations, something is true or it is not, and either you did it or you did not. It is important to differentiate between the constructive and destructive forms of denial. Of course we don't like it when people disagree with our point of view, but to those of us who welcome a friendly, informative debate once in awhile, denial of this sort can remove inaccuracies and educate us. To be able to outwardly disagree and support that disagreement with a sound argument is a hallmark of a competent communicator. For example, if you are negotiating an agreement and feel pressured or sense that you are being violated in some way, it is essential that you voice your objection.

It is the destructive forms of denial that affect the listening connection. For example, how often do we discount or reject another's perception of a situation? "It can't be that bad," or "You're making too much fuss about this," are perfect examples of subtle denial. Your child comes home from school after experiencing an embarrassing situation. You respond to the child's story of the event by saying, "I doubt if the kids were *really* laughing at you." Your child hears this as, "You're wrong. You are not telling me the truth. You made this up." In another situation, your child makes a derogatory statement about a classmate. By responding, "It's not nice to feel that way," or "You shouldn't say those things," you make him feel like something is wrong with him for expressing jealousy, anger, or resentment. A parent who makes a habit of denying his child's feelings is courting disaster; it is one reason kids keep things to themselves and share less and less with their parents. A mindful response could be, "That must have been very upsetting. Let's see, can we think of some ways to keep that from happening again?" This response comes naturally when you put aside your point of view and get into your child's movie.

If you encourage your teenager to share his feelings about break-ing up with his girlfriend, it may be difficult to listen to him verbalize his plans for revenge. It is easy to jump in and attempt to persuade him to act like an adult, but this not only denies your teenager's hurt feelings, it denies the fact that your child is a teenager, not an adult. Your job is to listen attentively, put yourself in his movie without interrupting and judging, no matter what he proposes. When the fury dies down, you might ask, "Are there any other ways you could let her know you are upset?" or "Would you like to know what I might do in that situation?"

In the movie *Patch Adams,* actor Robin Williams demonstrated the virtues of accepting the perceptions of others versus denying them. A fellow roommate at a psychiatric hospital was unable to sleep be-cause he had to use the bathroom. His nervous rocking in the bed kept Patch from getting any sleep. Patch asked why he didn't just walk to the bathroom. The roommate responded that he was afraid of the squirrels blocking the bathroom door. At first Patch tried to convince the roommate that he was hallucinating and that squirrels were gentle creatures, not to be feared. This only aggravated the roommate more. Then Patch got into his roommate's movie: he eliminated the squirrels in a make-believe shoot-out. Afterward, the roommate calmed down and they were both able to sleep.

Changing the subject, rolling your eyes, or ignoring your speaker's comments altogether is denial is its most pernicious form. How often do you hear Person A at the lunch table telling about her wonderful vacation visiting relatives in her home town, when Person B pipes in with, "Well, last summer we went to *Hawaii*, now *that* was a *real* vacation!" Person B has stolen the focus of the conversation and denied Person A the joy of reliving the experience and relating the exhilaration of the vacation to others. Person B has ignored the feelings of Person A. You can bet that Person A will never share any . experience with Person B again.

Imagine instead that Person B chooses to get into Person A's movie by responding, "That sounds like it was very restful. Your home town, whereabouts is that?" By sharing and validating Person A's enthusiasm, Person B has created a potential ally in the workplace.

In the case of children, a lifetime of denial responses teaches them to distrust their feelings and intuition and fosters insensitivity to the feelings and needs of others.

Interrogation is one of the most exhausting responses for a speaker to hear. Have you ever come home disheartened by a discouraging event and been subjected to cross-examination by your partner with questions like, "What went wrong today?" or "Why did you do that?" or "Are you crazy?" Questions that attack, criticize, or make assumptions come across to the listener as punitive. A man misplaces his keys, and in the middle of explaining his dilemma to his wife, she interrupts in a condescending tone, "How could you do such a thing?" Such responses make the speaker feel foolish and guilty, and the result is either silence or a nasty argument.

On the other hand, open-ended questions encourage the speaker to express his feelings and may point the way to a solution. "Can you remember where you were when you last saw your keys?" or "How was your day today?" or "How do you feel about that situation?" help the speaker to relax and put his difficulties into perspective. Occasional questions by the listener that request *clarification* help to assure that the information is received accurately, such as, "So, are you saying then that frozen vegetables are more nutritious than fresh vegetables?" or "What do you mean by 'fresh' vegetables?"

However, certain types of questions can become a way of getting control of the conversation. During an informative discussion with a biological expert, a probing question like, "How does the molecular structure of a frozen vegetable differ from that of a fresh vegetable?" may be appropriate. If you are speaking to a dietician though, these deeper questions may pull the speaker away from the original intent of her message (which just may be to improve your nutrition). Asking questions as a means of manipulating the conversation usually succeeds in discouraging interaction. A mindful listener asks questions to better understand the speaker and his views. A mindless listener asks questions to fulfill her own agenda.

Beware of turning a friendly contact into an interview in which you ask endless questions but volunteer nothing about yourself. This makes it very difficult for the person being questioned to exit the conversation. He may have a difficult time figuring out whether you are truly interested in the topic or have some ulterior motive. Leave interrogating to the police and you'll have much more repeat business.

Advice giving is often linked with denial. This is frequently the mode of consultants and the eldest child in a large family. Being the eldest of five, I was often accused of this. A rule of thumb should be, *Give advice only when asked and keep it short!* When you supply unrequested advice, you may feel you are doing your listeners a great favor, but you may be totally blind to the fact that they are very capable of solving their own problems.

Sometimes what you may consider sharing information can also come across like advice giving. A good example is the new, far-from-being-a-millionaire son-in-law whose hobby is the stock market. The father-in-law makes a statement about a potential stock purchase. In the hope of winning the respect of his new and already wealthy in-laws, he remarks about his new family's stock holdings and points out flaws in their approach to staying rich. The son-in-law ignores the rather blatant lack of interest on the part of his in-laws and persists with his advice. The in-laws, clearly annoyed, try to change the subject. The son-in-law ends up feeling thwarted by the very people he wants to impress. His in-laws resent the insinuation that they cannot manage their own affairs. This young man has now set the stage for a poor relationship with his new family.

Advice, unsolicited, sends the message that the receiver is not capable of solving his own problems; it is the ultimate put-down. Remember that take-it-or-leave-it information, like giving someone a free tip or mentioning a contact that might be of interest to them, is positive. It may not always be helpful, but it is not offensive. Unrequested advice frequently takes on a preachy tone, even if it is good, sound, well-meaning advice. Chronic advice givers relish a sense of power and altruism. There's nothing more self-inflating than leaning back in your chair, slapping the desk, and starting every sentence with, "If I were you I would . . ." This response style reinforces a judgmental and status-prone barrier toward the listener.

To top it off, quite often the advice being given suits the advice-giver more than the advisee. Imagine a muscle-bound, aggressive father whose meek and frail son has just been the target of the classroom bully. After hearing about the confrontation, the father states, "Listen son, the best way to drive off a bully is to let him have it, right between the eyes!" This kind of advice is double trouble—not only did the child not request it, but the advice was insensitive to the son's disposition and physical abilities. Instead of listening to how his son felt about the altercation and the bully, the father made his son feel worse. The advice may or may not have been the right thing to do, but it was given in a mindless manner.

Advice giving can be a major obstacle to close parent-child relationships. Some kids avoid discussing problems with their parents because they give unwanted advice. (Parents, in their defense, sometimes feel that they are responsible for fixing the problem and that their advice is needed to avoid mistakes.) Over half my students report difficulties communicating with their parents. The most frequent complaint is that one or both parents are consistently judgmental and force unwanted advice on their children, disguised as so-called "guidance." Probably these parents want only to help their children, but they often forget how they saw the world in early adulthood. Parents blinded by wisdom, experience, and hard knocks may find it difficult to get into the movies of their teenagers. It takes careful self-listening and control to avoid sounding critical. Other response styles, such as paraphrasing, silence, and reassurance, are more suitable methods of building trust. Once inside your child's movie, you may notice that she has already considered many solutions for herself. Your presence as a sounding board may be all she needs.

If you can restrain yourself from responses that impose self-judgment—advice giving, interrogation, and denial—your tendency to prejudge and discriminate may lessen. Along with a reduction in negative self-talk, this will enable you to adopt a more open mind to new ideas and different perspectives.

If you are particularly prone to advice giving, you may also indulge in **psychoanalysis (without a license)**. You may feel that some deity has bestowed upon you a gift of insight so much deeper and more knowledgeable than your conversation partner's that to abstain from getting to the root of her problem is an injustice. Looking back to my high-school days, it was an introduction to existentialism that made me question life's purpose and human behavior. After several semesters of psychology classes, it was tantalizing to look for symptoms of manic depression, schizophrenia, and obsessive-compulsive disorder that could be the basis of the physical illnesses of my troubled friends and relatives.

Hours of discussion and probing self-analysis (perspectives that changed with the weather) further galvanized my tendency to make psychological diagnoses. In addition to giving advice to my younger siblings and anyone else who had the misfortune of sharing their woes with me, my new bounty of book-born wisdom led me to feel responsible for their mental health. Exasperated at their lack of follow-through on my suggestions for a happier existence, I began to examine my own behavior in a more constructive way. I saw that psychoanalyzing only prevented friends and family from sharing their feelings with me. This is also common to those who have participated successfully in counseling sessions and are eager to share their methods for overcoming fear or depression. But this kind of well-meaning help can be perceived as an invasion of privacy, and it carries the undesirable characteristics of interrogation. Like advice-giving, psychoanalysis should be left to licensed clinicians. Unless you are qualified to play Freud, it is best to remain silent and mindful.

Those of us who admit to the overuse of advice-giving and psychoanalyzing our listeners might try to get comfortable with the next response mode—**silence.** Silence is one of the most powerful response modes, but—regrettably—the least practiced. (It is important to note here the distinction between attentive silence and silence born of anger, boredom, or lack of interest. Negative silence is accompanied by fidgeting, breaking eye contact with the speaker, or otherwise withdrawing your attention. This kind of silence can be destructive to any relationship.) If you can remain silent, keeping eye contact with the person who has just spoken, you hold the key to the treasury of information to come.

Our ancestors, even as recently as our great-grandparents, were more comfortable with silence than we are today. Long ago the world had a more homogenized view of silence, where women generally deferred speaking rights to their fathers or husbands, and wise men and the elders (including women) expected lengthy silence from children as a sign of respect.

But today, most of us feel uncomfortable with silence. Our ears have accommodated a threshold of noise pollution so that a moment or two of quiet is unsettling. Perhaps this is one reason why, when someone is talking, we start thinking about what to say next, just to keep that comfort level of noise constant. We feel compelled to jump in right away and make a comment or argue the point. This nervous talk is often why we are unable to get beyond surface information to the real depth of the message. We don't allow the speaker to develop his ideas or give him the opportunity to reveal the core of his concern. As long as you continue to believe that listening is an ego-active exercise, that you need to exert control in order for the interaction to be beneficial (interrupting, questioning, advising), it will be difficult to discover the treasure of silence.

In Far Eastern cultures, silence as a behavior is revered and cherished. However, in Western cultures where fast pace and constant action reign, silence is disdained as negative and unproductive. Those who are typically silent at meetings or in group discussions tend to be viewed as indifferent and unmotivated, not team players.

When two or more of us congregate, we feel compelled to fill quiet spaces by asking too many questions, talking too much, laughing too much, or completing sentences for others. To escape silence, we look around the room, sip a drink, or clear our throats. In an elevator we try to ignore silence by staring at the numbers or the floor.

Yet in the privacy of our homes after the children have fallen asleep or under the stars on a moonlit pond, silence is our friend.

Since most of us interact daily at work or in our communities with people from different cultures, it is important to be aware of and sensitive to the varying perceptions and misinterpretations of silence to avoid intercultural misunderstandings. A cross-cultural survey taken by Satoshi Ishii and D. W. Knopf in 1976 showed that the average person in the US converses twice as long (six hours and forty-three minutes) than the Japanese (three hours and thirty-one minutes). Westerners speak first, listen second, and observe third. Eastern cultures prefer a different order: observe, listen, speak.

An important feature of Japanese interpersonal relations is the notion of *enryo-sasshi*. In 1984, Ishii pointed out how the Japanese simplify their messages and avoid verbal elaboration of their ideas, depending instead upon the intuition of the listener to derive the full meaning. In his article, "Silence and Silences in Cross-Cultural Perspectives: Japan and the United States," Ishii describes "his or her psychological 'exit,' through which the encoded messages are sent out under the impact of *enryo* (reserve or restraint) is considered to be much smaller than his or her message-receiving entrance, called *sasshi*."

If you are a Westerner working abroad in an Eastern culture, it is important that you be attentive to the notion of *enryo-sasshi*, because if you talk too much and elaborate on ideas and feelings, you demonstrate poor *enryo*. This is considered rude. A person of good *sasshi*, on the other hand, is highly appreciated by others, because he is good at perceiving the whole message through the context, body language, and tone of the situation; he is viewed as wisdom seeking, open-minded.

As you begin to put mindful listening into action, your perception of silence changes. You start to notice more about the people around you. The unproductive act-like-you are-listening mode gives way to an information-gathering mindset. Your natural curiosity for learning is released from captivity after decades of stagnant, self-centered thinking. Relationships with family and coworkers become richer as silence creates space and time for understanding others.

Most of us have rarely experienced deep, true silence. We think of silence as being quiet on the outside. Deep silence, an uncomfortable bedfellow for many of us, means no internal noise either. If you've been faithful to your breathing practice, you may have experienced glimpses of true silence as the chatter in your head begins to settle down. During those rare moments, you are truly in the present, not thinking of your past mistakes nor anticipating the ones you are going to make. Uneasiness with silence of any kind is a major reason why so many of us have trouble listening. Yet, when we are given the gift of extended, attentive silence by a listener, there is a tendency to bask in its glow and reveal the depths of our soul.

One day, a statuesque, exquisitely dressed woman in her forties, whom I will refer to as Ellen, came to our voice clinic complaining about an intermittent loss of voice. Her throat exam had been normal and her voice sounded fine. She presented herself as cordial, confident, and cheerful. I began with my usual list of questions about how she used her voice every day. Ellen described herself as a high-powered executive, frequently on the phone and a presenter at meetings. For relaxation, she read voraciously, played the flute, and enjoyed a massage and facial once a week. As I imagined this lifestyle, interrupting to impose my agenda was the last thing on my mind. I was eager to determine how she was able to manage all these activities. Ellen, with her dazzling smile and somewhat boastful manner, continued to fascinate me with her enviable lifestyle as her voice became weak and breathy. She started clearing her throat, showing discomfort.

After several minutes, Ellen paused and took a deep breath. I sat stunned into silence and began to collect my thoughts in order to proceed with my assessment. Gradually, over a matter of ten seconds, a cloud came over her triumphant expression, and she began to cry softly. Now I really was in shock! I could have muttered something clinical at this point, but I didn't want to put a stop to the stream of thoughts I saw coming. In a still weaker and strained voice, Ellen spoke angrily about her troubled marriage, sick parents, and a pending lawsuit by a former coworker. More crying. Ellen finished her story with a voice very close to normal. Ellen was horribly embarrassed to have taken up my time in this manner, yet she felt tremendously relieved. She even admitted to keeping much of this information from her psychiatrist. It was clear to both of us that her episodic voice problems were stress related, and we were able to agree on an appropriate course of treatment. Looking back, it was a world's record for me to stay silent, yet it was the best thing I could have done for Ellen.

When you become absorbed with the speaker's movie, as I was (clearly my agenda took a back seat to Ellen's shocking accounts!), you don't worry about what to say next. Your speaker will appreciate your silence and relish the chance to get to the heart of the matter.

When you listen in the speaker's movie, you also tune into the silences between words—they scream with meaning. Disappointment, reluctance, heartbreak, anticipation, remorse, hopefulness, and anything else the speaker cannot effectively put into words become loud and clear in the silences. Many of the emotional casualties in our lives stem from attending only to the words, the footprints and shadows of the message, and we regard that as "listening."

Too often those moments needed to elaborate on a feeling are cut off by questions, comments, or a change of subject. I recall doing these same things because I felt uncomfortable with silence. It was important for me to take control of the session and get on with my agenda to treat the patient. It took Ellen to teach me that attentive, supportive silence is often the best treatment. For Ellen, it was the catalyst for her to see the connection between her anxiety and her voice.

There are similar situations with patients referred to me for presurgical counseling. They may have cancer of the larynx and must have the voice box removed. You cannot imagine how devastating this can be, particularly to anyone who uses his voice for a living. My job is to inform them of the alternatives for communicating after surgery. Occasionally I get a patient, angry about the upcoming surgery, whose voice complaints were ignored or misdiagnosed. They may have acquired reputations for being problem patients. These patients need to express their feelings, but are discouraged by hearing responses like denial and advice giving. The last thing they want to hear about is an artificial voice substitute. In these situations, I introduce myself and let them know that I will be able to help them communicate after surgery. Then I ask them how they are doing. From then on, I remain silent and get into their movie. Immediately, they recount their experience, tell about their families, or their deepest concerns. They may cry and even scream out their anguish. Sometimes they need to be reassured about the surgeon's credentials or their fear of dying in surgery. They cannot discuss many of these issues with their spouses. By the end of the meeting, they often apologize for their outbursts, and in the same breath, thank me profusely for helping them. Despite the fact that I never get to my agenda, they still feel I do them a great service.

Silence is virtuous in its ability to make your speaker feel good about himself. Silence allows the speaker's deeper thoughts to surface, thoughts that often contain solutions to problems. When you allow your speaker the time to think out loud in a supportive environment, you set the stage for her empowerment, and she will want to be in your company more often.

Silence is also a powerful negotiation tool. Your speaker's real priorities may not be the parcel of land or the salary. Perhaps what he really fears is loss of prestige or control. If a worker demands a raise and shorter hours, he may be complaining about the cost and flex-

ibility of the daycare center at your facility. By making room for silence, the real issues come to the surface, thus short-circuiting hours
of unproductive arguing and escalating antagonism.

On the lighter side, I must make a confession. I often find silence quite entertaining. In the past it was more common for me to
share my experiences equally with my speaker, but more often these
days I find it enjoyable to hold myself back from sharing my experiences, particularly when the speaker is having one heck of a time
telling hers.

For example, one day my husband and I were walking in the
woods with our dog. We came across another beautiful dog, Chester,
and his owner, Kate. Kate is a fascinating woman whom I run into
every so often. She always has some unusual insight to share. This
time she started talking about the spiritual nature of dogs and their
connection to man. Being a dog lover myself, I could relate to her
point of view. At first I felt a bit of an urge to jump in and share my
feelings and experiences, but drew myself back into her movie because she was so exuberant in support of her theory. My contribution
would have added little, and I didn't feel a personal need for feedback. It was just plain interesting to listen to her. Kate went on to
talk about yoga and how it had changed her life. I too practice yoga
regularly and find it extremely helpful. I would have liked to let her
know that I share her interest, but she left no room for interruption.
And the best part was that it was okay! I did not feel the least bit
slighted nor did I need to focus the conversation on myself—I was
totally in Kate's movie. As we neared the gate, Kate mentioned how
she hoped someday to write a book about dogs and asked me what I
knew about book writing. I mentioned that, as a matter of fact, I was
in the process of writing a book. She asked me the topic. I told her it
about listening. Needless to say, Kate was embarrassed by having done
so little listening throughout our walk. To reassure her, I told her
how interesting her insights were and how I thoroughly enjoyed hear-

ing her point of view. Kate commented, "Even though I did all the talking, it felt so good to have someone feel the same way I do!" I realized that silence is a form of sharing.

Notice too, when you are in your speaker's movie, how relaxed and tuned in your posture becomes. Chances are, you are keeping eye contact with the speaker, occasionally nodding your head, and leaning slightly forward. Silence is not so uncomfortable when you are in the speaker's movie, because you naturally listen with your whole body—just like at the theater! Your posture and facial expression naturally react to the message and the messenger. There is no space for self-conscious noise or thinking about past or future. Your mind is centered on receiving not only the speaker's words and gestures, but the feeling behind the message. (Later, I will discuss how silence can be a powerful ally when listening under stress.)

Comforting a friend suffering through difficult times is never easy. You feel you have to say something in order to show that you share their feelings. In these situations supportive silence is the best response. By offering silent support, you encourage your speakers to describe their feelings, vent anger and frustration, and relate their problems in detail. You *are* responding by simply not talking.

Closely linked to silence is appropriate and supportive **reassurance.** Statements like, "Yes, I see that your situation must be very difficult," or "I'm sure you'll do the right thing," restore confidence and courage. These kinds of responses are devoid of judgment and denial of their pain; they reassure your friend that you empathize with him. Although it can be comforting to know that other people have experienced the same feelings and survived, most persons in the immediate stress of job loss or family tragedy cannot derive comfort from hearing you relate a similar experience or pointing out the silver lining to their black cloud.

When reassurance is sincere, accompanied by a warm voice and a simple gesture, it is appreciated. For example, Bob comes home after a difficult day at the office. He laments to his wife, Kelly, that he is burned-out tired of the politics at work and feels no challenge. Both parties know there is no immediate solution to the problem—money is tight and the jobs in his field are not plentiful. If Kelly were to suggest he just quit, this would cause an argument. What Bob needs right now is reassurance and support. A comment like, "I know you try every day to make the best of this situation; I really admire your patience," is just the right touch. However, a reassuring response that lacks sincerity may come across as condescending or insensitive to the speaker's experience.

A medical student once told me about an attending physician who forbade students to tell their patients, "I understand." The physician warned that unless they had personally experienced the patient's disease and its emotional side effects, it was dishonest to claim understanding of the patient's predicament.

Many attempts to reassure someone after loss of a loved one often backfire. Old standby comments like, "At least she isn't suffering," and "You know he's in a better place," are subtle ways to avoid a bereaved person's movie. We don't want to be dragged down into their sorrow, so we say such things to distance the distressed person from his emotions and get back in control. What those beset by tragedy need is to talk about their loved ones. Attentive silence and empathy, not sympathy, are most appreciated.

Paraphrasing is one of my favorite response styles because it provides much for both speaker and listener. Paraphrasing is the act of repeating back your speaker's message for the purpose of clarity and reflection. It is a way to let her know you're doing your best to understand. It also serves as a way of hearing the message again to more deeply process the meaning behind the words.

Mindful listeners are sensitive to two variations of paraphrasing: *parroting* (repeating back as exactly as possible what the speaker says), and *summarizing* (putting into our own words the gist of our speaker's message). Parroting should be used when exact information like numbers, times and dates, or other precise details are concerned. For example, I say to my secretary, "Lori, please make three copies of that report. Send the original to Mr. Smith, and one copy each to Dr. Jones and Dr. Jackson. The third ones goes into my file." Lori parrots my request by saying, "So you want me to send the original to Mr. Smith, a copy to Dr. Jones, a copy to Dr. Jackson, and put the third copy in your file." By this response, I know with certainty that I have communicated the information correctly. I get a chance to hear back what I said and make any clarification that's needed, and I feel confident that the task will be carried out correctly. By parroting back the message, Lori had a chance to hear it again too. She feels confident that she can do what needs to be done.

This style of responding is most helpful when taking directions. How often have you stopped a stranger for directions and could not remember what he told you? Your negative self-talk distracted you from being in the moment. You thank him, roll up the window and try to find someone else.

Let's redo this scenario in mindfulness, using paraphrasing as a way to clarify the directions and store them in memory. You stop and ask the stranger for directions and visualize the route as he describes it. In your mind's eye, you see the left at the light, and the right at the stop sign. After he's finished, say, "Let me be sure I have this straight," and you proceed to repeat the directions. So far, I have never yet found a stranger who objected to this. Paraphrasing is a practical and time-saving approach to effective communication. When you correctly parrot back the information in your own words, both parties are satisfied that the message was received.

Summarizing to assure that the speaker's needs and/or feelings have been understood is usually the first step in firming up a relationship. This checking in to see if you're on the same page can be helpful in a stressful interaction or in a negotiation, because in heated discussions we are not good at hearing or saying the right words; then we get angry when the other person interprets us wrongly. As a mindful listener, you get deep in the speaker's movie, synthesize the words, gestures, facial expressions, and tone of voice to arrive at the best guess, but it is still only a guess. That is why you need to check with the speaker. It may mean asking a question like, "Are you saying that you'd rather I have more normal working hours?" Or it may be in a statement, like "I sense you're discouraged with this project and you'd like to switch to a different one." Sometimes it takes a mindful listener to sum things up for a speaker, to clarify the thoughts or the vibes they are sending out.

Irene, your employee, comes into your office one day and gives notice. She explains that a highway construction project near her home makes the morning commute impossible to predict, and moreover, she has a teenager with some serious behavioral problems. The result is that Irene is frequently late for work, and although she makes sure her phone is answered until she arrives, she feels guilty asking others to cover for her.

In this case, it would be clearly unproductive for you to parrot back all the grisly details. Instead, summarizing her explanation lets her know she's been heard. "Irene, I understand that things are quite hectic for you at home right now. You really enjoy working here, and I see that you've tried to make other arrangements, but you feel obligated to offer your resignation because you have to rely on others for coverage. Do I understand you correctly?" Irene nods her head, and the expression of relief on her face is unmistakable. Your summary of her problem opens the path toward a solution other than quitting her job, such as shorter hours or a different starting time.

When I summarize in this way, my conversation partners are often relieved—as Irene was—to hear the words that they *wanted* to say. Other times, my attempts to clarify the message are off the mark and I need to be set straight. In either case, paraphrasing by summarizing pays off. (In contrast, parroting in situations where feelings and volatile emotions are involved can come across as sarcastic or condescending. Summarizing, on the other hand, sends the subliminal message, "I am repeating what I think you said, because I really want to understand your viewpoint."

Paraphrasing is also a way—without being judgmental or hinting at advice—of getting people to reflect on what they communicate. Suicide-prevention hotlines teach their counselors to paraphrase as a way of clarifying a caller's view on a problem and getting him to continue talking. Since there is no visual communication, it is important to let the troubled caller know with more than a few "Uh-huhs" that the counselor is listening.

In my classes, the paraphrasing exercise can be painfully surprising. It exposes weaknesses in attention and memory, yet with practice it quickly improves focus and retention. One student reads a two- or three-step direction or a short, informative paragraph to a partner. The partner has to paraphrase. The reader then provides feedback on accuracy and, if necessary, clarifies the information. After the first several minutes of this exercise, it is easy to see why we often lose information and make so many listening mistakes.

Paraphrasing has been criticized as an unnatural way of responding. To these criticisms I say, yes, paraphrasing, like any other response style, can be overused and become mechanical. And, yes, it sounds strange to let your speaker know you want to be sure you got his message—but isn't that what good communication is all about? If you understand the purpose of paraphrasing, you will tend to be conservative in its use.

I make paraphrasing a regular component of voice therapy. At our first visit, I encourage my higher-functioning patients to ask questions if there is something they don't understand, because I'll be checking periodically to make sure they do. This immediately sets the stage for more active participation on their part. After explaining the goal of the session and going through a series of exercises to meet that goal, I often ask the patient, "Why did we do those exercises? What was the point?" If the patient cannot answer correctly, i.e., is not able to paraphrase the goal of the session, then I know the patient was not listening, did not understand, or I did not explain it clearly. In the latter case, the patient may not have given me any verbal or nonverbal indication that she did not understand.

With practice, the patient becomes more involved with the session because she knows that she has to make the link between what she is trying to achieve and how she is going to do it. After telling back her understanding of the session, she is more motivated to practice the exercises, since she understands the connection with the goal. I know this because she was able to verbalize it. I also apply these same techniques with my students. A student describes an exercise and carries it out correctly. At the end of the session, it might go like this:

Me: Today you came with questions about coordinating your breath support and vocal pitch. Now that we've reviewed that process, is it clearer?

Patient: Yes. I can do both now and it sounds and feels better.

Me: I need to be sure that I have explained these ideas clearly. Please tell me how you understand this method and then demonstrate the process.

After the student explains and demonstrates the exercise, I clarify any weaknesses. The student and I are both satisfied with the session. The student has achieved another skill level, and we have both made an investment in the learning process.

This form of paraphrasing is appropriate in any teacher-student situation because both share the same interest—to correctly execute the process to achieve a positive outcome. Many people are reluctant to ask questions. They don't want to appear stupid, they don't want to take up your time, and/or in the past they have not had patient instructors. In any teaching or sales interaction, encourage your speakers to tell back how they understand the procedure so you can be sure that you communicated the information correctly. Let them know that mistakes are fine. Do not judge their responses as right or wrong; just offer *clarification*. It is important to you, for instance, that they understand how to use the equipment you are selling them. Chances are, they will be grateful and remember the time you took to listen to their questions in order to make them happy customers.

Honest communication between customer and salesperson, teacher and student, or therapist and patient is essential to success; both parties must see themselves as equal partners. In a balanced, barrierless environment, students and patients feel comfortable enough to ask questions, clarify problems with the learning process, and openly discuss their progress. Paraphrasing invites this give and take. Make paraphrasing a habit in these situations, and note how your confidence in your ability to process information soars!

To be agile in the use of these and other ways of responding requires self-listening and practice. Remember that response styles are situation dependent. If, however, you let yourself into the speaker's movie and forget your own agenda for awhile, you will become more sensitive to their needs and hear yourself respond in a more varied and natural manner. Keep in mind the many different combinations of responses you may give. In the above examples, silence and reassurance are comfortable partners. Paraphrasing combines well with any of the response types when clarification is required.

Examining your habitual responses to your speakers helps you better understand your attitude toward listening to others. When you converse with others, you and your listeners find out who you really are. For example, advice giving, denial, and interrogation are *self-centered* response styles, and they send the message of aggressive, ego-driven closed mindedness. Conversely, paraphrasing, silence, and reassurance are *speaker-supportive* styles. If you develop these qualities, your speakers will perceive you as secure with yourself, open to new ideas, and caring.

Now, go back to the first exercise at the beginning of this chapter and label your responses. What kind of message about yourself did you plant? During your next conversation or while listening to others, notice how the majority of preferred listeners (those that we feel a connection with) predominantly support the speaker, while poor listeners support themselves.

Catch Yourself

1. As you read through this chapter, you were probably able to identify with a few habitual response modes. Notice how often you use these modes during an average day, and make note of the reactions you get. Think how you might have responded differently, using some of the other response types.

2. Sit back and listen to conversations. See if you can identify some of the more common response types. Notice the reaction of speakers to certain responses. Think of how you might have responded. Note too the combination of responses a good listener offers.

3. Here are seven statements that might be directed to you from different people. Using what you have learned about mindful responding, what would you say or *not* say in response to these statements:

- I'm leaving my wife.

- I have the hardest time meeting nice men.

- Do you think I need to see a counselor?

- The government should ship these good-for-nothing immigrants back home.

- My wife tells me I need Viagra.

- I just can't get into an exercise habit.

- I look fat and frumpy in this suit.

4. Pick one of the more powerful modes (such as silence or paraphrasing) and apply it at least once a day. Select a person with whom you frequently converse. Let her talk. Avoid interrupting. Don't take the stage from her. Don't try to teach her anything. Be silent, or if she looks like she wants feedback, paraphrase what she told you without making a judgment. Notice how much more she wants to share with you and how much more you learn about her.

5. Get more practice with paraphrasing. There are several ways to make this a habit. The next time you're out walking, stop someone and ask for directions to a nearby destination. Repeat the directions for confirmation. Both you and the person you stopped will feel good that the directions were communicated correctly. Another way is to paraphrase with someone who accuses you of *not* listening. Show that you are making an effort by repeating

in your own words what he said. Notice how after only a few times, he will likely make a comment that you are paying more attention. In some relationships, this little bit of effort on your part can mean the world to your partner.

6. Encourage others to paraphrase you. If your child has trouble following directions in school, ask him to repeat simple instructions like, "David, please go upstairs and get the blue sweater from your drawer and give it to Mike. Now, tell me back what I just said." Reward him for his cooperation and notice how every time he succeeds, his self-esteem zooms.

7. If you are faithful to your daily breathing practice, you will naturally become more comfortable with silence. As you center your concentration on the breath, notice how your mind noise settles down. Your tendency to start thinking about what you're going to say while the other person is still talking will be reduced. The more you practice, the longer you will be able to sustain a mindful listener's composure, free from barriers and internal distraction. Your responses will reflect your speaker's needs and less self-interest.

Listening to Ourselves

Part 2: The Listener's Pariahs

Blessed is the man who, having nothing to say,
abstains from giving us worthy evidence of the fact.

—George Eliot

I f we could listen to ourselves as we converse, we would probably be astounded at how often we speak mindlessly. We are so taken up with being the speaker that, quite innocently perhaps, we make insensitive comments, speak inaccurately, or talk too much, hardly aware of the effect of those actions. Mindless speaking is a proven listening stopper.

For example, I was recently corrected by a patient, notorious for her attention to detail, for using the word *girl* to refer to a twenty-year-old woman who worked at the desk. I meant no harm by that slip of the tongue, but in the eyes of my patient it was offensive.

Having heard that I was from Chicago, a native New Englander asked me if I noticed any differences between Bostonians and Chicagoans. In the past I might have mindlessly responded that I felt that people in Boston tend to be less friendly and more conservative. These words would have certainly ruffled his feathers. Now when I'm asked such a question, I try to consider my listener *before* I speak. I might say, "Bostonians appear to me to be more private," or "Bostonians take a little more time to get to know strangers." Both statements communicate my perceptions without hurting anyone's feelings.

The last time you were faced with an angry customer, did you make things worse by giving excuses or stating company policy? *Ugh!* According to Jeffrey Gitomer, public relations consultant, customers hate the word *policy.* The next time, shift your perspective to the customer's concerns. You might say, "Yes, that's terrible. The fastest way to handle that is . . ." It is likely that you will keep that customer.

Think of the times when others have offended you. Did they say those things on purpose? Couldn't they sense your embarrassment or irritation despite your smile? No, probably not. They were deep in their own movies, unaware of yours.

Mindless speaking is so annoying that perhaps it is one of the reasons we dwell more and more in removed forms of communication like e-mail, Internet chat rooms, and faxes. We make the connections we crave but avoid the hassles associated with face-to-face contact. Occasionally, I get students who sign up for my listening course at the behest of their employers. These students admit that they prefer to distance themselves from customers at all costs. They often complain about the inefficiency and dissatisfaction they experience in face-to-face or telephone contact, not just with customers, but sometimes even family and friends. Some avoid personal contact because people don't get to the point, they act foolishly, laugh too much, and beat around the bush. They interrupt, complain, judge, give unrequested advice, and talk too much. To them and a growing number of onliners, most people are to be avoided.

Denial, endless interrogation, or the dreaded advice-giving responses are just a few of the gaffs that can be avoided with a bit of mindfulness. Try being your own customer for a change. Call into your office with a question or a complaint, preferably late in the day (about ten minutes before closing time is good). How well are you treated? When you hang up the phone, how do you feel? Great or offended? Respected or resentful? Listen to your voice mail. What's your perception? Do you feel welcomed or like a number? Is there even a hint of sincerity in that voice about your call being important?

Interestingly, the more mindful you are of the movies of your speakers, the more sensitive you become to your own words. The next time you say something you regret, notice whether you were propelled by self-consciousness, ego fulfillment, or disrespect for the speaker's perspective. Smile at your newfound awareness, knowing that this discovery will prevent future mindless moments. Avoid putting yourself down. Instead, remember that your intentions were good. Next time, notice how much more appropriate your comments are when you are mindful of not only your intent, but the perspective of your listener. You will say less and learn more. Your mind won't wander around looking for a clever rejoinder so that your conversation partner can see how clever and amusing you are.

One of the benefits of meditation is that you learn to pause before you speak. Meditation deautomatizes your false self, the part of the ego that is self-conscious, insecure, righteous, and deluded by your barriers. If your foundation for listening is not based on meditation and mindfulness, it feels awkward and mechanical to stop and think before speaking. You have to first clear your mind of traffic, stop wondering what the other person is thinking about you, get comfortable with the silence, try to remember what the speaker just said, and formulate a response. Drudgery of this sort discourages you from making self-listening a habit. Fortunately, daily mindfulness practice makes it comfortable and natural to take in the whole message and choose your words carefully in much less time and with greater accuracy. Your words must match as closely as possible how you feel and what you want. However, there are many interpretations out there. Aside from words alone, other features of your speech can flip the meaning. Varying combinations of characteristics like speech rate, pauses, pitch contour, emphasis, loudness, facial expression, and eye contact may concoct a message well beyond your intent.

Mindful listening includes the ability to listen to what you say and make necessary changes. When writing a memo, you are more careful with word choice. Because you can *see* what you want to communicate, it is easier to review your message and edit vague or inaccurate information. Why should you be any less careful when speaking? How many times have you said "left" when you meant "right," or "Tuesday morning" when you meant to say, "Thursday morning" and later paid the consequences?

Just as you carefully watch your footing on a steep and rocky path, you should speak with the same care to avoid injury or costly mistakes. You make a statement, hear it back in your head, and study your listener to be sure it was received the way you meant it. If you notice frequent discrepancies between your intention and the reaction of your listener, you need to examine whether 1) your words accurately represented your thoughts, 2) your tone of voice or physical movements contradicted your intended meaning, 3) your listener interpreted your meaning from his unique cultural perspective rather than yours, or 4) your listener chose not to accept your point of view or did not process the information accurately. Listening to yourself, like listening to others, is an art. It requires mindfulness to match your intent with appropriate words and be sensitive to the way others perceive them.

Earlier, I described how barriers are serious impediments to your ability to listen to others. They also get in the way of listening to yourself. In the examples that follow, notice how status, personal agenda, and negative self-talk can sabotage the intent of your message. A mindful listener needs to eliminate these barriers when listening to herself and others.

Entering the movies of your listeners is as close as you can get to understanding them. You cannot read people's minds and walk on eggshells all the time, but you can prevent hurt feelings and careless errors by being more sensitive in delicate situations. The ability to listen to yourself while keeping your speaker in mind may include giving directions, personal heart-to-heart discussions, and interviews. Take a moment to think about situations when a bit more self-listening would have resulted in a better outcome. Let's take a look at some of our less desirable speaking habits.

Swearing, to spark a listener's attention or to show displeasure, should be avoided. More often than not, swear words or obscenities are a turn-off and suggest an inability to express yourself in a more intelligent manner. Even expressions like "gosh," or "darn it" have been known to ruffle feathers in certain company. Especially in formal settings, you should refrain from expressions that can be considered disrespectful or inappropriate, like "Jesus, Mary, and Joseph!" or "Gosh darn it!" These expressions may not only affect your credibility, they may also offend.

Are you a chronic interrupter? **Interrupting,** or cutting off the speaker and taking over the conversation, is *the* number-one most annoying conversation habit. It is a discourteous and egocentric way of conversation control. When you consistently interrupt, it is likely that your preoccupation with status or self is rearing its ugly head. You may also interrupt by finishing a sentence for the speaker. In doing so, you assure the speaker (and everyone else in the conversation circle) that you have saved everyone time by reading the speaker's mind and anticipating what he is going to say. How chagrined you are when you guess wrong!

These days, the length of the average doctor's appointment is between ten and fifteen minutes. Physicians are pressed to make the most of a very short period of time. Sometimes, out of necessity to complete the examination in a timely manner, interruption may be necessary, yet this is not always the case. Observational studies show that the average duration of a physician listening without interrupting a patient is seventeen seconds. If patients are allowed to speak until they finish, they stop talking in about forty-five seconds. Patient satisfaction measures show that if the physician interrupts, both parties are dissatisfied. If the physician listens without interrupting, both parties give higher evaluations of the visit.

It is easy for a consultant in any field to see the value of relinquishing control of the interaction for the first forty-five seconds or so. Think about it! *Less than a minute* can make all the difference between open, honest communication and feeling rushed and treated impersonally.

Yet not all interrupting is bad. At times you can break into someone's explanation in a positive way with an encouraging comment like, "Oh, yeah, I wanted to hear about this," or an emphasis that adds humor, such as, "Right, *very* big shoes!" These positive forms of interruption are inoffensive and demonstrate interest and coparticipation in topic development. If you listen hard to a group conversation, you will hear a wide variety of rude interruptions and some congenial interrupting-like behaviors. But where do you draw the line? When does merely interjecting become interrupting?

Deborah Tannen in her book, *Talking from 9 to 5,* uses the term *overlapping* to neutralize the negative connotation associated with interruption. Linguists Carl Zimmerman and Candace West (1975) describe overlapping as instances of simultaneous speech where a speaker other than the current speaker begins to speak at or very close to a possible transition place in a current speaker's utterance (i.e., within the boundaries of the last word). Tannen claims that an overlap becomes an interruption when the *balance* of the conversation is disrupted. If one speaker repeatedly jumps in on the original speaker with comments or attempts to change the topic and causes the original speaker to give way, the resulting communication is unbalanced. There is symmetry, however, when both parties equally take turns, that is, build on an idea or argue a point in which there is no winner or loser. Tannen says that a symmetrical struggle for the floor can be described as creating rapport in the spirit of ritual opposition analogous to sports.

Basic to whether an individual is overlapping or interrupting is the intent of such remarks. The quality of intent may be communicated by the timing of the interjection, the words used, and the show of emotion behind the words. If your aim is to support and establish rapport with your speaker, then your interjections will be considered positive. If, however, your intent is to take the floor and dominate your conversation partner, then a negative form of interruption is perceived. You need to be sensitive to the fact that many of your conversation partners may not appreciate even the positive forms of interruption. (On the other hand, in a debate, negative forms of interruption may be hailed as signs of leadership—and therefore positive.) Tannen states that in judging whether an overlap is an interruption, context is important (casual conversation versus a job interview), as well as a speaker's personal style (high- versus low-involvement types), and how different styles interact.

You may also interrupt the speaker in nonverbal ways. Frequent shifts in your posture or looking away are distracting to a speaker and can be interpreted as wanting to *break into* the speaker's monologue or *break away* from the speaker. When you are in the speaker's movie, your body language naturally conforms to the message. Your position rarely changes, your eye contact is fairly constant. You may interject a gesture or vocalization like a nod or an "Uh-huh," signaling "Yes, I'm listening." An overlapping or interruptive gesture may be a raised finger, a touch on the arm, or leaning forward toward the speaker. To allow for taking turns in a discussion encourages cooperative listening. A good listener encourages the speaker to continue developing her idea through a combination of silence, good eye contact, and verbal support. A good listener avoids any selfish attempt to interrupt the speaker's stream of consciousness.

Talking too much is quite often the result of the fear of silence. When a person is labeled as talking too much, it usually means that he talks on and on about things that interest only himself.

I am convinced that a speaker who goes on and on for days, totally oblivious to the glazed look in your eyes, utterly consumed by the sound of her voice, feels that she is doing *you* an immense favor. How many times have you been subjected to an extreme version of mindless speaking at a party or work gathering? To refresh your memory and make you take a closer look at your own behavior, let's relive a minute with a listener's pariah.

A friendly individual walks up to you, eager to talk, and starts speaking enthusiastically about some gossip at the office. You realize that, due to the inappropriateness of the subject material, this is *not* the movie you want to be in. The speaker does not pick up on your queasy facial expression, but instead insists on dragging you down into the abyss. You are stuck and at a loss as to how you can gracefully remove yourself from this one-sided conversation.

Or how about a situation in which the speaker takes *forever* to get to the point? Not only do you have to endure the introduction, but the worst is yet to come! These people are so into their movies that they are blind to the sweat dripping from your brow. They don't notice you fidgeting in your seat, shifting your weight, or looking around the room for rescue! They just keep talking, frequently looking off somewhere else. When this happens I get the urge to slip away to see if that person even notices I'm gone. I feel I'm being used as a prop for the speaker. Then, to make matters worse, they start dropping names or using buzz words they know you are not familiar with. By this time, you are praying for a miracle! Abduction by alien beings, a call from the IRS, even a small earthquake will do—*anything* but having to listen to this rambling! While the nausea still lingers in reliving this all too familiar scene, let's make a sincere commitment to avoid being a listener's pariah. Just because an experience was funny, exciting, or interesting to you, doesn't mean it will be to anyone else.

Mindful self-listening means answering questions directly, choosing topics that are appropriate to the conversation, and selecting your words carefully so that they reflect your true meaning. Avoid telling stories and opening up topics that are of interest only to you. Having to sit through a story that doesn't go anywhere or the relentless pursuit of a topic that bores or offends you is a particularly refined form of social torture. Some of these people won't quit unless you see things their way (you have to admit the virtues of red meat even though you are a staunch vegetarian, or vice-versa).

I once had a client who was a marketing consultant. His most valuable piece of advice was, "Stop talking after the customer says yes." After winning a sale, your excitement may open the door to mindless talking—making promises you can't keep, excessive thanking, putting down the competition. Your customer may wonder whether he made the right choice.

Quite often I am asked, "How do you deal with someone who just doesn't stop talking? What about the person who rambles on and on?" If you find yourself in an interview with a prospective employee, a customer, or someone at a cocktail party who talks mindlessly, there are graceful ways to cut to the chase without offending the speaker. One way to get the speaker back on track is to say, "Excuse me, John, perhaps I was not clear enough in my question. I asked if . . ." Often, the speaker has forgotten the question and just keeps talking in the hope of remembering. We hear this frequently on radio talk shows. The interviewer asks a two- or three-part question and the guest goes off on a tangent that answers only a part of the original question.

In healthcare it is not at all uncommon to have several patients a day who have a lot to tell; perhaps a visit to the hospital is the only social life they have. And as we will discuss later, being heard is the first step to healing. However, the reality is that healthcare and other kinds of workers who deal with the public have a limited amount of time to spend with each customer. I deal with this predicament by imagining the time I can spend listening each day as an armful of cookies. (As I get to be a more mindful person, I hope that I can add a few more cookies to my load). Unfortunately, I can carry only a finite number of cookies each day.

Some people may need more cookies than others, but the fact remains, I have just so many. After listening mindfully for as many minutes as I can spare, I may have to interrupt and say, "Excuse me, Mr. Johnson, I wish I had more time to listen, but I have to see the next person on my list. Would you write down anything else you'd like to tell me and leave that note in my box? I'll get back to you by tomorrow." Only occasionally do people feel that they need to leave the note. Sometimes, writing down their comments or questions helps them crystallize their thoughts or realize that those questions were already addressed. Being as honest as possible about why you need to stop listening leaves the customer satisfied and allows him to put closure on the meeting.

Many times I am asked, "If someone starts talking about something I'm not interested in, should I be polite and keep acting like I'm listening or interrupt the speaker?" Most people agree that they would rather be interrupted than have someone pretend that they are listening. And the longer you wait to exit the conversation, the more uncomfortable exiting becomes. In the rare case when I feel I do not have the patience, interest, or time to listen, I simply excuse myself early on in a polite tone and tell the speaker that I need to move along. I refuse to make up bogus excuses. It's bad enough when people don't want to hear what you have to say; to get a phony excuse for exiting is often more hurtful. Instead, I simply stay true to myself and my notion that I have just so many cookies to share in one day. Keep in mind, though, that there are times when people really need a few extra cookies (that includes ourselves!). That is when patience is most appreciated. Sometimes, the nicest thing you can do for someone is listen.

I had an opportunity to sit in on a meeting of a newly appointed vice president and his ten department managers. After reviewing the corporation's annual goals, the VP requested that each manager present a brief summary of his department's current projects and challenges. He asked, "In your description, keep in mind how you might relate to each other's circumstances so that we can team up on some of these projects." The VP added that the meeting needed to adjourn in thirty minutes, clearly, a polite request to keep it short. Only *four of the ten managers* appeared to be mindful of their responsibility. These four presented their projects in terms understandable to the other managers. Their descriptions were concise and details were kept to a minimum. These managers remembered the VP's request to link their concerns with the interests of the other team members. They made eye contact with everyone in the group and kept to their three-minute allotment. The VP, a mindful communicator himself, gleefully praised these managers' ability to focus and show respect to the other members of the group.

The meeting went eighteen minutes overtime, thanks to one manager who talked nonstop for almost ten minutes. To this day, when asked to give a brief update, he is often teased by his coworkers as one who needs a stopwatch. A reputation as a poor self-listener is often hard to shake. It was evident from the pressed half-smile on the face of the VP that he knew exactly whom he could count on to meet deadlines, think on their feet, and work as team players.

Does it seem like barriers were at work here? We see from this meeting that not only can those great walls separate you from the speaker (as discussed in chapter four), but they can isolate you from your listeners as well; your vice president is probably not the person from whom you want to estrange yourself. Ironically, most of these six managers were known to be very hard workers, staying late and often working weekends. In fact, at least four of the six showed such intense involvement with their agendas that they appeared totally unaware of their unteamlike approach and hard-to-listen-to presentations. Could they be any better listeners with their staffs? Not likely.

Other mindless self-listening behaviors that we often encounter in long-winded meetings include:

- using unfamiliar jargon and acronyms, such as "the MAC project"
- giving too many details
- inserting anecdotes
- incessant use of "um" or "uh"
- dropping names
- long pauses
- avoiding eye contact with the audience
- interrupting a speaker to ask tangential questions
- making self-deprecating comments

The last is frequently a vice of new managers; for example, "Well, I'm not very good at speaking by the clock," or "I hope I remember everything that's going on in my department." The care you take to choose your words and consider your audience tells much about your competency and your ability to respect others. If you are accused of talking too much, it may imply that you do not allow others to take a turn. Quite often we are so engrossed in our own movies that we neglect obvious signals that it is time to give someone else a chance to speak. A good rule of thumb is to keep your comments to twenty seconds or less. When you go beyond this limit, you push the listener's attention span. Be sensitive to nonverbal cues by others who may want their turn to speak. Such a person may

- shift her position in the chair,

- signal for a turn by raising his index finger,

- lean forward and audibly inhale,

- break eye contact with you,

- nod quickly and open his mouth as if to begin speaking.

Observe the difference between interruptive behaviors discussed earlier and preinterruptive gestures intended as turn-taking requests. Acknowledging these is part of being a mindful and considerate listener.

How often do you begin sentences with *I*? The syntax of the English language promotes the use of the first-person pronoun at the beginning of sentences to signal the arrival of your opinion or experience of the self. The use of *I* in a prominent position in a sentence reflects our culture's emphasis on self-interest. Your agenda (mentioned in chapter four), better known as the me-myself-and-I barrier, is the greatest obstacle to listening to others *and* ourselves.

The repetitive use of *I* has the tendency to alienate your listener. For example, at a recent medical conference, a woman in the audience frequently chimed in to relate her experience with whatever new methods of treatment the trainer introduced. She started most of her statements with *I,* or *I* was used prominently in the sentence: "*I* liked that approach because *I* felt it applied to the kind of patients *I* work with," or "*I* don't agree with that according to what *I* have researched." After a half day of this, groans from the audience signaled that she had alienated others in the group. Her lengthy comments were interpreted as arrogant and self-serving.

Recently, I attended a group swimming class taught by two well-known triathletes. Each student swam his heart out hoping for a helpful critique of his stroke. Each coach started with five students. Both coaches were equally friendly and experienced, but there was one crucial difference: one of the coaches *consistently* referred to himself when asked a question. For example, a beginner asked, "How can I improve my swimming speed?" The coach answered, "Well, when *I* started out *I* began using a stop watch and improved my time by a few seconds each lap." Subsequent answers included, "Well, *I* use . . ." and "What *I* do . . ." These responses were discouraging. What the students wanted were answers that took *their* unique situations, such as physical condition, years swimming, and level of ability into consideration. The use of the me-myself-and-I barrier was a listening stopper. The other coach gave pretty much the same advice, but couched it in different language, such as, "You might try timing your laps—that is, if you can already swim a half mile with some ease," or asking questions about what the student had already tried. Overuse of *I* tends to alienate listeners and decrease trust. Keeping your ego out of the spotlight when giving requested advice creates admiration and a willingness to follow through, because the needs of your speakers are taken into consideration.

This offensive use of *I* was pointed out to a friend of mine who lived with two other people who received few phone calls. Because 90 percent of the calls were for my friend, she innocently recorded her message on the answering machine as follows: "You have reached . . . . *I* am not able to take your call right now. Leave a message and *I* will return your call as soon as *I* can." First of all, it assumed that the caller knew who "I" was, and second, totally disregarded the possibility that the caller might want to speak to another member of the household.

There are ways in which you can communicate a personal intent without overusing *I*. You might begin a sentence with "It seems to me," or "It has been my experience that . . ." or "My feeling is . . ."

It's a sad commentary on the nature of our human relations that some people feel the need to apologize for sharing their thoughts. Once on a skiing trip, I found myself on the chairlift with a young father. He smiled and said hello. I said hello back and commented on the beautiful skiing conditions. He said what a great day he was having after watching his seven-year-old daughter take her first ski lesson. He beamed as he told me how proud he was and what a good attitude she had about learning. He was so happy that I couldn't help but get into his movie. I mentioned how that must *really* be a good feeling, and he went on to tell me more about his daughter. After only a minute or so, he stopped in midsentence and apologized with an embarrassed grin for dumping on me. Perplexed by this comment, I told him what a genuine pleasure it was to hear about how he felt.

Every opportunity to get into someone else's movie widens my scope of experience. It is a good feeling to truly share another's happiness. To put aside my ego and feel spiritually connected with another human being, even for a moment, is a profound experience. Every time you forget yourself and get into someone else's movie, you are closer to freeing yourself from the constraints of self-interest. And by the way, when you are in the movie, don't worry about losing your ego—it has a way of sticking around.

Here's an alarming fact: of approximately eight hundred thousand words in the English language, we use about eight hundred on a regular basis. Those eight hundred words have fourteen thousand meanings. By division there are about seventeen meanings per word. In other words, we have a one-in-seventeen chance of being understood as we intended. Perhaps you've heard of Chisholm's Third

Law—*If you explain something so clearly that no one can misunderstand, someone will.*

Again, this is where listening to yourself comes in. Be mindful of matching as closely as possible your words to your thoughts. Sometimes a short rehearsal on the way to an important meeting is a good way to hear back what you intend to say. Keep the number of words to a minimum. Outline the main issues in your mind or on paper. Weigh every word cautiously and check your listener periodically to see whether he is perceiving you correctly. Eliminate foggy words or phrases such as, "It is my determination that Johnny is demonstrating indicators of increased positive socialization with various classmates and his teachers," and replace them with "Johnny is getting along better with others." This word-by-word or phrase-by-phrase evaluation is particularly necessary when the discussion is complex or emotionally charged. As an extra check, encourage your listener to tell back or paraphrase your message to be sure it was delivered as you intended. These three steps—rehearsing, self-evaluating, and rechecking—can make you reasonably sure that you connected with your listener.

You must also be aware of comments or vocalizations that send a message you do not intend. For example, to some, nodding or saying "Uh-huh" suggests agreement. To others it simply means, "I am paying attention." There is no single universal interpretation of body movements or facial expressions. As our towns and workplaces become more culturally diverse, you must not expect people of different nationalities to respond nonverbally in the same way you do. A head nod in one culture (Japanese, for example), means, "I'm following you." In India, the same nod indicates disagreement.

Gestures and voice inflection should serve to *emphasize* and *reinforce* key words or phrases. These help the listener identify the important points, almost like using a highlighter pen to help you remember main ideas on a page.

In chapter four, I described silent negative self-talk as a barrier to attending to the listener. How about when you are the speaker? Making negative comments about yourself aloud in the company of others is double trouble. You must listen for these self-defeating remarks—even ask a friend to catch you in the act. You may cultivate very carefully other aspects of your image—wardrobe, punctuality, resume—so why in the world would you want to broadcast your inefficiencies? Every negative statement you make about yourself to others is instantly accepted as truth.

For example, Jim accidentally reads the wrong column on a document at an early meeting. He exclaims to the group, "Oh boy, I guess I'm not awake yet." Or upon misplacing an item, you may hear yourself announce, "I'd lose my head if it wasn't attached." These comments, meant to be excuses for your errors, seriously undermine your image and create a divide between yourself and exactly the persons with whom you are trying to develop a successful relationship.

To rid yourself of this self-defeating behavior, begin by becoming aware and extinguishing the silent negative self-talk (as described in chapter four). In situations where you find yourself in error or momentarily disorganized, excuse yourself and get back on track with the discussion. If you cannot locate an important document immediately or if your facts are incorrect, let others know you will locate the item ASAP or make the needed changes. *Period.* Avoid disparaging comments about yourself—no matter how badly you messed up.

Listen to yourself during informal group chit-chat. Do you speak negatively of others? Do you hear yourself gossiping or unfairly criticizing someone's appearance or berating someone's actions? You may be doing this to make yourself look better, yet this kind of talk only reinforces your status or prejudicial barriers. Instead of putting yourself in a positive light, you appear distrustful and insecure. Start by excusing yourself from those people-bashing sessions at the outset, and you will be on your way to eliminating a major adversary to mindful listening.

How often do you put your ego aside and sincerely compliment another? The proportion of negative to positive comments we make each day is startling. Once while waiting for my car to be fixed, I overheard about six different conversations between managers and their staff. After several minutes of listening to uncomplimentary and discouraging talk sprinkled with an occasional, "Thank you," or "Fine, thanks," I began a tally. Over a twenty-five-minute period I counted thirty-seven disparaging comments—and only two compliments or encouraging comments. The odd thing was that this dealership had a decent reputation and was fairly successful. I'd hate to be around if business got slow. The more I thought about it, the more I realized that these proportions are not unusual.

Is it any wonder we leave work discouraged? Why put in 200 percent on the job when no one really appreciates it? If we could hear ourselves as others do, we might be able to understand why staff turnover is high, why our kids avoid our company, or why our marriages get stale. Interestingly, we often think positive things about people but don't often let them know it. Why?

Many psychologists would say that we are too busy beating ourselves up with negative self-talk to give someone else a boost. If you begin balancing out negative self-talk with positive self-talk (suggested back in chapter four), it may be easier for you to vocalize positive comments about others. If you are compassionate with yourself, you'll more likely be compassionate toward others.

Sincere compliments like, "Hey, Gary, great job on that presentation!" or "Oh, Susan, that extra copy came in handy at the meeting today," or "Jenny, I really appreciate how you kept the noise down while I spoke with Mr. Smith," brighten up an ordinary afternoon. To forget yourself and your own neediness and let others know how they helped you out, performed well, or just plain did a good day's work will make you feel better about yourself.

It is very common to use preemptive comments like, "Excuse me, I know you must be very busy right now but . . ." or "You might not agree with me, but . . ." instead of getting right to the point. This kind of remark screams inferiority and insignificance rather than courtesy or respect. You probably make these tag remarks around certain people to whom you feel inferior—exactly the people you hope to impress. By getting to the point in a respectful rather than an obsequious manner, you establish a more symmetrical and productive relationship.

Tone and inflection carry their own sets of messages. An air of tentativeness is communicated when you make a question out of a declarative statement. "My first priority is to address the late-delivery issue?" or "The Jones account is a very important one?" indicate either a lack of confidence or a patronizing attitude.

I recall an administrator speaking like this to me when I was new to management. Perhaps she was trying to be motherly, but I found it condescending, as if she were checking that I comprehended her instructions, when she said things like, "Be sure to drop off your monthly statistics in my office?" However, she did the same thing in social situations, as in "I'm really glad I have a dog?" or "I felt it was the right thing to do?" This habitual rising inflection suggested ambivalence and created confusion. Listen carefully to the tone of your statements. Be sensitive to the reactions of your listeners. If you are perceived as indecisive or if people are continually questioning your stand on an issue, you may be asking for it.

Even more difficult to pay attention to are speakers who lack any inflection and lecture in a monotone. To those of you with these problems, I recommend voice therapy or a drama coach. Most of the time these vocal habits can be significantly improved. The hardest part is to listen objectively to the way you express yourself. The satisfying part is taking the steps to change.

Last but not least, listeners cringe at the sound of a voice that is too high pitched and nasal. Men are particularly irritated by women whose voices become shrill when they get excited or upset. When men get upset their pitch also rises, but not to levels that annoy the ear. Women's voices are usually about an octave higher to begin with, so when some females speak under stress, their voices often soar to much higher levels.

Hold Your Tongue

1. If you are a chronic interrupter, halt your interruption midsentence and say, "Excuse me. Please go on with what you were saying." In time, you will catch yourself *before* you interrupt. However, if from the start of the conversation you get into their movie, your focus will not be on your agenda anyway; you will be totally absorbed with understanding your speakers, and there will be less tendency for you to interrupt.

2. As a speaker, there are acceptable ways to stave off an interrupter. Watch some of the political group discussions on CNN to learn the technique. When someone jumps in on you to disagree or to dominate the conversation, hold up your index finger, signaling "Just a minute," and continue talking. If the verbal intruder persists, stop and say, "Let me finish and then I will listen to you." Continue with what you were saying. Be mindful that the speaker may have a practical reason for interrupting (i.e., you are out of time; there is an important call for you).

3. If *you* need to interrupt for a legitimate reason, raise a hand to chest level and address the person by name. "Bob, excuse me, but due to time, we must get back on track," or "Linda, we are out of time." Using their names gets their attention.

4. The next time you have to give a talk or present an issue, find a private place and tape yourself on video or audio. It is often astounding to hear yourself as your listeners will hear you. Reflect on your choice of words, tone of voice, and other aspects of your presentation. You may well want to revise a few things. (By the way, your voice sounds different on tape. Most of us are familiar with our voices as they reverberate through our skulls. The recorded voice is very close to the sound that other people hear.)

5. In our quest to become compassionate listeners, "friendly" is a good place to start. Come up with a new, friendlier greeting for your voice mail. Avoid the robotic phrases you hear on everyone else's voice mail like, "I'm either on the phone, or . . ." No kidding! Smile as you speak, as if you just received a great compliment from your boss. Now listen with the ears of a stranger. Does it make you smile or feel welcomed? In the words of Jeffrey Gitomer, author of *Customer Satisfaction Is Worthless, Customer Loyalty Is Priceless*, "Friendly makes sales—and friendly generates repeat business."

6. To combat frequent swearing, practice using more acceptable expletives. Brainstorm a variety of synonyms

to describe a person, situation, or anything else to which you might reflexively attach the swear word. For example, instead of saying, "That was the best f——— cheesecake I ever ate," you might substitute "most delectable" or "exquisite."

7. To practice choosing words carefully, take a piece of paper and draw an abstract design. Find a partner and give him a piece of paper and a pen. With your design visible only to yourself, describe the shapes and locations on the paper as clearly as possible. See if your partner interprets your words as you intended and reproduces the design exactly.

8. Look for the subtle negatives in your habitual responses and turn them into positives. For example, if you are the appointment scheduler, you may find yourself in a *rut response pattern,* saying things like, "I'm sorry there's nothing open for you till next week." That comment makes others feel unwanted and disappointed. If there's nothing you can do to create the desired time slot, try making the same message positive: "Mr. Jones, you're in luck! Dr. Smith has an opening next Friday!"

9. Below is a list of negative responses. Keep the same message but make your listener feel good.

- We won't have any more size twelves until Monday.

- Get in line with everyone else.

- You're really lost aren't you? Where's your map?

- You can't be serious about fixing this bike.

- Mr. Ramirez is waiting to get an important call. Call back later.

- Our new computer system has lost your file. Try back tomorrow.

Here are some suggested answers:

- Every Monday we get in a large shipment, including size twelves. May I put something aside for you next Monday?

- To be fair to those who have been waiting, we need to make a line.

- I'll help you get back home. Do you have a map, by any chance?

- I'm really sorry, but this bike can't be repaired.

- Mr. Ramirez is eager to speak with you, but he is helping another customer right now. May he call you back in a few minutes?

- Today we're having some computer difficulties. I apologize for the inconvenience.

Chapter Nine

Listening Under Stress

Loyalty to a petrified opinion never yet broke a chain or freed a human soul.

—Mark Twain

$\mathcal{U}$p to this point we have discussed listening in rather peaceful conditions—lectures, friendly conversations, interviews, and so on—where facts and figures are received without much emotional turmoil. When good or neutral feelings exist between you and the speaker, it is much easier to meet your listening objectives.

However, when a listening situation is uncomfortable, our ability to listen usually breaks down. Stressful listening situations may cover a broad range of circumstances. Aside from full-blown arguments and disciplinary events, they may also include job interviews, counseling sessions, talking to the boss, negotiation, getting directions from a stranger, or meeting new people. Your practice thus far has prepared you for better listening in these latter situations. Your improved ability to put aside your agenda, process information more accurately, and get into the movie of the speaker eliminates most of the anxiety associated with these situations. Your continued practice will make them even easier.

During heated arguments and confrontations, the listening demands are much greater. The challenge is to process not only the words and emotions behind the words, but to avoid becoming defensive and/or eventually offensive. To do this you need to *unconditionally accept* the reality of the other person as legitimate. You need to remain calm and focused in order to choose your words carefully. You can see how listening under stress is the ultimate test of the firmness of your foundation for mindful listening.

Interestingly, in my listening class, this listening-under-stress segment is very popular. Stressful listening situations are commonplace in our society. The pressures of school and the workplace are brought home and added to the mix of family problems. In these forum discussions, my students become very open and uninhibited about how their listening abilities break down when conflict arises. Many of us find it uncomfortable to disagree openly or make critical observations. One reason for this is concern about how the other person will take it.

Perhaps in the past your difference of opinion was not welcomed or the other person's reaction was threatening to you or the relationship. So now you prefer to nod, be nice, and agree with the opposing point of view while your true feelings fester. At that point you run up against a wall of self-recrimination that serves only to reinforce negative self-talk.

How can you start to feel comfortable when listening under stress and break this cycle of frustration? Before you can listen well in stressful encounters you must be able to

- recognize your barriers and work through the ones you can change. ("Ah-ha! Here comes George. I'm starting to cringe just thinking about his comments at last week's meeting. But

I'm going to try to keep an open mind and avoid getting bogged down by the past.");

- be able to put aside your agenda and get into the movie of the other in order to understand where he is coming from;

- be able to relax by controlling your breathing;

- have a genuine interest in establishing a positive relationship.

For centuries, the greatest martial artists, well equipped with weapons and fighting skills, have said that it is always best to avoid conflict in the first place. However, sometimes conflict is unavoidable, as in a self-defense situation. In the martial arts, the objective is not to kill the aggressor, but to put him in a situation where he is no longer a threat. Effective self-defense maneuvers require sharp mental focus; physical strength is secondary. Without practice in breath control, just the opposite occurs—your mental focus breaks down and you become more physically tense.

When you are fearful, your strength increases by at least 20 percent due to the strong rush of adrenaline. The liver demands more oxygen from the heart and lungs as it pumps sugar into the bloodstream. As a result of the blood supply being diverted to the extremities (the fight-or-flight response), the blood supply to the problem-solving part of the brain is significantly reduced. Similar to a martial artist, you need to maintain sharp mental focus to avoid becoming defensive and verbally provocative, which only intensify emotions. That is why breathing practice is such a major part of martial arts training and why I promote it as a basic skill for listening.

If stressful interactions are common in your home and workplace, try to identify the patterns of behavior that trigger them. Quite often you may be the recipient of someone's displaced anger, and the fact that you just happen to be in the same room is enough to spark a conflict. Other times, you may create situations that invite conflict. Purposefully bringing up the name of an old girlfriend, pointing out someone's bad habits, or rarely having anything positive to say could be the hot buttons for stopping the listening process. Unfortunately, the better you know someone, the better you know what irks her and how to get a reaction.

An insensitive response style or letting your barriers into the discussion also fuels the fire of conflict. If you are the guilty party, you are aware of and somewhat in control of these behaviors. But for some, due to psychological problems or a history of abuse, it may be very difficult to repress or eliminate them. If past issues chronically play havoc with your communications with others, psychological counseling may be called for. Yet many disagreements that incite stressful interactions with family or workmates can be resolved by acknowledging your barriers, trying to understand the disgruntled other, and connecting with your breath.

I make a point of staying in touch with students who take my class, particularly those who have had a hard time listening under stress. Some of them have very moody spouses or bosses. Others live with emotionally disturbed family members. After taking my class, these students report instant awareness of their barriers when interacting with these difficult persons. They admit saying to themselves and others, "He's been angry all week; why should today be different?" or "Here comes that nasty old Mrs. Hastings. Every time I see her coming I know she's going to complain about something!" Inevitably the interaction goes sour—just as the listener planned it! Now, when they peer into what makes these people act the way they do (get into their movie), the feelings transform from extreme dislike to curiosity, making room for empathy and compassion.

This perspective softens your reaction, and keeps you from becoming defensive in the face of adversity. Incidentally, compassion does not mean pity or sympathy; it means getting a sense of the other person's frustration. *Com* means "to connect with," and *passion* means "suffering." The Dalai Lama defines compassion in practical terms: "Compassion is a sense of responsibility. Compassion is wanting to share with others. We all have responsibility to shape the future of humanity. So (by being compassionate) let us try to contribute as much as we can."

The philosopher Martin Buber might also have been describing compassion when he suggested that you listen until you experience the other side of the argument. Make it your responsibility to understand the other side by getting into the movie of the other person. Dr. Richard Cabot described this experience when he said, "We do not understand an opposing idea *until we have so exposed ourselves to it that we feel the pull of its persuasion,* until we arrive at the point where we really see the power of whatever element of truth it contains" (emphasis added).

What makes us think that the only people we can effectively work and live with are people similar to ourselves? We make life more difficult when we avoid those who differ from us. Especially in our culturally and religiously diverse society, making a point to avoid interaction with those from different backgrounds shuts us off from seeing different perspectives on a problem and reduces our capacity for creative solutions. Making a point of interacting only with those who are like us creates *mental narrowing.* Many poor listeners are inflexible thinkers and resist ideas that bend the rules or break the mold. For these persons, advice giving and denial are the preferred modes of verbal communication; it's their way or the highway. Forcing our ideas on others merely escalates conflict.

In the workplace, poor listening limits productivity in many ways. First, it discourages information sharing that could make a product or service more desirable or enable employees to get more done in less time. Poor listening creates a desert where otherwise a forest of ideas would flourish. When a free flow of ideas is stymied, energy and enthusiasm are squelched, resulting in lost sales, poor quality, and costly mistakes.

From a Zen perspective, interpersonal conflict can be a means of personal growth. Of course, peace and harmony are preferable to anger and discontent, but if you recall from earlier chapters, strong preferences often get us into trouble by reinforcing barriers. Therefore, as unthinkable as it may seem in an angry moment, let's try looking for that golden nugget or the seed of opportunity for growth hidden deep within a stressful listening situation.

Professor Richard Walton, in his book *Interpersonal Peacemaking: Confrontations and Third-Part Consultation,* pointed out some constructive benefits of conflict, applicable to boardroom, bedroom, and classroom. Walton claims that dealing with conflict helps you see better into your own position. Having to articulate your needs in response to another's needs allows you to question the rationality of your own arguments. You may decide after all that something is not worth arguing about. You may have a weak supporting argument or no real support for your position. Perhaps there is a deeper issue underlying this surface problem. If you are the one responsible for inciting the argument, mindfulness may give you the courage to explore your internal conflicts.

Last, conflict can spur innovative approaches to problems. Especially when there is a diversity of needs and viewpoints and a heightened sense of necessity, motivation and energy are high. This chemistry releases creative potential for problem solving. As the philosopher John Dewey wrote, "Conflict is the *sin qua non* of reflection and ingenuity." Thomas Crum, in his book *The Magic of Conflict,* suggests that we see conflict in a positive light in which neither side loses and a new dance is created. He points out that Nature uses conflict as a primary motivator for the creation of beautiful beaches, canyons, mountains, and pearls. Being able to listen well in conflict, according to Crum, begins by unhitching the burden of belief systems (barriers) that prevent us from appreciating our differences.

Let's take a common example in which Mary, a not-so-favorite co-worker, is promoted as your new manager. If you remain rigid in your perception of this new arrangement, your knee-jerk response may be denial, anger, or resentment. You may even consider looking for another job or going to a new department—anything to avoid Mary. Here is an example of superficial thought processes that focus on the concrete aspects of this relationship. Notice how surface thinking drags negative self-talk into the process:

- Mary has never taken my knowledge and experience seriously. *This won't change.*

- Mary is *younger* than I am. *I can't deal* with these new-wave approaches.

- Mary's background is administration; *she doesn't understand* field work.

The other option is to stay in your present job and take on the challenge of understanding what divides you and Mary. (These same issues usually follow us from job to job anyway.) You can begin by pinpointing the barriers that separate you and Mary. These may include age, race, gender, past experiences, or a host of others. Now look at the source of these barriers. What you may see is an overwhelming focus on your self-interests and a lack of concern for the big picture. Perhaps you are fearful of comparison or not being included in key meetings. Ask yourself: Why do I feel this way about myself? Is there any basis for my fears? Has this happened before? If yes, did I take the steps necessary to turn these weaknesses into strengths?

The answers may make you uncomfortable, but at least you recognized that your agenda and status are major barriers in effectively interacting with Mary. At this point, you can choose to remain stuck in the mud with this attitude and make your life miserable, or you can perceive the situation from a more creative and flexible point of view.

Are there any points on which you and Mary agree? Can you find balance between your experience and what Mary has to offer? How could you and she together turn a potentially disagreeable arrangement into a positive team effort? Shifting the focus from yourself to the big picture is the next step toward personal growth.

As much as it may physically and mentally tax you to accept this challenge, it is possible that you, the company, and your coworkers may derive long-term benefit from this arrangement. Hence, you have established the mindset of the flexible thinker—one who is willing to consider a range of alternatives to reduce potential stresses with Mary. Your list might look something like this:

- Mary and I have had a rocky past, but perhaps we can put that behind us and see how we can meet today's challenges.

- Perhaps getting some fresh ideas will spur us to brainstorm as a group; after all, the old routines don't seem to be working.

- Maybe if I had a better understanding of the administrative side of things, I would be able to provide customers with more answers. This knowledge would make me feel more confident in my job.

Look for the synergy between you and Mary. Perhaps you and she are more compatible coworkers than you think. Mary may appreciate your independent approach to things, but it could also be necessary for you to become more of a team player. Would this challenge not benefit you? Can you imagine (and I recommend that you try visualizing a similar situation during breathing practice) a relaxed and fruitful conversation about how the team can best achieve its goals for the coming year, or brainstorming ways of raising money for a project? Just as you can shape the outcome of your meeting with Mrs. Hastings and create stress, you have the power to create a stress-free and potentially creative situation with your new boss.

If you are going to meet with someone and you anticipate difficulties, try dissecting the problem in its spark stage instead of allowing the chain reaction of emotions to reach an explosion. I described this process in chapter four as a way of using meditation to dissolve the emotions associated with barriers. Matthieu Ricard describes how to break down potential anxieties that cause us so much suffering. He suggests that we

> . . . grasp the nature of thoughts and trace them to their very source. A feeling of hatred, for example, can seem extremely solid and powerful, and can create a sort of knot somewhere in our chests and completely change the way we behave. But if we look at it we see that it is not brandishing any weapon, it can't crush us like a boulder could or burn us like a fire. In reality the whole thing began with a tiny thought, which has gradually grown and swollen up like a storm cloud. From far away, summer clouds can look very impressive and solid. You really feel you could sit on them. But when you get inside them there's hardly anything there. They turn out to be completely intangible. In the same way, when we look at a thought and trace it back to its source, we can't find anything substantial. At that moment the thought evaporates. This is called "liberating thoughts by looking at their nature," meaning to recognize their "emptiness." Once we've liberated a thought, it won't set off a chain reaction. Instead it'll dissolve without a trace, like a bird flying through the sky.

I've tried this approach successfully several times with issues that troubled me, both personal and professional. Once I was called into the vice president's office to defend my proposal for a major project at the hospital. I was given several days to prepare; this also gave me sufficient time to build up a storm cloud of anxiety over it. From the moment the meeting was called, the knot in my chest started to ache, so I tried to liberate it before it got worse. I traced the anxious feelings to my fears: 1) losing my job, being replaced by someone who commanded a lower salary, 2) the job-seeking process, 3) disappointing my family and causing them worry, 4) the possibility of having to relocate, and 5) not being persuasive enough.

I discovered that at the heart of all these fears was an ego that felt threatened. My list did not include more critical issues like whether or not I would be able to pay my bills. It all had to do with facing the possibility of a major change and losing face. I chuckled to myself. The knot in my chest was loosening already. This wasn't such a big problem after all. Sure, I'd like to keep my job, but the possibility of moving out west had always been exciting. I could get my chance! This meeting might be a disguise for a new opportunity! I was prepared to defend the proposal; I knew I had done my best. Now I was no longer dreading the meeting, I was only curious to see where it led.

The reason that listening well under stress seems, at first, so daunting is that when we hear something unsettling, our thinking turns inward. We become preoccupied with ourselves. We see the issue as inseparable from our emotions. Stepping back to determine where these emotions are coming from helps loosen their grip on the psyche.

Linda, a student from my class, successfully applied this tracing-back approach when her son announced that he was planning to drop out of college. He felt stifled by academic life and saw more opportunities outside the college environment. He wanted to seek out these opportunities and perhaps return to school at some later time. Linda's reaction was shock and anger. Tracing back her reaction to her son's announcement, she realized how attached she was to conventional barriers: the perceptions of her friends and what they would say about her as a mother, her son labeled a dropout, jealousy that her friends would see their sons graduate and she wouldn't. Linda faced the barriers of status, negative self-talk, and wanting to control her son's choices. She acknowledged that these barriers were fears based on pride and ego. Of course, Linda remained disappointed with her son's decision, but by discovering the source of her turmoil, she was able to diffuse her reactions to the point of caring more about her son's present unhappiness and his optimism for the future. Linda was free to get into his movie and understand her son better.

We can't expect ourselves to ignore feelings of anger, resentment, or fear that present as obstacles to hearing someone out. Yet we can search for the source of these feelings, and quite often it is our egos expressing greed or hatred for some person or idea. Let's say you are very angry with your brother for something he said to your parents, and you are about to have a conversation with him. Beforehand, get to the source of the bad feelings you have toward your brother. How realistic is it to expect that you can protect your parents from insults and hurtful situations? If you show anger toward your brother, will he be any more sensitive to your parents? If the answer to these questions is "no," you have begun to face the source of your negative feelings. You are not denying your anger; you still feel bad for your parents, but you have separated yourself from a situation you cannot change. Just like in dealing with our negative self-talk in chapter four, let a positive thought or idea cancel out a negative one. Neutralize your anger by thinking of an admirable trait or some positive action your brother demonstrated. Try to wish him well instead of wishing him ill. If you find this difficult, it may mean that you are still battling with your own negative self-talk. Before you can be compassionate with others, you have to be compassionate with yourself.

Mindful listening under stress begins inside and works outward.

Another student, Karen, a marketing representative for a large pharmaceutical company, came to my class because she felt uncomfortable with networking. She was getting pressure from her boss to participate in activities that would draw in more business. Despite the many opportunities she lost as a result of not attending networking functions, the thought of having to "shmooze" with strangers was stressful. Karen had even considered changing careers.

When I asked Karen what she disliked about networking, she reported that she felt she had to act a certain way—overly friendly, insincere, witty, and animated. Because of her nervousness with her self-imposed pressure to perform, she was rarely able to walk away with any usable information; therefore, networking was a waste of time. Karen admitted that there was a lot of negative self-talk going on in her head, and she agreed to work on that problem until our next meeting. Shortly after completing the listening class, she began meditating. She became more comfortable with silence, plus there was a lot less negative noise going on in her head. At that point, Karen began getting into the movies of friends and family members. She started to experience freedom from her self-consciousness. She could listen mindfully to others and put her own mind traffic aside for longer and longer periods of time.

Karen began to experience listening as an adventure. She claimed, "The more I put my agenda aside, the more I can sense the whole message coming through." Karen enthusiastically accepted her next networking invitation. Afterward, she reported that "time flew by." She didn't feel the pressure to perform because she cast the spotlight on her speaker instead of herself. By giving of herself in this way, Karen got more than she had bargained for: repeat business and word-of-mouth referrals, much to the pleasure of her boss. She formed new contacts, better understood her competition, and made a few relationships with customers that had long-term potential. Karen now teaches mindful networking skills to her staff.

Those who choose not to be so rigid about people and things, seeing all approaches as necessary for the balance of the common good, turn out to be the best listeners. For some of us, a change in mindset may be sufficient, but for the majority of us, a consensus between mind and body is necessary to take on such a challenge. Never before have we been exposed to such high levels of anxiety in our everyday lives. Global concerns about AIDS and other mysterious viruses, drug addiction, wide swings in the economy, and threats of terrorism top the list. Then there are the garden varieties of anxiety that we bring on ourselves—extreme attachment to material wealth, obsessions with weight and dieting, procrastination, the need for instant gratification—that have rerouted our consciousness. The alienation brought on by a thriving economy, a skyrocketing stock market, explosive technological innovation, and instant wealth creates an unprecedented amount of stress. Philosopher Peter Koestenbaum refers to the "new-economy pathology" as the affliction imposed by the need to meet ever-higher objectives in all realms of work, wealth, and lifestyle. "A terrible insensitivity to basic human values," Koestenbaum warns, is the result of placing emphasis on the price of a stock over what it really means to be a successful human being (*Fast Company*, March 2000).

Understanding the different kinds of anxiety helps us know which need managing and which are conducive to personal growth. In addition, different people will experience different degrees of listener anxiety depending on the situation and their genetic predisposition.

Robert Gerzon, in his book *Finding Serenity in the Age of Anxiety*, describes three different kinds of anxiety:

- *Natural anxiety* (the good anxiety) acts as a warning mechanism, but also alerts us to moments of opportunity. The theme of natural anxiety is "just do it." I compare it to a level of mental energy needed to focus on a challenging and enjoyable task.

- *Ontological* (or existential) *anxiety* is born of grappling with issues of the purpose of life and life after death and is related to a heightened need to answer questions about our existence.

- *Toxic anxiety* arises from the refusal to face the other two. Instead of acknowledging natural anxiety and ontological anxiety as necessary and appropriate, we ignore them, with the result that they fester into a poisonous mental state. Freud called this *neurotic anxiety,* the kind of mental dysfunction that takes the form of depression, addiction, or mood disorders. It can become so extreme that it overwhelms our ability to listen and think clearly. If unresolved, toxic anxiety leads to violence, alienation, and—eventually—to physical illness.

Natural and ontological anxiety are the most conducive to mindful listening. They imply a state of readiness and hunger for knowledge, both prerequisites for attending to and concentrating on the message. However, extremes of natural and ontological anxiety can lead to toxic states. Obsessive type-A personalities or religious zealots are familiar examples. Unless these types learn to channel their anxieties toward positive achievement and spiritual growth, they may plummet to the depths of frustration and paranoia.

Negative self-talk, mentioned earlier as a major barrier to listening, is an internal source of anxiety. It creates an inner noise that foils our attempts to listen effectively. We overreact to these thoughts, real or imagined, causing our blood pressure to rise and our normal bodily functions—breathing, digesting, and speaking—to become dysfunctional. Negative self-talk subverts the mind-body balance needed to think clearly and act effectively, particularly in stressful encounters.

Look back on a recent situation in which you were verbally confronted. Perhaps it was an angry boss, spouse, or child. What did you do as they ranted and raved? Chances are, your body was tense, you had to swallow hard, and you felt yourself blushing. You might have thought negatively of yourself and even more negatively toward the person shouting at you. Perhaps you started thinking about the consequences of this verbal attack—would you be fired, divorced, ignored? All the while, this noise in your brain prevented you from taking that first positive step toward a successful resolution—focusing on the issue. Say it was a personal accusation, such as "You are always fifteen to twenty minutes late!" The real issue is that in that span of time, the business loses out on ten calls that could generate hundreds of dollars in revenue. You have the choice to perceive this as a personal attack or you can see the complaint as a functional problem that affects the whole system: *the company is losing out on so many calls; this affects everybody in the group. There must be a way to plan ahead so I can get to my desk by eight o'clock.* The former response is anxiety producing, laden with barriers that prevent self-understanding and growth. The latter response focuses on the issue (missing valuable calls) and includes an action step. It is unrealistic to expect yourself to shut out feelings of anger and resentment when you are under attack, but you can put the issue in the foreground and the noise in the background. This way you can get on with *solving the problem,* which is the outcome both parties desire.

In *The Art of Happiness,* the Dalai Lama comments on how we tend to overreact to minor things and blow them out of proportion by endlessly recounting the situation, further feeding the anger and dislike. This is the way we create our own suffering and anxiety. He explains:

For example, say that you find out that someone is speaking badly of you behind your back. If you react to this knowledge that someone is speaking badly of you, this negativity, with a feeling of hurt or anger, then you yourself destroy your own peace of mind. Your pain is your own personal creation. On the other hand, if you let the slander pass by you as if it were a silent wind passing behind your ears, you protect yourself from that feeling of hurt, that feeling of agony. So although you may not always be able to avoid difficult situations you can modify the extent to which you suffer by how you choose to respond to the situation.

Similarly, in the art of *jiujitsu,* the way to defend against an opponent is to yield to the full force of the attack, but turn it in the opposite direction to avoid being harmed. Perhaps you have seen documentary films of martial-arts masters who demonstrate the ability to turn away an attacker by directing the negative energy back toward the aggressor with a calm eye and barely a flick of the wrist. It does not require years of martial-arts training to determine how great or how small a problem is. With a basic foundation in mindfulness, you can calmly evaluate the situation and judge to what extent you want to take your stress levels.

It requires a sense of calm in order to rationally deal with the onslaught of verbal conflict. In describing how matadors deal with a charging bull in the ring, Ernest Hemingway said in *Death in the Afternoon,* "To calmly watch the bull come is the most necessary and primarily difficult thing in bullfighting." Our tendency, when the bull or verbal aggressor is on the attack, is to interrupt, begin objecting, or leave the room. This only angers the charging other more, escalates bad feelings, and postpones a positive outcome. If you have any prior notice of an impending confrontation, prepare with a few deep, slow breaths and continue breathing slowly and fully as you listen.

Unsuccessful attempts to communicate under stress give you

the sense of a split between mind and body. Your breath gets out of control and your heart rate speeds up. Notice how your breath becomes shallow and how your shoulders and neck tense. The mind is on the defensive, erecting barriers and shooting words from the hip. Perhaps this state of intense discomfort is the reason we so dislike conflict and avoid it at all costs.

Regular breathing practice, *daily meditation on the breath,* helps restore balance and connection between mind and body. You can easily learn to revert from tight, shallow breathing to a deep abdominal breath, which relaxes the neck and shoulders. You may not see instant results, but over several days or a few short weeks the changes are apparent.

Meditation increases the brain's alpha waves, which elevate our sense of well-being. For centuries, Eastern cultures have promoted meditation as a means of attaining peace. Meditation practice helps you attain a sense of deep relaxation that allows you to step back and see situations in a clearer light, unobstructed by barriers and noise. This alert, calm state of mindfulness, achieved through regular practice, begins to permeate every interaction. Whenever you are teaching, consulting, conversing, or whatever your day brings, it is this deep relaxation that brings quality to the moment. You will begin to notice that situations that once would have caused an excessively emotional reaction are now resolved in a calmer, more productive manner.

If some of these suggestions for listening under stress are difficult for you to apply right now, try not to be discouraged. Continue to work on your foundation for being a mindful listener in more laid-back contexts. Your confidence in your ability to communicate with others will increase as you become more efficient and notice others responding to you more favorably. To consistently process auditory information accurately *under pressure* is the aim of even the best listeners!

Getting a head start in relaxation helps set your mind to focus on the issue at hand rather than the negative noise competing for your attention. As your conversation partner launches into her complaint, continue to keep your breath steady and slow. If you have practiced the relaxation exercises in chapter three, this should come easier to you. Withhold the temptation to interrupt and start defending yourself. Instead, encourage the speaker to tell you more. Ask questions like, "Is there anything else that has upset you?" or "What do you mean by slacking off?" Quite often the opening remarks are just the tip of the iceberg. The real issue is usually several minutes down the road.

Getting into their movie is crucial to being able to listen well in situations where someone you care about is under stress. The focus is not on yourself, but on seeing the other's viewpoint. Saying, "Is there anything else?" is the *last* thing a speaker expects to hear, and it signals that you are eager and receptive to solving the problem. In many cases, this request calms the waters. The speaker senses that she will not be interrupted and does not have to race against the clock. Her body relaxes and her volume drops down. Allowing those extra minutes for the speaker to verbalize her whole concern reduces the chances of another stressful encounter on the same topic days or weeks later. However, there are times when that invitation to speak her mind gives the speaker license to open the floodgates and bring up other issues unrelated or indirectly related to the topic at hand. This may give you more insight into the problem, i.e., a general discontent with life, not enough free time, problems at work, and so on. Just as with the silent response discussed in chapter seven, the speaker may, by hearing herself expound on the problem, arrive at her own solutions. If the speaker appears to be straying from the topic, it may be necessary to refocus on the main issue. Either way, asking the angry person to elaborate on her complaint helps get to the bottom of the problem.

Remember the power of silence? Sometimes people may start

off with what appears to be a trivial complaint. You may say to your-self, "How could he get so mad about me not dumping the garbage?" But this is often just a starting point. Keep eye contact and let him continue until he is finished. Watch your breath and keep it slow and steady. Pause for several seconds and *wait*. At that point, the person may sense that you are giving him the go-ahead to get to the heart of the problem. Or he may have truly finished and not dumping the garbage on a regular basis is the only issue. Either way, begin by briefly paraphrasing what was just said to you. Try to avoid sounding too clinical with phrases like, "So, what I hear you saying is . . ." or "So, to recap, what you're telling me is . . ." Be natural and remember why you are telling back what you heard—to better understand the speaker's point of view. Simply say, "I want to make sure I'm getting everything you are saying to me. Let me see if I understand . . ." Leave out foul language and dramatic imitations. This lets the speaker know you heard him and gives him a chance to amend inaccuracies. After you have paraphrased your understanding of what was said, ask for clarification. "Is my understanding of this problem correct?" You may ask questions to get more clarification. Then state your case briefly and to the point; then offer to brainstorm possible solutions. Listening to your words during stressful discussions is essential to avoid fueling the fire.

Whenever loved ones are angry and upset, our goal as listeners is to help them feel understood, not put down. Get into their mov-ies. Being silently attentive is particularly helpful while listening to angry, upset children. If your child comes home complaining about something that a teacher said, you may be tempted to try to talk him out of his feelings, as if they are not to be taken seriously. If you can put your "shoulds," interrogation, and advice aside and instead re-main silently attentive, your child will feel safe about revealing his emotions. If you still feel pressed to give your advice, wait until he has finished all he has to say. Then you might say, "Would you like to hear what I might have done if I had been in your shoes?" If he wants to know, let him ask.

Try to avoid cross-complaining. ("You say *I* never take out the garbage? Well, *you* never do the laundry!") Avoid using absolutes like *never, always,* and *every.* Absolutes and *should* are hot-button words that can easily shut down your partner's willingness to listen.

When someone is yelling at you, keep your voice soft and steady, just like your breath. This voice response can be very helpful in quieting your partner's voice. It is often difficult for us to listen to swearing and other expletives delivered in a loud, hostile tone. Our bodies naturally tense in response to threatening behavior. But, just like the matador, we will most certainly lose the battle if our fight-or-flight tendency takes over.

Agree with what you can. There may be something you both can agree on, such as, "You are right about that. I don't take out the garbage most nights. But this is because I don't think of it. I'll try to pay more attention." The issue may well be that you don't follow through on household responsibilities. If that is the case, try to treat this as an *issue,* not an attack. By this time, your adversary may be calming down too. He was given the chance to say all that was bothering him. He sees that there is no need to continue screaming, because by paraphrasing, you have shown that you truly listened (you care). Now he feels, even in a small way, indebted to listen to you. At this point you have set the stage for a successful negotiation of the problem.

There may be times when it is not appropriate to continue the discussion. You may not be in a good mood, the setting may not be conducive, or time is a factor. In that case, ask to continue the discussion at another time, preferably that day. This shows good faith and gives you an opportunity to set the stage for a more positive outcome.

There are certain individuals who, due to lack of emotional and physical control, make it unsafe and unreasonable to get into their movies. With persons who pose a danger to you, emotionally or physically, it may be best to leave the room or remain silent. The last thing you need to get from these people is more. They may require a combination of psychological counseling and restraint. You may have to seek guidance for special ways of dealing with these dangerous individuals.

A mindful listener sees all interactions as equal. Pleasant conversations reinforce a positive relationship and hold promise for future interactions. Conflict poses opportunities; the process of working through conflict contributes more to personal growth than the resolution itself. If you look to the less desirable relationships or contacts in your life as an opportunity for achieving balance between mind and body, you will not find yourself wanting to hide your head in the sand when conflict arises. This attitude takes the stress out of the discussion. If your purpose is to resolve the issue to the extent where all parties are satisfied—versus winning the argument—you may become less resistant to situations where opinions differ. When there is less emphasis on the outcome and more emphasis on the process of listening, a relationship is established.

Did you ever think of a complaint by a customer or disgruntled other as code for "I want to continue a relationship with you/your company, but something is amiss"? Try to see complaints as coming from a concerned individual who wants things to go smoother between you. If salvaging the relationship were not the case, she would have ceased contact. A complaint is an opportunity to set things right.

Allowing silence, getting into her movie, paraphrasing her complaint, are perceived by the disgruntled other as action steps in restoring the relationship; they act as the cornerstone for future resolutions. Take the anxiety out of listening in difficult situations by seeing them as a challenge to your personal growth.

Hardiness, a term coined by Salvatore Maddi and Suzanne

Kobasa, describes the tendency of certain individuals to respond to threatening situations by transforming them into manageable challenges. Thich Nhat Hahn says, "In Zen everything one does becomes a vehicle for self-realization, every act, every movement is done wholeheartedly with nothing left over."

A note to those of you who work in the customer complaint office: try this exercise and finish each day with a sense of accomplishment instead of burnout. Using the suggestions above for listening under stress, keep a count each day of how many unhappy customers you turned into happy customers. Set a quota and inspire others in your department to do the same. Call back the most disgruntled customers as soon as possible to let them know you followed up on their complaints or changes in their service. Because you listen, they will reward you with continued business and new referrals because they know you cared.

Let Stress Be Your Teacher

1. Relaxed attentiveness is a necessary first step. Stay true to your daily breathing practice. Meditate about twenty minutes twice a day (if you can) every day for a week. Find a quiet spot, sit up tall, relax your eyes (eyelids closed or half-open) and breathe slowly. Focus only on how your breath moves in and out of your body. Other thoughts may enter your consciousness, but let them pass and refocus on the breath. It may be helpful to count the breaths silently if focusing on just the movement of the breath is difficult. (For specific guidelines, please see Eknath Easwaran's book, *Meditation.*)

If you find thoughts about a particular person or an up-coming event interfering with your practice, take a few minutes to make this situation manageable. Relax and close your eyes, breathe for a few minutes, and settle yourself. Think of pleasant, relaxing experiences, like sitting by a campfire, fishing on a quiet lake, sipping tea, or listening to music. Notice how you feel void of any tension in your body. After a few minutes, start to think of communication interactions that make you mildly self-conscious or intimidated. Begin by seeing the positive traits of this person or situation. See yourself reacting calmly. See the interaction going smoothly—standing tall, arms relaxed, feeling confident, able to converse fluently. Breathe through these thoughts at the same relaxed pace you started with. See yourself relaxed and calm. See yourself not doing the things that created negative outcomes in the past, such as interrupting, use of absolutes, or cross-complaining. See yourself listening attentively, fully in the speaker's movie, with good eye contact and a composed posture. Avoid feelings of criticism or defensiveness. If any negative thoughts creep into your scenario or if you feel your body tense, get back on track by checking your breathing—slow and steady. Go back to the beginning until you can see a calm response to whatever is said, from start to finish. See the interaction ending successfully with good feelings on both sides. Think about how much you both accomplished. Continue easy breathing for a few more minutes, savoring the process by which you accomplished this result. Gradually open your eyes and go make that appointment!

2. Be empathetic with another's view on a controversial subject. Find a friend who will try this exercise with you. Pick a topic over which you disagree. Take turns defending your friend's viewpoint; enthusiastically develop your argument. After this exercise, do you still feel as convinced of your original point of view? Is it a little easier to listen to an opposing viewpoint on other topics?

3. Before dealing with a personal conflict, plan your discussion on paper. Without too much attention to structure and neatness, write out key ideas and sentences as they come to you. Now look at what you wrote and edit out the vague, rambling portions. Will your listener immediately understand your intent and get the message? Clarify your thoughts, review your word choice, and cut it down to size. Notice how much more direct and effective your message is.

4. When a customer makes a complaint, let him finish and then respond on a positive note, with:

- That's my favorite problem!

- I'm sure we can find a way.

- Consider that taken care of!

- I will try to get an answer for you as fast as I can.

- Thank you for bringing that to my attention!

Conclude with a tell-me-more: "Is there anything else I can help you with today?"

Chapter Ten

Boosting Your Listening Memory

A good listener is not only popular everywhere,
but after a while, he knows something.

—Wilson Mizner

In almost every listening class I teach there are a handful of people who think that they are losing it—because they have become scattered or absentminded. Mindlessness, if allowed to go wild, fragments our attention with the result that many minutes and hours in our lives go unnoticed. When our thoughts are scattered somewhere in the past or future, our minds are absent from the present reality. This kind of suffering creates needless havoc in our lives and makes us feel inadequate and stupid.

Mindfulness practice helps us to reassemble our dispersed attention, restore concentration, and build self-esteem. To attain mindfulness requires regular application, but most importantly, it takes a sustained commitment to do away with *mindlessness*. It often helps to have a vision of the kind of listener you want to be—calm, focused, and able to process and remember whatever you choose.

Now that you have invested some time in self-awareness and regular breathing practice, it is time to apply mindfulness to the most common listening concerns of the Information Age. These include:

- Do I have attention deficit disorder?
- Continuing to sharpen the saw
- How to listen better in meetings or classes
- Remembering people's names
- Listening hygiene
- Skillful listening

If you have been faithful to your daily breathing practice, you probably notice an improved ability to direct and maintain your attention. One of my students, Adam, a sales manager at a software company, complained that his main problem with listening was that he was easily lured by other information sources in his environment. When listening to a customer or employee complaint, he was tempted to pick up a memo, glance at his e-mail, or answer the phone. He felt anxious about not getting enough done during the day and missing out on opportunities coming at him from all angles.

Eventually, Adam was able to see that his scattered attention and his negligence of customer and employee relationships was the true source of his anxiety. He spent so much time having to put out fires brought on by mindless inattention to people that he had nothing left over for his office work. After a few weeks of meditation practice, Adam reported that he was less fidgety and more able to resist the urge to give in to the computer and the phone. Adam discovered that he could shift his attention back to listening in the movie and solve problems more efficiently, to the satisfaction of both his customers and his employees. This gave him more free time to stay informed, read his e-mail, and return calls. He said:

> I started to see the connection after a few days of breathing prac-
> tice. Before then, when someone came in with a problem, I couldn't
> keep still enough to focus on the issue. Other things seemed so
> much more important to me. I felt scattered between the work on
> my desk and this person talking, so by the end of the day I paid
> the consequences. After I started meditating, the same distrac-
> tions didn't pull me away as easily. Now I'm able to stay with my
> breath for longer periods without other thoughts competing for
> attention. Without being hard on myself, I calmly notice these
> other thoughts and then return to my breath. That was the turn-
> ing point. Now I'm more patient and able to get into the movie of
> the person talking. Even on a people-busy day, I have more time
> left over to do my desk work.

Do I Have Attention Deficit Disorder?

Some students arrive at my listening workshops fully convinced that
their listening problems are related to attention deficit disorder, better known as ADD. Even without an official diagnosis, it is easy to
convince yourself that this is your problem. The name itself, *attention deficit disorder*, sounds precisely like what ails many of us—namely,
difficulty staying focused. ADD appears to be tailormade for our
high-tech, fast-paced culture. There are so many auditory and visual
stimuli and so little time to process them that we struggle to stay
afloat in a sea of information. Researchers at Washington State University found that in 1995, office visits made to a physician for the
treatment of ADD had doubled to 2,357,833 since 1990. Evan I.
Schwartz, writing in the June 1994 issue of *Wired* magazine, describes
ADD as "the official brain syndrome of the information age." True

adult ADD, however, can include several behaviors, ranging from mild to severe. Some of the most common include:

- Inability to maintain attention to structured tasks
- Difficulty following directions
- Sticking to deadlines
- Fidgeting, difficulty sitting still
- Excessive interrupting
- Impulsive behaviors

It should be noted that although millions of people suffer with ADD, the disorder is present in less than 5 percent of the adult population, and that a true diagnosis of ADD can be made only by an experienced physician or psychologist. ADD may be difficult to diagnose because it can be masked by other conditions—depression, obsessive-compulsive disorder, thyroid gland dysfunction, or anxiety. Also, there is no standard test that can definitively label an adult as having ADD. Currently ADD is thought to be a neurobehavioral disorder of self-control that usually starts in childhood and persists into adulthood. Although ADD is thought by some researchers to be a genetically transmitted disorder, the behavior characteristics of ADD are becoming so common (the average kindergarten through eighth-grade teacher may report five or more children correctly or incorrectly diagnosed with ADD per classroom per year) that many psychologists believe that it is culturally induced. A school nurse recently told me that she spends more and more of her day running from classroom to classroom, administering medications to children who have been labeled with this syndrome.

Information comes at us from all angles: TV, radio, the Internet, fax machines, e-mail, voice mail, and regular mail. There are so much data available to us that we have a difficult time sorting out what is relevant and important. As the public is made more aware of the symptoms of ADD, it is tempting to joke about having this disorder as an excuse for the mindless listening habits we display daily. However, an adult with true ADD experiences these behaviors *consistently,* not just a few times a day.

It is even more desirable to consider a drug as a quick solution to the problem instead of looking deep within ourselves for the answer. Our barriers, our ever-expanding must-do lists, and forgotten sense of calm actually prevent us from focusing on any one thing.

Diagnosis of adult ADD begins with a visit with your primary physician. She may suggest a consultation with a psychologist to rule out depression, anxiety, or stress-related illness. If the diagnosis is confirmed, the usual and most effective course of treatment is medication. Frequently prescribed medications for ADD include Ritalin, Cylert, Norpramin, Torfranil, Dexadrine, Prozac, and Aderall. It is wise to discuss treatment options with your physician, including any long and short-term side effects of the prescribed medication.

Remember that medication alleviates only the symptoms and side effects of ADD—what may remain are the old coping behaviors that need to be deconstructed and rebuilt. Dr. Kevin Murphy, chief of the ADD clinic at the University of Massachusetts Medical Center, reports that once a patient is relieved of the mental storm associated with ADD through the use of medication, it is still necessary to modify the habits of communicating that accompanied the old ADD behaviors. This is also true for persons clinically diagnosed with depression or anxiety disorders whose balance has been restored with the use of medication. For example, after years of Ritalin or Prozac, some old reflexive patterns may persist, such as inattention, self-absorption, impulsive speaking, and negative self-talk. In a more mentally and emotionally balanced state, thanks to medication, the person is now in a position to rekindle old relationships and take advantage of new opportunities. This is where mindful listening helps a person to

- experience a formerly unattainable state of relaxation
- widen the comfort zone for new ideas that once were threatening
- concentrate better in lectures and discussions
- put aside self-concerns to understand others

Continuing to Sharpen the Saw

It is widely accepted that a certain amount of memory loss can be attributed to biological changes associated with age. However, some percentage of memory loss may be a conditioned expectation. We may have witnessed grandparents becoming absentminded and forgetful, but we may not have been aware of other factors contributing to their memory changes, such as depression, reduced socialization, illness, or hearing loss. Very few of our grandparents' generation went on to pursue continuing education or new careers after retiring from the jobs they held for thirty or more years. Therefore, we expect memory loss to creep in and perhaps allow ourselves to become lazy when listening. My neighbor, a gentleman in his late seventies, told me about his memory loss.

> After all, people my age are all slowing down a bit and changing physically. Why should we hold ourselves to younger standards of mental sharpness? Nobody expects us to remember everything the same way as before. Even people who don't know me see that I'm older and assume that my mind is old, too. They speak louder and talk to me like I'm a baby sometimes . . . simple sentences, to help me understand and remember, I guess.

Even though more and more people over age sixty are going back to school and starting up businesses, the majority of seniors feel due to stereotypical thinking that their capacity for new learning is diminished.

Many historical and contemporary studies of brain activity support the fact that at least five auditory-association areas of the brain participate when we listen to spoken language. Both left and right hemispheres are activated during listening tasks. The more complex tasks (i.e., listening for details, use of visualization, linking dates with events requiring silent rehearsal) involve even more brain activity.

As the amount of auditory stimuli increases, we run the risk of listening on autopilot—skimming the surface for information that falls into the category of our self-interests or supports our biases. Analysis and comparison take too much time and threaten the status quo. After all, it's much more convenient to just skip over what doesn't fit . . . or is it?

Long-term memory (LTM) (also called *semantic* memory) is the filter that chooses what information to save for short-term storage, awareness, and long-term storage. LTM determines what is relevant and worth capturing and what can be discarded. It is an efficient way to manage massive amounts of information. Anxiety can thwart the process, either as a result of too much information assailing the system at once or as an ever-present condition that blocks all data needed to make a decision or take appropriate action. The source of the anxiety that affects our ability to listen mindfully is often related to the barriers discussed in chapter four.

In normal activity, millions of brain cells die every day. Research shows that when our brains are active, we retain more brain cells and are able to sprout new ones. Listening invigorates the brain. Positron emission tomography (PET) scans show that blood flow increases to many parts of the brain during listening. As we age, our lives become more routine and predictable, but this approach offers little opportunity to expand our repertoire for new knowledge and new ways of thinking. There is evidence that we can slow down the inevitable aging process of the brain by simply putting our brains to work *more* every day rather than less.

Many of us can boast acquaintance with an elderly person whom we describe as "sharp as a tack." Through *accelerated* brain use versus *stagnant* brain use, these individuals defy the connection between old age and senility. It is still possible to develop Alzheimer's or a similar dementia if it runs in your family, despite attempts to actively use the brain. However, the majority of us can prevent or postpone dysfunctional memory loss by continually sharpening the saw every day through mindful listening.

In my workshops, I like to shock my audience with the benefits of mindful listening. In one exercise, I tell them that they will be listening to a five-minute commentary from a radio talk show. Half of the group is instructed to listen for the name of the speaker, her background, her main argument, as least two points that support it, and to tell how the speaker felt about the issue. The second half of the group is asked to just listen.

Each group is unaware of the instructions given to the other. Without fail, at least 90 percent of the group that was given specific instructions are able to recall considerably more information than the group that was told to "just listen." A short quiz hours later at the end of the workshop reveals that the mindful-listening group still retains at least 75 percent of the commentary. If you want to retain the information, it makes sense to embark on a listening opportunity with certain goals in mind:

- Get to know the speaker's name and background. What life experiences led him to these conclusions?

- What is his main point? What facts or observations support his position?

- How does he feel about the topic?

- How does his point of view add or change your view of the issue?

Depending on the nature of the conversation, you may want to listen with more or less structure. For example, if your customer is telling you about her new job or your child is complaining about too much homework, your only concern might be to learn how the person *feels* about her situation. The degree of vigilance you employ depends on the extent of the information the speaker is willing to share and how much you want or need to remember.

From a listening perspective alone, your ability to focus, select, and process auditory information bombarding the airwaves every day is a daunting task. If you haven't tried this recently, notice how difficult it is to process two speakers simultaneously. You begin to follow speaker A's message, and as you shift your attention to speaker B, notice how speaker A might as well be speaking a foreign language. You may be able to process some of the gestural and vocal cues of speaker A, but not the verbal message. This shows that you can really listen to only one thing at a time.

To remember better, you need regular practice at being absorbed with the speaker and what he has to say by getting into his movie or listening in a mindful way. This gives you the chance to involve both sides of the brain—the left side, which processes the logical meanings of words, and the right side, which takes the speaker's tone and nonverbal gestures into account.

Hence, when you are totally absorbed, your brain is actively engaged on many levels over a period of minutes. Compare that level of mental aerobics with the typical listener's attention span. With regular application of breathing meditation and the movie mindset, you can shift into gear and stay there throughout an interaction.

Get practice staying in the movie in noisy places. Even if familiar people walk by as you listen to your speaker, resist the urge to nod or wave. Nothing else matters but the person you are listening to. With this kind of practice, just think how much easier it will be to focus your listening in quieter environments.

If you continually challenge your listening capacity, you will be exercising more of your brain. Most of us use only 7 to 8 percent of our brain power daily. Dr. Patrick Turski, of the University of Wisconsin Hospital, has patients listen to Charlton Heston reading passages by Nietzsche. This is done for the purpose of mapping areas of the brain involved in verbal processing. In 1997, during a surgical procedure to remove a congenital malformation from the brain of a thirty-one-year-old woman, it was essential to locate these sites of speech and language processing prior to the actual surgery in order to avoid brain damage. Nietzsche was chosen because, according to Dr. Turski, complicated philosophical literature encourages more brain activity and concentration, and requires the listener to utilize higher orders of verbal processing. Not only are the primary listening centers activated, but also the association areas of the brain. Compare the complexity of a philosophical discussion with the complexity of the average sitcom. Given the fact that many of us spend more time watching TV than engaging in intellectual discussions, is it any wonder that our attention and concentration skills are dwindling?

How else might we exercise our brains? Radio talk shows, books on tape, and continuing education courses are low-cost ways to improve attention and comprehension. Paraphrase the speaker's ideas back to yourself aloud. This allows you to clarify new ideas and store them in your memory bank.

To improve your ability to process and recall factual or technical information, take ten to twenty minutes every day to listen to a radio interview, self-help tape, or lecture. At the midpoint and at the end of the segment *say back aloud* some of the key points you heard. Elaborate on one or two of them, if possible. Just like in the paraphrasing exercise in chapter five, unless you can paraphrase the key points out loud to yourself, you will not know whether you have processed the information. With practice, this daily exercise can considerably increase your confidence in your memory! Experts in memory agree—*use it or lose it.*

Commercials can be helpful in giving us that minute of recall opportunity. After listening to a portion of a TV or radio interview, for example, use the commercial time to recall issues and key points. Review aloud so you can hear the completeness of your ideas. If the material is of particular interest, go one step further and jot down these ideas on paper. Occasional review of the material helps keep the information accessible for future use. You'll be surprised to see that later that day, you will be able to relate to others several points on that particular issue.

Another way to improve your ability to concentrate, particularly when the information is technical or complex, is to *picture the words* as they are being spoken, like a teletype in your mind's eye. This definitely takes practice, but it can be very helpful in a dry lecture or a technical explanation. Some of us learn better when information is presented visually, while some of us learn even better when information is presented visually *and* aurally. An advantage to this method is that it eliminates external distractions because you are so busy listening *and* seeing in your mind's eye every word that is being uttered.

Many people feel that taking notes should be reserved for the classroom, or that it is a sign of poor memory to take out a notepad and jot down a few points. Most speakers would agree, however, that any sign of conscientious listening is appreciated. At least you can be sure that the message was received. In addition, writing down and seeing the information in print, even if you discard the notes shortly afterward, means that there will be a better chance of recall at a later date.

Once you choose to remember some piece of information, dwell on it for *at least one minute*. This allows the association areas of your brain to get in on the act and take that piece of information to a deeper level. Douglas J. Herrman, the author of *Super Memory*, claims that anything given less than a minute of thought will fade from memory. Once the words are perceived and you choose to remember the idea, it takes several seconds of rehearsal or repetition of the information to make it to short-term memory. For example, when you have to remember a phone number, you usually repeat it several times before you call. Yet by the time the call is complete, you may have forgotten it again. Occasional rehearsal of your new association keeps the information in long-term storage. (For specific help with memory, please see the bibliography at the back of this book.)

Dr. Tony Buzan introduced an effective means of note making/taking called *mind mapping*. This technique is contrary to the standard system of writing out full sentences or making an outline. Dr. Buzan states that the traditional style of note taking uses *less than half* of the capacity of the brain to learn new information. In fact, traditional note taking works against the brain's natural inclination to learn by making associations and looking for patterns. Traditional note taking obscures key ideas, is monotonous, uses listening time inefficiently, and fails to stimulate the brain to remember. Consequently, we diminish our powers of concentration, view learning as time consuming and unproductive, lose confidence in our ability to learn, and because we are working against the brain's natural tendencies, we become frustrated with learning. In contrast, mind mapping incorporates images and pictures with printed words. Ideas hover around a central theme. Various modes of print and the use of spacing and symmetrical designs help the brain remember ideas associated with the central theme.

You may ask, what is Zen-like about mind mapping? Mind

mapping doesn't restrict us to just the words of the message. Our map can include emphases, contrasts, feelings, and complexity unlike a flat list of words and phrases. Mind mapping is liberating. It frees the brain from barriers to learning—monotony, frustration, and poor self-esteem. It is also a mindful activity because it promotes concentration and creativity.

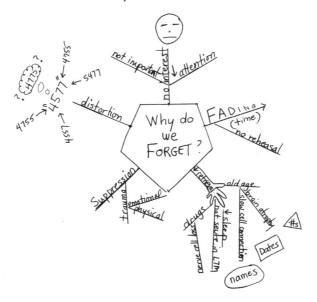

How to Listen Better in Meetings and Classes

If you do not give your full attention to the speaker, the information will not have a chance to get into your memory. Students frequently ask how to maintain attention during large meetings, particularly the boring ones. CNN recently claimed that at least 38 percent of people polled have difficulty paying attention in meetings.

Why are certain meetings more boring than others? A poll taken from thirty students chosen at random from my classes revealed the following. When asked to fill in the blank: "A meeting is considered

boring or a waste of time because it _____."
Most students completed the sentence in one of four ways: 1) "will require no input from me or the people in my group," 2) "lacks an agenda, or does not stick to the proposed agenda," 3) "accomplishes nothing," 4) "is led by a poor speaker."

Students also feel resentment that they are forced to listen in these situations, and subsequently, find it difficult to tune back in when necessary. In the next chapter, you will see how you as a meeting presenter can keep the number of poor listeners to a minimum. But for now, as potentially gifted listeners, how can you become mindful in meetings and get the most out of them?

Just calling a meeting or a presentation "boring" implies that it has no purpose and that it is a waste of time. But if you tweak your attitude toward these kinds of activities and approach meetings as an archeological dig or a challenge to discover an idea you may not have otherwise encountered, you will benefit. Some of the great entrepreneurs of our time say that great ideas come to them in unexpected situations. A word or phrase triggers a series of associations that leads to a new invention or a solution to a problem. Use you ears' *downtime* (the lag between the mind's ability to process information and the speaker's rate of speech) to review what has been said and its relevance to current trends, articles you've read, or implications for future endeavors. Remember that your focus, although broadened by the associations you are making, is still in the present with the speaker in the foreground. Find out how this piece, this topic, is part of the big picture.

For example, I was required to attend a manager's meeting at our clinic about the employee parking problem, a topic that might be considered well within the definition of boring. Instead of taking that attitude, I sat back and was astounded to hear a wide variety of solutions. Some were practical, others convenient but costly, several were creative. One person presented an ethical approach. By combining a few of these ideas, we were able to strike a majority vote and arrive at a remedy. If I had given myself twenty minutes to come up with all the possible solutions to the parking problem, I would have thought of only a couple at best. Listening with barriers down to these diverse perspectives widened my scope for solving my own business problems that day.

If a more active approach is necessary, take a bold step by offering to take the minutes of the meeting. This requires you to be totally focused. Firsthand experience taught me the value of getting involved in this way, even when I assumed that the meeting had little to do with me. Given the task to take the minutes (the secretary was out sick), others depended on me to become absorbed in the issues discussed. As I took notes, I realized that the ideas being proposed would help a coworker who was having problems with one of her projects. I became invested in the concerns of the group. By the end of the meeting, not only was I able to provide the team leader with an accurate and detailed report, but I had picked up some tips for my friend and learned quite a bit for myself.

The usual mindset would have set me apart, twiddling my thumbs and watching the clock in boredom. I also felt guilty, thinking of other meetings in the past that I had classified as boring— what lost opportunities! Students in my listening classes admit that at first, they are reluctant to take the minutes because they doubt their ability to catch everything; they have been such passive participants for so long. But with practice, the rewards are immediate, and they jump at the chance to give the secretary a break!

Taking the minutes, like other listening exercises described in this book, is a daunting task for some—it challenges our barriers and concentration skills. But these are the missions for the mind that wait at your doorstep every day.

Remembering People's Names

We love it when someone remembers our name. It makes us feel good about our uniqueness, the impression we made, or the possibility of a future relationship. When someone says they remember our face but (sorry!) not our name, we are not as enthusiastic.

Forgetting names is one of the most common communication complaints, but it is fairly easy to remedy with practice and the proper mindset. Comedian Paul Rieser had a great solution to this dilemma. He suggested we eliminate names altogether and refer to each other according to our unique physical characteristics. Instead of saying "Hey Jim, meet Mary," we could say "Hey, Broken Glasses, come on over here and meet Food in Her Teeth!" In a way, this approach has merit.

Think about the names you are able to recall and ask yourself why that is. Of course we remember the names of family members, but can you explain why you remember Harold, a brief acquaintance from twelve years ago? Is it that you recall the coincidence of going to the movie *Harold and Maude* and joking about his choice in movies? Or was it that he was the "spittin' image" of your Uncle Harold? Nevertheless, the names of people that you spent much more time with twelve years ago may elude you. Chances are, it was the association of the name with something already familiar that set Harold's name in stone.

Try this: every time you meet someone new, associate a prominent characteristic with his name. For instance, someone named Jim may be very slender, so it's handy to think of him as "Slim Jim." The next time you run into Jim, his outstanding feature—his slimness—will pop into your mind and "Jim" will surface. Or you may recall a Jim in your past who looks very much like *this* Jim.

My favorite method of remembering names is to repeat the name during the handshake and a few times during our conversation. This means: 1) at the introduction, 2) when initiating a comment, and 3) at the close of the discussion. People love to hear their names, but don't overdo it. During this time you are in their movie and assimilating information about them with their name solidly in the mix. Repeating a person's name throughout the conversation assists you in making the connections needed for recall later on. When your intention is to develop a working relationship with that person, your occasional repetition of his name will feel more natural. If, on the other hand, you treat a new acquaintance as a meal ticket, your use of his name will come across as phony.

As extra insurance, soon after the discussion, write down the name and any notes about a new acquaintance. Review the information occasionally, rehearse the association, particularly when you might run into your new acquaintance again. Rehearsal (seeing the person's face and what was discussed while repeating the name) is particularly helpful with unusual names.

As our society becomes more culturally diverse, we encounter more and more unfamiliar names. This renders the association approach practically useless. In my clinic, I frequently come across physicians and nurses from other countries. Names like Fanghua, Sangbaek and Thanatip are difficult to pronounce correctly, much less remember. These foreign-born associates already feel isolated by the language barrier and cultural differences, and this may be exacerbated by American-born colleagues who are hesitant to initiate conversation for fear of mispronouncing their names. We welcome the nicknames that are more familiar to us, like Bob, Mike, or Liz, yet we cannot expect foreign-born people to change their names just for our convenience

Most people heartily appreciate being addressed by name. When I teach foreign-accent reduction classes, I see it as a personal challenge and a necessity to learn twenty or more students' names within a week. Establishing this link sets the stage for openness and self-discovery. The first step is to be sure to pronounce each name correctly. When you meet someone with an unusual name, *insist* upon getting the pronunciation correct. The spelling might not help, so grab a piece of paper and write out phonetically, as closely as possible, the right pronunciation. Getting comfortable with the pronunciation is a necessary first step, and I have yet to meet a foreign-born person who is not willing to persist with me until I get it right. Then I repeat the name a few times during our conversation. Shortly thereafter, I recall the conversation and the name. This takes consistent practice, but the rewards will encourage you to make it a habit.

By the way, if you do forget someone's name, ask it again and give this process another try. Otherwise, you know how it goes—you'll be playing the search-my-brain-for-the-name game while completely tuning out what he is saying. My students are at first reluctant to accept that the forgotten other will not be upset with them. On the contrary, he or she whose name you forgot sees your request as admirable (admitting the mind-slip up front) and confident (taking action to get it right the second time). It also lets them know you care enough to admit your flaw.

A very considerate gesture when running into people you know only marginally is to immediately reintroduce yourself. They will be very grateful to you for the minirefresher, and both of you can concentrate on your message rather than playing the name game while you speak.

Using the person's name during the conversation may feel odd at first, but with a couple tries, it will start to feel natural. We are used to trying to relate to someone while standing outside the theater. With the names attached to the movie, you can both get down to knowing one another.

Listening Hygiene

From a physical point of view, there are things you can do to improve your ability to listen. First, ask yourself a few questions:

Do you get enough sleep? If your mind is not awake and alert, how can you be a mindful listener? Most of us need at least seven to eight hours of sleep a night in order to attend and concentrate efficiently. According to James Maas, the author of *Power Sleep*, we may find ourselves falling asleep during meetings, not because of the content, the room temperature, or the heavy lunch we just consumed, but because these conditions expose the level of sleep deprivation in our bodies. Because our consciousness during sleep doesn't appear to have the same continuity and focus as waking consciousness, most people think that when we are asleep the brain is turned off. Quite the contrary. For example, REM (rapid eye movement) sleep, the state of sleep associated with dreaming, is known as *paradoxical sleep* because, despite the relaxed tone of the body, the brain and respiratory system are very active. REM sleep stimulates neural circuits that retain ideas and memories. Without strong memory circuits acquired during REM sleep, we may have difficulty remembering what we hear over the course of a day.

How do you fuel the fire for listening? Sometimes our most important meetings of the day occur right after lunch. Rather than listening to the message, our bodies are preoccupied with digesting. Overeating can lead to drowsiness, which impairs our ability to pay attention. On the other hand, being hungry and drinking too much caffeine can make us jumpy and easily distractible. Some people feel that they are better communicators after a few alcoholic drinks. They report being more relaxed, less inhibited. Unfortunately, *accurate* processing of the message is poorer under the influence of alcohol, and after a few drinks it may be difficult to stay awake. Over time, the effects of alcohol have been found to seriously impair memory.

Gingko supplements, used with caution (gingko should not be taken with certain heart medications), have been advertised as memory enhancers. However, there appear to be no well-controlled studies to support this claim yet.

In order to maximize your readiness to listen, get to know the amounts and kinds of foods that best enable your brain to perform at its best. To exceed that threshold spells disaster for attention and concentration.

Are you anxious or depressed? Anxiety and depression make it difficult to get into the movie or to be mindful. Our barriers (described in chapter four) cause major distractions, or you may be preoccupied with internal struggles, as discussed in chapter five. Your ability to listen mindfully may also be affected by physical tension, which, as I have stated throughout this book, can be mitigated significantly through meditation.

When was your last yearly physical examination? Physiological imbalances can cause difficulties with memory. We already discussed the effects of alcohol and caffeine, but certain medications may also affect your ability to process and recall information.

Hormonal imbalances have also been cited as responsible for memory loss and learning difficulties. Women who are estrogen deficient may also suffer from cognitive disorders. According to a study in the *Journal of the American Medical Association,* "Effects of Age, Sex, and Ethnicity on the Association Between Apolipoprotein E Genotype and Alzheimer Disease: A Meta-analysis" (Vol. 278, No. 16), women are also two to three times more likely to develop Alzheimer's disease than men. Dr. Roberta Diaz Brinton at the University of Southern California claims that "some, not all, estrogens will promote the cellular mechanism responsible for learning and memory and protect them from the damage that occurs from free radicals and some of the insults that are associated with Alzheimer's disease." Diabetics should also consult their physicians if memory problems are noted.

Skillful Listening

Mindful listening provides the basis for skillful listening, or decision-based mindful listening. Some of you may be familiar with the term *critical listening*. In our information-laden world, we simply do not have the time to listen to everything that comes our way, so we have to make decisions between listening to things we *should* hear and what we *want* to hear. There are approximately eighteen hundred radio talk shows in America. When one comes on about how to reduce your risk of heart disease, it is quite tempting to see what the fight is about on the Jerry Springer show. Sometimes we merely want to be entertained by watching unusual people do unusual things, or we may be just plain curious about the motives of a mass murderer. We must ask ourselves, "Will this show benefit me in some way? Or will it add more noise or bolster a barrier I've been trying to get rid of?"

It is necessary to seriously examine the quality and integrity of the discussions, advertisements, and news reports that influence what car to buy, what candidate to vote for, what vitamins to take, how much coffee to drink, what stocks to buy, and how much exercise we need. Because of our limited attention spans, we are drawn to the more sensational speakers and advertisements and tempted to tune out the lengthy, less attractive presenters that may be the most informative.

As mindful listeners, we take an objective stance in listening for the truth. We are aware of the methods used by the media to persuade and sell. For example, an advertising agency discovered that despite our years of quality education our attention span is about twenty-two seconds. Ah! Just about as long as the average commercial! Nowadays, infomercials push our limits to fifteen minutes or more. They frequently feature fast-talking, enthusiastic, handsome celebrities who repeat over and over again the benefits of the product.

But as mindful listeners, we know how our eyes frequently take precedence over our ears. Lesley Stahl, a reporter on the television show *60 Minutes,* describes in *Reporting Live* how television overpowers our reason. She cites a news report she prepared on the theme of how President Reagan used television to create an image of himself that was contrary to his actual stand on issues such as funding for the disabled and housing for the elderly. In support of her thesis, Stahl used footage of Reagan presiding at the opening of a nursing home and presenting medals to Special Olympics athletes. Despite her voice-over describing Reagan's actual position on these issues, the Reagan White House was overjoyed with her reportage. They insisted that Stahl's critical voice-over had made no impact on the viewing audience, that only the video portion of her report was important. A short time later, Stahl's piece was shown without the sound track to an audience of 100 people. When they were asked what the report was about, they claimed it was a political promo. The clip was replayed, this time with Stahl's critical audio commentary. Still, over half the audience insisted it was a very pro-Reagan news report!

Stahl says, "Unlike reading or listening to the radio, with television we 'learn' with two of our senses together, and apparently the eye is dominant. . . . We get an emotional reaction: the information doesn't always go to the thinking part of our brains but to the gut." As voters and consumers, we need to be aware of this tendency to perceive information in an unbalanced way. By strengthening our listening abilities, we become more competent decision makers.

Here are some questions you might ask yourself while listening to TV or radio: What are the pros and cons in what the speaker proposes? Skillful listening means making associations with what the speaker is promoting and what you know from prior knowledge or experience. Aside from just getting the facts, is her argument well supported? If not, why? Is she an expert in her field? What are the short and long-term implications of what this person is suggesting? What is her bias?

Pharmaceutical companies are well aware of our listening weaknesses, particularly of the less medically educated market. A fast-growing segment of the population spends billions of dollars on health and beauty products directed toward promoting longevity and youthfulness. Even if you purchase only vitamin C tablets every few months, you are a target for the industry. It is tempting to think that a pill can improve your memory or give you more energy. After all, pills are effective for losing weight, eliminating depression, and keeping you awake. Why not trust a pill that will make you smarter?

The companies selling herbal remedies must include credible sources in their commercials, just like advertisers of aspirin and antacids. At best, they may have a few satisfied customers (or people paid to act like satisfied customers) and an endorsement by a believable person. Is that enough to convince you to spend twenty dollars or more on a pill? Sometimes. But to make sure, these companies often cite a research study claiming positive findings. What the average listener does not hear is whether the studies performed included a sizeable and representative population, were well controlled for accuracy, or overseen by a reputable association like a major clinic or scientific organization.

In addition, it is difficult—or perhaps impossible—to quantify an intangible benefit like energy or memory. Feeling younger and smarter is in the eye of the beholder. The unskillful listener will slap down cash not knowing what to expect and without hearing any hard evidence to support the claims. Health product advertising is only one venue that requires skillful listening.

How well are *you* prepared for listening in the twenty-first century? Developing your foundation of mindful listening will ready you for the onslaught of information, advertising, diversity, and hype predicted in this millennium.

Ask yourself

- Are you a fair listener?

- Is your listening focused and concentrated in order to use the knowledge base you have acquired to examine the validity of the evidence?

- Can you process information contrary to your beliefs with out becoming defensive or argumentative?

- Can you look beyond physical attractiveness and sensational claims to evaluate the validity of the product or service?

- Is your negative self-talk under control or do you mistrust your gut feeling?

Cortical Calisthenics

1. Prior to a listening opportunity like a TV or radio interview, review the list of questions above. Discuss your answers with a friend who also saw or heard the same show. Agree with a partner to regularly practice mindful listening in this manner.

2. Sign up for an adult education class. Most large towns or cities have at least one adult education program. Some colleges and universities offer adult education programs also. These affordable classes can run anywhere from two to eight hours on a single day to two to four hours once every six weeks, depending upon the format. You can take in a minilecture or learn a new skill.

3. When you go to view an exhibit at an art museum, spend a few extra dollars and take the tour on tape. These audio guide programs can be very entertaining and will enhance your appreciation and understanding of the work by narrating the history surrounding the piece, the artist's mood, or events that shaped the work.

Chapter Eleven

How to Help Others Listen Better

*It is no use walking anywhere to preach
unless our walking is our preaching.*

—Saint Francis of Assisi

Why aren't we taught listening skills in school? Given the fact that it is the basis for learning math, science, and reading, not to mention many other life skills, you would think that listening classes would occupy a prominent position in the academic curriculum. Browse through your local library and you will find dozens of books on how to write or how to be a better public speaker, but you will find very few books on listening—the nation's greatest communication weakness.

As we mature into adulthood, listening acquires several negative connotations. For instance, when someone says, "Listen to me," we interpret that as "Agree with me," or "Do as I say," thus relinquishing control and taking a back seat to the speaker. Isn't it ironic that the number-one request of teachers is to "pay attention"? When I was a kid, that was code for, "Look up you heathens, stop doing what you're enjoying and suffer while I talk."

These unpleasant associations give listening a bad rap. By the time we are adults, we view listening as passive and speaking as a leadership activity. Rarely in commercials are political candidates shown listening. Because listening is an internal, silent process, it lacks the visual flashiness needed to grab voters' attention. In actual political life, however, the average politician claims to spend at least 70 percent of his job listening. Therefore, wouldn't it make sense to vote for the better listener?

In July 1999, Hillary Rodham Clinton launched her listening tours as part of her campaign for the New York Senate seat. It was a novel strategy and it made a lot of sense. First of all, the people of New York knew Mrs. Clinton better than she knew them, and she had, compared to her competition, little time to get to know voters. She chose the most direct route to developing a relationship with voters—letting them know she *wanted to listen.* At the time of the writing of this book, the outcome of the race is not known, but if Mrs. Clinton listens like she said she will, it will be interesting to find out how voters react to this refreshing campaign approach.

In American schools, about twelve years of formal education are focused on teaching us how to read, write, and speak. Yet according to Madelyn Burley-Allen in *Listening—the Forgotten Skill,* only about half a year, doled out in bits and pieces without any structured format, comprises listening training. Yet our ability to excel in reading, speaking, and writing depends on the strength of our listening and concentration skills. Studies show that elementary students are expected on the average to spend 57.5 percent of their classroom time listening; high-school students 66 percent; and college students, anywhere from 52 to 90 percent.

Perhaps listening is one of those skills that teachers assume we learn at home. Those of us who were fortunate enough to have frequent family discussions practiced turn-taking, debate, and critical listening from an early age. This preliminary coaching prepared us for learning how to reason, analyze information (spoken or written), and the give and take required in making friends.

Even dogs need some basic training from their mothers before they can be adopted by humans. Prior to bringing home my beloved Spud from the litter next door, I read a book called *Mother Knows Best*. It explained how mother dogs instinctively discipline their pups to take turns feeding, to be submissive, to clean themselves, and protect their food. The mother sets up certain conditions, and it's up to the human owner to follow through immediately with the next stages of training.

The lack of preschool home training makes classroom learning difficult for so many children. If basic attention and listening skills were emphasized in the home from an early age, teachers would be able to use their talents to teach instead of having to constantly discipline children who have never been prepared to learn. More time spent on teaching would probably result in better SAT scores and more fulfilled adults. I propose that daily discussions about everyday moral dilemmas, vacation planning, household chores, sports, and so on, be standard topics at the dinner table, on automobile trips, and during bedtime conversation.

Signing our children up for a listening class may not be the best way for them to become better listeners, especially if it is not given the same credibility as science or math. Children learn best by observing and imitating their parents. Be a good model of listening not only in the home environment, but also in social situations. Show your children how disputes and differences of opinion can be tolerated and, in some cases, even welcomed.

Teach your children at an early age that a different way of doing things does not have to be accompanied by a judgment. When you watch a movie together or see a different mode of dress, avoid judgmental remarks. Balance the negative aspects of any experience with positive observations. Allow for some gray areas before a final decision is made. Pick out routine activities and demonstrate different ways of achieving the same solution. For example, when driving to a familiar destination, choose a different route and notice your child's reaction. Reassure her that there may be some delight in taking a slightly longer route once in awhile. Or take your kids to an ethnic restaurant. To increase the chances of your child appreciating this break from the cherished pizza-and-burger routine, ask the waiter which foods on the menu are particularly favored by children their age. They still may not like the cuisine, but you can emphasize that this is a chance to see how kids in other lands eat every day. A new experience does not always have to be a favorite one in order to be beneficial.

Kids learn how to listen by being listened to. And just like adults, kids want to share those good feelings by listening to others. In my listening utopia I envision families sitting down to meditate together for ten to fifteen minutes every morning before work or play. This would settle down mental distractions and fine tune their abilities to absorb the contents of the day. More attention would be paid to calm discussion instead of mindless TV and radio. As the result of good listening, parents and teachers would receive respect and loyalty, the difficult people in our lives would receive compassion, and the thoughts and perspectives of people from other cultures would be welcomed.

Another awakening experience occurred to me during my work as a voice coach. Managers thrust into the world of public speaking, salespeople, and budding political candidates made up my "Enhancing Your Vocal Image" classes. The main theme of the class was "It's not *what* you say but *how* you say it." This class became increasingly popular as media experts shared their insights about political candidates, particularly around election time. We heard commentators hail Ronald Reagan as "the great communicator," not because of how he listened or chose his words, but because of his charismatic voice and

224

commanding presence. He also had an excellent speechwriter. George Bush presented a striking contrast. His weak, whiny voice and agitated responses under stress earned him a reputation as a wimp. The eighties taught us much about the image makers in politics and big business, and how we could get ahead using some of their techniques.

My voice-image class focused on creating a physical presence on stage, using techniques borrowed from actors' workshops and the professional image makers to wow the audience or win the sale. Many students claimed that these methods earned them the vote, the sale, the promotion, despite the fact that the presentation was often badly prepared or the sales pitch failed to make sense.

Those admissions, despite the students' delight at beating out the competition, gave me a queasy feeling. I began to rethink the purpose of passing down these gems of knowledge and experience from my days in theater. Not long after that revelation, I had an opportunity that forever changed my way of communication training.

In 1992, I was invited to visit Senator Paul Tsongas and convince him to improve his vocal image. He was a presidential candidate for the Democrat Party, and although he was well respected for his knowledge and integrity, he was handicapped by voice characteristics and a presentation style that lacked the power and punch expected of the leader of the most powerful country on Earth. Senator Tsongas listened patiently to my dissertation on what I could do to improve his speaking style. A few supporters who were also present urged him to consider the coaching. Soon after our meeting, however, I received word that Senator Tsongas chose not to follow through with voice coaching. Despite his desire for victory and the knowledge that his lackluster speaking style could cost him the nomination, Senator Tsongas could not bring himself to sound different to his wife and children. What I judged as a small concession for a big prize, Senator Tsongas saw as a threat to what mattered to him most—his honesty with himself and others.

From that point on, I continued to teach the same skills, but with the motive of helping others to listen better and understand the message rather than swaying an audience to act in our self-interest.

To help others listen when we speak involves

- connecting with your listeners, making it easy for them to get into your movie;

- forming a trusting relationship with them (how many products you sell when your presentation is over, getting your kids to clear off the dinner dishes, or getting your husband to mow the lawn are secondary);

- being mindful about what your audience wants and needs to know;

- knowing their barriers toward you.

If you want others to listen and understand you better, think about what makes *you* want to listen. High on your list may be compliments, words of encouragement, expressions of support, appreciation, and love, unambiguous comments and questions, or invitations to do things we like. It's easy to give orders, make demands, and criticize for the sake of getting things done, but how often do you offer an appreciative comment, compliment, or praise?

For example, my husband and I love to eat out occasionally at little ethnic restaurants, where we typically discuss our projects, family issues, or home improvements. I often think about how great it is to be with someone who enjoys these evenings too, but I couldn't remember the last time I had told him that. The next time we went out, I waited for the right moment, reached across the table and squeezed my husband's hand as I explained to him how much our evenings out meant to me. My husband smiled warmly with a glow of mutual agreement and said it made him very happy to hear that.

For the rest of the evening, my husband's attentiveness to me, even with topics that would have normally stretched his interest, was spectacular.

Every parent and spouse knows the frustration of being tuned out by a loved one. As external distractions mount in our environment, being tuned out is more common than being tuned in. If you ask teenagers (specialists in this field) to tell you why they are reluctant to respond when spoken to, they will give you several reasons:

- I know what's coming . . . the dishes or something.

- It's usually homework related or something I screwed up.

- My dad always has *suggestions* for how I could do some job better next time.

- It's never anything I'm interested in hearing.

- I can't tell whether it's my mom talking or the TV—they kinda sound the same.

The message here is that teens don't see their parents' interests as relevant or interesting. Kids start building barriers toward messages with punitive overtones—like advice—at a young age. This tendency persists into adulthood and is the cause of many an unnecessary hearing test and divorce.

If by now you've discovered the joys of forgetting yourself to go to the movies, you may find it easier to let your family member finish watching the game on TV or logging off the computer before you begin talking. As I have already mentioned, meditation practice can increase the generosity of your spirit. Even though what you have to say is important, you find yourself respecting what others find more important at the time.

By letting someone finish something that is important to him, you show that he is valued and respected. That is the first step in getting someone to listen to you. Then when you are engrossed in a movie or a book and others want to interrupt, they will be more likely to show you the same courtesy. In this way, when you really need to be heard immediately, you'll have a much better chance of getting their attention.

Getting kids to listen is fraught with frustration unless you think from a mindful-listening point of view. We can become pariahs to our kids if we persist in speaking to them from our perspective. It often amuses me that the typical comments or questions, despite their inefficiency, get passed down from generation to generation. Every day we hear young parents in their twenties and thirties saying exactly the same things we grew up hearing: "Now, if you do that one more time . . ." or "Look at me! What did I just finish saying?" And how about "Wouldn't it be a nice change if we turned down the TV so I can hear myself think?" And don't forget the infamous "How many times do I have to tell you . . . ?"

After observing kids and parents interact in this manner, I doubt if the kids comprehend these threats and demands. They infer from tone of voice and body language that they're in trouble, but they don't have a clue what their parents really want. The most effective caregivers I have observed, those who succeed in keeping their kids tuned in, are the ones who say exactly what is on their minds in a nonthreatening but cooperative tone, explaining why their actions are necessary and using words kids understand: "Let's clean out the garage together today," or "Please turn down the TV. I can't hear what your father is saying."

Being flexible enough to offer choices (if choices are available) gives teenagers some say in a situation. "Your room needs to be cleaned tonight. You choose—right after dinner or before you go to bed?" Kids and adults become engrossed in external distractions like TV, CD headphones, and the Internet. Therefore, instead of repeating yourself louder and louder, get physically closer, in full view of your listener, and speak in a normal tone. To get someone's undivided attention, try saying, "What I have to say to you right now is very important, so I need you to listen for the next ten minutes or so," or "I have something that concerns me very much that I need your opinion about," or "I know you'd rather listen to music right now, but what I have to say concerns both of us." Asking for their opinion and their assistance, using the word *important* with care, and appreciating what they are engrossed in will save you many minutes of mindless aggravation.

Perhaps your job or community requires that you give spoken presentations, or perhaps you supervise or train people at work. Getting adults to listen to you and take desirable action can be almost as challenging as getting your kids to do their homework. Adults are exposed to the same distractions as kids, and our internal distractions are greater.

Think about some of the most effective public speakers you have heard in the past.

Chances are, the ones who made the best impressions were those who did not speak *at* you but *to* you; they were sensitive to audience perspective, showed enthusiasm, and left you with a good feeling. Memorable speakers are *genuine* communicators. They care about forging a relationship with their audience. Here are sixteen ways to connect better with your audience and help them listen more effectively to the information you have to share:

1. **Get to know your audience.** Before preparing a talk for a large group, gather some information about your audience. In an impromptu situation or in a one-to-one meeting, I first get into their movie by getting them to talk so I can save time and focus my presentation on *their* best interest. This time also gives me valuable in-

sight into their barriers. I will be able to set the stage for a better relationship if I know how they like to receive information, if they already have a bias about the topic, or if they feel uncomfortable talking to me.

2. **Keep your environment free of noise and visual distractions.** Make arrangements ahead of time for a quiet room. If you are making a presentation in an auditorium, check the microphone and adjust the lighting. Are your audiovisual aids in good working order, set appropriately, and ready to go? Ask if there are personal FM listening devices available to hearing-impaired participants. Avoid the use of distracting physical mannerisms—repetitive hand gestures, flicking back your hair, or playing with a pen or piece of jewelry.

3. **Listen first.** In gripe sessions, start by listening mindfully. When it is your turn, your speakers will be more likely to listen to you. It is so rare to come across a good listener that when we do, we feel indebted to listen to them in return. Make sure they have said everything on their minds before you begin. Allow plenty of silence between their thoughts. Until they have stopped talking, they are not ready to hear you anyway. If time is at a premium, let the audience know early on that you want to hear from as many people as possible. This will help keep each speaker to a time limit. Be flexible with your response styles.

4. **Use a bit of humor to open a presentation.** Start off with a statement that gets their attention. Comedy writer Gene Perret once said, "Humor is not a condiment; it's not a main course. It's not a trinket. It doesn't need justification; it's essential." Humor does many things to encourage listening. First, it is relaxing, and they must be relaxed in order to listen. Joking about universal human faults and frustrations reduces tension and often makes a point better than a

thousand words. Humor is entertaining and adds needed sparkle to a dry subject. Humor also helps connect you with your audience by establishing rapport. Test your jokes and stories on others before you tell an audience. Be sensitive to words that could be taken the wrong way—*girl* versus *woman,* for example. If your joke is in bad taste or poorly executed, it will have the opposite effect—it can make your audience tune you out!

5. **Use audiovisuals as supplements to highlight key ideas.** Audiences appreciate colorful slides or laptop presentations. Contact a Toastmasters club or adult education program in your community for a course in laptop presentations or listener-enhancing slide presentations.

6. **Draw diagrams to help your audience understand difficult concepts.** When speaking one-on-one or to a small group, a diagram or mind map is a great note-taking aid, often worth many words. Diagramming a simple flow chart while you speak will be retained better than a string of sentences. This approach allows more listening time and less note taking. If you are going to meet with someone whom you know in advance is not a good listener, offer her paper and pen to take notes.

7. **Emphasize key phrases by changing the pitch and pace of your words.** The use of a pause before or after a key phrase also helps to break up the hypnotic monotony of continuous talk. Research shows that a speaking rate of 275 to 300 words per minute is most conducive to listener comprehension. (See the exercises at the end of this chapter to check your speaking rate.)

8. **Encourage the audience to use their visual memory.** Use visually descriptive words to make a point. For example, if you are

proposing a new public library in your community, you might say, "Imagine the lack of information as a dry, barren wasteland devoid of resources. Build a library and watch the land bloom green and fruitful."

9. **Ask frequently for feedback from your audience.** If you know their names, use them. When someone asks a question, do not assume that the whole audience heard it. Keep everyone involved by repeating the question. This also clarifies the question and helps you target your answer. After answering, inquire, "Does that answer your question?"

10. **Stir up attention by breaking into a discussion format.** An audience is typically more engaged when an active discussion is taking place. If you are giving a lecture and you notice that people are beginning to get that glazed look, open up the floor for discussion or debate. You may be surprised to learn that the real interests of your audience are very different than you or your meeting planner anticipated. For example, when my dad was diagnosed with prostate cancer, I was eager to attend a lecture on the topic. The surgeon/lecturer, well known in his field, spent the first forty minutes explaining prostate anatomy and the symptoms of prostate cancer. Although this was important information, the gentleman beside me started snoring sporadically. I also sensed that many of the participants were getting restless. Finally, one bold member of the audience stood up and asked if the surgeon could discuss sex after prostate surgery, specifically his own patients' experiences. Amid the chuckles and respectful hurrahs, the surgeon smiled at his own oversight and cheerfully acquiesced. He put his notes aside, turned off the overhead projector, and got the audience involved. He did not insist on completing his agenda. Instead he unselfishly addressed the main concerns of the people who took the time to attend his lecture. He worked in some key points necessary to patients contemplating surgery, but generally stuck to

the interests of the group. The audience overwhelmingly thanked him, and several participants made arrangements for consultations. If the surgeon had continued with his agenda as planned, these relationships would not have transpired.

11. **Encourage group participation with brainstorming.** The rules of brainstorming include any and all ideas, without judgments. Most certainly a few ideas will attract a few groans and chuckles, but this should be discouraged—every speaker deserves respect and every idea has equal weight.

12. **Make eye contact with members of the audience.** This creates an atmosphere of conversation and discussion, which is a more favorable listening situation for your audience and a more natural speaking situation for you. Some of the most memorable public speakers I have heard made me feel that they were talking directly to me. One particularly outstanding speaker told me, "I try to make everybody feel like we are all just sittin' around my livin' room havin' pie 'n' coffee while sharin' some new ideas."

13. **Highlight the *benefits* versus the features of the product or service you offer.** An audience listens more to the *benefits* they stand to gain than the features of the product or service. Use your voice and gestures to underscore these points: how the product or the service can save them money or time (use statistics) and how it is an investment of their resources.

14. **Get to the point.** Tell people what they need to know. If your audience already knows the problem, you might open with the solution and then expand your comments.

15. Eliminate distracting speech impediments. If you have a speech impediment like a lisp, stutter, or strong foreign or regional accent, don't let it get in the way of your ability as a public speaker or group leader. These behaviors may be distracting, but they can usually be treated successfully by a speech-language pathologist.

16. Summarize the key points at the end of your presentation. It is your responsibility to be sure your information gets across. Remember in chapter six how your ability to tell back the message is the true test of how well the message was processed? Therefore, periodically—and definitely at the end of a session—ask various students to tell three things they learned. If you let students know that periodic feedback will be a part of the class, they will be more apt to pay attention. This helps students remember the information better and clears up any confusion. This also gives you information about how well you are communicating.

Share Your Movie

1. Take a class in public speaking or join Toastmasters to get practice applying the above suggestions. Seek out a few sessions with a voice coach (contact a university drama school) to help you discover your expressive abilities; be willing to experiment.

2. To determine your average speaking rate, select an article from a newspaper or a magazine. Count out 100 words. Turn on a tape recorder and set a timer for sixty

seconds. Then read your 100 words aloud over and over until the timer goes off. Repeat the exercise two or three times to get a realistic average number of words per minute. Listeners best process information spoken at a rate of 275 to 300 words per minute.

3. Critique your presentation. As painful as it may be, tape a segment of your speech and listen back for utterances like "um," or "uh." Do you repeatedly end sentences with "Okay?", "Right?", or "Everybody with me?" These expressions can seriously detract attention from your message.

Chapter Twelve

Mindful Listening Is Good for Your Health

Listening is an attitude of the heart,
a genuine desire to be with another
which both attracts and heals.

—J. Isham

M indful listening benefits the physical and psychological health of the listener and the speaker. Edward Hallowell, M.D., of Harvard Medical School reported in *Bottom Line* magazine (February 2000) several studies that linked low death rates with feelings of connectedness. According to one study (*Journal of the American Medical Association,* 1997), the most protective factors against violent behavior, severe emotional distress, suicide, and substance abuse among twelve thousand adolescents were feelings of connectedness with family members, schoolmates, and teachers. Several studies in both the United States and abroad involving different age groups support the link between well-being and frequent and positive social encounters. Face-to-face contact with other people has been shown to reduce susceptibility to cold viruses, boost the immune system, and lower pain sensitivity. E-mail and chat lines serve only to increase social isolation.

Dr. James Pennebaker found that when people were given a chance to discuss a stressful event in their lives with willing listeners, their blood pressure decreased. He also reported that having a confidante strengthened the immune system. Being heard lifts self-esteem; we feel important when someone takes the time to hear us out.

Sidney Jourard in his visionary book, *The Transparent Self,* differentiates between inspiriting and dispiriting transactions and their dramatic effects on our health. Because listening is such a powerful connector, it is no surprise that we feel close to our psychiatrists or counselors. *Inspiriting* activities, like being listened to, give us a sense of worth and purpose. Conversely, *dispiriting* transactions, such as failing a test, family arguments, or performing poorly at an interview, make us feel unimportant, worthless, and frustrated. Jourard's hypothesis is that dispiriting events render us vulnerable to illness, while inspiriting ones promote wellness.

Dr. Joyce Brothers (the *Today* show, March 22, 1999) claims that listening to your partner is one of the most important ways to fight fairly when disagreements arise. Unfair fighting (criticizing character versus behavior, cross-complaining, unending accusations, etc.) serves only to depress the immune system.

Dean Ornish, M.D., author of *The Program for Recovering from Heart Disease,* designed a cardiac rehabilitation program with an added feature—group discussions. These groups enable participants from various backgrounds to share their problems with other recovering heart patients. One participant reported his experience:

> It was so interesting to find people from all walks of life with the same basic problems. We all got to know each other as friends with a similar concern—wanting to stay alive. We were above judging each other. Titles, incomes, backgrounds did not matter—we

spoke to each other as human beings with similar problems. I could go to an Ornish group discussion and tell things I would never share even with my spouse. I am convinced this opportunity to be heard and accepted was paramount to my recovery.

Dr. Ornish claims that if we are able to make changes at the psychological and spiritual levels, then the physical heart can begin to improve. On a radio talk show (May 5, 1999, *Fresh Air,* National Public Radio), Ornish suggested that the health benefits attributed to red wine are likely the result of activities associated with drinking wine, namely, lively conversation, the company of other people, and personal disclosure.

Support groups such as AA (Alcoholics Anonymous), or MOMS (Moms Offering Moms Support) are some of the best venues available for mindful listening. Participants share a similar movie, and most of them have experienced many of the same problems. It is the nonjudgmental empathy shared by the group that is often more effective than a session with a counselor who does not share the same experience. A person who is HIV positive is much more likely to be understood by someone else who is HIV positive. Support groups dispel the notion that you are alone, that your anger is shameful, or that you are exaggerating your pain. Participants give each other respect—time to say what's on their minds and hear what works for others.

Those who lead isolated lives experience chronic stress, depression, and decreased immunity. A mindful ear gives a lonely person a chance for self-disclosure and unburdening. This lightening of the load, as crisis counselors will attest, prevents self-inflicting injuries and suicide attempts. Caregivers and patients who participate in support groups have overall better outcomes for survival, are less depressed, and more proactive in directing healthcare decisions.

What makes these groups so health-giving is the sense of

community each member contributes. Most people I spoke to expected to just get information; few expected to experience a connection with the group, and even fewer thought they would want to attend these meetings regularly. The majority agreed that after attending several group meetings, they felt more positive, more eager to contribute to their communities and their friends' lives, and were more patient with strangers.

Dr. Larry Scherwitz found that another risk factor for coronary artery disease is ego indulgence. He noted that when all other factors were controlled, patients who used the pronouns *I, me,* and *my* most often were more likely to develop cardiac problems. Self-focused people, in contrast to other-focused people, are more likely to experience higher levels of dissatisfaction, poorer health, and greater vulnerability to stress.

Perhaps this is what the Zen masters mean by the power of the *sangha,* or group. Zen teaches us that our innate compassionate state would reveal itself more easily if we thought of humanity as one being, one *sangha* with one goal—to help each other get along.

Our dependency on one another may range from obscure to obvious, but in some way, we all depend on each other. For example, the owner of the local hardware store may be the only one for miles who stocks a certain brand of fertilizer that doesn't make you cough or sneeze; your neighbor's dog keeps the rabbits away from your lettuce patch, perhaps the ninety-year-old woman who drives the old blue Nova at twenty miles per hour in a forty-mile-per-hour zone during rush hour is the one who prevents you from spinning out on the oil slick and crashing through the guard rail minutes down the road.

The simple to complex ways that we depend on each other still exist, but gated communities, exclusive clubs, and excessive interaction with computers instead of people physically isolate and dehumanize us. Our great-great-grandparents were master networkers.

Dependency among neighbors and the larger community was the means to sheer survival; each person was a resource. Listening to each other was easy because everyone was in the same boat; barriers and distractions were few and far between. What mattered was the trust established between neighbors, trust built on listening to one another. Nowadays, few of us can name more than three neighbors.

At this point in your listening practice, you may have noticed that you are calmer and less anxious. Not only are you a better listener, but you have also begun to be aware of the thinking and feeling states that influence your ability to process spoken information. Does mindful listening lead to a healthier cardiovascular system?

In *The Language of the Heart,* by James J. Lynch, the author describes a study in which hypertensive patients were hooked up to a computerized blood-pressure monitoring system while they conversed with the experimenter. Blood-pressure readings soared as patients discussed themselves or when their listening became defensive and self-conscious. However, when the experimenter set up a nonthreatening situation by telling the patients a personal experience or reading a passage that helped give a patient another perspective, blood pressure dropped to the lowest levels that patients had enjoyed in years. During these drops in blood pressure, patients momentarily focused on something outside themselves, much like getting into the movie of the speaker. This suggests a connection between our attention mechanisms and the cardiovascular system. Lynch noted the same connection between people and dogs. When you stroke your cat or dog, your blood pressure drops as you temporarily forget yourself and direct your attention to your pet.

Putting aside your agenda and taking the spotlight off yourself is exactly what you need to do when listening under stress. Through regular meditation practice, you can achieve that calm state, set aside your barriers and other defenses, and more directly address the issue. Of course, you may feel strong emotions while listening, but they will not overpower your attempt to understand the speaker and the source of the stress. Instead of wasting time haggling, your meditation practice allows you to clear the mist and get to a solution faster before the stress affects you physically. Epictetus, a first-century Roman philosopher, described the stressful impact of barriers when he said, "Man is disturbed not by things, but by his opinion of things."

Sometimes when I listen in mindfulness to another, it is as if I am in a meditative state. My eyes are open and I am fully aware of my surroundings, but I am totally calm and focused on the speaker. He may make alarming statements, annoy me with his attitude, or be wearing unusual clothes and jewelry that momentarily distract me. Just as in meditation, I note the distraction and gently return my attention to the speaker. When I recognize the mental hijacking in progress, getting back to the breath helps bring my body and mind back to their state of balance.

What exactly happens in our bodies during meditation that allows us to calm down and focus? One theory is that meditation lowers the body's responsiveness to the stress hormone norepinephrine. This theory belongs to Robert Benson, M.D., president of the Mind/Body Medical Institute at Deaconess Hospital in Boston, Massachusetts, and author of *The Relaxation Response*. In one study, subjects were presented with a stressful situation while heart rate and blood pressure were monitored. Subjects who had meditated twice a day for a month did not experience a rise in heart rate and blood pressure despite a rise in norepinephrine. Subjects who had not meditated experienced the usual increased blood pressure and heart rate. Many programs designed to help people with weight control, coronary heart disease, smoking cessation, and depression now encourage meditation as part of the treatment protocol.

After a day with difficult people, you might think that going home to solitude would be healthy. Think again! In 1998, researchers at Carnegie Mellon University studied the social and psychological effects of Internet use at home. One hundred sixty-nine average Internet users were asked to complete a questionnaire that measured psychological health and featured a self-rating scale that indicated their degree of depression and loneliness. You might assume that Internet users would be happier, since they spend more time interacting on chat lines, bulletin boards, and e-mail. Instead, researchers found a deterioration of social and psychological life. They hypothesize that cyberspace relationships do not provide the kind of psychological support and happiness derived from real-life contact. Professor Robert Kraut claimed, "Our hypothesis is there are more cases where you're building shallow relationships, leading to an overall decline in feeling of connection to other people."

Another concern unique to the computer age is our children. By introducing them to computers at very young ages, are we taking away valuable time needed to develop social skills? Will these computer whizzes grow up to be robotic, communicatively inept beings? According to Jane Healy, author of *Failure to Connect: How Computers Affect Our Children's Minds—for Better and Worse,* "If computer time subtracts from talking, socializing, playing, imagining, or learning to focus the mind internally, the lost ground my be hard or impossible to regain." There is evidence to support a critical period for learning language and social skills, a sensitive sliver of time, generally between the ages of one and seven years. The window of opportunity for mastering computer skills is much greater, as many midlife computer masters can attest. However, during the time between preschool and second grade, children learn to comprehend language, rehearse their sound repertoire, build vocabulary, and acquire the foundation for expressive language ranging from the concrete to the abstract. Coincidentally, this is also the time when children can more easily learn second and third languages. Early conversation practice forms the basis for reasoning, comprehension of complex language, reflection, problem solving, exchange of ideas, empathetic listening, tolerance for different communication styles, and soul building. As parents we must ask ourselves whether computer superiority is worth eroding our children's potential for becoming socially successful human beings.

If you spend a few hours every day communicating with people online, you are getting a taste of the electronic distancing that could become the overwhelming trend in the twenty-first century. It's fast, cheap, and gets a message across. *Which* message is the question. Remember that I mentioned how only 7 percent of thought content is carried by words alone? We derive 93 percent of what a person *means* by gestures, voice tone, and facial expression. Because so much is lost through e-mail or chat-room talk, we are setting ourselves up for a degree of miscommunication and mistrust never before imagined. Might a lack of sufficient face-to-face real-time personal interaction create an emotional fallout that could shorten our life spans? Could we forget how to create meaningful relationships with family members and how to make friends *off* the Internet? Could our people skills become extinct? Might feelings of compassion and caring be only fond childhood memories? Might our children view compassion and caring as an awkward or disturbed behavior? We must ask ourselves, "Is high-tech chat really more convenient and effective?"

Meditation has been shown to quiet the symptoms of anxiety and depression. Unlike medication, however, meditation has no negative side effects, naturally calms the source of the symptoms, and thus eliminates the need for medication. (When meditating, our oxygen consumption is reduced by 20 to 30 percent, which decreases blood lactate levels and results in fewer anxious feelings.)

Physical problems such as pain may inhibit listening. Meditation is reinforced as a way of connecting mind and body for many purposes; listening has been shown to benefit significantly from mind/body synchrony. Studies that show how blood pressure, heart, and breathing rate change as a function of mindful listening. Conversely, the health of speakers is affected positively by mindful listeners. Mindful listening can take place only when the listener's mind and body are balanced. The result is that the listener receives the whole message (words and intent) and processes it to the desired depth of memory. Your daily meditation practice prepares you to experience that mind-body link—your mind is calm, your breathing is slow and steady.

Chapter nine described ways of listening more effectively in stressful circumstances. Mindful listening under stress can eliminate the increased blood pressure and heart rate associated with the fight-or-flight response. Daily breathing practice establishes a higher overall threshold for anxiety, reducing our over-responsiveness to stressful situations. In an emergency, we are more likely to react quickly and intelligently and panic less. Breath control, if practiced regularly, can be elicited at will, which can reduce the activity of the sympathetic nervous system. By purposefully executing breath control, we can make healthful changes in the sympathetic nervous system. With regular practice, the physical and mental changes produced by daily meditation counteract the unhealthy effects of stress.

Most of us value our health more than any car, house, or job. It is essential, then, that both doctor and patient engage in mindful listening. Norman Cousins, a patient who recovered from a near-fatal illness, wrote an article called "The Anatomy of an Illness" (*New England Journal of Medicine,* 1976). His experience emphasized how being listened to played a key role in his recovery. "If I had to guess, I would have to say that the principal contribution made by my doctor to the taming and possible conquest of my illness was that he encouraged me to believe I was a respected partner with him in the total undertaking."

Both parties must take responsibility for the outcome. For you the patient, that means asking straightforward questions, describing symptoms and patterns of symptoms as accurately as possible, providing the most helpful information for the doctor to arrive at the proper diagnosis. You should be aware that most doctor visits may be fifteen minutes or less, so good preparation is appreciated. To make the most of the visit, the doctor should allow at least sixty seconds for the patient to speak without interrupting.

Mindful listening is *empathetic,* not sympathetic. In the doctor's office, as in any consultant-customer situation, empathetic listening means the ability to understand what a person is experiencing. When we give sympathy, we are attentive and reassuring, but removed from the speaker's experience. Mindful listening between doctor and patient creates trust, which has been shown to yield better outcomes from medical treatment. In fact, Dr. Herbert Benson, in *Beyond the Relaxation Response,* claims that trust and a belief in the doctor's advice can "actually alter the patient's physiology—and effect the cure or relief of bodily diseases."

I see this phenomenon often in the clinic. A patient comes to us from an outside medical practice seeking a second opinion. The doctor's advice may be the same as the first opinion, but because the patient felt that he established rapport with the second physician, his symptoms markedly improved even if there was no direct treatment given.

Benson cites a study in which two matched groups of patients were about to undergo similar surgery. One group was visited by the anesthesiologist and given a cursory explanation about the upcoming surgery and a projected recovery time. The second group was visited by the same anesthesiologist, who this time spoke warmly with his patients, listened to their concerns and worries, and answered questions in detail. He also informed them what to expect regarding pain and discomfort during recovery. After surgery, clear differences were noted. The second group recovered sooner and were discharged from the hospital 2.7 days earlier than the first group. That translates into big savings for a hospital. Clearly, our ability to heal can be significantly improved with mindful listening. (It should also be mentioned that mindful listening has, by definition, a positive focus. A patient or customer may not remember everything you told him, but his anxiety and eventual outcome will be significantly affected by dealing with a positive person.)

A doctor's concluding remarks and recommendations should include clarification of medical terms and explanation of side effects of prescribed medications. A responsible patient will repeat back or paraphrase how she understands the recommendations. If time runs out and there are more questions or concerns, some doctors ask the patient to write them down with the assurance that the doctor will call them back at a later time. A visit to your doctor that ignores these crucial points may set off a chain reaction of faulty interpretations, incomplete dissemination of information, misunderstood instructions, noncompliance with treatment suggestions, and—more seriously—a lack of trust.

There is no reason to stay with a physician who is not a good listener. In light of the competitive nature of today's healthcare environment, hospital administrators are becoming more sensitive to the need for patient-friendly physicians. The surge of interest in alternative healthcare such as acupuncture, massage therapy, herbal medicine, and meditation appears to be a direct request from consumers for a more mindful approach to healthcare. Dr. John Abramson, a family practitioner at the Lahey Clinic in Hamilton, Massachusetts, claims that there are two reasons people seek an alternative approach: "People are motivated to use alternative healthcare services for two very different reasons: one is that they are seeking techniques or medications that are not offered in mainstream medicine, but the other is that they desire a different kind of relationship with their caregiver."

The *New England Journal of Medicine* reported that the care and attention delivered in alternative medical practices is causing them to grow by leaps and bounds. Traditional business practices of all kinds would benefit from the implications of this message from patients to traditional medical establishments: people want to be heard, valued, and connected with the decision makers who determine the service or product they are receiving. David Siegel, web guru and author of *Futurize Your Enterprise: Business Strategy in the Age of the E-Customer,* says that customer-driven businesses will be common-place by 2005. He claims that the way to make the transition from a management-led business to a customer-led business is "First, learn to listen. And listen and listen." Siegel claims, "Markets are really conversations." Can you afford to let distraction get in the way of these conversations?

This book concludes with a story about a king who sought to understand others outside his royal circle. He gave up a life of worldly possessions and false comforts to discover the value of compassion and to share his knowledge with those bound by barriers of prejudice and inhumanity. He listened to and experienced the suffering of others as a way to connect with his fellow human. After several years, he awakened to the reality that we are all dependent on each other to make our lives happy and peaceful, no matter what our status. This man, Siddhartha, came to be known as "the Awakened One" (or Buddha) to his students. He is revered today not as a god, but as a model for patience, sincerity and openness.

Mindful listening in this Age of Distraction is needed as never before for our personal and professional survival. You can choose today to take steps toward understanding your true nature and using your intelligence in a more profound and productive way. The Zen principles discussed in this book—mindfulness, compassion, equa-nimity, forgetting ourselves long enough to get into movie of an-other, and meditation—form the basis for truly understanding our-selves and one another. Along the way, like Siddhartha, we can teach others, not by force, but by our example.

Let mindful listening be your guide to continuous self-renewal and compassion toward yourself and others.

Bibliography

Austin, James H. *Zen and the Brain: Toward an Understanding of Meditation and Consciousness.* Cambridge: MIT Press, 1998.

Banville, Thomas C. *How to Listen—How to Be Heard.* Chicago: Nelson-Hall, Inc., 1978.

Benson, Herbert. *The Relaxation Response.* New York: William Morrow & Co., Inc., 1975.

————. *Beyond the Relaxation Response.* New York: Times Books, 1984.

Bolton, Robert. *People Skills.* New York: Simon & Schuster, Inc., 1979.

Burley-Allen, Madelyn. *Listening—the Forgotten Skill.* New York: John Wiley & Sons, 1982.

Buzan, Tony, and Barry Buzan. *The Mind Map Book: How to Use Radiant Thinking to Maximize Your Brain's Untapped Potential,* New York: Plume Books, 1996.

Carew, Jack C. *The Mentor: 15 Keys to Success in Sales, Business and Life.* New York: Penguin Putnam, Inc., 1998.

Covey, Stephen. *The Seven Habits of Highly Effective People.* New York: Simon & Schuster, Inc., 1989.

Crum, Thomas F. *The Magic of Conflict.* New York: Simon & Schuster, Inc., 1987.

Czikszentmihalyi, Mihaly. *Flow: The Psychology of Optimal Experience.* New York: Harper-Collins, 1991.

Dalai Lama and Cutler, Howard C. *The Art of Happiness.* New York: Riverhead Books, 1998.

Easwaran, Eknath. *Meditation.* Tomales, Calif.: Nilgiri Press, 1991.

———. *Words to Live By: Inspiration for Everyday.* Tomales, Calif.: Nilgiri Press, 1996.

Gitomer, Jeffrey. *Customer Satisfaction Is Worthless, Customer Loyalty Is Priceless.* Austin, Tex.: Bard Press, 1998.

Hallowell, Edward M., and John J. Rately. *Driven to Distraction: Recognizing and Coping with Attention Deficit Disorder from Childhood through Adulthood.* New York: Simon & Schuster, Inc., 1994.

Hall, Edward T. and Mildred R. *Understanding Cultural Differences: Keys to Success in West Germany, France and the United States.* Maine: Intercultural Press, 1990.

Healy, Jane M. *Failure to Connect: How Computers Affect Our Children's Minds—for Better and Worse.* New York: Simon & Schuster, Inc., 1998.

Herrmann, Douglas J. *Supermemory: A Quick-Action Program for Memory Improvement.* Emmaus, Pa.: Rodale Press, 1991.

Kabat-Zinn, Jon. *Wherever You Go There You Are: Mindfulness Meditation in Everyday Life.* New York: Hyperion, 1994.

Kurtz, Howard. *Hot Air: All Talk, All the Time.* New York: Times Books, 1996.

Langer, Ellen J. *Mindfulness*. Reading, Mass.: Perseus Books, 1990.

———. *The Power of Mindful Learning*. Reading, Mass.: Perseus Books, 1997.

Lown, Bernard. *The Lost Art of Healing*. Boston: Houghton-Mifflin, 1996.

Maas, James B., with Megan L. Wherry, et al. *Power Sleep: The Revolutionary Program That Prepares Your Mind for Peak Performance*. New York: Villard (Random House), 1998.

Maslow, A. H. *Dominance, Self-Esteem, Self-Actualization: Germinal Papers of A. H. Maslow*. Monterey, Calif.: Brooks/Cole Publishing Company, 1973.

Murphy, Kevin R. and Suzanne Levert. *Out of the Fog: Treatment Options and Coping Strategies for Adult Attention Deficit Disorder*. New York: Skylight Press, 1995.

Nhat Hanh, Thich. *The Miracle of Mindfulness*. Boston: Beacon Press, 1987.

Nichols, Michael P. *The Lost Art of Listening*. New York: Guilford Press, 1995.

Revel, Jean-Francis, and Matthieu Ricard. *The Monk and the Philosopher*. New York: Schocken Books, 1998.

Rosenberg, Marshall B. *Nonviolent Communication: A Language of Compassion*. Del Mar, Calif.: PuddleDancer Press, 1999.

Samovar, L. and R. Porter. *Intercultural Communication: A Reader*. 7th ed. Belmont, Calif.: Wadsworth Publishing, 1997.

Schafer, Edith Nalle. *Our Remarkable Memory.* Washington, D.C.: Starrhill Press, 1988.

Shlien, John. "A Criterion of Psychological Health." *Group Psychotherapy.* p. 1–18, 1994.

Spence, Gerry. *How to Argue and Win Every Time.* New York: St. Martin's Press, 1995.

Stahl, Lesley. *Reporting Live.* New York: Simon & Schuster, Inc., 1999.

Stone, Douglas, et al. *Difficult Conversations: How to Discuss What Matters Most.* New York: Viking Penguin, 1999.

Tannen, Deborah. *Talking from 9 to 5.* New York: William Morrow and Company, Inc., 1994.

Watts, Alan W. *The Spirit of Zen.* New York: Grove Press, 1958.

———. *The Way of Zen.* New York: Vintage Books, 1999.

Wolvin, Andrew, and Carolyn Coakley. *Listening.* 5th ed. Dubuque, Iowa: Brown & Benchmark, 1996.

Woodall, Marian K. *How to Talk So Men Will Listen.* Chicago: Contemporary Press, 1993.

Ziglar, Zig. *See You at the Top.* Gretna, La.: Pelican Publishing Company, 1993.

Zimmerman, Don H., and Candace West. *Sex Roles, Interruptions and Silences in Conversation in Language and Sex: Difference and Dominance.* Rowley, Mass.: Newbury House, 1975.

The author and publisher are grateful for permission to reprint passages from the following copyrighted material:

From *See You at the Top by Zig Ziglar* © 1975, used by permission of the publisher, Pelican Publishing Company, Inc.

Charles Pappas, "MacKay's Selling Secrets," *Success Magazine*, vol. 46, no. 2, Feb. 1999. Used by permission of *Success Magazine*.

The Monk and the Philosopher by Jean-Francis Revel and Matthieu Ricard © NIL Editions, Paris, 1997; Shocken Books, New York, 1998.

From *Words To Live By* by Eknath Easwaran, founder and director of the Blue Mountain Center of Meditation, copyright 1996; reprinted by permission of Nilgiri Press, Tomales, California.

Les Kaye, *Zen at Work*, © 1996, Crown Publishers, Inc.

Cousins, N. "Anatomy of an Illness (As Perceived by the Patient)," *New England Journal of Medicine*, vol. 295, Dec. 23, 1976, pp. 1458-1463.

Steffan Heuer, "Talking the Talk," *The Industry Standard*, Feb. 7, 2000.

From *The Miracle of Mindfulness* by Thich Nhat Hanh Copyright © 1975, 1976 by Thich Nhat Hanh. Preface and English translation copyright © 1975, 1976, 1987 by Mobi Ho. Reprinted by permission of Beacon Press, Boston.

From *The Art of Happiness: A Handbook for Living* by the Dalai Lama and Howard C. Cutler, copyright © 1998 by H. H. Dalai Lama and Howard C. Cutler. Used by permission of Putnam Berkeley, a division of Penguin Putnam Inc.

QUEST BOOKS
are published by
The Theosophical Society in America,
Wheaton, Illinois 60189-0270,
a branch of a world fellowship,
a membership organization
dedicated to the promotion of the unity of
humanity and the encouragement of the study of
religion, philosophy, and science, to the end that
we may better understand ourselves and our place in
the universe. The Society stands for complete
freedom of individual search and belief.
For further information about its activities,
write, call 1-800-669-1571, e-mail olcott@theosophia.org,
or consult its Web page: http://www.theosophical.org

*The Theosophical Publishing House
is aided by the generous support of
THE KERN FOUNDATION,
a trust established by Herbert A. Kern
and dedicated to Theosophical education.*